MW00398557

Solomon's Sieve

(Black Swan 7)

Victoria Danann

Copyright 2014 Victoria Danann

Published by 7th House, an Imprint of Andromeda LLC

Read more about this author and upcoming works at
http://VictoriaDanann.me

I love them all but I think my Favorite character is Deliverance. A happy-go-lucky sex demon. He is all you could want and more in the bedroom as long as that is all you want. Outside the bedroom he is an impulsive teenager who only has respect for his daughter and granddaughter! I find it quite sad that he found love once with Litha's mother and will never know that again.

Dee Bowerman

For my assistant, Sarah Nicole Blausey, who starts my morning – no matter how early - with a cheerful, "Good Morning," every day, sometimes including weekends and holidays even when she's not scheduled to work. I can tell how much others appreciate her by the fact that she's so often included in posts, comments, and email communication.

Thank you, Sarah, for always being on my side no matter what.

For the fan-in-chief, my daughter, Kelly Danann, who was the first person to read My Familiar Stranger and convince me that it really was good enough to publish. Forever indebted. Annnnnd, guess who's YOUR biggest fan?

Thank you, Kelly, for always being on my side no matter what.

For my husband, who is my counsel-in-chief. Whenever an Indie business question arises, he's my first stop. Whenever someone has left a review that makes me want to never write another word, he's my first stop. And with every celebratory milestone, whether it's an award nomination or another hundred reviews, he's my first stop.

Thank you, Tom, for always being on my side no matter what.

For the proofer-in-chief, Julie Roberts, I write with super confidence knowing that you're going to find the gnarly stuff. It takes a very special sort of editor to understand when NOT to edit and to adjust your style to the eccentricities and egomania of the author. Love you for that!

For Simon Whistler (Rocking Self Publishing Podcast) and Arial Burnz (PNR Radio) who boosted my profile this year with guest features on their podcasts. Thanks guys. You're the best.

For all the bloggers who have written phenomenal reviews that help me fake it as a legitimate literary figure – drinks on the house!

If you bought one of my books, THANK YOU for making me a full-time writer. If you told someone else they should really read Knights of Black Swan, thank you even more.

Three times blessings on you all.

If you're interested in serving on the best street team anywhere, email blackswanjunkie@gmail.com or visit here http://victoriadanann.me/the-street-team/.

A TEAM MEMBERS

Anna-Marie Coomber
Bobbi Kinion
Brandy Ralston
Cheryl Lewis Fennimore
Cindy Hunt
Cristi Riquelme
Crystal Lehmann
Debera Smith
Dee Bowerman
Diane Nix
Elizabeth Quincy Nix
Ellen Sandberg
Fawn Phillips
Gina Whitney
Janine Fromherz Diller
Joy Whiteside
Kim Staley Schommer
Lindsay Thompson
Lisa High
Lisa Lopez
Maggie Nolan
Michelle Stein
Mountain Crew
Nelta Baldwin Mathias
Pam James
Patricia Smith
Rebecca Stigers

Renay Arthur
Robyn Byrd
Shanyn Clark Doan
Tabitha Schneider
Tifinie Henry

TABLE OF CONTENTS

So far ...

This series is also a serial saga in the sense that each book begins where the previous book ended.

There is a very old and secret society of paranormal investigators and protectors known as The Order of the Black Swan. In modern times, in a dimension similar to our own, they continue to operate, as they always have, to keep the human population safe. For centuries they have relied on a formula that outlines recruitment of certain second sons, in their early, post-pubescent youth, who match a narrow and highly specialized psychological profile. Those who agree to forego the ordinary pleasures and freedoms of adolescence receive the best education available anywhere along with the training and discipline necessary for a possible future as active operatives in the Hunters Division. In recognition of the personal sacrifice and inherent danger, The Order bestows knighthoods on those who accept.

BOOK ONE. *My Familiar Stranger:*

The elite B Team of Jefferson Unit in New York, also known as Bad Company, was devastated by the loss of one of its four members in a battle with vampire. A few days later Elora Laiken, an accidental pilgrim from another dimension, literally landed at their feet so physically damaged by the journey they weren't even sure of her species. After a lengthy recovery, they discovered that she had gained amazing speed and strength through the cross-dimension translation. She earned the trust and respect of the knights of B Team and eventually replaced the fourth member, who had been killed in the line of duty.

She was also forced to choose between three suitors: Istvan Baka, a devastatingly seductive six-hundred-year-old vampire, who worked as a consultant to neutralize an epidemic of vampire abductions, Engel Storm, the noble and stalwart leader of B Team who saved her life twice; and Rammel Hawking, the elf who persuaded her that she was destined to be his alone.

BOOK TWO. ***The Witch's Dream:***

Ten months later everyone was gathered at Rammel's home in Derry, Ireland. B Team had been temporarily assigned to The Order's Headquarters office in Edinburgh, but they had been given leave for a week to celebrate an elftale handfasting for Ram and Elora, who were expecting.

Ram's younger sister, Aelsong, went to Edinburgh with B Team after being recruited for her exceptional psychic skills. Shortly after arriving, Kay's fiancé was abducted by a demon with a vendetta, who slipped her to a dimension out of reach. Their only hope to locate Katrina and retrieve her was Litha Brandywine, the witch tracker, who had fallen in love with Storm at first sight.

Storm was assigned to escort the witch, who slowly penetrated the ice that had formed around his heart when he lost Elora to Ram. Litha tracked the demon and took Katrina's place as hostage after learning that he, Deliverance, was her biological father. The story ended with all members of B Team happily married and retired from active duty.

BOOK THREE. ***A Summoner's Tale: The Vampire's Confessor***

Istvan Baka was captured by vampire in the Edinburgh underground and reinfected with the vampire virus. His assistant, Heaven McBride, was found to be a "summoner", a person who can compel others to come to them when they play the flute. She also turned out to be the reincarnation of the young wife who was Baka's first victim as a new vampire six hundred years before.

Elora Laiken was studying a pack of wolves hoping to get puppies for her new breed of dog. While Rammel was overseeing the renovation of their new home, she and Blackie were caught in a snowstorm in the New Forest. At the same time assassins from her world, agents of the clan who massacred her family, found her isolated in a remote location without the ability to communicate. She gave birth to her baby alone except for the company of her dog, Blackie, and the wolf pack.

Heaven was instrumental in calling vampire to her so that they could be intercepted and given the curative vaccine. Baka was found, restored, and given the opportunity for a "do over" with the wife who had waited for many lifetimes to spend just one with him.

BOOK FOUR. *Moonlight: The Big Bad Wolf*

Ram and Elora moved into temporary quarters at Jefferson Unit to protect mother and baby. Sol asked Storm to prepare to replace him as Jefferson Unit Sovereign so that he could retire in two years. Storm declined, but suggested twenty-year-old trainee, Glendennon Catch for the job.

Litha uncovered a shocking discovery about the vampire virus by accidentally leading five immortal host vampire back to Jefferson Unit. Deliverance struck a deal with Litha to assist Black Swan with two issues: the old vampire and an interdimensional migration of Stalkson Grey's werewolf tribe.

In the process of averting possible extinction of his tribe, the king of the Elk Mountain werewolves, Stalkson Grey, fell in love with a cult slave and abducted her with the demon's assistance. He eventually won his captive's heart and took his new mate to the New Elk Mountain werewolf colony in Lunark Dimension where the wolf people's ancestors had settled centuries before.

Throughout this portion of the story, Litha's pregnancy developed at an alarming rate. Since there had been no previous instance of progeny with the baby's genetic heritage, no one knew what to expect. The baby arrived months ahead of schedule. The birth was dramatic and unique because Storm's and Litha's new daughter, Elora Rose, "Rosie", skipped the usual delivery with a twelve inch ride through the passes and appeared on the outside of Litha's body.

BOOK FIVE. ***Gathering Storm***

Book Five opened with Storm and Litha enjoying quiet days at home at the vineyard with a brand new infant. Sol shocked Storm with the news that he was getting married to Farnsworth and asked Storm to help Glen run Jefferson Unit so that he could take a vacation – his first ever – with his intended. Storm agreed, but when Rosie reached six weeks her growth began to accelerate drastically.

Deliverance was to pick Storm up every day, take him to Jefferson Unit so that he could spend two hours with Glen and supervise management of Sol's affairs, then return him to Sonoma, but the demon lost his son-in-law in the passes en route to New Jersey. Every paranormal ally available was called in for a massive interdimensional search. Finally, Deliverance was alerted that Storm had been located.

The demon picked him up and dropped him in Litha's bedroom, but it was the wrong Storm. B Team, Glen and Litha all undertook a project to do a makeover on the fake Storm so that nobody would find out that there was a huge flaw with interdimensional transport.

Jefferson Unit was attacked by aliens from Stagsnare Dimension, Elora's home world, with nobody there to offer defense except Elora, Glen, the fake Storm, Sir Fennimore, the non-combat personnel and the trainees.

BOOK SIX. *A Tale of Two Kingdoms*

The book opens with a look behind the metaphysical scene. It seems that the strings governing Earth related operations are being pulled by a group of misfit adolescent deities who were, eons in the past, given the planet and its derivative dimensions as a group project.

Kellareal leads the elves and fae to discovery of the truth that they were once the same people, but were separated in the distant past because of a tragic estrangement of siblings. After believing that they had escaped the politics of their families, Duff and Song were captured and separated. With the angel's help, however, they were reunited. Meanwhile, Aelsblood, Ram's older brother was removed as monarch and his son, Aelshelm, succeeded as king in name only under the agreement that Ram's father, Ethelred Mag Lehane Hawking, would reign in Helm's place until he is old enough to decide whether he will join the family business and accept a career as king.

PROLOGUE

The beach Cape May, New Jersey

Sol

Regrets? Well, sure. Nobody dies without regrets.

The only way to avoid that would be to sleep even less than I did and be rearranging your priorities every minute. Of course, if you rearranged your priorities every minute, then there'd be no time for anything else and, at the end of your life, you'd regret that you'd wasted your time working so hard at trying to reach the finish line without regrets that you never got anything done.

What's my biggest regret? The first thing that comes to mind isn't exactly a regret, but more a disappointment. I wish I'd had more time to spend with Farnsworth.

I never expected to find love so late in life. Neither did she. I asked her once why she'd never married. She said she was waiting for the right crusty old bastard to come along. I liked that answer. I liked just about everything about Farnsworth.

All those years I would stop off at the Hub and grab one of those rank strong coffees with a cheese and ham and egg thing they nuked while I waited, which was never long because the way I stared at them made them so fidgety they could hardly wait to give me my order and get me the hell out of their space. Makes me smile just thinking about it.

So every morning I was just steps away from where Farnsworth was in Operations, really running the whole show at Jefferson Unit while I was taking credit for it. Fuck me. She's one of a kind.

It's funny to think that all those years she was right there and we just never made that connection. I guess it's not exactly funny.

Now that I have one foot on the other side, the pieces all fit together better and it's easier to see things clearly. Got to stop and laugh at my own jokes, because who else is going to? That was funny because I only have one foot. Looks like the damn dune buggy cut off my leg. And my life. I'm bleeding out, listening to the weeping of the only woman I ever loved and that's the hardest part.

The only reason I can joke about this is because it's temporary. I can't stay gone. There's too much going on.

I was planning to wait until I got back from the first vacation I ever took in my life to inform the interested parties, that would be almost everyone I know, that the great bright promise of curing vampirism with a vaccine... well, it's not working. And, unfortunately, the conclusion is that it's not going to work. Ever.

It's starting to look like it would be easier to rid the world of cockroaches and we all know how that's going. No one doubts that, in the end, cockroaches will be the last life form left on Earth.

So I don't have any plans for crossing to the other side and dancing in the sunshine or singing "Kum Ba Yah" with people who don't have anything better to do. I'm going to lie here and wait until this body gives up the ghost, while this magnificent woman beside me cries her heart out. Then I'm going to raise hel until they find a way to bring me back.

CHAPTER 1

New York

The facilitator looked at him like she'd rather have him thrown out than help him get caught up to speed. Yes. He was late. Yes. He was a mess. "Is that blood on your face?" she'd asked, looking down her nose.

That's only one of the shitty things that's likely to happen when you pick the wrong fight in a battle with extra-dimensional assassins. Among others, you could end up locked in a freezing basement cage for hours.

His answer was to stare in bald challenge. "Just tell me where I'm supposed to be."

She hesitated, but decided it would be less disruptive to the event to go along with the maniac than to cause a scene. "Very well, Mr...," she looked down at the card, "Nightsong. Everyone will be changing stations in..." she looked at her stop watch, "five, four, three – go to station seven now – two, one." She raised her voice. "Time everyone! Move on to the next table."

Raif spotted the number seven and headed in that direction, clearing a path as people took one look and gave him a wide berth. When he got a look at the woman who had just sat down to wait for him at table number seven, he felt his dick jerk and that infuriated him. He flopped into the empty chair seething about the past twenty-four hours, about having to comply with a speed date because he'd lost a bet, about how unsatisfying his work for Black Swan had become, and about the fact that the cutie was getting a response from his pants that was not in line with how tired and dejected he was at the moment.

He refused to look at her. Instead, he looked around the room with a smirk. Speed dating. What could be more ludicrous for a guy like him? He had a progression of pleasure-giving penis piercings, commonly known as a ladder, and a reputation with women that was nothing to be ashamed of. Well, depending on who you talked to. But he'd never been on a "date" in his life.

His present discomfort was his teammate's idea of a joke, the price of a wager that misfired.

"I'm Mercedes."

The sound of her voice brought him back. He let his eyes roam over what he could see above the table top slowly, way too slowly for speed dating. It was an intimidation tactic intended to make her uncomfortable, deliberate or not. She was buttoned up all the way to the neck and he thought the closed tight look was out of place on a natural redhead with freckles that seemed to say, "Underneath this disguise, I'm as unruly as the pigment in my skin."

"Rafael Nightsong."

Her lips parted and stayed open for a minute, like she was thinking about repeating his name, but she recovered quickly and that look vanished. "So. What do you do?"

"Vampire hunter," he said as nonchalantly as if the answer had been insurance salesman.

She supposed he must have been attempting some sort of theatrical goth look. The style was outrageous, but those eyes were such a pale shade of blue, framed by midnight black hair and lashes, they drew her in, compelling her to look and preventing her from looking away. One could almost believe that he actually was a vampire hunter.

Gathering her composure, she smirked. "I see. You must be too shy to talk about yourself. So, let me just refer to your card then." She picked up a white four by six index card with the number seven in bold at the top. "I see you like long walks on the beach and pina coladas." He barked out a laugh in spite of himself. He had to give it up. Torn Finngarick was a funny guy. "Let me guess. I'll bet you also like getting caught in the rain."

"Yes. I'm a simple guy, easy to read. Long walks on the beach and pina coladas are my idea of fun." Her rust-colored eyelashes swept down and to the side as she looked away. "Sooooooo. Let's see what your card says about you." He shuffled through cards and held one up pretending to read. "Here we are. Little Miss Sheltered McManners. For fun you like spraying with Lysol and wearing stilts. All the better to look down on other people."

"Mr… you know, really, the most interesting thing about you is that you chose Nightsong for a fake name. I don't need stilts to look down on you. I could be lying face down on the floor and wouldn't have any trouble."

One of his brows arched. "Well, well, well. Honesty. Wasn't expecting that."

The facilitator's voice rang out, "One minute."

"Sixty seconds." His malicious grin was sexy in spite of its intent. "Just long enough for me to say that I'll bet your cunt is buttoned up tighter than your sweater. I'll bet it's so sanitary that it doesn't even smell like pussy. A shame because I *like* the smell of pussy. For one thing it's honest."

Mercy didn't think of herself as prudish, but hearing that tirade come from the mouth of a complete stranger sitting on the other side of white linen was shocking. While she was trying to make up her mind between blushing and blanching, he decided to add one parting comment.

"You know, hives is not a good look for you."

"Time!"

She wasn't about to allow that to be the last thing said between them. "You're an authority of good looks? Have you seen a mirror? When did post-apocalyptic remnant become the new GQ? You look like an extra from a zombie movie set."

"Time!"

He glanced toward the facilitator at the front of the room, who had repeated herself, more forcefully, for *their* benefit.

"Good. 'Cause we're done here." He shoved the chair back as he stood, throwing his splayed hands out in front of him to punctuate his exit like a petulant teenager who'd been wronged.

"Excellent. Because I couldn't have stood the smell a second longer."

Three minutes later they were still standing at table seven, locked in an argument that seemed to be spiraling into a frenzy instead of winding down. While the other would-be speed daters turned spectators looked on, the facilitator kept helplessly calling "time" and was ignored.

Finally, Raif ended it by storming out of the restaurant and walked for two blocks in dense New York City pedestrian traffic before ducking into an alley. He stopped and put his forehead on the cold composition wall of the closest building.

"Gods' teeth, why am I *such* an asshole? A big mouth, broken asshole?"

Fingers shaking, she gathered her purse and jacket without meeting the eyes of any of the onlookers. If she'd ever been more humiliated, she couldn't remember when. She got almost to the end of the block before bursting into tears. So much for speed dating.

She was glad it was windy and cold for the six block walk back to Columbia. People would assume the color in her face was from weather and not from crying.

CHAPTER 2

Sol in Shamayim

He could pinpoint the moment when the well-oiled machine jumped its tracks. In fact, on reflection, he sensed she was going to be trouble the minute she materialized in midair and plopped on the floor as a bloody, oozing, pile of goo. He didn't know what it was, but he knew it was a harbinger of change. *Elora Fucking Laiken*. Turned things upside down and inside out and, if it ever got back to 'normal' after she arrived, it never stayed that way for long. Babies at Jefferson Unit! Unbelievable!

In the beginning, after she recovered from the interdimensional journey and was given conditional freedom of the facility, he was resistant as stone to the idea of using her in Hunter Division. The idea of a female knight in Hunter Division would remain eternally ludicrous even though the gifts she acquired through transition to a new dimension outfitted her perfectly for the job of slayer.

There was only one thing that might change his position on the matter. It just so happened that the one thing was what they had to have – the help of a very old vampire. Luckily the vampire in question, Istvan Baka, took a fancy to the young lady. First he wanted a private audience, private being a highly relative term given that his every move was monitored by Knights of the Black Swan through a glass enclosure.

After he signed a contract to act as consultant, the vampire more or less embarrassed Sol into using Laiken's unique talents by pointing out that she was very likely Black Swan's most powerful asset. Yes. That's exactly what he'd said during the same phone call when he'd asked for cleanup because the girl had just taken out a vampire. Alone. Without any training. With a toothpick!

After that he couldn't really say no without looking like a chauvinistic ass wipe. So he let her replace Sir Landsdowne as fourth member of B Team. He'd hoped the three remaining members would draw a line, but two of them gave her an "up" vote.

For a little while it seemed like it might work out okay. Then Sir Hawking was disabled in a confrontation and she responded rash and ready, which got her eaten and infected by vampire. Well, that may have been overly harsh. No one asks to be eaten. Exactly.

Her partial conversion to vampire made for a fairly tense twenty-four hours, but it led to a miracle of science, courtesy of Laiken's blood and Monq's brilliance, Or so they believed.

Certainly the advent of a vaccine that would cure the vampire virus was heralded as the most important development in Black Swan history and none of them doubted it. Why would they? It seemed that centuries of dedication would resolve the vampire part of the organization's activities with a feel-good win. Something no one would have ever thought possible.

It was The Order's first ever cause for real celebration. Sol would never forget the slogan that popped up right away. "Shoot to cure."

Of course it benefitted Baka. The vaccine gave the old vampire a new humanity card. Twice. No cause for complaint there. He was even tapped to head up the task force to convert hunters to healers, another great Vaccine Era slogan. He formed a network of rehabilitation and treatment centers for vampire who had been successfully reconverted to human.

The original target date of how long it should take to effectively stamp out vampirism was calculated based on the best guess estimate of the number of vampire, number of active hunters, and the amount of vaccine being produced and dispersed.

At first there was a marked decline in vampire activity. So much so that Jefferson Unit was quickly and efficiently reconceived as a research and training facility. Too quickly and efficiently in Sol's opinion.

Of course J.U. had always been a research and training facility, but it had also been one of the crown jewels of the Black Swan Hunters Division, home to the most elite slayers on the planet. There was such a certainty that the vaccine was going to be the end of the vampire plague. The rush to reorganize and redistribute resources left Jefferson Unit feeling like a ghost town. The hunters and all the staff who supported them, including medical, were transferred. The facility felt sad, abandoned, and retired.

If that was the whole story, you might be inclined to say that it was a good time to die. And, if that was the whole story, he might have been inclined to agree. But he was privy to information about the progress of the "Great Vampire Inversion". That was the name given to the era of revolution, when humanity would free itself from the most dangerous and most rampant of the monsters that make prey of people. It was a phrase that later mocked the hope it implied and made them seem childlike in their naïve and gullible rush toward belief in the vaccine as a fait accompli.

The reports had come in during his time away from work with Farnsworth. Sol had been called to Edinburgh for an urgent meeting and had to leave Farnsworth where she was and not knowing whether he'd make it back before the clock ran out on their vacation time. As a fellow employee of Black Swan, there was no question that she understood, but that didn't make it feel less like leaving her on her own in the middle of their long-planned romantic interlude was a shitty thing to do.

Farnsworth though? In Sol's opinion she was a great dame. She didn't make him feel worse by looking disappointed, didn't even mist up when he kissed her goodbye. The first ten years she worked at J.U. she saved most of what she earned by living in the small onsite apartment that came with the job. With food, utilities and housing included, she was able to sock away enough to make her modest dream come true.

She bought a precious yellow cottage on the beach at Cape May and spent whatever needed to be spent to keep it maintained to perfection. It was less than a two hour drive away from Fort Dixon, but it was a world away. Every chance she got she retreated to her little bit of private heaven.

When the question arose about where they would go for a romantic escape, she suggested her getaway.

"Don't get me wrong. I appreciate a cheap date as much as the next guy, but I've got a lot of unused vacation funds. I could take you anywhere you want to go. Do anything you want to do."

She gave him that special smile that never failed to make him feel like he was made of pure gold. Made his cock feel just about that hard, too.

She turned her chin up at an angle and kept a hint of that smile on her lips as she said, "Can I have a rain check on that? Next time I might just rise to the challenge of spending all your vacation stash, but this time I'd like to just hide you away and have you all to myself."

Damn if that didn't make Sol fall even more in love with her. Before that he would have said he couldn't love her more, but she just kept stretching the limits. Like she was bringing a withered heart back to life and gradually filling it with healthy fluids, making it swell bigger and bigger.

"Whatever you say, beautiful." She saw both love and amusement on his face when he reached up and tucked a stray tendril behind her ear. "Have me all to yourself, huh? I like the way you think."

When the big day came, Sol borrowed Storm's silver convertible Porche roadster. Storm had never driven it to California because he didn't need it there. It had been parked in the underground at J.U. for months without use, but it turned over when Sol pressed the ignition. There were two seats in the car and not much room in the trunk, but most of what Farnsworth would want and need was already at her cottage.

It was too cold to put the top down, but convertibles are romantic even when the tops are up, wind noise and all. They have a way of making a vehicle's occupants feel young. And sexy.

On the trip down they chatted easily about places where they'd been, people they knew in common, and bucket list items even though it was still early in life for them to be composing bucket lists. When they were twenty minutes away, they made a grocery stop at the last supermarket en route. They bought more than the space left in the trunk, but Farnsworth was a good sport and laughed about sharing the passenger seat with one of Sol's duffels between her legs.

It was cool but sunny when they arrived and the March wind was doing its reputation proud. Sol pulled the car underneath the house between thick weathered support pillars. There was a store room and guest room next to the carport, but the two floors she used as real living space began twelve feet above ground level.

He carried groceries and bags up the stairs while she opened up the house. That involved engaging the motorized storm shutters, lighting the pilot and turning on the heat plus her favorite part of the ritual - affixing a unicorn flag to its holder on the deck.

"There," she said, turning toward Sol with a grin. "Now we're officially in residence."

He stared at the flag for a minute. "A unicorn?"

She laughed. "Beautiful, isn't it?" It was a blue and white unicorn on a light gray background. And it was beautiful. As unicorns go it was dignified with a fine proud head, flying mane and long elecorn.

"I guess," he conceded. His scowl was more obligatory than sincere, lip service to the code of macho.

Using an armload of logs from the half cord of firewood on the deck, Sol built a fire to warm up the cottage while they were waiting for the small gas furnace to do its job. When everything was put away, they drank a glass of wine and made love in front of the fire on a white rag rug that was so thick it felt like a pallet.

When Sol had assured her that he had the resources to take her anywhere she wanted to go, she had immediately formed images of having him in her house. And, once that vision had taken root, it appealed to her more than anything else she could think of.

Farnsworth was so accustomed to relaxing at the cottage and letting work stress dissolve away that her nervous system responded to the environment automatically and put her in getaway mode. Sol, on the other hand, had muscles that were knots on top of knots on top of knots. If he had ever known how to relax, it had been decades in the past and, certainly, the idea of "vacation" was foreign to his nervous system.

So he fidgeted and paced and suggested things to go and do. She sat watching him, casually sipping chardonnay, in a yellow cable sweater the same cheerful color as the cottage.

"Let's go for a walk on the beach," she said.

He stopped abruptly, his gaze going toward the ocean. "A walk on the beach?" He looked and sounded as if he'd never heard of such a thing.

"Um-hmmm."

"What for?"

She chuckled and shook her head. "Just because. Go put on enough layers to keep you toasty and we'll go see what there is to see." He looked dubious. "Come on. It'll be fun. I promise."

"You promise?" His face split into a grin.

"I do."

He swore he liked the sound of that, but he would have also sworn that he would hate walking on the beach. Maybe that would have been true under other circumstances, but doing things with Farnsworth just made them different. She had a way of transforming ordinary experiences into extraordinary events, simply by virtue of being there.

She taught him to like walking on the beach by changing his perspective. She pointed out sights like little birds that ran on the sand so fast you almost couldn't see their skinny little legs and little crabs that ran out of holes on some unseen errand and then retreated to safety just as fast. Now and then she'd point to the remains of a seashell and tell him what kind it was. Through her eyes his consciousness was raised to appreciate the way sunlight dances on water, the way the color of the ocean changes to try and match the color of the sky, the way brightly colored windsocks whip in the wind against a blue sky background and make the whole world feel festive.

He began to see through her eyes, hear through her ears, feel her sensations, and little by little, day by day, the layers of tension fell away and she saw, for the first time, what his face looked like when the muscles were lax and not held rigid as steel.

One day he picked up a stick and threw it for a retriever someone was walking on the beach. When he turned back to her with a laugh and a glorious heart-stopping grin she said, "Solomon. You're so lovely when you let go."

His grin resolved into a smile. "Lovely? If you say so."

"I do."

He liked the sound of that every time he heard it. "I was just aiming for nice-looking. Did I overshoot?"

She laughed. "Indeed you did. By fathoms."

"I think I'm keeping you"

He pulled her into a kiss that was far too passionate for a beach they shared with passersby. She thought about pulling away, was sure that pulling away was the appropriate thing to do, but her body was making the case that life was too short for propriety. So she returned his kiss with enough fervor to make sure he knew she meant it.

The days melted away into the closest thing to pure happiness that Sol had ever known. He didn't remember feeling that happy or carefree even in childhood. And that was the state of his euphoria when the call came that he was needed at Headquarters immediately. The furrows in his brow reappeared instantly, the lines around his eyes were deeper, and the smile that had become perpetual disappeared.

She nodded as he promised to come right back if he could. He gave her the keys to Storm's roadster and a soft, lingering kiss goodbye. When he reached the end of the deck he turned back once to see her watching from inside the glass door. She waved and his heart responded with a reluctance to go. He'd never before had a hard time with the call of duty and he cursed under a heavy sigh when he confronted just how much he didn't want to leave her or that place. He would have given just about anything to stay right where he was.

But he didn't.

He took a cab to Ocean City and paid dearly for a jet charter to New York where he could jump on a company transport to Scotia.

When he got to Simon's office, Baka and heads of some of the other units that would be most affected by the news were already there. Sol thought he'd been in grim meetings before, but nothing compared to the somber vibe in Director Tvelgar's conference room as he delivered the message that the tide had turned on the Inversion. Not only had the vaccine ceased to work, but the resurgent strain of virus mutation was stronger and faster than before, converting human to vampire within minutes of contact with the bloodstream.

As they went over the projections, each man present had felt his heart sag as he realized that the short, hopeful reprieve was turning into a bigger problem than they had before. Instead of reducing the number of knights in rotation, they were going to be hard pressed to meet the increased demand. They would have to recall every able-bodied retired hunter to active duty and begin inducting the trainees sooner than optimum.

The Hunter Division had developed a tradition of waiting until their knights-to-be were twenty-two before sending them into the field, although exceptions were made on a case by case basis. Though they might be physically capable by the time they were eighteen, they were generally thought to lack the judgment crucial to keeping them and their comrades alive. There were only three training facilities in the world. They were the units in London, Brasilia and New Jersey.

Dr. Tvelgar turned to the three men who were Sovereigns of those facilities and told them that they were to go home and begin gearing up by submitting requisitions for support staff and sending formal notices to a lot of retired knights who'd gone to bed that very night believing they'd seen their last hunt. They were informed that the active duty knights who had been transferred would be returned to their former units with no additional paperwork being necessary. They were also instructed that they were to begin the process of selecting trainees to "go" early. They would each need to contribute three to make the numbers work.

Somehow that was harder for the Sovereigns to digest than the idea of compelling retirees to return to a dangerous occupation from which they thought they'd successfully escaped and lived to tell the tale. They agreed they wouldn't bring up any retirees over the age of forty, which was palatable enough. But the idea of sending the young against vampire before the age of psychological readiness was difficult. It smacked of sacrifice. And the training unit heads didn't like it one bit.

At the same time they were told that people were being pulled from other Order duties to expand Recruiting and that they should prepare for larger incoming classes of fourteen-year-olds. The Sovereigns – looking older and grayer by the moment - glanced at each other with a taciturn solemnness and even the least sensitive of them was aware of the air grown heavier in the room. Still, they looked downright giddy compared to Baka.

Leadership had always required dedication and concentration, but the burden had never felt cumbersome, like lead weight. There wasn't one person in the room who wasn't silently wishing that they'd never heard of the vaccine. It was turning out to be three steps forward, ten steps back. And each step back represented deaths that they, as Sovereigns, would be responsible for cataloguing.

As they filed out of Simon's office, Sol looked at Baka. "Looks like you better make a bigger effort to stay human this time."

Baka turned toward Sol and cocked his head. "I suppose it could be said that the only good thing that came out of this was that I got my humanity back. No doubt there'll be many in the future to say it wasn't worth it."

"What's the final verdict on the others?"

Baka grimaced. "We didn't have as much success with rehabilitation as we had hoped." He looked away and lowered his voice like it hurt him physically to say the next sentence. "Nearly half became suicides."

"Well, you know that thing about historical distancing and the big picture. Who's to say how it will look in the annals when the dust settles?"

Baka tried a smile that didn't quite work. "Good to see you, Old Man."

Sol barked out a laugh. "You're calling me old? Now *that* is funny." When his smile died he said, "What are you going to do? You're welcome to join my hunters at J.U. Storm always said you missed your calling, that you would have been a great vampire slayer."

"No irony there." Baka drew in a big breath. "Thank you for the offer. I guess I need to have a sit down with my wife. And, of course, we need to decide how this affects the, um, do you call them Animal House, too?"

Sol smirked. "Everybody calls them that but you."

Baka nodded. "Well, we need to decide what part, if any, they're going to play now that we've changed direction. Can I get back to you?"

"Anytime."

Baka gave a lift of his chin as he started walking away, but stopped and turned. "The hardest thing is that there are some out there who could still be cured, but knights in the field have no way of recognizing which strain the infected are carrying, new or old."

"No. They don't," Sol said slowly.

"So they all have to be treated as incurable hostiles."

"I'm afraid so. I'm sorry."

"Yeah. It's a shame. Huh?"

Sol had hung back and lingered in Simon's outer office hoping to talk to him privately before he left.

"So, where were you when we called?"

Sol smiled, but it didn't reach his eyes. "On holiday with my girl. First one I'd ever taken. Wouldn't you know?"

Simon sat behind his desk and cocked his head while he considered that. "First girl or first vacation?"

"Funny. First vacation."

"Did you take her home or leave her stranded?"

"Neither. I left her at her vacation house at Cape May. Told her I'd come back if I could."

"Hmmm. Well, I don't see how taking another couple of days would make such a difference. We'll be stipulating that your transferred knights and former staff have twenty days to report for duty. Why don't you go finish your holiday on a good note? It may be a while before you get another."

Sol nodded again. "Suspect truer words were never spoken. Thanks. I believe I will. She works for The Order, at my unit. So same goes for her."

"Oh? Do I know her?"

"No idea. Her name is Farnsworth."

Simon leaned back and laughed. "You and Farnsworth? Well, yes, I know her by phone. I've talked to her many times over the years, a marvel of efficiency." He looked at Sol like he was studying him through a new filter. "Yes. I can see the two of you together. Is she a handsome woman?"

Sol smiled at Simon's very British expression. "None can compare."

"Well, then."

"Well, then." Simon stood, shook hands with Sol and walked him as far as the door of the outer office.

When Sol learned that he had to wait six hours to get a company jet back to New York, he decided to use the time productively. Baka told him about a jeweler a couple of blocks away. So he set out on foot to, as Farnsworth would say, "see what there was to see".

Between waiting on the jet at The Order's private hangar to refuel and get a maintenance check, the flight to New York, the charter to Ocean City, and the cab ride, he was traveling for eighteen hours. He tried to give some thought to the monumental tasks awaiting when he returned to J.U., but all he could think about was getting back to Farnsworth. He cursed himself for acting like a fifteen-year-old who had just found out that sex is even better than it sounds.

He texted her from the hangar at Edinburgh. *It will be tomorrow, but I'm on the way back.*

She responded almost immediately. *I'll be here.*

"I'll be here." He repeated it in his head. He loved the sound of that. Sure and steady. His girl was somebody who could be counted on. Grounded. Mature. Ready for whatever came. She was so perfect he was sure she must have been made for him in some grand metaphysical scheme of things.

It was early morning when he made it back to the yellow beach cottage. Farnsworth wasn't dressed yet. She was standing in the kitchen with a mug of coffee, her hair down and falling around her shoulders, wearing her navy blue Japanese silk robe. And Sol thought the smile she gave when she looked up to find him standing on the deck on the other side of the sliding glass door was by far the sexiest thing he'd ever seen.

He grabbed her before she'd opened the door all the way and backed her up to the kitchen counter with her giggling like a teenager. When he lifted her up and stepped inside her thighs, she gasped.

"Solomon, The door. *Anybody* could climb the stairs and walk up to the back door the same way you just did."

"Then let's give 'em a show," he growled into her neck.

They spent the rest of the day driving each other to exhaustion, like they were trying to make up for not having been together since they were young. When it started getting dark, Sol made pasta while Farnsworth – still in her robe, took a shower and changed. He lit a fire and was going to open a bottle of wine, but couldn't find the opener.

When she came in, hair still damp at the ends even after blow drying, he stopped and stared like he hadn't seen her before.

"What?"

A corner of his mouth went up. "Sorry. I guess I just, uh, like all your looks."

She seemed embarrassed, like she wasn't used to getting compliments on her appearance. Her eyes drifted toward the stove. "Smells good." She looked at the bottle of wine sitting on the counter. "The Red Guitar. It's my favorite. How did you know that?"

"Lucky guess? Oh. Where's the wine opener?"

She moved toward a drawer that hadn't opened when he tried it. "I keep the opener and the family heirlooms in the trick drawer." He watched as she demonstrated the key. "You have to kick the baseboard underneath the bottom cabinet and pull at the same time."

The drawer slid right out for her like magic.

He reached in for the wine opener not being able to help noticing the contents. "Family heirlooms huh?"

Shaking her head she looked at the drawer. "Well, the ice cream scooper did come from my grandmother's."

"Then I guess she made an honest woman out of you." She laughed. "So how did you figure that out?"

"I didn't. The realtor showed it to me when I took possession of the house." Sol looked back at the drawer. "I know what you're thinking. You're wondering how many different things the former owners tried before they came up with that."

"That *is* what I was thinking." He let his eyes drift lazily down the front of her creamy knit sweater. "Know what I'm thinking now?"

"Hold on, Mister."

He gave her that sardonic grin that never failed to make her heart stutter. "That's Sovereign," he said as he leaned closer.

"I'm hungry. Love slaves have to be fed."

He leaned back on his heels and cocked his head to the side. "Is that negotiable?"

"Feed me."

"Beg."

"Please."

"Oh. All right." He turned back to the stove. "Now look what you made me do. The pasta is mushy."

She started laughing. "I *made* you do that?"

"Yes. You came in here teasing me with shiny wavy hair and skin flushed from a hot shower and showed me tricks with a drawer. And all the while you were talking dirty."

"I was talking dirty?"

"You kept saying family jewels."

"I said no such thing. One time I said family heirlooms."

"Jewels. Heirlooms. Same thing."

"They are not!"

"I'll show you mine…"

"Do I have to go down the road for takeout?"

"...you show me yours."

"Or maybe I need to call 911." He smiled. "I thought men your age were supposed to slow down in that department."

He smiled bigger. "Who would have thought a woman your age could get me so hard? And keep me that way?"

She blinked. "Mushy pasta is okay with me."

"You want me to go get you takeout?"

"Just put something in my mouth." He leered. "YOU KNOW PERFECTLY WELL WHAT I MEAN!"

He flipped the dishtowel over his shoulder, poured a touch of olive oil over the ziti and swirled it around the colander like he did it every day. He dumped generous portions onto two plates, used tongs to deposit grilled chicken strips on top of that, covered it with marinara and green peppers, then topped it off with shredded parmesan.

When the plate was set before her and a glass of her favorite red was poured, she inhaled the steam and gave him a smile that was all the gratitude he needed. Sol sat down across from her and waited with anticipation while she paired a bit of chicken with two pieces of ziti to make one forkful. She put it in her mouth then immediately closed her eyes and began making yummy sounds.

"Stop."

Her eyes flew open. She chewed quickly and swallowed. "Stop what?"

"Stop making those sexy humming noises if you want to get through dinner."

She chuckled. "Have I ever told you that you're the best thing that has ever happened to my ego?"

As soon as she had finished the last morsel on the plate, Sol moved her to the couch in front of the fire where he made love to her as slowly as if he thought it would be the last time ever. Something about it made her want to cry, but she didn't. Farnsworth was not a crier. But she recorded the feeling and promised herself that she would take it out and look at it another time. An emotion potent enough to threaten tears was worthy of pondering further.

Later Sol covered them both with a blanket, but they stayed pressed against each other, skin to skin, as they talked about their future in hushed tones with the rest of the world far, far away.

After a while he slid off the couch and strode off toward the kitchen looking for the jacket left by the door.

He'd left Farnsworth watching him walk away in the full bounty of nakedness. She was constantly amazed at how the only signs of age on his body were the gray around the temples, the deep set crinkles around his eyes and the permanent vertical "perfectionist" lines between his brows. If viewing him from the neck down, a person would guess twenty years younger.

She was lost in appreciating and applauding his strong youthful body when he returned and knelt beside the couch. She hadn't moved. She was waiting to welcome him back into their blanketed cocoon of a love nest.

Pinched between his fingers was a ring that he held up at her eye level. "Fa..., uh, Susan. Marry me."

She looked at the ring. Farnsworth wasn't materialistic and wouldn't have cared if it was a cigar wrapper, but she was a woman and it was sparkling in the firelight like it was a living thing, just inches in front of her eyes. She couldn't avoid looking at it.

It was perfect. A five carat marquis cut solitaire on a simple white gold band. She didn't know much about diamonds, but she'd read enough to know that diamonds that pick up all the colors and lights in the room and reflect them back like a prism… well, that's as good as a diamond gets. It had robbed her of her identity as an intelligent independent woman and reduced her to a creature who was mesmerized by a shiny object.

Wielding a rock that size might take some getting used to, but she decided she was up to the challenge and wanted Sol to believe that, of all the rings in the world, it was the very one she would have chosen for herself.

Her hesitation was starting to make Sol anxious and self-conscious. "I hope it's right. I thought it looked like you. The guy in the store said it's simply elegant, simply unique and I said, 'Yeah. That's her. That's definitely her.'"

As fantastic as the ring was, the compliment was even better.

Farnsworth's eyes slid to his as she swallowed the golf ball size lump that had formed in her throat. She didn't speak, but didn't hesitate either. She just nodded and smiled as she sat up, took his hand and guided it toward her ring finger. Little did he know that he would have made her happy with a proposal and a cereal box prize.

"Move over," he chuckled as she made room for him to nestle back into his place. "Let's do it before we go back."

He was too close to see the surprise on her face.

"Do what?"

"Get married."

"What?"

"We could pack up tonight. Go to Las Vegas tomorrow and we'd be back before my deadline."

"Solomon. I may be middle aged, but I still have a mother who would never forgive me if she didn't get to attend her only daughter's wedding."

"We could bring her along?"

She laughed and pushed his shoulder. "Stop."

He kissed her softly and lowered his voice. "So you need a big to do."

"No. Just a few people." She planted a row of kisses on his collar bone. "I know for a fact that you have a few people who would be livid if you left them out."

He blinked a few times. "Who?"

"You really don't know there are people who care about you? B Team, for instance. Glen."

"Pffffft." She nuzzled her face into his neck. "Those fakers have got you believing that?" She smiled against his skin and subtly inhaled his scent at the same time. "Okay, but soon? I'm too old for long engagements."

Raising up so she could see his face, she planted a kiss on his chin. "Soon."

"Next month."

"What's the rush, Sol? Are you worried about something?"

"Baby. Things are going to get busier than ever before, maybe out of hand."

Farnsworth had worked at Jefferson Unit long enough to know that "busy" was code for "dangerous".

"Okay, next month. Maybe they'd let us use the chapel on base? It would be just the right size."

"Sure. I can arrange that." He squeezed her in his arms. "I can't wait. You want to marry me as much as I want to marry you?"

She shook her head back and forth against his chest, but said, "I do." She felt as much as heard the rumble of his soft laughter. They lay together in the companionable silence of true lovers for a while. "What are you thinking?"

"Um?"

"You're stalling. What exactly was on your mind when I asked the question?"

"I was wondering how different our lives would have been if we'd found each other when we were young. If, maybe, we would have had children."

Her flinch at the word "children" was slight, but she was pressed so close to him that there was no mistaking it. "What was that?"

"Nothing."

"It was something. Tell me."

"I..."

He rearranged their bodies so that she was tucked under him, so that he could see every emotion and reaction on her face. "There's nothing you will ever tell me that will make me feel differently about you or love you less. One of the things I love about the fact that we both work for The Order is that there's no reason for secrets between us.

"So much about our lives revolves around keeping secrets, it would be good to know that when we're together, we're in a truth zone."

The fact that she knew what sort of man he was and knew that she could trust and believe him didn't really make it any easier. "I had a baby. A girl. I was sixteen."

Sol's eyes softened in sympathy. He gently moved a strand of hair behind her ear and kissed her softly on the cheek, encouraging her to continue.

"My parents were trying to do the best thing for me. They were loving and supportive and took me to an agency that counsels girls in, uh, that situation." She stopped for a minute. Sol waited patiently, but lifted his head so she would know he wanted to hear the rest. "The counselors laid out my options, but they made such a good case for adoption that I ended up feeling like the worse thing I could do for my baby was to keep it. They swore that my baby would have the best life possible, parents with good values and good resources who wanted a baby more than anything and would give mine the world."

She paused again, while a lone silent tear slid out of the corner of her eye and downward toward her ear. "I thought I was doing the best thing. The right thing. When she was born I didn't get to see her or hold her. I asked and they said she was a girl."

Sol cleared his throat and swallowed. "And you regret the decision."

"Every hour of every day. She'll be twenty-eight soon."

Looking at the wishful and wistful expression on her face, he had to ask, "Have you thought about looking for her?"

"Of course, but what would I say? I was so young that my brain wasn't fully developed yet? I thought I was doing the right thing, but I wasn't and by the time I understood that it was too late?"

"Yes," Sol said with exquisite simplicity.

Farnsworth breathed in a big sigh that made her chest heave. "I guess it looks simple from your vantage point."

"Yeah. I'm not you. I get that. I know mistakes can't always be corrected, but sometimes some of the sting can be soothed."

"You think I should look for her?"

"You curious?" She smiled and nodded as a couple of tears slid away from her eyes. "Well," he said as he placed little kisses on both sides of her face, "it just so happens that I work for an outfit that can pretty much find out anything."

She laughed. "Yeah. I might have heard of them, but you didn't answer my question. Do you think I should look for her?"

"Yeah. I do."

The next day they got up determined to make their last days of vacation so special that the memory would last a lifetime. If necessary.

Sol looked out at the Atlantic while he sipped his coffee. The surf was high. The wind wasn't just noisy, but pushing against the piers and posts that the elevated house was built on. He was looking at the high surf and thinking that it had been hard to get any sleep with the house moving around. Still, he wasn't complaining.

He knew he couldn't fully enjoy the sensations of being cuddled next to Farnsworth's warm body when he was asleep. So he took pleasure in holding her in his arms, feeling her breath on his chest, and listening to the phenomenon of a howling Atlantic wind.

A slight rustling alerted him that she was coming up behind him. He turned and gave her a big grin.

"Let's go rent a dune buggy and then fly a kite." He set down the coffee, grabbed her and twirled her around.

"Have you lost your mind?" He shook his head like a little boy, still grinning. "You can't charm me into doing something insane. I'm too old for that."

He grabbed his crotch and said, "I've got somethin' right here that says that's not true."

She looked from his face to his crotch and back to his face. He wiggled his eyebrows, which was so cheesy it made her burst out laughing in spite of her determination to draw a boundary in defense of his outrageous behavior. Outrageous behavior that was both fun and unexpected.

"Come on. Get dressed. Let's go get bacon and eggs and pancakes at that diner up the beach and then wake up the dune buggy guy."

"Sol, it's too cold out there. The dune buggy guy isn't going to open up until June."

He stepped back and looked serious. "Where is the Farnsworth who can perform miracles?" She blinked slowly and opened her mouth. "Okay. Just pretend with me. I'm one of the knights. I'm standing in front of your counter telling you that I have one day off and it's my fondest desire to get a dune buggy rental on Cape May. Today. What are you going to do?"

She continued to stare for a couple of beats, but then smiled sheepishly. Her pride in her work trumped her bluff and bluster. "I guess I'd find a way to make it happen."

He laughed. "And that's my girl."

Two and a half hours later they were bundled against the cold, full of diner pancakes, and flying down the sand in a glittered magenta fiberglass dune buggy. Sol whooped and hollered every time they hit a bump that temporarily lifted them out of their seats. It wasn't her favorite recreational activity, but he was having such a good time that she wouldn't put a stop to it even if she turned into a popsicle.

She turned to look at him just as he let out a huge whoop. Then the horizon was turning the wrong direction and the ground was coming toward her like it was falling down on top of her. When she landed on the wet hard pack sand, her breath was knocked out of her and every last nerve ending was frozen in shock from the impact. Lying there, she had no way of predicting whether that paralysis was temporary, permanent, or some sort of prelude to dying.

After an agonizing minute that felt like hours, she was able to rake in a breath. It took longer to mentally check over her body for injuries. She felt stunned, but not seriously injured. At least not in terms of bleeding or breakage.

She'd landed on her front side with her head turned toward the water. From that position all she could see was the ocean and sky. The wind was cold, punishing, and relentless. When she was able to lift her head and turn it the other direction, she saw that the dune buggy was turned over. She tried to call for Sol, but with the wind so high she wasn't sure she'd actually made a sound. All she'd managed to do was get a mouthful of sand.

With nothing to help her but will and determination, she managed to get to her hands and knees. She started crawling toward the wreck while spitting sand out of her mouth. If it was June the beach would be populated with people walking dogs, jogging, building sand castles with their children. But the beach at Cape May in March seemed as deserted as the Siberian tundra. There was no one to help.

She couldn't see Sol so she assumed he was on the other side of the dune buggy. When she got close enough to touch it, she got a grip on the undercarriage frame and used it to pull herself to an upright position. Her body protested loudly, letting her know that she needed to prepare to be one solid bruise for a while.

She tested her ability to walk with a small step, still holding onto the buggy's frame. It wasn't pleasant, but it was possible. She continued gingerly inching her way around to the other side.

"Sol," she tried calling again. "You're scaring me."

She thought she heard him answer, but couldn't be sure. So she kept going that direction.

There was nothing that could have prepared her for the trauma of what she saw when she came around the front and could see the other side. Sol lay on his back, his leg pinned underneath the buggy where a monstrous pool of blood had formed. His face was white as snow.

The sight swept her off her feet as surely as if she'd been physically knocked down. She fell to her knees and crawled the rest of the way. She heard a strange hiccupping sound through the wind. When her muddled mind put together that the sound matched the jerking of her chest, she realized it was coming from her, that and sheets of tears blown dry by the wind almost as soon as they fell.

When she reached him, she saw his eyes cut to her face. He opened his mouth and tried to say something, but nothing was coming out.

"I've got to get help. Got to get help." She started jerking her outerwear off and covering him up with it. The whole time she was chanting, "Got to get help," in between sobs. She couldn't leave him and couldn't help him without leaving him. Finally, the cloud in her mind cleared away enough for an image of a phone to form. "Phone," she said out loud.

She started looking around and spied the red crocheted bag she'd brought along on their outing. It must have fallen out of the vehicle when it started to roll because it was lying on the sand about thirty feet away. She pulled herself up and tried to make her body run for it. She fell twice on the way, the second time she was close enough to scramble on hands and knees.

The phone was in the bag and perfectly fine. She called 911.

"911. What is your emergency?"

"My... my fiancé is caught underneath a dune buggy. I think his leg is... is..."

"Where are you?"

"On the beach. We're... I don't know."

Someone in one of the nearby houses had finally looked out and seen what was happening. He'd come running as fast as seventy-year-old bones could bring him and arrived just as she was telling the 911 operator that she didn't know where they were. She couldn't hear the man come up behind her in the wind, but she was in too much shock to be startled when he took the phone out of her hand and began speaking.

"Near Spirit of Cape May. Beach patrol knows where that is."

She didn't know how long it was before the ambulance arrived, but he was dead before they got there. She overheard one of the paramedics say to the other that, if she had applied a tourniquet that, it wouldn't have saved his leg, but it might have saved his life.

The resident who had come to her aid asked if he could take her somewhere. It was easy for him, with no medical training whatever, to recognize shock by the glazed and distant expression on her face.

"Look here," he said to the paramedics. "The young woman is in shock and needs to go to the hospital herself."

"Yes sir. Another unit is on the way."

"All right," he said. "How long will that be?"

"Hard to say." They handed him a blanket from the ambulance. "Keep her warm until they get here."

The ambulance drove away. When no one had come an hour later, the good Samaritan said, "I'm going to get my car and drive it as close as I can. Stay here until I get back. I'm going to take you to the hospital myself."

On the way to the emergency room, he tried to get her to name someone he could call to come and help her. When she didn't speak, he resorted to calling contacts on her phone.

Sol had fought to keep his eyes open as long as he could. When they finally closed of their own accord and refused to reopen, he'd been freezing cold, lying on wet sand, with the worst imaginable sounds ringing in his ears, the combination of howling wind and Farnsworth weeping. He'd been angry about the entire turn of events and ready to take names.

When he opened his eyes again he saw sunlight filtered through gently rustling leaves in a tree overhead. Looking around he saw that he was lying on grass so green it looked fake. He heard tinkling wind chimes and people nearby laughing like they were playing. Playing like children. The sound of a flute might have been coming from a distance, but he hoped he was imagining that part. The flute was just enough maudlin overkill to make him want to beg to be put out of his misery.

He checked himself for pain, but no. There wasn't any. Matter of fact all physical sensations were pleasant. Maybe even nice. Or they would be if the flute would find something else to do.

He thought about sitting up and found himself jacking to a sitting position quickly and smoothly without feeling any muscle strain at all, which was a little weird because, on his best day, a sit up could still be felt.

From a sitting position he could see idyllic pastoral scenes in every direction. Flora and fauna abiding in a state of otherworldly perfection, Spring-time harmony on steroids. Grassy hills, flowered paths, trees with silver-dollar-shaped leaves danced in the little breeze and birds sang in a way that would probably be pleasing to most people.

Sol had already been losing his battle with flute irritation. The birds just ratcheted his annoyance up several notches. He was trying to remember how one gets birds to shut it or move on, when his attention was pulled toward the sheep. They were fat and fluffy, snowy white, with pretty black faces and shiny dainty hooves. And one of them was staring straight at him instead of being down with the phony-looking grass like his brethren. Sol tried staring the sheep down and eventually concluded that the animal was too stupid to realize that Sol had just alpha'd the crap out of him.

"Hey. Eyes to the grass!" Rather than having the desired effect, Sol's instruction to the curious sheep seemed to make him more interesting to the creature.

That, added to the irritation of the birds and flute was just too much.

"WHAT IS YOUR FUCKING PROBLEM? YOU ARE A HAIR'S BREADTH AWAY FROM BECOMING A LAMB PIE!"

In response the sheep bleated, but Sol knew all the way to the bottom of his core that it was intended as a raspberry.

He was in the process of standing with plans to throttle the errant ovine, when he noticed that he was wearing a toga. A white toga. Complete with one shoulder and a skirt that ended above the knee. No shoes, and a quick check confirmed that there was nothing underneath the toga either. Nothing supporting or protecting or covering the package, that is.

The bad news was that he was shoeless and naked except for a short ass toga. The good news was that some of his anger dissipated when he realized that the sheep actually had a legitimate reason to be looking at him funny.

When Sol got to his feet, the sheep bleated again.

"Yeah. That's what I think, too," he grumbled.

Looking in the direction of voices, it seemed the most logical possibility for determining where he was, how he got there, and, more importantly, how to recover his clothes and get the hel out.

CHAPTER 3

Jefferson Unit, Fort Dixon, New Jersey, Loti Dimension

"Hello?"

"Hey."

The caller didn't need to identify himself by name. Litha knew his voice very, very well. Well enough to hear every layer of weariness and to note the absence of his usual exuberance.

"Hi, Glen. How are you? Haven't heard from you for a while."

"Yeah."

Litha was nothing if not patient. She could wait him out no matter how long it took, but as the silence stretched, she felt a maternal need to rescue him from awkward conversation. "We've missed you."

He cleared his throat. "Am I still invited to Thursday night dinners?"

She smiled at the phone. "I think you know the answer to that. Standing invitation for Thursday or anytime at all. Shall we expect you tomorrow?"

"I'd, um, like that."

"Sure. I'll come get you. You know Rosie's not here though. Right?"

There was another pause. "Not there as in…what do you mean?"

"Not here as in gone, Glen."

"Gone where?"

"We don't know. Precisely."

There was a pause. "For how long?"

"We don't know that either. Actually I was hoping *you* might shed some light on the situation. I know it's prying and might only be considered my business indirectly, but do you think her sudden need for time away has something to do with you?"

After another pause, he sighed. "Maybe." He said it quietly with a hint of something that might have been embarrassment.

"Well? Talking or leg breaking? Which will it be?"

"You don't scare me, Mrs. I know you're more powder puff than demon."

"Yes, well, I admit to being fond of you, but understand this. I'm obligated to like Rosie more. Capiche?"

He chuckled softly. "As you should. Given the threats, I'm going to need some guarantees of my safety before I risk dinner. Not to mention the passes."

"No worries. I'll be bringing the handcuffs."

"Funny."

"You know I'm not joking. No handcuffs, no passes. That's the rule. You have a reprieve until tomorrow night. Then you have to face the parents and blab."

Again, he didn't answer right away. "What are we having?"

She laughed. Any doubt that the caller might have been masquerading as Glen dissolved with that question.

"Nine o'clock. Your time."

"Okay. I'll be the cute one in the hallway outside Sol's conference room. I mean outside the Sovereign's conference room."

"The cute one?"

"Okay. I'll be the only one there."

She chuckled at him and disconnected.

Glen sat on the edge of his bed and continued to stare at the phone wondering why he'd thought there was something, anything, in the world that could override the ache in his heart from being separated from Rosie. When she'd issued an ultimatum, "Call by Thursday night or else," he'd reasoned that starting a long-term relationship with caving to demands would set a dangerous precedent and an expectation of servitude. Nothing about that sounded appealing to a werewolf. Even a quarter werewolf.

So he had deliberately let the deadline slide thinking her burn would cool and they would work it out. He was practically watching for the clock to roll over midnight, just past ultimatum, so he could call. She had said supper Thursday. He did the math. The Storms usually had dinner at seven Pacific time. There was a three hour time difference between New Jersey and Napa Valley. That meant ten his time. So he decided to wait a couple of hours past to prove his point, save his pride and their future.

At exactly midnight he tapped her contact number. She didn't answer so he left a message and followed that with a CALL ME text. No reply.

It was the first time he'd gone for ten days straight without seeing Rosie since she'd been born and he was feeling the loss in painful ways. He couldn't begin to estimate the number of messages he'd left. A hundred maybe.

He didn't think there was anything funny about being forced to call her parents for information, but he was getting borderline desperate. He needed to get in touch with her and sort it out.

Storm was in and out of Jefferson Unit frequently, helping out with keeping things in order until the new Sovereign took over. Although no one knew when that would be because there was no one on the horizon.

If people with the profile and qualities of potential Black Swan knights were rare, the profile and qualities of a Sovereign were practically non-existent. It had to be someone who had once served as an active duty knight, who could tolerate administrative work, with the common sense of a problem solver, the judgment of a sage, and the charisma of a leader.

Good luck finding all that in one package.

Storm made a point of taking Farnsworth into the club lounge for coffee in front of the fire or having lunch with her twice a week. Nobody had ever specifically taught him that friends look out for the widows of friends, but he felt like that was the right thing to do. Although Sol and Farnsworth hadn't been married when he died, Sol had told Storm that he was surrendering his bachelorhood in the very near future.

Farnsworth was touched by Storm's attentions and came to lean on him for emotional support, which he offered freely. When the initial haze of grief began to lift from her heart, she occasionally had thoughts about something other than the hole left in her life.

"Sir Storm." She set her cup into its saucer and looked over at Storm who sat cattycornered in a plush chair. "The night before Sol died, we talked about something from my past. I had a teenage pregnancy and gave the baby up for adoption on the advice of counselors."

Storm looked solemn, his dark eyes reflecting a little of her sadness. On several occasions Farnsworth had thought that she'd never known a better listener. He nodded for her to continue.

"Sol thought I should try to find her and I feel..." She paused to take a couple of deep breaths and look away. When she felt like her composure was restored, she said, "I feel like I need to do that for me and also for him."

"You want Black Swan to locate her? Gather some information?"

Farnsworth nodded. "Her birthday is April 22nd. She'll be twenty-eight. The adoption took place in Fall River."

"Is that in...?"

"Massachusetts."

"I'll get the ball rolling. The report will come into the Sovereign's office. Do you mind if Glen sees it? I might not be there whenever..."

"No. I don't mind. The course is locked in. Really has been since I made the decision to tell the story to someone. To Sol," she added.

"Is there something else?" Storm's question was prompted by instinct. He couldn't have explained it, just the feeling that something had been bothering her since Sol's death. Something beyond mourning.

She blinked like she was surprised and looked around like she was afraid someone had heard her thoughts. She looked at Storm and swallowed.

"Whatever it is, you can tell me. You know I'll never break your confidence."

She stared at Storm for a minute and then smiled. "A confessional."

"You need to confess something?"

"You'll hate me after you hear it."

"I seriously doubt that."

The expression on her face changed from uncertain to determined. And hardened.

"I killed him."

Of all the things she might have said Storm wouldn't have guessed that in a thousand years. His jaw dropped and he gaped openly while his brain tried to piece together how she might have come to such a conclusion.

"Were you driving?"

"No."

"Then what makes...?"

"I heard the paramedics who put him in the ambulance that took him away. They said that if I had done a tourniquet, that it wouldn't have saved his leg, but it would have saved his life."

Storm's face transformed into an expression of the most abject sympathy. He couldn't imagine how hard it must have been for her to believe that she'd not only lost the love of her life, but that she was also responsible for his death.

"Susan. Have you ever been instructed on how to apply a tourniquet field dressing?"

Her brow furrowed and she searched his eyes. "No?"

"It was a thoughtless thing for those idiot medics to say and an easy thing for them to say. Tourniquets are second nature to them. They know how to do it. They know it so well they don't remember when they didn't know how to do it. Plus, *they* weren't in shock. You almost certainly were. Weren't you thrown from the vehicle when it turned over?"

She looked down at the floor. "Yes."

"Did you lose consciousness?"

"I think so. I don't know for how long."

Storm cursed under his breath. "Please excuse me. I've got to go get some morons fired and the Cape May Emergency Services Department is going to give you an apology or there'll be the devil to pay." Realizing what he'd just said, he hoped she didn't know about his mixed heritage.

"No, Storm, I don't want this made public."

"What they said…it's not right. Passing judgment like that, on an injured, traumatized person?" Storm's gaze jerked up to hers. "Did they send just one ambulance?"

"Yes."

"Where did they have you ride on the way to the hospital?"

"They didn't."

"What do you mean they didn't?"

"They left me on the beach."

Storm stood up so fast she flinched. He looked furious, but what he was feeling was even darker and more intense than that. "You can't ask me to do nothing. That goes so far beyond incompetence."

Looking around to see who was watching, she took his hand. "Sit down. Please."

He sat, but wasn't having much luck controlling the battle urges. "How did you get to the hospital?"

She studied him for a few seconds trying to decide whether or not to answer, because she knew that anything more would just be throwing kerosene on the fire. Finally, she decided that Storm might have a point. She didn't know how to apply a tourniquet and she bet that those paramedics didn't know how to do many things that were so routine to her that they were second nature.

"The paramedics said that there would be another ambulance coming. The man who helped me, he lived in one of the houses on the beach, waited with me, but the ambulance never came. Finally, he got his car and drove it as close to where I was as he could. He took me to the hospital, took my phone and started calling contacts. When he called the Operations office, one of the trainees answered and got Glen. At least that's what I heard."

"Gods Almighty. It's a marvel you aren't a suicide. It's the cluster fuck that just keeps on giving."

"What?" Farnsworth's eyes darted to Storm. He'd never used language like that in front of her before.

Storm leaned to the side so he could pull his phone from his pocket and touched Monq's name. "Code P. Someone has a story for you. We'll be down in five minutes." Storm ended the call and looked at Farnsworth. "Now listen to me.

"It hurts my heart that you've been carrying the burden of somebody else's mistake. I'm glad you told me, but I'm sorry you waited this long. You're not responsible for what happened to Sol in any way. It was an accident.

"You may not believe me, but I'm just a retired knight. We're going to go downstairs and tell your story to somebody who *can* actually help you sort this out."

"Who?"

"Monq."

"I don't know, Storm."

"He can be a character. I admit it. But he's good at what he does. Let him help you through this.

"You survived. I'm very glad you did and Monq is going to set you on the path of healing so you can live the rest of your life the way Sol would have wanted you to."

Storm saw the shift that took place in her demeanor when he mentioned what Sol would have wanted. She took in a breath. "Okay."

"One last thing. Please. I'm begging you, for Sol's sake and mine, too. Give me permission to get justice from the assholes who wrongly blamed and then abandoned you."

"Okay."

CHAPTER 4

Overseer Dimension.

"He's one of those."

Huber had rushed into the Council room to let them know they had a troublemaker whose status had been escalated to need-to-deal-with.

Heralda looked up. "Whose child is he?"

"Oh, you know, could be anybody's."

"If he's causing *that* much trouble, he couldn't be anybody's. He couldn't be Theasophie's, for example. Or Etana's."

Huber pursed his lips intending to look thoughtful, but it ended up looking more like Baby Huey pouting.

"Stop that," Heralda said.

"Stop what?"

"That ugly thing with your lips."

Huber looked offended. "Humph." He crossed his arms over his soft tummy and glared.

"Huber, try and stay focused. What are his traits?"

"He's sure he knows everything and should be in charge. His spirit was sent to Summerland on Saturnia because the stories his grandmother had told him were the closest thing he had to religion and an idea of hereafter.

"His behavior has been disruptive to the point of being disturbing. We even tried an immersion treatment in the River of Rebirth."

"Yeah?"

"What happened?"

"Nothing. He's one-of-a-kind stubborn."

Heralda looked at Culain. "Thinks he knows everything and should be in charge?"

"Got to be Ragnal's," said Culain without even looking up from what he was doing.

"No doubt," added Ming.

Heralda turned to Huber. "So go get Ragnal and tell him to fix the problem."

Huber stomped his biker boot clad foot and his belly jiggled noticeably. "Don't order me around like I'm an Elemental. I'm a peer!"

"Of course you are. I would go myself, but I'm really in the middle of something. Would you mind? Please?" Heralda used her most persuasive tone. "I'll look at your dragon babies later."

"You will? All right. I'll go this time."

"Thank you."

Huber waited outside Ragnal's harem, if not patiently. He paced, fumed, and muttered something about Viagra. He stopped in front of one of the massive androgynous Elementals guarding the door.

"How much longer?"

The guard's face never changed expression. He slid a dispassionate almond-shaped gaze Huber's way but said nothing.

"Fine!" Huber said. "Just give him this message."

Huber turned his back to the door and wrote a cursive message in the air with his index finger. "Urgent Council biz. GG wants to see U. Tired of waiting. Call me. – HQ"

The black letters hung in the air at eye level. Huber looked them over and decided that cobalt blue would be better. He waved his hand and stepped back to better see the result. Satisfied with the new look of his airborne graphic, he made a face at the guards and vanished.

Huber had made sure that Ragnal couldn't help but see the message when he emerged from his fuck fest.

But Ragnal chose to interpret the word "urgent" as "when you get around to it". After all, according to his personal version of hierarchy, he saw the other Council members as working for him.

The others had let him get away with the self-delusion for centuries, but he was on the verge of pushing it one too many times.

"He what?" Heralda asked.

"His guards wouldn't let me in. I left a message, but he hasn't returned my call," Huber said.

"Did he know it was Council business?"

Huber nodded. "Used the word urgent and told him you said."

The room rumbled underneath their feet. *Uh oh.*

Heralda was more than a little upset that Ragnal had ignored Huber's message, which was virtually the same thing as a summons. She stormed out of the Council room and materialized in Ragnal's private foyer, but unlike Huber, she didn't bother with polite protocol which entailed asking the guards for entrance. As far as she was concerned, Ragnal had used up his chances to play by guidelines and be social. Good manners don't hold integrity for long without being a two way exchange.

She bypassed the guards and went straight to where Ragnal was enjoying felatio as performed by a creature of indeterminate genetics. When Heralda grabbed the giver of head and pulled her away, the sudden loss of suction – which had apparently been sincere – resulted in a wet pop and the lolling of a Council member's rapidly deflating penis.

Ragnal stood, making a noise that resembled a howl, raised his hand to Heralda, but thought better of it just before he struck. His brain reengaged in time to remember that she had a reputation for holding a grudge and fighting dirty. He lowered his hand.

"What do you want, Heralda?"

She deliberately looked down at his flaccid godhood. "Let's start small. Cover that up and we'll talk about bigger issues."

He sneered as he pulled a robe over his head. "Better?"

"Will you join me at Council willingly, Ragnal?" He hesitated one beat too long for her patience. "Or..."

"Oh all right."

Within the blink of an eye they were in the Council room and he was being apprised of the situation.

"What makes you think he's one of mine?"

Huber snorted.

Ragnal looked at him like he'd farted instead of snorted.

Heralda more or less strutted to her rococo chair and made a show of sitting down. "Comparing his qualities to yours, there can be little doubt."

Ragnal's eyes roved over the Council members present before fastening on Heralda. "And what is it you want me to do about it?"

"Your child. Your problem. Figure it out."

He glared at her for a bit before saying, "Where is he from?"

She looked at Huber, who answered, "An inconsequential little cell of a layer on the fringe of the ellipse."

Ragnal let out a long sigh managing to communicate without words that he was perturbed, put out, and prickly.

"And where is he now?"

"Saturnia," Huber answered again.

"Show me."

CHAPTER 5

Shamayim

It seemed to Sol that he'd spent an eternity in Hel. The caretakers on Saturnia had tried everything imaginable to calm the soul who insisted his identity remained that of Solomon Nememiah, even though he'd left his physical body behind. Since he hadn't forgotten the details of his former life, he was not adapting well to his spirit's vacation between incarnations.

He was supposed to be basking in the sensory perfection of Saturnia's Summerland and rejoicing in the initial stages of Phase One, but what he was doing instead was trying to incite other sojourners to riot. He'd demanded to be told what the caretakers were talking about when they repeatedly referred to Phase One. When they refused to answer, his response could only be described as a fit – a display the caretakers were not accustomed to seeing in a passively pleasant dimension like Saturnia.

The caretakers' reply was always the same. Sol's response to that was always the same. They would stare at him as he demanded to see the person in charge and blink slowly when he threatened them with a sound throttling.

During brief periods when he would take a regrouping break from his full on assault of the status quo, he would return to the grassy knoll where he first awoke to find himself trapped in a nightmare that, to him, made Dante look like Disney. He was perpetually pissed off by the oversupply of pristine and pastoral. How he longed to hear someone, other than himself, object to something! Anything!

He swore that, if he ever escaped the madhouse, he would never complain about complainers again.

The grassy knoll, which he had come to think of as his personal space, was replete with aggravating birdsong, but at least he didn't have to look at the serene beatific and creepily robotic expressions of humanoids whom, he concluded, must have been lobotomized.

The biggest drawback to his retreat was not birds that never slept, but a sheep that hadn't anything better to do than stare. Sol began to wonder if it was a robot spy, equipped with camera and sound, observing and recording everything he did. The thought sounded paranoid even to him, but that thought was always followed by the admonition that all conspiracies are not imaginary.

Sol was sitting on his knoll studying the sheep, envisioning ways to dismember it, wondering how the legs would look Frenched and how it would taste with mint sauce. That led him to the realization that he hadn't either eaten or been hungry since arriving. Nor had he consumed liquids of any sort. Because he was lost in that thought and because he didn't anticipate company, he was startled by a nearby voice.

"Solomon Nememiah?"

He jerked his head in the direction of the inquirer, a man with tan skin, tan pants and a black Ravi Shankar tee shirt with long sleeves and three long slits across the torso that were evenly spaced like claw marks. He was medium height with strong facial bone structure, brown eyes and hair cut so close to the scalp it was impossible to tell its actual color. But by far the most striking thing about him was the no-nonsense expression he wore. The guy wore a presence that screamed, "I am not a pussy."

"Yeah?"

"I hear you've been requesting to speak with someone in a position of authority."

"And would you be that guy?"

Ragnal's face wore a ghost of a smile, but it didn't change the hard look one bit. "What do you think?"

Sol met the confrontational gaze eye to eye, but knew without asking that the fellow was altogether a different sort than he'd encountered since arriving in that godsforsaken place. He got to his feet so that the newcomer wouldn't be looking down on him. Literally.

"It seems you have me at a disadvantage."

The ghost of a smile grew slightly bigger. "How's that?"

"You're dressed. I'm not."

Ragnal's eyes drifted down to Sol's bare legs and feet. Then he put back his head and laughed. "Yes. You're one of mine all right." Sol had no idea how to respond to that, but his eyes narrowed. Ragnal's laughter ended in a sigh, a smile, and a shake of the head. "What would you like to wear? Never mind. Just think about your preference."

Before Sol could ponder the bizarre instruction, he had, in fact, formed an image in his mind of what he would like to be wearing – his favorite old jeans that had been washed so many times they were buttery soft, the ones with a hole in the knee for character, a plain white tee shirt, and coffee-brown Ropers. He knew the instant his clothes had changed because he no longer felt grass between his toes, no longer felt a breeze ruffling his, um, skirt, and he did feel the familiar comfort and security of having his package supported. Even though he knew what he'd find, he looked down for confirmation.

Yes. Those were his favorite weekend jeans and his broken-in boots. He passed a large hand over his chest and abdomen reveling in the feel of the tee that covered his upper body. To his mind there was nothing better than the freshness and classlessness of a plain white, soft fresh cotton tee.

He didn't understand how physics worked in hel, if that's where he was, but he did understand saying thank you to someone when they did you a good turn. "Thank you."

"You're welcome." The guy nodded once. "I assume you have something to say? Would you like to stand, sit, walk?" Ragnal cocked his head, tilted his chin up as he looked at Sol and said, "Never mind. I know the answer."

In less than a blink of an eye, Sol found himself sitting on a leather barstool in front of a well-aged oak bar, being handed his favorite long neck by a kindly-looking bartender who winked when he set it down. Sol swiveled around to take a read on his environment. Old vampire hunter habits never seem to fade away. There were only three people in the bar. Himself, the bartender, and a yet-to-be-named companion.

"I'm Ragnal."

"Just Ragnal?"

"Yes."

"It seems you already know my name."

Ragnal gave a slight nod. "What I don't know is why you've been causing such a ruckus."

"I need to get out of here."

"I see. And where do you want to go?"

"Back."

"Back?"

"Yes. You know. Back to where I was before I was here."

"Oh." Ragnal paused before adding, "I see."

The bartender walked to the end of the bar and disappeared around the corner as he slung a damp towel over his shoulder. Sol thought that was a nice realistic touch. The guy must have gone to the Elia Kazan school of acting.

Ragnal grasped the long neck that sat in front of him. It was covered with the telltale condensation caused when glass-bottled beer is chilled in ice. "So this is your favorite, huh?" He took a sip and pursed his lips. "Hmmm. Not bad."

Sol looked at his own beer. He liked the way it looked sitting in front of him, but he just didn't have a desire to reach for it. "So. About going back?"

"Ah, yes. About that." Ragnal looked into Sol's face. "Just out of curiosity, can you tell me what you were doing at the moment of your death?"

That question shouldn't have come as a shock to Sol. He'd put it together shortly after arrival... that he must have died. But still, having someone just say it out loud like that made him feel funny. Inconsequential somehow. He heaved a big sigh even though he'd also discovered shortly after arriving that inhaling and exhaling were purely optional.

"So I really am, uh, dead."

"Let's not play games, Solomon. You know you've moved on to another phase in the process."

"Sol."

"What?"

"If you're going to call me by my first name, call me Sol."

"All right. Sol. What were you thinking at the very last?"

Sol looked down at the bar, looked at the beer, then looked at his hands. "I was thinking that I couldn't check out because too much depended on me. I was thinking that, if it turned out there was an after-existence that was supposed to make me happy, I would have to convince somebody that the only thing that would make me happy is being returned to duty where I belong."

When he turned back, Ragnal searched his eyes like he was looking for something in particular. "And what sort of 'duty' is it that's so important?"

Sol drew up short, realizing for the first time that he would have to discuss Black Swan business with an outsider. That presented a dilemma. He couldn't get out of there without breaking his vow of secrecy.

"This is a pickle. I took a vow of secrecy."

"So you need me to pledge confidence?" Sol nodded. "Very well. You have my word that I will not divulge what you tell me without first gaining your permission to do so."

It wasn't perfect, but Sol decided he had no choice but to accept it and be satisfied.

"We were in the middle of a vampire crisis. We thought we'd found a cure, but it didn't work out and, if anything, we made it worse. I was instrumental in the correction. A world of people, some who know about the impending danger and some who don't, were depending on me. So I *have* to get back."

Ragnal's expression gave away nothing except that Sol thought there might have been a flicker of recognition when he'd said the word vampire. But by the time he'd finished speaking, Sol could see that Ragnal looked confused.

"I'm not understanding. There's a problem relating to vampire?"

Sol's shoulder sagged. "Yes. There's a problem relating to vampire and you just made me the king of understatement." Ragnal scowled. "So you know about vampire?"

"I know a little about them. I didn't know they were posing a problem."

Thinking about Animal House, Sol realized that Ragnal might be aware of the variety of vampire that are relatively harmless, the kind that, like mosquitoes, just take their blood and go without causing more than a minor irritation.

"Vampire have been a plague on our world for at least thirty generations and perhaps forever. A bacterial virus turns humans into monsters who are serial killers of women and contagion to men, infecting them with the disease.

"We learned recently that there is something particular to the environment in our world that caused an adverse, viral, reaction."

Sol stopped to make sure that Ragnal was following.

"Go on."

"I work for a very, very old organization that was founded for the purpose of keeping humans safe. If it wasn't for the effort we've made to contain the epidemic, it would have grown exponentially and rendered humans extinct a long time ago."

Ragnal stared at Sol as he took another drink of beer. "And why do you believe you are indispensable to this... cause?"

"You think it's ego. It's not ego. It's like there's a tsunami on the way. We need all hands on deck. It's not so much that I'm indispensable as it is that I'm useful. I've been doing this work most of my life and I'm responsible... was responsible... for a contingent of people who are most qualified to combat what's coming.

"Sure. Somebody could eventually take my place, but I'm ready to hit the ground running now. And that's what they're going to need to survive."

After a second Ragnal gave Sol a smile that looked a little like a smirk. "You think you should be in charge. I get it." Ragnal stood up. "Let me see what I can work out." He looked around the bar. "Where would you like to wait for your answer?"

"You got a library?"

"That can be arranged."

Sol found himself standing in front of a Greco-Roman building at the bottom of steps, flanked by two huge lion statues, leading upward to a bank of doors that appeared to be glass framed in gold. The building was the only structure in a countryside that was unaltered by road or building.

As he began to climb the steps, he told himself that he would be grateful for small favors if he opened the doors to find no birds, wind chimes, flute music, or sheep inside.

Ragnal found Heralda cooing at some sort of cat-sized reptiles in a large terrarium. She looked up as he was approaching.

"All taken care of?"

"No. Turns out it's not my problem," Ragnal said. "It's *your* mess and you're the one who needs to clean it up."

"What are you talking about?"

"One word. Vampire."

"Cut the cryptic games and say what you mean to say before I lose patience with you twice in one day."

"Your vampire's saliva interacted badly with the unique organic composition of the subject's little world. Turned homo sapiens into cannibals intent on wiping out their own species."

Heralda paled visibly as she thought about the possibility of giving Pierce cause to extend their Earth sentence. Extensions can be a real bitch when time is infinite. The vampire project was supposed to be for *extra credit*. How ironic was that!

"You're sure?"

"That's what he says. Why would he lie?"

Heralda turned to the elementals standing by the inner doors. "Get me Kellareal!"

CHAPTER 6

Overseer Dimension

Heralda was a vision sitting in her white and gold room with her hip-length black hair moving in slow motion around her body. It was lifted by an invisible force so that it appeared to be floating. She was wearing a blood-red dress that matched her blood-red mouth and was tapping her blood-red fingernails on the massive arm of her rococo chair. That's how Kellareal found her, lost in thought, when he entered the room.

She looked up. "Why am I just now hearing about this?" Her tone was accusatory, but Kellareal wasn't easily made to feel defensive.

"The vampire in Loti Dimension?"

"YES! THE VAMPIRE IN LOTI DIMENSION!"

His throat moved as he tried to swallow his frustration and not yell his response at equal volume. "I've attempted to bring the situation to your attention *many* times. Perhaps you were distracted?"

She glared at Kellareal for an uncomfortable minute as if it was his fault that she hadn't been paying attention. "All right. Whatever. I'm listening now."

Kellareal explained the history, confirming that the vampire virus had first appeared around two thousand years ago and, as Solomon Nememiah had said, would have rendered the human population of Loti extinct if the secret society of vampire hunters had not intervened.

Heralda rose from her chair and began pacing. "Who sponsors this Black Swan thing?"

"They've been operating independently."

She raised her eyebrows. "No sponsor?"

He shook his head and angel dust fell freely around him like platinum glitter. "None."

Heralda pursed her beautiful lips while she continued to pace.

Huber entered uninvited, didn't bother to cast Kellareal a glance, and plopped down on Heralda's very grand, temporarily vacated chair. "If you don't stop doing that thing with your mouth, you'll end up with smoking wrinkles."

"Hmmm?" She hadn't been paying attention. "Huber, I don't have time for your silliness right now."

He slunk off to his play corner, sat down at his table, and began making motor lips noises.

"Not having a sponsor might make it easier to correct this situation. No objection. No interference. No blowback."

"Yes, ma'am," Kellareal agreed.

She looked at Kellareal. Really looked at him for, perhaps, the first time in centuries. "I'll probably need your help."

"Yes, ma'am."

"Huber. Stop that and come here!"

Huber looked up from what he was doing, which appeared to be stirring the beginnings of a tropical storm in the Gulf of Mexico. He dropped his hand like he'd been caught doing something naughty and shuffled over to stand at the foot of Heralda's dais.

"Go talk to this mortal mischief-maker. Find out if he's the sort who could keep his mouth shut if we give him what he wants."

Huber stood up ramrod straight, gave an exaggerated mock salute, and attempted to click his heels together. It looked a little ridiculous in his everyday costume of white toga and biker boots. The boots more thumped together than clicked.

Heralda rolled her eyes. "Hurry up."

"Why is it again that you don't ever run your own errands?" She turned a glare on him that included bared, clenched teeth. "Okay! I'm going!" he whined as the doors flew open to let him pass.

Sol had spent a long time in the library. At first he'd found it amusing to walk around shouting, "Hello," and then listen to the echo. But as much as he thought of himself as the antithesis of a people person, the solitude grew tedious after a stretch of time and he was ready to break up the boredom, even if the only way to do that was to listen to birds pretend to be birds.

He was lying on his back on his grassy knoll watching the shimmer of aspen-like leaves in the trees above him, remembering the silky feel of Farnsworth's hair and the way her eyes would get so bright when he kissed her the way a woman like her should be kissed – thoroughly. He wondered about how she'd felt when he'd left his body behind, if she'd taken it really hard. If she was doing all right. If she was still wearing his ring.

He didn't hear anyone approach and jumped a little when someone nearby cleared his throat. Sol raised his head and looked in the direction of the sound.

There was a curious character standing about eight feet away wearing a goofy expression, a toga, biker boots, and a ridiculous laurel wreath on his head. Sol wouldn't be mean enough to say the little guy was misshapen, but it did cross his mind that a few pushups and laps around the pasture could only do the figure good.

Sol remained in a semi-reclining position, but propped himself up on his elbows. "I was here first," he deadpanned.

Huber giggled. "I know."

"Well? What do you want?"

"I've been sent to ask a couple of questions."

"Did you bring snacks?"

Huber giggled again. "You want snacks?"

"No. Just thought I'd ask."

"Oh."

"You want to sit down?"

"Okay."

Sol watched, fascinated, while Huber crossed his legs meditation-style in midair before floating down and hovering just inches above the grass.

"Neat trick."

Huber looked momentarily confused, as if he hadn't thought about the fact that everyone couldn't defy gravity at will. His brow cleared when he realized what Sol meant. "Oh, yes. I have others."

"I'll bet. How about raising the dead?"

Huber waved his hand and said, "Sometimes," offhandedly. "And speaking of that..."

Huber stopped midsentence, seemingly preoccupied by other things.

"Speaking of that..." Sol prompted.

Huber's unfocused eyes cleared and he brought his attention back to Sol as he reached up to straighten his laurel wreath, which hadn't moved at all. "Let's play a game of 'What if?'"

"Okay. *What if* I don't want to play?"

Huber pouted a little. "No fair. I get to ask the questions."

Sol made a little twirling gesture with his hand to indicate, "Go ahead."

"What if we sent you back?" That got Sol's attention. He sat up. "You know we couldn't send you back to your old body because it's, you know, gone."

"Gone?" Intellectually Sol knew that made sense, but emotionally it felt like the bottom dropped out of the elevator. "Oh. I... guess that's right."

"If we sent you back, we'd have to put you in a new body." Sol's mind was racing trying to figure out how to make that work. "Don't get ahead of yourself. For now, all I want to know is if you think you could keep a highly unusual secret."

"Look. I work for a highly unusual secret organization in top level management. I'm not bragging. That's just how it is. Now. My turn. How am I supposed to get back inside in a different body without telling them who I am?"

Huber looked down and frowned. "That is a puzzle. Set that aside for the time being. Assume we could get around that part and get you inside this 'highly secret organization'..."

"Are you mocking me?"

Huber looked sheepish. "Just a little. Are you sensitive? You don't look sensitive." Sol glared at him. "So? Can you keep a secret?"

"Yes."

"Very well. Good boy." Huber started to leave. "Um. As you were." He vanished.

While Huber was gone, Heralda called the other available Council members together. She would have rather had lashes than admit to her six peers that there'd been an unfortunate and undesirable side effect to her prize creation, the vampire. But she knew it was useless to try and hide the mistake now that Ragnal knew about it. The only thing stopping him from broadcasting the news throughout the multiverse was that they were in the project together. If one made a mess, so far as Overseer Pierce was concerned, the mess belonged to the whole group.

The only logical play for her was to get out in front of the story and confess the error in a contrite show of character and humility.

So she called a meeting and did exactly that. The others seemed to take it well. Heralda interpreted that to mean that they had their own little missteps they'd just as soon keep under wraps.

"Send him back in a new body?" It was technically a question, but not one that Theasophie expected to be answered. "That's risky business. If it gets out, it will create an explosion of religious fads. Every human will want a new young body when the old one ages out."

"Like hitting a reset button," Ming added.

The doors opened and Huber floated in.

"Well, Huber. What do you think? Does the human strike you as someone who could keep that sort of secret?"

"He's a grouchy sort, but he's all about the duty and the honor, blah blah blah blah blah blah."

"If we agree to helping you out of this bind," Ming said, "you'll owe us."

"Oh here we go." Heralda suspected the negotiation was coming.

CHAPTER 7

Rio de Janeiro

Rev Farthing walked with as much stealth as possible on the old and unevenly worn brick alleyway in the old Colonial part of the city. His team had just split into pairs to try and head off a couple of vampire pulling at a young girl who, judging by her dress, was part of the Samba School Parade.

If being a vampire hunter wasn't already a nightmare, try adding Carnival week to the mix. Anything within blocks of the Sambadrome was an all-you-can-eat vamp buffet and the crowds of dancers, tourists, and revelers were too thick to do anything about it. They unwittingly provided both bountiful feast and perfect cover for vampire for one week every year.

Every night when he went out on patrol he told himself the same story. That if he died that night, it wouldn't be a tragedy because he'd lived a lot in his thirty-one years. He'd seen a lot more of what the world had to offer, good and bad, than most. He'd also given the past sixteen years to the service of humanity through an outfit called The Order of the Black Swan.

He'd spent his childhood in England, but his father had been appointed British ambassador to Portugal when he was ten. By the time he was recruited by Black Swan, he spoke perfect Portuguese, which was why he was sent back to Brazil after he was inducted into knighthood.

There was no one to grieve for him. His parents and older brother had been killed in a sailing accident off the Spanish coast near Barcelona and there was no other family that would recognize him as an adult without being told who he was. No wife. No steady girlfriend. Not many regrets. Like the Native Americans supposedly said, it was a good day to die. That was what he told himself every night when he went out to hunt.

He was moving as quickly as he could, keeping to one side of the alley. He wore dark clothes and was glued to the shadows on the wall while his partner mirrored his actions on the other side. He was so intent on reaching the girl in time, that he never saw the shadow in front of him take form until it had sunk its teeth into his trapezius. He yelled out from the shock or the pain or the anger at being overtaken.

In less than five seconds his partner had staked the vampire from behind. It slumped to the ground between them. The two knights stood and stared at each other in the dim light, a world of communication passing between them. It was a rookie mistake. He'd let his emotions, his desire to save that girl, override his training.

Rev had been partners with Jorge for seven years. The bond they shared couldn't be described to anyone who'd never had the experience of being certain they were going to die. He'd shared that experience with Jorge many times.

They couldn't say how long it would be before Rev was overtaken. The resurgent strain was converting humans much faster than the old virus. Minutes.

In the darkness he could see the shine of tears streaking down Jorge's face. There wasn't anything to say. They both knew the score. They both knew that, if Jorge had been given the choice, he'd trade places with his partner. For seven years they'd patrolled together. And for seven years each had silently reaffirmed that he would give his life for his partner. If it came to that.

Rev didn't look panic-stricken. He didn't even look upset. He simply smiled at his partner and Jorge would never forget what he said. "I love you, brother. Quit this madness. Find a girl. Live a long life. Give your babies a kiss from me. And remember there's never a good day to die." Then he held his arms out to his sides.

According to the explicit instructions they'd been given on how to proceed in such a circumstance, they both knew what had to be done. Jorge raised his stake, but the uncontrollable sobs were racking his body so hard he was afraid he would miss Rev's heart. He knew he had to get control of his feelings long enough to dispatch his friend or cause unnecessary suffering. And there was already enough suffering. He loved Rev Farthing far too much to let his execution be anything besides quick.

So he sucked in two deep breaths, gritted his teeth, gave his head a vigorous shake, and screamed at the same time he summoned all his might toward driving the stake into his fellow knight's heart. He did a good job. Rev didn't linger. Jorge sank to his knees next to the body and called the cleanup location in to his Sovereign.

For a while he sat motionless next to his partner's corpse, feeling a hundred years old and wishing he had died, too. Then he leaned down, planted a kiss on his Rev's cooling forehead, left the cell phone lying on top of the body and walked away. Away from the alley. Away from his partner's corpse. And away from Black Swan.

When cleanup arrived a few minutes later, all they found was one dead vampire and Jorge's cell phone lying on the ground not far away.

The following morning, the Rio Unit Sovereign set down his coffee, opened his portaputer and TOP SECRET file on the transfer of Sir Farthing to Jefferson Unit in New Jersey. Everything seemed to be in order. He'd just never heard of an urgent middle-of-the-night transfer before. "Nice of them to tell me," he grumbled before getting to work on revising the schedule rotations.

Shamayim

Kellareal found Sol in the library that had been created for his benefit, sitting at a table in the middle of an immense room with a four story ceiling and gallery views of the stacks on every floor. Sol was looking down at the book he was reading, but looked up when he caught movement in his peripheral vision. He watched the angel approach and stop in front of him on the other side of the table.

"Mind if I sit?"

Kellareal was wearing the white robe that was his customary uniform when he visited the planes of Phase One. Sol's eyes drifted over him before making a conciliatory gesture toward a chair on the other side of the table. He closed the book he'd been reading. "Do I know you?"

"The answer is no, but only because of chance. We narrowly missed meeting. There was an incident involving one of your knights and I ended up being in and out of Jefferson Unit for a while. You were away on holiday."

"What incident?" Sol's brow furrowed as he instantly slipped into caretaker mode and became more concerned about the fact that one of his knights was involved in an "incident" than about the fact that he was stuck in some kind of pastoral purgatory. "Which knight?"

Kellareal responded with the barest of smiles. "All was resolved and is well. At present, the topic of conversation is what to do about you." The angel glanced around. "Let's get out of here."

Instantly they were seated at the bar where Sol had conversed with Ragnal over a beer. The same pleasant-looking bartender put two chilled Lone Star beers on the bar.

"Anything else?" He looked from Sol to Kellareal and back to Sol.

Sol shook his head.

Kellareal said, "No. Thank you," and watched the man until he was out of sight. His black eyes slid back to Sol.

"You were saying..." Sol did revolutions in the air with his right hand to hurry the Enforcer along. "...what to do about me."

"You know, your sense of self-preservation doesn't seem to be fully developed."

Sol searched Kellareal's face. He'd made note of the angel's height and unusual looks. White blond hair and black eyes wasn't exactly a common color combination.

"You want me to be afraid of you?"

The angel grinned. "No." He scraped a hand back and forth over his chin. "But most people are." Sol started to open his mouth, but Kellareal held a hand up. "I know. You're experiencing some anxiety and you want me to move toward the point."

Sol waited.

"Well, it's good news."

"Really?"

"Yes. We found you a body. One that's perfect as a matter of fact. Actually better than your old one."

"Hey. There was nothing wrong with my body."

"Okay. Simmer down. I'm just saying you might accept the transition easier if you consider this an upgrade.

"A thirty-one-year-old Black Swan knight was the victim of a vampire bite in Rio last night while on patrol. He was staked by his partner, according to procedure. But I guess you know all about procedure. We recovered the body in time to heal the wounds and purge the bacteria that interacts so badly with human biology in your world.

"We also forged transfer papers to New Jersey. As far as his former unit commander knows..."

"Sovereign."

"Yes. His former Sovereign. As far as he's concerned Sir Farthing is on his way to Fort Dixon right now."

If Solomon Nememiah had ever been more excited, he'd lost track of that memory. He was going back. He tried out the name to see how it felt on his tongue. "Farthing." He realized that he probably shouldn't be giddy about some poor devil's fate, but he told himself that it was circle of life stuff. One creature benefits from another's misfortune.

"Wait a minute. The vampire bite... it wasn't, uh..."

"No. No. Relax. It was pure fate. The man was in the wrong place at the wrong time and that's all there was to it.

"Sir Reverence Foster Farthing. Rev for short. There'll be a scar over your heart where he was staked so you'll need to come up with a cover story in case you're asked. Bicycle accident as a child or something like that."

Kellareal grinned. "And I know you don't care one way or the other, but most people who see you in your new body? The first thing they're going to think is that you're good-looking."

"Yeah. You're right. I don't care about that. What I do care about is the catch."

"Catch? Ah. The fine print. Very astute because indeed there is some."

"Thought so. Let's have it." Sol gave his beer bottle several rotations on the bar without lifting it up.

"First, you have to agree formally that you will never tell anyone who you were."

Sol nodded.

"Second, some of Farthing's memories may be embedded in the brain circuitry and that could cause some confusion. Could take some getting used to."

"I'll handle it."

"Last, you'll be deposited into a healthy new body on its way to Jefferson Unit to take up the position of active duty knight. We're putting you on the chess board with all the tools you require. What happens after that is up to you."

"I guess it's the best I could hope for."

Kellareal smiled and put his hand on Sol's shoulder. "It's better than I thought was possible. You fought the law and damned if you didn't win. Everybody knows it doesn't get better than that."

"I guess I owe you a thank you. So. Thank you. When do I leave?"

The angel laughed.

Sol blinked and when he opened his eyes he was on a company jet that was taxiing. He looked out the window to a view he knew very well. The plane was pulling up to The Order's private hangar at Fort Dixon. He moved his hands to unbuckle his seatbelt, but the action felt unfamiliar. No hint of carpal tunnel or reminder of the finger he'd broken in Seville.

He looked down at the young strong hands in his lap, the long fingers and large knuckles, the smoothness and even skin tone, the healthy veins. All of a sudden he couldn't wait to stand up and get to a mirror.

When Kellareal had talked about his looks, he told the truth when he said that was the last of his concerns, but facing the very real prospect of a new identity put that in a different light. The desire to know what he looked like was as intense as a compulsion.

When he felt the plane's brakes make that final stop, he swung up and out of his seat with the easy athleticism of a much younger man. The flight attendant came toward him. She wasn't just smiling. She was flirting.

"Let me get that for you, sir." She pulled a bleached duffel down from the overhead and put her hand on his bicep in a way that was clearly invitational. "Did you enjoy your flight?"

He smiled back at her, appreciating the attention as someone who had once taken sexual magnetism for granted, then woke up one day to realize that he was no longer turning heads. "I must have. It seemed to go by really fast."

She giggled.

A jeep was pulling up just as he descended the last step and set foot on the tarmac.

"Airman Konolkin, at your service, sir." The young driver took Sol's duffel and put it in the back of the jeep.

"Airman." Sol nodded once and swung up into the vehicle. "Nice day."

"Indeed it is, sir. Have you been to Fort Dixon before?"

As Sol stared straight ahead he was overwhelmed by the deluge of memories that question evoked. He felt his face soften into a small smile. "Yes. I have. Looking forward to being back."

"Yes, sir."

When he was dropped in front of Jefferson Unit, Sol shouldered his duffel and stood staring at the front of the building. If he was honest with himself, he hadn't really believed he'd ever be back in a body entering J.U. again. He heard his stomach rumble and laughed out loud. He was hungry! Hungry and eager to see what he looked like.

He stepped inside the door and was standing on the outer circle of The Hub a few seconds later. There was definitely more hustle and bustle than the last time he'd stood in that spot. The extra activity looked good on J.U. His entrance hadn't garnered any attention so he took the moment of temporary anonymity to turn right toward the men's room.

A man was coming out, someone Sol didn't recognize, but who had to be a hunter based on his age and the way he carried himself. He breathed a little sigh of relief thinking there was no one else in the restroom, but had to rethink that when he turned toward the mirrored wall.

His first thought was that there was someone else and that he'd have to wait. Then he realized that the stranger looking back at him, mirroring his every movement, was Rev Farthing. He let the duffel slide to the floor and approached the mirror, slowly examining every detail of the reflection.

Cripes! No wonder the flight attendant was a little gaga. That angel fellow didn't lie. The kid in the mirror was damn good-looking. Light brown hair, dark brown eyes, and tanned skin pretty enough to be a woman's. At least he thought that would be the case once he shaved off the travel scruff. He hesitated at the top button of his shirt feeling a little gay about peeping, but by the gods, it was his body and he deserved to have a look at it.

He pulled the sides of his shirt apart to reveal well-defined abs kept in top working condition. His eyes followed a natural path to the happy trail. He asked himself if he had a good excuse for a look at the package and decided that a piss stop was as good an excuse as any. So he unzipped, pulled out, looked up into the mirror and grinned at himself. Yeah. The angel was right. He could have done a lot worse.

Once he got all that pretty hair buzzed away from his head he'd start to settle into the new house of flesh.

Overseer Dimension

"Enforcer. You need to keep an eye on the vampire aberration on that outpost." Heralda didn't bother to look at Kellareal when she addressed him.

"Very well. What does 'keeping an eye' entail?"

She stopped what she was doing and looked at him. "We'll assist that band of boys. What was the name?"

"Animal House?"

"No. The human boys."

"The Order of the Black Swan."

"Yes. We'll give them just enough support to begin turning the tide their way, but not enough to raise suspicion of divine intervention or something of the sort. The last thing we need is another era of people claiming to have gods on their side."

"You're going to sponsor them? Black Swan, that is?"

Huber barked out a laugh, stopped abruptly and began sniffing the air in every direction. "Does anyone else smell irony on the grill?" he giggled. "The mother of vampire is sponsoring vampire hunters. If this ever gets out..."

"Shut it, Huber." Heralda heaved a sigh while she considered goosing Huber with a small lightning bolt. She turned back to the angel, appearing more bored than anything. "Yes. I will sponsor them. Keep me posted."

"All right. Do you have a goal in mind?"

"Um. How do they count time?" Kellareal showed her a vision of time in year increments. "Two hundred years." Kellareal didn't move or change expression. "Too long or too short?"

"In terms of their life spans, that's eight generations."

"Oh. Make it one hundred years then."

The angel bowed and vanished before she changed her mind. He knew her habits all too well.

CHAPTER 8

Jefferson Unit, New Jersey

Rev Farthing went straight to the Sovereign's office. He recognized the kid sitting at the assistant's desk in the outer office. Bo Barrock.

Bo looked up. "Yes, sir? Can I help you?"

"Rev Farthing reporting for duty." He looked toward the closed door. "Who's the acting Sovereign?"

"Sir Catch. Glendennon Catch."

"Sir Catch? Not Sovereign Catch?" Sol felt the same little rush of pride he always felt when one of his boys was inducted into the knighthood. That feeling of accomplishment never seemed to get old.

"No sir. It's kind of a long story. Basically though, the unit Sovereign passed away and Glen, um, Sovereign Catch is one of the people filling in until he can be permanently replaced."

"Thank you, Mr.," Sol made a point of leaning back to read the on-duty-now name plate on the desk, "Barrock. Would it be possible for me to speak with Sir Catch?"

"Just a second, let me ask." Bo rose and turned his back to Sol to knock lightly on the Sovereign's door. He opened it, stuck his head in, and said something to Catch.

In another couple of seconds, the door was jerked wide open. Bo had to step out of the way as Glen advanced on Sol smiling with his hand out.

"Glendennon Catch. So glad to have you here." Sol shook his hand. "You stiff from the flight? What is it? Ten hours?"

"Yeah. About that. And, no, I'm doing all right."

Glen waved toward his office. "Good. Good. Come on in. You want something?"

"Well, to be honest, I haven't had breakfast. I was going to check in with you and then try to scare something up."

"No hunting necessary. We like to take first things first. Bo," Glen turned to his assistant, "Get the kitchen to bring us the works." Turning back to Sol, he said, "What do you like?"

"American all the way. Eggs. Bacon. Hash browns. Biscuits. Orange juice. Coffee."

"No pancakes?"

Sol grinned at Glen. "A side of pancakes with warm maple syrup would be heaven."

"Heaven, huh? Well, let's see what we can do." He motioned Sol into the office while he told Bo to bring the food to the conference room and call when it arrived.

When they were both seated in the office, Glen turned to Sol. "So. Again. Welcome. Bo said you asked to speak to me?"

"I did. I want to apply for the job of Sovereign."

Glen had just raised a coffee cup to his lips and sputtered a little which caused some of the liquid to go down the wrong way and some to land on his keyboard. When Glen started wheezing, Sol stood up, but Glen stopped him with a wave. "Just give me a second," he said in a strained and breathy voice as he tried to return his breathing to normal.

When he was once again in control of respiratory function, he looked across the desk at Sol with eyes slightly narrowed and a studious look on his face.

"What makes you think the position is open?"

"The HELP WANTED sign on the door."

"Very funny."

"I heard that you're in line for impending field duty. Do you have somebody in line to take over here?"

Glen shook his head slowly, trying not to do a Snoopy dance in his chair or look otherwise too eager. Personally, he couldn't imagine why anyone with faculties functioning properly would want the job, but if the guy in front of him turned out to be the real deal, he just might be the recipient of the first kiss Glen ever bestowed on another guy.

He didn't really care how Farthing knew about the opening. He just hoped he was looking at a real replacement candidate for somebody who couldn't really be replaced.

"Why do you want it? And what makes you think you have what it takes?"

The two questions that went straight to the heart of the matter. Sol was proud enough of Glen to bust the buttons on his shirt.

"I could give you a bunch of baloney answers, but I'm going to tell the truth even though it's going to make me sound like an ass."

"Okay." Glen looked intrigued.

"I like to run things and I'm good at it."

Glen stared for a minute and then started laughing. "You want to know what's funny about that answer?"

"What?"

"That's exactly the kind of thing the former Sovereign would have said. And there was never one better at the job. Ever." Sol would have been lying if he didn't admit that he enjoyed the flattery. It was nice to know that he'd left life with people thinking good things about him. "And what makes you think you can do the job?"

"Give me a try. No harm. No foul. Let's negotiate a probation period."

"Well, it's not quite that easy to get hold of command around here, but I accept your application.

Gladly. And will get the two other people who will be most instrumental in making a decision to conduct your vetting."

"Could I ask who the other two are?"

"I doubt you know them. The head of science, research, and development, Dr. Thelonius Monq and knight emeritus, Sir Engel Storm."

"You're right. I don't know them, but I have heard of both of them. I'll look forward to the meeting or meetings, whatever the process may be."

They chatted about various issues of running Jefferson Unit for a while longer until Bo stuck his head in to say breakfast was served. They moved the conversation into the conference room where Glen almost got the feeling that he was the one being interviewed.

The questions that Farthing asked about J.U. were so germane, so pertinent, that with each passing minute Glen was more and more certain that the perfect guy had just come walking through the door asking for the fu...

"If this is an example of the food around here, then I'm in."

"You know, Farthing..."

"Call me Rev."

"Sure. I'll tell you what. There's an outside chance I might even get the two decision makers in here to talk to you right away. If it's up to me, we'll get your tryout." Sol smiled. "You got a resume?" Sol's face dropped and Glen started laughing. "Gotcha. Just kidding. Not a resume kind of job. Nothing could prepare somebody. Believe me. Wait here."

Glen left and, while he was gone, breakfast dishes were taken away and replaced with a fresh coffee service. Since there was nothing else to do, he poured himself a cup of black and settled into a chair. Waiting wasn't his favorite thing whether it was lying on a grassy knoll or sitting at a conference table. He'd already heard enough to know that time was being wasted, but he understood the need to convince his own people that he should be in charge. It was just weird.

Twenty minutes later Glen opened the door and held it as Monq and Storm entered. It was harder than Sol could have imagined pretending that he didn't know them. He'd shared considerable history with both those men, but had to act like they were strangers.

They sat down at the table and conducted the interview informally, more like a casual conversation than a tribunal. Sol didn't have a resume on paper, but he was able to recite his qualifications on demand and make a case for why he should be given a try.

It was a tricky mental exercise, using key points that could only spring from his personal working knowledge of the position without revealing that he actually had personal working knowledge of the position.

He noted the glances that passed between the three as punctuation to some of his answers. After a couple of hours, Storm said, "Will you excuse us for a few minutes, please?"

"Of course," he said.

In less than two minutes, the door reopened and they filed back in. He guessed from the grin on Glen's face that he was going to be sitting in his old chair real soon.

"You're in," Glen said, looking a little elated and a lot relieved. "Ninety day probationary position. If all goes well, there will be a review by higher ups at the end of that time and then it will be made permanent. Don't screw up because we," he motioned between himself and Storm, "don't want the job back."

Storm stuck out his hand. "Welcome to Jefferson Unit, Temporary Sovereign Farthing." Sol took his hand and Storm used his other hand to slap Sol on the shoulder.

"If you'll excuse me," Glen said, "I need to make a call to get everything ready. We'd made arrangements to house a new knight and hadn't planned on opening up the Sovereign's apartment."

"Anything is fine. I just need a bed. I'm ready to get started."

"Come on," Storm said. "Let me walk with you and help you get situated with credentials and a tour while they're getting your quarters ready."

They were chatting as they walked. Unbeknownst to Storm, Sol was asking sly questions for the purpose of getting up to date and up to speed on what was going on in his absence.

He was totally focused on that conversation when Storm stopped and said, "Okay. I'm dropping you off here, but I'll catch up with you in a little while."

Sol nodded and turned his attention to where he was.

There were two things that almost caused him to give himself away. The first, and by far more traumatic, was standing behind a counter a few steps away. The sight of her almost made his knees buckle and, at the end of his life, he would say the hardest thing he ever did was to keep from vaulting over the counter and pulling her into his arms.

"Can I help you?"

He thought she looked much the same, but with a touch of sadness maybe. She was wearing her business persona: crisp, efficient, determined not to miss a single detail. Few Black Swan employees had ever seen Farnsworth off duty and relaxed.

A lifetime of discipline helped with the control. Instead of grabbing her up and showing her how much he missed her, he stared and swallowed until she repeated herself.

"Is there something I can do for you?"

His presence of mind snapped into place and he knew he had to play the role of newcomer. He stepped back outside the door, pretending to read the placard. "Operations, right?"

"Yes. This is Operations."

He walked up to the counter and smiled with the sort of warmth she didn't usually get from the knights.

"Rev Farthing. Reporting for credentials." She lowered her eyes and reached for the clipboard that held her docket. "And what's *your* name?"

"Everybody calls me Farnsworth," she said without looking up as she reached for the packet sitting near her right hand.

"Farnsworth. I'll bet our names will be next to each other on the revised list of J.U. personnel."

She was distracted and only halfway listening to what he was saying. When she realized he'd been speaking to her, a little line formed between her brows. "What?"

When she looked up, she met his eyes and registered that his gaze was intense.

He pointed to the personnel manifest. "Farthing. Farnsworth."

"Oh. Yes." She placed the packet on the counter in front of him, "Here it is," then turned her head to the left to speak to a trainee who was doing office time. "Mr. Chorzak, take Sir Farthing on a thorough tour of the facility."

"Yes, ma'am." Spaz hurried around the counter and waited by the door.

Sol leaned so far toward Farnsworth that she took a small step back. The fact that he'd put her in a position of retreat pushed at least one of her buttons and made hackles rise. With satisfaction he saw that fire could still be brought to her eyes.

He held onto her gaze like he was trying to cast a spell. "That's *Sovereign* Farthing." He said it softly with a slight smile, making it sound more like a promise than a correction.

"Sovereign?" She looked confused and a little flustered, which she tried to hide by looking through paperwork. He noticed that she wasn't wearing the ring, but wasn't surprised. She was no longer engaged. "I don't have any documentation to that effect."

"Just got the job. Technically I'm on probation for ninety days."

"Oh," she said softly. "Well, um, congratulations, Sovereign Farthing."

It was hard for her to imagine someone else filling Sol's role, but intellectually she recognized that the page had to be turned.

If Farnsworth wasn't acutely aware of the difference in their ages, she would have thought the probationary head of Jefferson Unit was flirting with her. But she'd just reviewed his file that morning as she prepared to complete the transfer of a knight. She knew that he was thirty-one. That put her at a whopping thirteen years older.

Internally, she scoffed at her imagination for sending the thought of flirtation across her radar. She told herself that she was old enough to be his mother, at least in a few drastically primitive and barbaric cultures.

The time she'd been without Sol crystalized in her heart the fact that no replacement for Sol was ever going to walk through that door. He was one of a kind.

"Sovereign Farthing, my function as head of Operations is to make things work here. If you find that you're in need of feminine companionship, I can make arrangements for you to connect with a variety of, ah, establishments frequented by young women."

He held her gaze for a moment longer than necessary, then cocked his head slightly, gave her a suddenly wicked smile, knocked on the counter with his middle knuckle and turned toward the door where the trainee was waiting patiently.

"Let's take that tour, shall we? Mr. Chorzak, is it?"

'Yes, sir. Everyone calls me Spaz."

Sol looked down at him. "Not really."

Spaz grinned. "Yes, sir. Really."

"Well we may have to do something about that. Even my knights-to-be deserve more respect."

"It's alright, sir. I don't mind."

"Well. I do. So far as I'm concerned, you're Mr. Chorzak."

"Yes, sir." Kellan Chorzak offered a small, shy smile. He really didn't mind being called Spaz. He knew it was done good-naturedly and almost affectionately. Still, the idea of being 'respected' had its own appeal, particularly when that respect was coming from the new head of J.U.

Farnsworth had been working in that office for twenty years, since she was twenty-four years old. The first decade and a half, she received her fair share of attention, and flirting, from the knights who drifted in and out. They were used to being admired by the female sex and they typically came with a certain swaggered poise that said they knew they were looking good.

She couldn't pinpoint when the flirting had stopped, but one day she realized that nobody had tried to impress her with a smile or a bedroom voice in, well, years. So naturally having one of the young knights, or, er, administrators, regard her with something other than professional courtesy was a little bit noteworthy and a lot flattering.

All morning her thoughts returned to the encounter with the new Sovereign. Her instincts had told her he'd been deliberately charming, but her intellect contended that he couldn't possibly be genuinely interested in her. And, even if the Earth tilted on its axis and he was interested in her in that way, she wasn't ready to try to move past a love affair with a man like Solomon Nemamiah and didn't know if she ever would. A woman just never gets over a man like that. Ever.

The second time Sol almost gave himself away because of an inappropriate emotional response was the stop on Chorzak's tour at The Chamber. Sol stepped inside trying to pretend to see it for the first time, but his breath caught in his throat when he saw the portrait hanging on the west wall.

Chorzak had been prattling away when he noticed that Sol had stopped. He turned to see what had grabbed the attention of Big Boss.

"That's a picture of the last Sovereign."

"Oh?" Sol said simply as he started moving toward it.

"Yeah. Everybody around here thought he was the sh..., um, thought he was the best."

Sol smirked down at Chorzak. "Did they now?"

"Yep. I'm afraid you got big shoes to fill, sir."

"Watch the impertinence, Mr. Chorzak."

Spaz stood up a little straighter. "Yes, sir."

Sol kept going until he was close enough to read the plaque.

In honor of
Solomon Neuhm Nememiah
Jefferson Unit Sovereign
and Distinguished Knight
The Order of the Black Swan

"The Lady Laiken... She's our martial arts teacher? She had the portrait done by the same guy who paints the heroes. I guess she's the one that decided what the words should say."

"The one *who* decided."

"Sir?"

"She isn't the one *that* decided. She's the one *who* decided."

"Yes, sir."

Thinking through how he would handle things if he was new to J.U. and had never held the job of Sovereign before, Sol decided he would want to brain pick the people who had done the job previously. So he called a meeting with Storm and Glen for the dinner hours that very night. Exercising one of his brand new privileges, he had the club lounge closed and had Crisp deliver dinner for three where they could dine and talk privately away from curious, prying eyes and ears.

At several points in the conversation he pressed his lips together in an expression that was familiar to Storm and unique, or heretofore unique, to Sol. It would have been impossible for Storm and Glen to recount their history with the job without memorializing Sol in the process. He sat back and looked amused while they chuckled over Sol stories.

After dinner he withdrew a small box of pencil thin black cigars from his pocket and offered them to Storm and Glen. Glen shook his head, but Storm quietly took one and waited to see what would happen next. Storm thought that it would be a curiosity of synchronicity if two people attracted to the J.U. Sovereign position happened to smoke the same brand - the same obscure brand - of imported Turkish cigars.

While Storm was mulling that over, the new Sovereign reached into the same shirt pocket and produced an old-fashioned lighter, the kind that requires lighter fluid. He noticed Storm eyeing the lighter. He looked down at it and said, "Found this in the Sovereign's apartment. I guess it belonged to the former resident. Would you like to have it? As a memento?"

"No. He'd probably enjoy knowing it was being used. Not many people want to fool with them these days."

Sol was pleased with the cover. He lit Storm's cigar before lighting his own, then placed the lighter on the table and proceeded to give it lazy quarter turns, exactly as Sol had done when he was alive. It caused goose bumps to rise on Storm's skin.

As they talked, understanding began to settle around Sol like an unwelcome shroud. It didn't take long for him to deduce that neither Storm nor Glen had been apprised of the information which he'd come by when called to Edinburgh in the middle of his holiday. *Before* he died. Which meant unit personnel were way, way, way behind in making preparations for the massive overhaul needed to get J.U. ready for a swarm of new or returning residents.

What was worse, if Storm and Glen didn't know, that meant that Farnsworth didn't know either and she would be ninety-nine percent of the reason for the success or failure of relocating a steady stream of Black Swan immigrants. Sol couldn't believe that something so big could have fallen through the normally sealed shut Black Swan cracks. He supposed that between the sudden and unexpected need to replace him as Sovereign and the immediate crisis of a viral mutation, the briefing had just gotten lost in the stampede.

Maybe Simon Tvelgar had thought he'd had a chance to pass on the intel before he passed. He took a drag on his little cigar while thoughts whizzed through his brain at Mach one. Instead of weeks to get ready, they had days. Truthfully, in his opinion, Storm and Glen were not prepared to implement far-reaching changes of that scope. And after all, wasn't that exactly why he'd fought so hard to get back there? Because he honestly believed that nobody else was as passionate about walking the tight-rope dichotomy of ridding the world of vampire while trying to take care of Black Swan knights at the same time.

Unfortunately acting on that information meant making some of the people that he most cared for very unhappy.

Sol thanked his temporary replacements for the informal briefing and, before they parted for the night, told Glen he would like to see him in the office the next day at ten o'clock. Storm received a similar instruction, but he was given a time of three o'clock instead.

Storm agreed, but added that he would be making himself scarce now that a suitable replacement had been found.

Sol gave no reply, but turned and walked away.

CHAPTER 9

The first decision Sol made as the new head of Jefferson Unit was to put his old identity to rest in his own head. He needed to stop thinking of himself as Sol and begin thinking of himself as Rev Farthing, Sovereign on probation who took over for the late Sol Nememiah. On the first night of residence in a comfortably familiar apartment, he held a memorial for his first incarnation with a bottle of Scotch, vowing to rise the next morning, reborn, and ready to conquer Life: Part Deux.

At exactly ten o'clock Glen came to stand in the open doorway on the threshold of the Sovereign's office and waited for an invitation to enter.

Rev looked up and motioned him in. "Sir Catch?"

"Good morning, Sovereign," Catch said with a grin as he stepped into Rev's new office.

"I would return your greeting in kind, but can't because I can see into the future."

Glen looked intrigued. "You're clairvoyant, sir?"

"Not at all, but I can still predict that you won't be looking quite so cheerful fifteen minutes from now."

"Uh oh. First day on the job and you're already busting as..., um, enforcing the discipline that's been lacking since the former Sovereign passed away."

Rev gave him the toothy grin his shit-eating comment deserved. "Sit. We put out the smokes last night."

"Yes, sir."

"I see that one of Z Team retired."

"Yes, sir."

"And that you're throwing in with them?"

"That's right."

Rev nodded and looked decidedly unhappy about that. "I see. Well, let me say this then. I haven't known you long and I don't know you well, but you seem like a nice sort. A nice sort with an outstanding and impeccable record. You would have to be remarkable to keep this place running. So I'm compelled to ask.

"Are. You. Sure?"

Glen smiled. "I see their reputation has made it south of the Equator."

"Oh, yes. They're infamous enough. I doubt there's anyone connected with Black Swan in any capacity who hasn't heard some Z story at some time or other."

Glen laughed. "Yes. And maybe some of it is even true!" Rev's scowl brought Glen's levity to a full stop. "I appreciate your concern, sir, but I expect I'll be able to..."

When Rev's mind unexpectedly flashed on a memory of an encounter with Z Team, he gasped from the assault of bright, vivid images and feelings of both excitement and anxiety. The memory came through crystal clear, complete with sounds, voices, and music. That would have been fine if he had always been Rev Farthing, but the memory he was witnessing – in his own head – was a recreation of somebody else's experience.

After a couple of seconds he realized that it was probably an episode of the memory cross-over phenomenon that Kellareal had warned him about.

Glen had come around the desk and was standing over him looking concerned. "What's wrong? You need medical?"

Rev swallowed and pushed the visions aside. "No. Of course not. An old injury. I just turned the wrong way and pinched a nerve. First time that's happened in years."

"You sure?"

Rev pointed to the chair. "Sit down over there and let's finish this talk." Glen hesitated, but did as he was told.

"So you have the crazy idea that you're going to rehabilitate that gang of miscreants?"

Glen smirked. "Why don't you just tell me how you really feel about them?"

"Just did."

"Maybe I'll learn something from them. Maybe they'll learn something from me. Maybe everybody benefits, The Order most of all. At least that's the plan."

"Well said, Sir Catch. You're a big boy, but you're a green knight. Being able to count on your team in the field is everything. Do you think these men are worthy of that trust?"

Glen had learned a lot about maturity while playing the role of Sovereign. Not wanting to rush into an answer without giving it due consideration, he took a moment and mulled the prospect over in his mind. "I appreciate your concern, Sovereign. I really do. As to the issue of trust, I honestly don't know, but if that's truly at question, they should be relieved of hunter duties."

Rev sighed and reached for his coffee cup. The kid was right. Their antics always seemed to stop just short of the discharge line.

"Next order of business. The vampire virus has mutated. Not only is it no longer affected by the vaccine, but evidence points to the new strain being stronger and more aggressive. At least the conversion process has accelerated. Vamps can be made in minutes."

Glen paled visibly and almost whispered, "Minutes."

Rev continued as if he'd just delivered the stock market report. "I need a report on housing for knights immediately, as in two weeks ago. We're recalling some of the retired to active duty and some of the trainees will be processed early.

"Including, Z Team, who will be staying here." He looked at Glen pointedly when he said it. "And the married couples… We now have eight in residence. We'll need housing for twenty more."

"Twenty?" Glen's eyes bugged out. "There hadn't been twenty-eight hunters in residence even in the days before the vaccine."

Rev nodded. "Your point?"

Glen moved his head back and forth in an odd motion that indicated discombobulated disbelief. "We don't have the staff to support that."

"That's right. But we will. They're on the way." He glanced at the calendar. "Should be starting to arrive in three days."

"Three days?" Glen repeated like he didn't believe it.

"You and your co-temporary-administrator were not made aware of the crisis or told to prepare for these changes in status, which was an oversight."

"Uh, no. We weren't. How is it that you know so much about it when you just got here?"

"That is no longer your concern, Sir Catch. You weren't told. It's not your fault, but it is a problem that's going to require diligent management and long hours."

"Yes, sir. Sorry for overstepping."

"In addition to the report on housing, I also need to see your recommendations on which three of the trainees could be made ready for field work right away."

"We don't have any trainees ready to go now, sir."

"Hard times, Sir Knight." Glen perceived from Rev's piercing look that he wasn't happy about the request, but it was what it was. "Every training unit has been tasked with repurposing. We have to come up with three to hit the numbers. You're in the best position to judge *which* three are most ready."

Glen looked as if he'd aged years within the last few minutes. 'Most ready' is not the same thing as ready. Nobody in his right mind wanted to pit kids against vampire. And, if it *had* to be done, nobody – least of all he, wanted the job of choosing which kids it would be.

Rev turned to his computer screen in dismissal. "Seems we've got a lot to do and not much time in which to do it."

"Yes. That is how it would seem," Glen replied.

Rev tried to look around Glen. "Who's on duty right now?"

"Bo Barrock."

"Please tell him to call Operations and ask Ms. Farnsworth to come for a briefing as soon as possible."

"I will. Is there anything else, sir?"

Rev looked at his watch. "Could you request the presence of Sir Hawking and the Lady Laiken in my office at 3:00?" Glen seemed to hesitate. "Is there a problem?"

"Um, well, sir, the problem is that I don't yet know you well enough to know if that's a true request or an order." In response to that, Glen received a stare so piercing that a lesser man would have squirmed. "Let's say that it's a request unless declined. Then it's an order."

"Yes, sir." Glen turned to leave. "Don't forget to tell Mr. Barrock to get Farnsworth in here. If we're going to pull this off, it will only be because she has miracle-worker in her skill set."

Glen looked curious. "You know her, sir?"

Rev glanced up from the computer screen. "Only by reputation and a brief introduction yesterday."

"Farnsworth has a reputation," he repeated. "Huh." Glen was clearly bemused about the idea.

"That's all."

At 11:00 Farnsworth knocked on the door.

Rev had been just about ready to grab his ears and scream, but when he looked up and saw her, a calmness descended and he was sure no task was impossible.

"Come in," he said softly.

"Sovereign." Her tone was crisp. She had her beautiful hair pulled back into a bun at her nape and held with crocheted netting. She wore tailored black pants, black heels and a sleeveless green silk blouse that fell to her hip line. It fit close enough to reveal the lines of her body without being overtly clingy. Elegant. Professional.

She sat in front of his desk and opened her portaputer with efficiency, apparently readying to take notes.

Rev stared openly for a couple of seconds, then rose, walked around the desk, closed the door which she'd left standing open, and returned to his chair.

"How are you?"

Farnsworth looked confused. "How am I?"

"Was that too intimate a question?"

Her face flushed instantly. "Intimate?"

"I don't want to make you feel uncomfortable, especially in light of the fact that I have bad news."

He spent the next few minutes explaining the crisis and the fact that they were weeks behind. She was cool, calm and collected through receipt of the news and all the implications for her and her department. It was also noteworthy that the only thing that got a reaction from her was his use of the word 'intimate'.

"So. Now that I've lowered the boom, as they say, I'm eager to hear your reaction."

"My reaction? That's why they pay me the big bucks?"

He tilted his head. "I know how much you make. It's not big bucks."

She smiled. "It was a joke."

"Of course, the big bucks." He returned her smile and held her gaze for a second. "What do you need from the rest of us to make this happen?"

"I need to see the report. Who? When? What do they do for The Order? We can hand off requisitioning medical supplies to medical, food to Crisp, and make housekeeping responsible for readying the apartments and dorm rooms that have been closed. I've got to have a total count on beds really soon though.

"Oh, I'll also need the flight schedules. My trainee assistants can coordinate pickups at the hangar. So long as someone else has made sure that there is enough support staff, we'll be okay."

She stared for a moment as if she was expecting Rev to say something.

"Yes?"

"Would you like me to double check the duty apportionment data to make sure we have the right ratio of support staff to knights and trainees?"

"That would be very much appreciated. I don't like unpleasant surprises." She laughed out loud. "What?"

"Well, who does? By the way, I'm not getting involved with anything to do with the armory."

Rev nodded. "Do you think you'll have an idea on where we are by tonight?"

She pursed her lips. "We better. They're coming ready or not. Right?"

"Right. So, in that case, would you like to have dinner with me and go over your thoughts, insights, discoveries…?"

She blinked several times. "I can make a report to you here." She looked around his office like it was safe.

"Yes, but you have to eat. I have to eat. Think of it as multitasking."

"Business dinner."

"Strictly business."

"All right then."

"I'll come by the office at eight. That is, if you think you'll be working late."

She snorted and immediately regretted the sound she'd made, even though she told herself that she didn't care what the new Sovereign thought of her. At all.

"Yes. I will be working late. I'll stop for dinner and then get back to it."

Rev's eyes roamed over her appreciatively. "I wish I could tell you that wouldn't be necessary. But the fact is that this entire convergence depends on you."

She met his gaze and saw that he was being sincere and not just polite. "Thank you for noticing. I'll do my part."

She caught the twinkle of amusement in his eyes when he smiled. "I know you will. Eight o'clock."

At three o'clock Storm, Ram, and Elora were waiting in the hall outside the new Sovereign's office wondering what in the world he might want with them. There was no one in the outer office because there was a shift of trainee duty at that time of day.

Storm was in midsentence telling the other two what he knew about the new guy, when the inner office door swung open.

Rev motioned to them. "Come in." Short. Terse. Authoritative. He acted like a man who'd been running that office forever, not like someone who'd just arrived and was feeling his way around. "Come on in and take a seat."

Storm took his customary place leaning against the back wall. Ram took his customary place at the end of the sofa closest to the Sovereign's chair and next to the Courtpark window. Elora sat in a leather chair facing the desk and was thinking that she'd been in that office countless times and had never sat anywhere else.

"I recognize you from your files, of course. My name is Rev Farthing, but you've..." He motioned at Ram and Elora. "...probably heard that already.

"I wish I had better news."

Rev spent a few minutes catching them up on the crisis. Of the three, the only one who had anything to say was Ram. He scrubbed a hand down the front of his face and punctuated the gesture with, "Great Paddy."

"Yes. Well, insofar as this predicament affects the three of you, and this does come from on high, every able bodied knight under the age of thirty-five is being recalled to active duty."

Ram jumped to his feet. "Active duty! For Paddy's sake, man! We have an apartment full of boxes packed for movin'. Look at my mate. You see that fuckin' nice bloom on her cheeks? 'Tis 'cause she's daydreamin' about a stack of an old house in Ireland, raisin' elflin's and black and silver pups!"

Elora had remained seated. "We have a baby, Sovereign."

The softening of Rev's face was barely noticeable. He'd been playing hard ass for a very long time. "Many of the retired knights have children, Lady Laiken. Perhaps even most." He glanced at Storm. "Sir Caelian is being recalled as well.

"You have seven days before B Team rotation begins. Six hour shifts every other day." He turned to Elora. "Sir Catch is preparing a report on which three of the trainees he thinks are most ready to go early. As martial instructor, I'd like to have your input on that as well."

At that, Elora jumped to her feet. She was incensed. "Stop right there! Putting seasoned knights back on the street is one thing, but you're not getting my boys before they're good and ready to go."

"It's not up to me."

"Of course it is. You're not getting them. And as far as B Team goes, two of us have a child together. Do you understand that that's a *special* circumstance?"

Rev seemed to be considering that. "You're right. You can't both be out on the same patrol. Take turns and I'll be B Team's fourth."

"What?"

"You heard me."

Storm spoke up for the first time. "You can't handle the duties of Sovereign *and* be on rotation."

"I absolutely can. And I will." Storm opened his mouth to speak, but Rev cut him off. "So long as I'm in charge here, it's not up to you."

To Storm, he said, "Go spend time with your wife and report in seven days."

To Ram and Elora, he said, "Go unpack. You're not going anywhere until we can replace you."

Watching as Ram and Elora looked to each other, an onlooker would have sworn an entire silent conversation took place through the connection they made with their eyes.

Ram turned back to Rev. "If our boy is going to be in danger..."

Rev interrupted. "If we're talking about vampire, this facility, which will soon house twenty-eight active duty knights and twenty trainees, is the safest place the child could be."

"Aye." Ram looked dubious. "I once thought the same."

The three members of B Team filed out into the hall, but didn't speak until they got into the elevator. Storm punched Hub level and turned to Ram. "How about a drink?"

"You read my mind, brother."

After they had settled into a booth near the bar Storm sat back and shook his head. "I'd rather take a horse-whipping than deliver the damn edict to Litha."

"'Tis no' *your* doin'. You're the victim here, the victim of vampire virus once removed. If anythin' she should be coverin' you with sympathetic kisses and cooin' about how The Order is king of mean."

Storm smirked at Ram. "Once removed? You have always had the oddest way of looking at things."

"Just another reason why you're incomparably fond of me. Wonder what Kay's goin' to say about this unwelcome development."

"Wonder what *Katrina* is going to say."

Storm looked at Elora across the booth table between them. "You're being uncharacteristically quiet."

Realizing that was true, Ram turned his head to watch her reaction. When she didn't speak right away, he put his arm around her shoulder. "What's goin' 'round in that beautiful noggin, my girl?"

Elora raised her gaze to meet Ram's, looked across at Storm, and then lowered her eyes to the table. "You heard him," she said quietly. "The vaccine, which came from *my* blood, has compounded the problem so that it's worse than it was before."

The two men knew her well enough to extrapolate her reasoning at the same time. Guilt.

"Elora," Storm began, "you can't possibly be thinking of taking on responsibility for this. For gods' sake, woman, you're just a plaything of the Fates. Like the rest of us."

"Stormy's right, love. You thinkin' 'tis you... well 'tis daft and there's nothin' for it."

Storm rolled his eyes at Ram's lack of delicacy. "What Rammel means to say is that, if we were going to place blame, which we're not, but if we were, it would be on Monq. Not you."

"AYE! 'TWAS MONQ!" Noticing that his outburst had drawn the attention of the few other people in the bar, Ram self-moderated his behavior, a rarity to be certain, and lowered his voice. "The whole thin' is a result of the quack's experiment and lays no' at your feet."

Elora looked up and searched Ram's eyes like she was looking for evidence that he believed what he was saying. When she seemed satisfied with what she saw, she looked over at Storm and found no accusation there either.

"Should I volunteer as an incubator to try and convert the new strain?"

"NO!!" Storm and Ram answered in unison, without hesitation, and with conviction. If Elora was a normal person, she would have been startled enough by the suddenness of their response to jump from her seat.

After a few seconds of silence, she said, "Okay." Looking between the two, she said, "I remember how I used to feel, thinking about you patrolling without me." She let her gaze settle on Ram. "I honestly don't know how I'm going to be able to sit at home wondering..."

Under the table she felt Ram's big warm hand cover hers. She interlaced her fingers with his. "Maybe I should..."

Both men knew what she was about to say. Again the response was quick, sure, and in unison. "NO!!"

When a couple of beats had elapsed, Ram said, "No doubt 'tis harder on the one stayin' behind." He gave her the signature killer smile. "You'll have to endure the discomfort just like..." His smile faltered when he allowed images of himself being the one waiting for her to return from patrol. "Fuck."

Storm looked at him with sympathy.

Elora took in a deep breath and blew it out. "As to the matter of my boys, I'd rather kill that pretty bastard than let him send my babies out before they're ready."

Ram scowled. "Pretty bastard?" He pulled back and looked at Elora like she'd grown a horn in the center of her forehead. "You mean the new Sovereign? You think he's pretty?" Ram sounded distinctly unhappy about the idea.

"Way to miss the point, Ram." She leaned into her husband so that her upper body was pressing against his arm. "Of course he's nowhere close to walking perfection. Like you," she purred.

His forehead cleared of lines as he smiled down at her, their faces inches apart.

"Gods of Halla. When are the two of you going to settle into old married life like the rest of us? To your point, Elora." She looked over at Storm. "You can't kill the new Sovereign. Without even broaching the morality of it, they would either send a replacement with the same orders, or order Glen and me to stand in. In which case they would also send the same orders. This is not going to be one of those times when you have a shot at fighting City Hall and winning."

"City Hall?"

Elora had been in Loti Dimension for nearly two years, which was long enough to glean most cultural differences, but not all.

"Metaphor for authority."

"Oh."

"So. What do you do when you disagree strongly, but can't fight?"

"Find a way to accommodate while preserving as much integrity as possible."

"Yeah. Exactly."

"You're saying that, if I have to give up three boys, I can at least control the situation to the extent of picking the ones that stand the best chance of surviving."

"Yep."

Elora stared at Storm for a few minutes while various candidates filed through her head. When every one of them ended with a vicious vampire bite, she finally shook her head and said, "No. The new Sovereign has to die. He and every replacement they send. Storm, if that's you, I'm sorry. You've been a really good friend. And rescuer. I'm auntie to your little girl and BFF to your wife, but I'm not sending lambs to slaughter even for you."

Ram chuckled, slouched into the booth leather, and threw back a shot of Irish whiskey.

"Elora..." Storm started.

She hissed at him. "We're supposed to be keeping the innocent safe from monsters, Storm. That includes those boys. I don't have any kids who are ready to be knights."

"I've got two Solomon Nememiah Medals of Honor that say otherwise."

Elora looked at him like she'd been slapped. She opened her mouth, but having lost her breath, it took her a while to whisper, "No."

The challenging expression on Storm's face melted into regret when he saw how deeply she was affected by the possibility that she'd have to give up the two boys who'd saved her own life. She looked at him like he'd just suggested throwing her own children to wolves.

"I'm sorry. I know you've gotten close to the trainees since you moved back here." He nodded toward the surroundings in general. "I don't mean to be so hard ass about it. What can we do to help?"

She took in a shallow breath like she was fighting for emotional stability and shook her red and pink head. "There's no good angle. If you put the trainees with veteran knights it's not only dangerous for the trainees, it's dangerous for the knights..." She stopped like she'd just received a message from the gods. "That's it! I need to be scheduled to go with them when they draw on rotation. I'll be their fourth!"

"NO!!" They answered in unison.

"The two of you are beginning to sound like the narrator's chorus in a Greek tragedy," she scowled. "And, in the words of the new Sovereign, it's not up to you."

"The fuck 'tis no'."

"Elora, you're a member of B Team and we're one of those outfits that's hard to get into and hard to get out of once you're in. I know what you're thinking. It's on your face plain as the day is long. You can't babysit knights. Not even very shiny new ones."

"I can."

"No," he said firmly. "You cannot. If The Order is going to give them the title, then you have to give them the respect that goes along with it. Compromising their confidence, which is what you'd be doing - and they're not dumb - threatens their safety more than a nest of vampire ever could."

Lines formed between Elora's brows as she let that sink in. She looked over at Ram, who responded with a slow nod. "Give the fucker his due, love. He's no' always right, but this time he is."

"After he put that out there, even if I didn't think he was right, I couldn't go with them now. Just on the off chance that he *is* right. Thanks a lot, Storm."

He shrugged. She was being sarcastic, but she should have been giving him genuine thanks because he *was* right.

"I've been so preoccupied thinking about what this means for me." She looked at Ram. "And you." She looked at Storm. "And you. And my boys. I hadn't even thought about how awful this must be for poor Baka. He was so, I don't know, euphoric about the vaccine putting an end to the plague. I'll bet he's taking this really hard."

"Well, I'll tell you one thing," Storm said. "He'd better make sure he keeps his ass away from fangs because there won't be any 'third time is the charm'."

Ram snickered.

"That's not funny," Elora scowled at Ram whose smile didn't waver in the least.

Storm's cell vibrated against his hip. He pulled it out and glanced across the table at Ram and Elora. "Kay."

He opened the connection with a tap. "Yeah?"

Storm jerked the phone away from his ear. Ram and Elora could hear Kay yelling from across the booth. "Hold... (pause). Hold... (pause) Hold... (pause) HOLD ON JUST A MINUTE!" I'm putting you on speaker. Ram and Elora are here."

"Well, hail, hail the gang."

The three looked at each other. Sarcasm wasn't Kay's typical style.

"Look. We're all in the same boat," Storm said. "Nobody's happy about this."

There was a long pause before Kay said, "What's the real story? There's got to be more to this than just report in seven days." Kay made some sort of indescribable noise. "SEVEN DAYS!!"

"We're not ALL in the same boat. Ram and Elora have got each other. I can't bring Katrina to J.U. and you can't bring Litha either."

Storm looked around the table. His gaze fell on Elora and stayed there. "That's partly true. Since Litha's an employee, she *could* move in here temporarily if she wanted to, but one thing is for sure. Wherever they are, Trina and Litha are not going onto the patrol schedule."

Kay's sigh was long and heavy enough that they heard it over speaker. "Yeah." He was sounding a little calmer. "That is something on the positive side." (Pause.) "I'd like to say that Elora is equipped to take care of herself, but we all know that's not true."

"Hey!" She jumped in while they chuckled. "Getting hung like meat while biters feast on your naked body and try to drain you isn't exactly a picnic." They stared at her without saying anything, each caught in the throes of his own memory. "Well. I guess it *is* a picnic if you're vampire." She smiled, not wanting to remain in that memory a second longer.

"So," Kay said. "Seven days. You told Litha?"

"I'm not calling from the hospital."

Kay laughed darkly. "Yeah. She could do it, too. What I'm likely to get out of it is a very sullen, unfun wife and a very dry wick."

"Hey!" Elora repeated. "Ladies present."

"Oh?" Kay said. "Who else is there?"

She snorted. Ram grinned. "No' a problem, lover boy. Just flip the switch in that great room of yours and start the mirrored ball goin' round. She's a sucker for your Disco Dino. I give her less than three songs to be callin' your wick wicked."

He wiggled eyebrows at Elora when he said the word "wicked".

"You're never growing up, are you?" she asked.

"From here it looks like growin' up is highly overrated," he said as his hand was slowly creeping up her thigh under cover of the tabletop.

She gave him a receptive smile, but moved his hand away and whispered, "Later," into the beautiful pointed ear that was closest to her.

Storm abbreviated the events that culminated in the necessity for recall and, after Kay fully understood the gravity of the new developments, he resumed the Kay persona that they knew, loved, and counted on.

"Better get to it. I've got a lot of wrapping up to do if I'm going to be there in a week. So what are they saying about how long they're going to need us?"

The three in the booth looked from one to another and shrugged. "They didn't say. The new Sovereign..."

"New Sovereign? That's news you left out. Who and when?"

"Guy who's been hunting in Brazil for a few years. Seems okay so far. The biggest surprise is that he's kind of taking to it like a duck to water. I swear you'd think he'd done it before."

"That's got to be a load off you and that kid."

"Seems to me Glen and I just jumped out of the room temperature pan and into the fire. The Sovereign gig comes with headaches and long hours, but at least it's a desk job."

"You have a point."

"Speaking of points, you in shape for hunting? I bet you have a paunch."

"Yeah? I'll see you on the mats. 'Bout a week from now."

"Count on it."

Storm looked over at the famous couple across the table. "No point in delaying the inevitable. Better let the better half know what's up."

"She's got to come pick you up anyway. Have her come join us for drinks right now. We'll all four talk it over together," Elora said.

"You don't think that will make her feel like it's an ambush?"

"I think there's no *good* way to say this. I think that if she sees that none of us want this, but that we don't have any choice, it will go down easier."

He pulled out the phone and pushed a contact. She answered. "What are you doing?"

"I'm at the Farmers Market. Glen's coming to dinner. He's still a growing boy and I want to feed him good stuff."

Storm grunted at that. "Growing boy, huh? What about me?"

"You're a boy, but your body has finished growing."

"Well, can it keep? What you bought? I'm having drinks with Ram and Elora. Something important's come up and we were thinking you could join us for a little while."

"What is it?"

"Tell you when you get here?"

There was a pause that made Storm visibly nervous. "Are you in the lounge?"

"Yes. We're in one of the booths."

She hung up.

A few minutes later Storm reached for his tumbler and raised it to his lips, but jumped when she appeared next to him.

"Gods Almighty, woman!" He set the glass down and started swiping at the spilled whiskey. He motioned to the bartender and pointed to his shirt. Within seconds he was holding a damp white linen towel.

"'Tis goin' to take more than that to cover the aroma of that fine whiskey you're now wearin'."

Litha wiped Storm down with the damp towel doing a terrible job of hiding the fact that she was amused.

"I ordered you a double foam latte with cinnamon, but it may have cooled off."

"Not a problem." She curled her fingers around the mug and four seconds later steam was rising along with an enticing aroma newly refreshed.

As she brought the cup to her lips Storm smiled and shook his head. "Some things you just never get used to."

She took a sip and moaned approval as her eyes slid closed. When she opened them, she looked around the table. "So what's up?"

Elora spoke before Storm had finished his internal deliberations on the best way to proceed with breaking the news. "We've been recalled to active duty."

Litha was at full attention instantly. She jerked a big-eyed gaze to Storm. "What does that mean?" she asked him point blank.

"Well..." he started, but Elora beat him to it again.

"It means B Team is back in duty rotation in ten days. All of us. Including Kay."

Litha cut right through the turbulent emotions circulating around the table. "No," she pronounced with an emphatic shaking of her wild curls.

"Baby..."

Storm didn't get far with whatever he was going to say.

"No. And that's the end of it, buster."

There was nothing funny about the situation and Storm knew that making light of it wasn't the best way to handle a worried wife. But she was cute when expressing authority and he couldn't help but chuckle a little. "Buster?"

Unconsciously he reached over to push a wayward tendril back from her face. She slapped his hand away. "I'm not kidding!" A noticeable flush was creeping into her cheeks. "I have to get dinner started. We're having company tonight." She was looking around for her purse.

Storm looked across the table.

"Sorry," Elora mouthed.

He shrugged. "I'm gonna catch a ride with her." He looked like a kid on the way to the principal's office. Ram and Elora nodded silently and sympathetically.

As soon as Storm cleared the booth and stood Litha snapped a purple sheepskin lined handcuff on him and they were gone.

Ram looked at Elora. "So. That turn out like you were thinkin'?"

She gave a little shrug that Ram found charming and feminine, maybe even adorable. Of course he found most things about her charming and feminine. And the rest he found adorable.

"I hoped we could soften the news, but we didn't really get a chance. I haven't seen her that upset since…"

As Ram leaned into Elora he caught and held her eyes. "Since her da' lost him in the passes. That what you were goin' to say?"

Elora took in a deep breath. "Maybe she hasn't had enough 'normal'. It's always something. A long lost demon dad. Having a baby in record time. Storm being lost. Rosie growing up in a few months. Then leaving. I guess we just witnessed the last straw up close and personal."

"I would no' be surprised if she took him straight to some other worldly hideout and left him there where she thinks she can keep him safe, sound and all to herself."

She looked at Ram with an open mouth. "You're wearing that you-can't-tell-what-I'm really-thinking face, but I know you're joking. Litha isn't the sort of person to take prisoners. And especially not her husband."

Ram leaned back and put both arms across the back of the wide booth in a display of masculine territorialism. "If you say so."

"Besides. Can you see Storm accepting that? Meekly submitting to being a love slave?"

Through the thin fine cotton of Ram's tee, Elora saw his abs contract with silent laughter. "Love slave is it? 'Tis a fantasy of yours?" He arched an eyebrow and canted his head to indicate interest in the subject as he brought his face closer. "You been holdin' out on me? 'Cause I'm thinkin' *I* would go willin'ly and comply eagerly."

Her lack of rejoinder coupled with the serious expression on her face made him stop teasing and sit up suddenly. He glanced around, leaned into her and dropped his teasing tone about an octave. "Are you entertainin' an image right this second?"

She looked away, but couldn't hide a telltale blush.

Ram's eyes twinkled with wickedness as his smile returned. "You *are*!" He slid closer and put his mouth next to her ear, grinning. "Tell me."

"No." She pushed him away playfully.

"Aye." He doubled down by drawing a finger up her outer thigh. "Tell me, love. I'll die if I do no' know."

She started laughing. "You will not die, Ram."

"Oh. I will. I swear." He said the words into her hair, her ear, and her neck.

"Stop it," she said giggling. "Drink your whiskey."

He looked down at the tumbler sitting half full on the table, but it didn't distract him for long. Within a second he was right back on target, enjoying the game of extracting information from her as much as a hunt.

"The whiskey can wait. What I'm after now is a look inside that beautiful head."

"Gah. Rammel. Some things are personal. Just mark that door private and move on to something else."

He sat back. "Private? Personal? These are no' words I'll be acceptin' if there's somethin' I could be doin' to please. Somethin' that's been left undone."

"You mean you've never thought about anything, um, sexual and kept it to yourself? Really?"

The tiniest scowl formed between his eyes. "Considerin' the inventive nature of our private and personal sex life, I'm a little taken back by the question."

"Yes, but it's entirely different when *you* suggest, uh, things."

He wasn't laughing at her exactly, but his amusement was evident. "'Tis only different if you make it so. I see now that I've been remiss in no' pressin' for your own imaginin's. There's no' a thin' in this life I want more than to see you pleasured."

"You *do* pleasure me, Ram."

"In every way possible," he corrected.

Seeing that he was taking the idea seriously and was so sincere, she couldn't help but smile. He glanced at his watch. "We have eighty-three minutes before we need to gather Helm. Let's go to our place where I can get you naked and tickle you into revealin' everythin' I want to know."

Unlike men who let the zest for life drain out of them when they become responsible for families, Ram still carried a party with him wherever he went. And that was just one of the things she loved about him.

She cut her eyes toward him and smiled slyly. "Do any of your fantasies involve unpacking moving boxes? Because there's a lot of that to do."

He snarled and bit her on the neck so suddenly that she shrieked. Looking around she saw that they'd drawn the attention of the few people in the lounge. "You're embarrassing me, Ram." She slapped at him playfully.

"Embarrassed?" Ram looked around the room and chuckled. "Elora, those fuckers are so jealous of me their balls are a semi-permanent shade of ugly cobalt blue."

She shot him a pretend glare and slid out of the booth.

"What? If you do no' believe me, pick one out. I'll take his pants down so you can see."

"Rammel. Ugh!" And that was the last thing she said before giving him the pleasure of watching her walk away. An activity of which he never tired.

When Rev showed up at the Operations Office at eight, Farnsworth glanced up and then did a double take. He looked freshly showered and enticingly damp. She, on the other hand, felt old, ill-used and in need of a long soak in a hot receptacle with scented bath oils.

She had dismissed the trainee assistants hours earlier so that they could complete their study and elective requirements for the day, which meant she was in the office alone.

Rev nodded at her. "First to arrive, last to leave?"

She smiled in a polite way that didn't reach her eyes. "Always." There was a folder sitting on the right side of her desk. She stood, grabbing that and her tablet. "I keep most things in digital form these days, but I printed some reports. I didn't know if you prefer hard copy."

Rev shrugged. "It's easier when you're reviewing details with a second person. Would you like me to carry it?"

She was so surprised by the question she laughed out loud. "No. I've got it. Lead the way."

Farnsworth's normal pace was more along the lines of a brisk determined stride, but she consciously decided that, if the new Sovereign thought there was time to stroll, she would follow his lead.

His eyes slid sideways as they ambled toward Mess. "I hope there are lots of pages in there that we both need to see at the same time." Her brow crinkled momentarily with an unanswered question. "It'll give me a chance to get close. Smell your perfume."

He grinned and winked while she practically gaped.

She started to turn into Mess when they reached the doors, but he gently took her elbow and pulled. "We're over here tonight."

She kept walking, but took a second look back at the Mess entrance. "Where are we going?"

"I asked Crisp to find us a place where we could have a business dinner with a little more privacy because some of the details we discuss may be sensitive, clearance-wise."

"Oh."

"Nice man." He decided to fill the silence with small talk because he sensed that she was feeling as awkward as if it was a first date, which it was in a sense. She just didn't know it. "Here we are."

He opened the door to one of the small rooms off the fountain court and gestured for her to enter. The table was set with forest green linen and fine German china with a Black Swan emblem in the center and the presentation was all the more appealing because of an arrangement of calla lilies and white tapers that had already been lit. A bottle of chardonnay was chilling in a bucket of ice next to the table.

Farnsworth's eyebrows rose almost to her hairline. "Fresh flowers and candlelight?"

Rev cleared his throat. "Well. Seems Crisp went all out. Very nice, isn't it? You know how to do things in style at Jefferson Unit."

He pulled out her chair and waited. When she looked at his face she thought she saw a little uncertainty and a lot of hopeful expectation. She told herself it couldn't hurt to have their dinner meeting alone.

As she sat she said, "It is very nice, but Crisp must have misunderstood. We're going to need more light if we're going to look at reports." She watched as Rev seated himself, then said pointedly in her most professional tone, "After all, I don't have twenty-year-old eyes."

He leaned back in his chair, studying her. "No. What you have is better."

She sucked in a breath. "Sovereign, if I've given you the impression that..."

"I don't want to make you feel uncomfortable and I'm sorry if that's what's happening here. Look. I'm new in town," he smiled, "as you well know. Could we just enjoy a nice dinner, get to know each other a little, and then we'll dive into the stacks."

He noticed that her shoulders relaxed. She sat back just enough to cross her legs, which he tried very hard not to notice, then looked over the table. "I do love calla lilies," she said.

He smiled, but stopped himself from saying, "I know."

For the next three quarters of an hour the new Sovereign asked the Operations Manager all manner of questions about herself. Whenever she tried to return the favor he neatly steered the conversation back to her. After getting her to reveal that she had been engaged to the former Sovereign and that it had ended tragically, he asked for her insights as to how successfully Jefferson Unit had been operating since then, adding that she – above all others – was in a position to know.

She seemed to open up and lose her reserve when talking about the day to day details of running the New Jersey complex. It was the closest he came to seeing the spark that used to fire in her dark eyes when she was emotional about something and she wasn't shy about holding his gaze when the subject matter was work.

Rev watched the lady pick at her dessert and cast her gaze around the room. Finally she said what was on her mind. "We need to bring the lights up so we can see the files or else move the meeting someplace more conducive."

When Farnsworth met his eyes as she waited for his reaction, she thought she saw a touch of sadness, but he covered it quickly with a smile just as Crisp entered and said, "I hope everything was to the lady's liking, sir."

Farnsworth thought it was strange that he'd directed that comment to her companion. "I'm right here, Crisp. If you want to know something, just ask me."

Crisp moved his head in her direction in a gesture that was more a bow than a nod. "Of course, madam. Did you enjoy your dinner?"

"I did, Crisp. Thank you for asking."

"And will there be anything else?"

"Not for me."

He turned in Rev's direction. "And you, sir?"

"More than satisfactory. Will you have this cleared and turn up the lights? Oh and have someone take the flowers to Ms. Farnsworth's office." Rev looked in her direction with a twinkle in his eye. "She likes calla lilies."

"Very good, sir."

"I'll have a coffee. You?" he asked Farnsworth. She nodded and Crisp withdrew taking the wine and flowers with him.

A couple of hours later Rev was satisfied that he was fully informed on every conceivable detail of running Jefferson Unit, other than duty assignments for hunters, which was entirely the purview of the Sovereign. Likewise, Farnsworth was fully informed of everything that must be accomplished to bring the facility back from training and research facility to fully staffed hunter unit.

Farnsworth leaned into a stretch of her back and shoulders and couldn't quite suppress a yawn. When he chuckled at that, she smiled as shyly as a teenager and he thoroughly enjoyed that expression of vulnerability it had taken him hours to win from her.

CHAPTER 10

New York

After the speed dating incident, Mercy had decided it was time for a change. So when she received an invitation to apply for a highly specialized position with a Scotia-based charity organization, she retrieved it from the shredding bin and rethought her initial reaction. She pulled the letter out and reread it thinking that it was not superstitious to believe that opportunity knocks in mysterious ways.

Teaching positions at universities like Columbia didn't grow on trees. They had to know that she wouldn't give it up lightly.

She couldn't imagine why a charity would need an historian/archeologist who specialized in Slavic studies and artifacts, but if the price was right and the work was worthy, it might be fun to earn more than subsistence pay. For a change. And, after all, change was exactly what she'd called to her.

"Be careful what you wish for," she whispered to herself just before she picked up the phone and made an appointment with a Dr. Monq in New Jersey.

"What!?!"

Mercy jumped at the response coming from inside the door upon which the young escort had just knocked. She turned to the young man with wide eyes, but he just grinned in response. He seemed brave for someone who appeared to be about fifteen years old.

"Don't let him scare you. He just acts like that. Bark, bark, bark, bark, no bite at all."

Mercy smiled uncertainly as she watched him knock again.

The door jerked open. "I SAID...!" Seeing the young woman standing there looking unsure of herself, Monq looked at his watch and said, "Oh." He mumbled something about where time goes. "You must be Dr. Renaux."

"Yes. If this has turned out to be a bad time…" She was turning away, but he stopped her.

"No. No. I'm always getting lost in my projects. The "zone" as they say. I didn't mean to be off-putting. Please come in." He motioned to one of two wingback chairs sitting in front of the fireplace. "Send us some hot water and tea complements, Monty. Would you, please?"

"Yes, sir."

The young man smiled and winked at her as he turned to go, which she thought required a measure of audacity beyond his years. Mercy sat in the chair that had been pointed out and watched the boy, whose name was apparently Monty, close the door.

"How was the bridge crossing?"

She thought that was odd wording. People didn't usually make it sound so adventurous or romantic. "Oh. I took the tunnel."

"Did you? Well, you're braver than I. Something about an entire ocean of water pressing on the ceiling right above one's head…" He shuddered dramatically.

"I understand that reaction isn't uncommon." Monq had been scurrying around his office while seeming to chat mindlessly and half-heartedly. "Please forgive me for rushing you, Dr. Monq, but my curiosity really has the best of me. I can't wait to hear why a charitable organization would be interested in someone with my particular skill set.

"I'm also dying to know why a charity would be located in the middle of a highly restricted military base."

"Both excellent questions!"

Monq snatched up a file from one of the piles on his massive carved desk, opened it and handed her a document that appeared to be several pages in length.

The title page read, "Vampire skeletons unearthed in Bulgarian monastery."

She looked up at his face for a clue that it was a joke. When she saw that his expression remained passive and serious, she read it one more time. Despite the fact that Dr. Monq's face was seriously passive, she laughed. "Bulgarian vampires."

"Actually that's vampire."

"What?"

"Vampire. The plural of vampire is vampire. No cause for self-recrimination. Most people get it wrong." He glanced down at the memo in front of her. "Read on. Take your time. I'm in no hurry."

She paused for a couple of beats to search his face then lowered her eyes and began to read the body of the text.

Archaeologists in Bulgaria have unearthed two skeletons from the Middle Ages pierced through the chest with ploughshares, apparently to either keep them from turning into the undead or to keep them firmly in place.

They are the latest in a succession of finds across western and central Europe which shed new light on just how seriously people took the threat of vampires and how those beliefs transformed into the modern myth.

Bulgaria's national history museum chief, Bozhidar Dimitrov, said: 'These two skeletons stabbed with rods illustrate a practice which was common in some Bulgarian villages up until the first decade of the 20th century.'

According to pagan beliefs, people who were considered bad during their lifetimes might turn into vampires after death unless stabbed in the chest with an iron or wooden rod or stake before being buried.

People believed the rod would also pin them down in their graves to prevent them from leaving at midnight and terrorizing the vicinity.

According to Mr Dimitrov, in Bulgaria alone, the corpses of over one hundred buried people were stabbed according to rituals to prevent them from becoming vampires.

Dimitrov: 'Because of the persistence of the folklore surrounding vampires, commoners believed that people who were evil when alive would rise from the dead as vampires and continue to torment the innocent. That is why vampires were so often aristocrats or clerics,' he laughed.

He added, 'The curious thing is that there are no women among them. They were not afraid of witches.'

However last month Italian researchers discovered what they believed to be the remains of a female 'vampire' in Venice - buried with a brick jammed between her jaws to prevent her feeding on victims of a plague which swept the city in the 16th century.

Matteo Borrini, an anthropologist from the University of Florence, said the discovery on the small island of Lazzaretto Nuovo in the Venice lagoon supported the medieval belief that vampires were behind the spread of plagues like the Black Death.

The skeleton was unearthed in a mass grave from the Venetian plague of 1576 - in which the artist Titian died - on Lazzaretto Nuovo, which lies around two miles northeast of Venice and was used as a sanitarium for plague sufferers.

Borrini said: 'This is the first time that archaeology has succeeded in reconstructing the ritual of exorcism of a vampire.

'This helps ... authenticate how the myth of vampires was born.'

The succession of plagues which ravaged Europe between 1300 and 1700 fostered the belief in vampires, mainly because the decomposition of corpses was not well understood, Borrini said.

The shrouds used to cover the faces of the dead were often decayed by bacteria in the mouth, revealing the corpse's teeth, and vampires became known as 'shroud-eaters.'

According to medieval medical and religious texts, the 'undead' were believed to spread pestilence in order to suck the remaining life from corpses until they acquired the strength to return to the streets again.

'To kill the vampire you had to remove the shroud from its mouth, which was its food like the milk of a child, and put something uneatable in there,' said Borrini.

'It's possible that other corpses have been found with bricks in their mouths, but this is the first time the ritual has been recognized.'

The article was supported with photos of the archeological site. The most interesting, by far, was a detailed close up of one of the skeletons. Dirt and debris had been brushed away, but it was otherwise untouched.

When she had digested the memo, Mercy put it down on the table in front of her. Monq noticed that her hand continued to rest on the paper after she looked up at him.

"Very interesting. Certainly I understand how my specialty might dovetail this discovery. What I don't understand is why a philanthropic institution might be investigating Dark Age beliefs in vampires," she caught herself, "um, vampire, and practices of rites of disposition."

Monq sat back in his chair. "What if I told you that vampire are as real as you and I?"

She didn't laugh, but did look around the room, almost as if she was scanning for hidden cameras. Perhaps either consciously or subconsciously that's exactly what she was doing.

"I would say that I have absolutely no reason to believe that might be true."

"Fair enough. A prudent answer and wise as well. Should I take that to mean that you discount my claim as patently false or that you are reserving judgment?"

She pursed her lips. "If you're asking if I'm able to keep an open mind, that is the very nature of science, even social sciences such as anthropology. I will proceed with an assumption that vampire stories are myths until I'm persuaded by evidence to the contrary."

Monq smiled. "What sort of evidence would convince you?"

She cocked her head. "Well, an actual vampire..."

"Are you the sort of person who is self-aware enough to know that you would, in fact, believe your own eyes if you were face to face with a vampire?"

"Look here, Dr. Monq. I'd like to know where this is going."

"Well, Dr. Renaux, I'm attempting to establish that you will accept the presence of an actual vampire as evidence. Before I go to the trouble of showing you one."

"Honestly, I don't know what to say to that."

"Well, either say, yes, a vampire will convince you or, no, it would take more than that."

"I will give you a non-prejudicial commitment to believe what I see pending such an event as you producing a vampire. By all means, please proceed."

Monq glanced at his watch, stood and pulled out his phone. He quickly factored for the time difference and determined that Baka's team would be going out on patrol.

"Baka. I'm in need of a quick demonstration. Could you please send Javier to my office?" He began to pace. "Yes. I know the last time you sent them here there was the devil to pay for it, but this time he is not only expected, but invited. I only need him for a minute to convince a young lady that vampire do exist. Please make sure he understands it is not an invitation to the, uh, dance." He looked over at Mercy. "Yes. I got it. As a matter of fact, this has to do with that." Pause. "Good."

He put the phone back in his pocket, sat down, and began drumming his fingers on the table lightly.

Mercy stared at Monq, hoping he would take the hint that she was expecting him to speak. When it became clear that he had nothing to say, she decided to take control of the conversation. "I don't mean to seem impatient, but what are we doing now? Waiting for a vampire to appear out of thin air?"

Just as Monq opened his mouth to answer, Javier appeared next to them, out of thin air, with a charming smile and an enthusiastic, "Salut!"

Mercy shrieked and scrambled backward with the intention of standing, but lost control of the wheels on her chair. She came to rest on the floor looking up at a handsome teenager.

Javier leaned down and offered his hand to help her up. "Sorry, mademoiselle," he said with a heavy, and unmistakably sexy, French accent. "I am clumsy. Please do not allow me to also be rude."

He offered his hand, which looked perfectly innocent, and smiled. When Mercy's heart rate and breathing began to resume normalcy, she reached to take his hand. As he helped her up he never broke eye contact. She was halfway up when he grinned, showing sparkling white fangs with points that looked as sharp as ice picks. She shrieked, for the second time in her life. Prior to that interview she wouldn't have been able to describe exactly what a shriek was or how one sounded. Out of reflex she brought her hands up and pushed away from Javier, which meant that she'd landed on her ass, on the floor, twice in under a minute.

She heard Monq chuckle, which was a gift because it made her mad. And anger replacing fear was a good thing. Her head whipped toward the sound of mirth. "What exactly is so funny?"

"I hope you'll forgive me. Someday. It's just that you were so well put together, in every way, and then you were on the floor making that noise that, well, I'm not sure what that was." He dropped his head in an effort to suppress more chuckles.

She got to her feet and glared at Javier. "So you're supposed to be the vampire, are you?" Javier simply smiled and shrugged a shoulder as elegantly as a Bolshoi dancer. "Open your mouth."

Javier looked at Monq, seemingly for confirmation that he should obey the highly strung female. Monq nodded.

Mercy tilted Javier's head back and felt all around the gum from which his left fang protruded. Javier looked at Monq questioningly as if to ask him to put a stop to the examination. When she was satisfied that the fangs were not surgical implants, she withdrew her hand, but scraped it on the way by. The fangs were every bit as sharp as they appeared to be.

She saw a thin line of blood begin to well from the scratch. "Ouch. How do you manage to not constantly be cutting yourself open?"

Mercy looked up for Javier's response, but what she saw stopped her breath. The vampire's interest was rapt and focused on her wound. His eyes had also gone dark and hooded, while his breathing became deeper and faster. She wasn't big on expletives, but that didn't keep one word from echoing around the space her brain occupied. *Shit.*

"Let's assume I believe you."

"Are you sure you don't want a more personal demonstration? Javier would be happy to show you that he can bite without pain and without much damage."

"The demo was bloody convincing, I assure you."

Monq laughed. "Bloody convincing. I like your sense of humor, Dr. Renaux." To Javier, he said, "Thank you for your help. That will be all."

Javier seemed mesmerized by the blood. He didn't move or look away from Mercy and had Monq thinking that he should have asked for the older vampire, Jean-Etienne. "Javier!"

Javier grabbed her finger, stuck it in his mouth and closed his eyes in ecstasy.

"She said no, Javier. Cease that sucking at once!"

Javier slid his tongue along the finger that Mercy was too spellbound to retract while holding her gaze and said, "Your coloring is magnifique, mademoiselle. It reminds me of autumn in Paris. Your ancestors were from Normandie, no?"

"Thank you, Javier. That will be all," Monq repeated more firmly.

Javier dragged his eyes away from his prey reluctantly and shot Monq a look that gave him pause. It was a look that implied, "Just because I look like an adolescent human doesn't mean that I am one. Just because I'm typically affable doesn't mean that's my only side. So watch yourself, mortal."

The vampire kissed Mercy's hand, his eyes not leaving hers. "Should you ever require my company, I will be at your service, beautiful lady."

Throwing a last look of longing toward Mercy, the young immortal vanished.

She stared at the space he'd occupied for a full minute after he'd disappeared before shaking herself and saying, "Geez. What would have happened if I'd said *yes* to the expanded demo? Never mind. I don't really want an image of that. I actually couldn't look away. " She shook her head. "Worse. I didn't *want* to look away. All I can say is, wow."

"They are, apparently, made for seduction and, I've been told, they can be quite difficult to resist." Monq waved toward the chairs in front of the fire. "Please sit."

Monq asked for a fresh pot of Earl Grey, took his seat and waited for Mercy to calm. Within the hour he was telling the story of Count Jungbluth, Dankvart der Recke, and the founding of Black Swan.

Sitting in Monq's study on a rainy afternoon, sipping tea with a heavy and heavenly aroma of bergamot, in front of a realistic-looking gas fire, she fell under the spell of Monq's baritone and was enthralled by the recitation of Black Swan's beginning. When he finished, she sat still and quiet for some time longer, wishing there was more and not wanting the experience to end. Monq sat watching, patiently waiting for her reaction.

Finally she said, "I have a question that's really neither here nor there, but if you wouldn't mind indulging me."

"Of course."

"Do you know of someone named Rafael Nightsong?"

Acting was not on Monq's incredibly long list of impressive accomplishments so Mercy noticed the slight widening of his eyes at the mention of the knight's name.

"I must amend my response. What I meant to say was of course I will answer any and all of your questions after you have accepted our offer and given your vows of loyalty and secrecy."

Mercy leaned over and placed her Rosenthal tea cup on the table nearest her right hand before looking back at Monq.

"I agree to the assignment and to your terms. I also give you my pledge of loyalty and secrecy. When do you want me to begin?"

"Welcome to The Order of the Black Swan, my dear. We're honored to have you with us. Normally vows of loyalty and secrecy are made formally with witnesses and signatures, but I have a good feeling about your sincerity.

"As to when we would like you to begin," he looked at his watch, "eighteen hours ago."

Mercy felt the laugh bubbling up. It was out before she knew it. "I don't mean to be disrespectful, Dr. Monq, but people are counting on me to fulfill previously made commitments to the university."

"Yes, well, please forgive me for saying so. Likewise, I don't mean to be disrespectful, but the interests of The Order of the Black Swan are more important and you're the right person for this job." She opened her mouth to protest, but he held up a hand to stop her. "Do you know Dr. Fornizia? Universidad de Sao Paulo?"

Mercy sat back looking a little confused, but willing, for the moment, to indulge Monq by letting him lead the conversation in what would seem to be a strange and unrelated direction. "In my field, I would have had to be spending the last ten years in a hermit cave to not have heard of him. Why?"

"He's prepared to move his projects to Columbia and take over your classes and other duties until such time as you may wish to return."

She couldn't have been more astonished if she'd been instantly transported to the Congo and met by Dr. Livingstone. "When?"

"Immediately."

"What makes you think that will be cleared with the school?"

Monq laughed and waved dismissively. "Not a problem. We have ways."

She mulled it over while studying Monq's face. Would she ever forgive herself if she passed up what seemed to be the offer of an adventure of a lifetime? The answer was no. She wouldn't.

"Okay then."

Monq smiled and rubbed his hands together. "Okay then. Go home and pack as if you were vacationing and spelunking in Eastern Europe. Gather the research tools of your preference. Anything you need and don't own personally can be expensed."

"Anything?"

He nodded. "Anything." He started to stand and show her the door.

"Wait a minute." He sat back down. "Rafael Nightsong?"

"Oh, yes. Indeed I do know him."

She searched Monq's face. "He's a vampire hunter, isn't he?"

Monq cocked his head. "He told you that?"

"I met him under, um, unusual circumstances. He didn't think he'd be believed. And he wasn't."

"I see." Monq sounded concerned.

"By the way, did anything unusual happen on March 2nd? Anything that would cause Mr. Nightsong to look like he had barely survived Armageddon?"

"*Sir* Nightsong." She raised an eyebrow at that. "March 2nd? Not precisely, but the night before this entire building was under attack and was practically reduced to rubble." She nodded, looking thoughtful. "I take it that, when you met him, he looked the worse for wear?"

"That's putting it mildly, but yes."

"We will send someone to pick you up day after tomorrow at 7 am." He scrabbled through the pile system on his desk until he withdrew a card. "If you need anything between now and then, contact Ms. Farnsworth in Operations. Her title should be Miracle Worker." He turned abruptly and picked up a little parchment-colored book. "And read this."

"All right."

She looked down. *Field Training Guide.* Opening to the first page, she read the first indexed item out loud. "The plural of vampire is vampire." She looked up at Monq. "Really?"

He smiled and opened the door for her. "Welcome home, Alice."

Monty was waiting for her in the hallway.

"Dr. Renaux," he said as he gestured for her to walk with him. He escorted her all the way to her car and never said a single word, but when she unlocked the car door, he opened it for her and grinned. As she drove away she looked in the rear view mirror and saw the kid wave goodbye. *Weird.*

On the drive back to the city her thoughts turned to the beautiful and angry speed dater. Crossing the bridge she was thinking that the asshole had turned out to be a truthful asshole. It just proved that there was one universal constant that could be counted on and that was that life was strange. Good luck with *ever* getting her to call him "Sir" though.

CHAPTER 11

Jefferson Unit

As the migration back to Jefferson Unit began, even Rev was constantly amazed at Farnsworth's seemingly superhuman ability to anticipate every need. When she was presented with surprises she couldn't possibly have planned for, she managed to pull a Plan B out of her invisible magic hat. And so far as Rev could determine, if Plan A didn't work out, you could bet your last dime that Plan B would.

Part of that genius was knowing her own limitations. When she knew she couldn't do it all, she requisitioned an assistant. Director Tvelgar flew three candidates to J.U. for Farnsworth to interview. She awarded the position to a young Frenchwoman from the Le Triomphe Unite in Paris. Mademoiselle Bonheur was both smart enough to recognize the opportunity and ambitious enough to take advantage of it, which meant she was eager to learn from Farnsworth and had no trouble whatsoever with deference.

The size of the Operations Department had always been just barely big enough to function and that was only because Farnsworth was masterful at keeping an organized, uncluttered space. So Farnsworth confiscated a storage room next door and had the stored items taken to the unused space from where Kellan Chorzak had announced the Battle for Jefferson Unit during a raid by assassins. She felt safe in assuming that lightning wouldn't strike the same spot twice.

She pulled workmen away from other projects in progress and gave them a maximum of three days to complete her changes. Knowing that she was in charge of scheduling, they had powerful motivation to please her.

They hung a plastic curtain before they began tearing out the wall, but there was nothing to block the noise. And work had to go on. The good news was that they finished ahead of schedule. The trainees who worked part time helped moved everything according to Farnsworth's direction and a reconceived Operations Department was ready for business. She and Mlle. Bonheur both had desks that were counter height, built adjacent to the counter that separated Operations from walk-ins. They sat in ergonomic chairs as high as stools unless someone stood on the other side of the counter in which case they would stand and face the visitor.

One thing Farnsworth had not counted on was how different the environment would feel with additional estrogen present or how taken the boys would be with Genevieve Bonheur, the new Assistant to the Chief of Operations. After the third kid stood star struck upon seeing her for the first time, Farnsworth took a good look. The younger woman had a tight petite little body, big caramel-colored eyes, shiny mahogany hair cut into a chic Parisian bob and a ready smile.

Everyone soon learned that the smile was quickly replaced with spitfire when her name was mispronounced. If one of the knights or other personnel called her Genevieve with typical English pronunciation, she would grab her triangular name plaque from the counter and point to her name, saying, "Zhawn. Vee. Ehv," slowly followed with, "Zhawnveyev," spoken quickly. When the employee requiring assistance repeated it back correctly, her smile returned and all was well.

Thus it went until the day that Kristoph Falcon walked in to relay a request from the Lady Laiken. Mlle. Bonheur quickly slid off her chair to help the cutie that seemed to have 'trouble' written across his forehead with invisible ink.

"May I help you?" she asked with a French accent that the men seemed to find hypnotizing.

Kris stared for a second before glancing down at her name plate. "You're new, um, Genevieve?"

He was captivated by the transformation. Her face scrunched into the cutest scowl he'd ever seen. "No!" She went through her routine, holding up the name plate as if to say, "You idiot. Anyone can plainly see it is Zhawnveyev and not Jinaveev."

With a sober expression that would challenge a judge, he repeated, "Jinaveev."

After three such exchanges, she stomped her foot, which made the cute haircut bounce in a delightfully young and athletic way. She took a deep breath and determined to try one more time.

On the outside Kris appeared to be seriously trying to get it right. On the inside he was sure he had never been so entertained before in his life. On his fourth attempt, he caught and held her gaze and said, "Jin. Ah. Veev."

She took the triangular name plate that she still held in her hand and cracked him on the head with it as she let out a stream of French that had the unmistakable tone and cadence of cursing, recognizable in any language. As soon as she realized what she'd done, she gasped and swung to look at Farnsworth with her face growing paler by the second.

"Ow," said Kris, rubbing his head and laughing at the same time.

Farnsworth, who had observed the entire incident while pretending to be otherwise occupied, was exercising all the maturity she could muster to keep from rolling her eyes. Finally she interceded with an unmistakable tone of warning, "Falcon."

"Yes, ma'am." He looked at Farnsworth momentarily attempting to cover the sheepishness vying to claim his expression.

Kris returned his attention to Mlle. Bonheur and treated her to a rare smile that was nothing less than dazzling. In perfect French, he said, "Mademoiselle Genevieve Bonheur, welcome to Jefferson Unit. I hope you will be happy here."

Her eyes narrowed when she realized he'd been toying with her. "Chieur."

He laughed, "I know what that means." He turned to Farnsworth in mock outrage. "Do you know what she just called me?"

Farnsworth sighed. "State your business, Falcon. The playroom is Sublevel Three."

"Yes, ma'am. Lady Laiken says we need enough exoarmor and helmets so that, in the event of attack on the facility, every person who might be called upon to defend would be outfitted. She said to tell you that includes *all* the trainees and some of the satellite staff who've had combat training."

Farnsworth nodded. "Tell her it shall be done."

Falcon's eyes twinkled. "Shall it be written as well?"

"What?"

"You know. Let it be written, let it be... Never mind. I'll tell her. Thank you."

"Falcon."

"Yes, ma'am?"

"When the unit was attacked, weren't you one of the ones who was left without protective gear?"

"Yes, ma'am."

He glanced at Genevieve compulsively hoping that she might be impressed, but her smug haughty expression hadn't changed even a little. He thought she was good for another reaction so he put his hand over his heart and blew her a kiss on his way out. As expected, her face went slack with surprise.

Kristoph Falcon walked away from Operations chuckling, his mood especially light considering how seldom he found things amusing.

As more and more newly transferred J.U. personnel reported for duty, Rev had enough knights on hand to get a rotation schedule underway. That was, after all, the business of the Hunter Division. With so much going on he found lots of excuses to stop by Operations and flirt with Farnsworth.

He began keeping a personal-best score of how many times he could make her blush per visit. The young assistant, Zhawnveyev, loved to see him coming. She'd become his biggest supporter, playing the role of silent cheerleader on the sidelines of the game he played with Farnsworth. When his efforts at being charming or seductively suggestive met with her approval, she would smile and nod. She was like a human date-o-meter.

Rev never failed to ask Farnsworth to go out with him, even if he was there six times in a work day. And she never failed to turn him down. Until she didn't. Unbeknownst to the Sovereign, Genevieve had been acting as more than a silent ally. Every time Rev left she found another way to respectfully phrase the idea that she thought Farnsworth would be crazy to continue being hard to get or that she thought they made a perfect couple.

"You work so hard. What is the trouble with having some pleasure in life as well? Few men would ever work so hard for the attentions of a woman in this century, especially when they are so charming and lovely as the Sovereign."

"He's too young." Farnsworth almost always responded with some variation on that theme.

"Pish. Pish. Pish. Ridiculous. In France such a thing would never stand in the way of love."

"Love!?! I think you're carried away."

"It is not I who is carried away. He has his heart set on you. Can you not see this?"

"Genevieve, we have work to do. Don't make me use the boss card."

With that, or something like it, the issue would be set aside until the Sovereign's next visit, which would usually be within two hours.

Then one day he didn't come in at all. Genevieve noticed Farnsworth looking at the doorway and knew she was wondering if she'd rejected his pursuit one too many times.

He was absent the following morning and early afternoon. It was then that Genevieve delivered, or perhaps detonated, a perfectly timed question.

"I see now that Sovereign Farthing is wasting his time. Since you are so clearly not interested, then perhaps you wouldn't mind if I try to ease his heartache."

Genevieve controlled her features so that she looked as innocent as a lamb, but on the inside, when she saw the look on Farnsworth's face, she was wearing a triumphantly wicked grin.

At two o'clock Rev came through the door with an armful of calla lilies and a big smile.

Farnsworth accepted the flowers. When he looked at Genevieve, she smiled and nodded. "You said you like these?"

"I do. They're my favorite."

"I believe you, but it seems odd."

"Why?"

"Because they're beautiful, but colorless and you're so... you know, colorful?"

"You think I'm colorful?" Farnsworth was a little taken aback because that would probably have been the last adjective she would have used to describe herself. Genevieve was beaming, thinking the man should have been French.

"Well, yeah. You don't think so?" Her answer was to blush and bury her nose in the blooms. "I have to get back. Sifting through the reports of what's happening in the field."

"Oh."

Did she sound disappointed? He thought she might have at first, but decided it was wishful thinking.

"So. See you soon?" He started to turn and leave.

"Wait!" She blushed again thinking that might have sounded just a little too forceful. Rev turned around and stepped back up to the counter. She dropped her eyes. "Don't you have something else to, ah, ask me?"

He looked momentarily confused, but any spectator could have easily read the emotions on his face, which softened when he realized what she was implying. He leaned closer and lowered his voice to a level of greater intimacy. "Will you go out with me?"

"Yes." Not the least hesitation or timidity. It was emphatic and it was assent.

Genevieve clapped her hands and shrieked quietly. Rev wouldn't have thought that possible, but she *was* French.

"Tonight?" Farnsworth looked discombobulated. It was evident her mind was racing around and jumping through work hoops, clothing hoops, hair and makeup hoops. "Tomorrow night." She smiled, looking pleased and shy.

"Meet me at the Whisterpad at eight and wear something red."

She looked terrified, but Genevieve interceded. "Tee shirt red? Or sexy with high heels red?"

Rev grinned and looked back at Farnsworth. "Sexy yes. High heels? Probably not. We may walk a little."

If he'd known that his comments would send his Operations Manager into an afternoon-long tailspin of how one might go about looking sexy in low heeled shoes, he would have taken it all back and said jeans and sneakers.

After he left, Genevieve said, "Do you have something red?"

"Oh. Yes. Sol liked to see me in red."

"Then they are alike in this way. Yes?"

Come to think of it, Farnsworth realized that Rev and Sol were alike in a lot of ways. She had the brief thought that perhaps she was a magnet to men who were predisposed to be Jefferson Unit Sovereigns, but she dismissed it as quickly as it flew by.

In the end Genevieve came up with a perfect solution. She loaned Farnsworth a designer bag big enough to hold a pair of shoes so that she could switch from heels to flats when necessary.

That was the moment when Farnsworth predicted a long and illustrious career in problem-solving for her talented assistant.

The construction underway to reconfigure parts of the facility was being supervised by Operations, of course, and that was one of the main reasons why Farnsworth had needed to take on an assistant.

It was a new chapter in the history of Jefferson Unit. There would be more active hunters in residence than ever before and there were additional housing issues such as the marital status of recalled knights. Those who were married to other employees of The Order were to be allowed family quarters, which were slightly bigger. There weren't many of those, but enough so that it presented a planning consideration.

Ram and Elora already occupied an apartment big enough for themselves, a child and a very large dog. Elsbeth and Sir Fennimore were getting married and three other knights qualified if they so desired.

Fennimore had taken his physical therapy seriously. Between that and the constant hands on care and encouragement of his wife-to-be, he was out of the wheelchair, walking with a cane and telling everyone he'd be ready for rotation in a few days. When people smiled, it wasn't an indulgence. They gave him an odds-on chance of doing whatever he claimed.

Of the other two, one hunter was married to a surgeon – always a welcome addition to an active hunter unit. The other was married to a scientist whom Director Tvelgar arranged to have transferred to Monq's research unit.

All was handled with relative ease. A little paperwork. A little shuffling. The last couple to be granted married quarters, however, was a surprise.

Reports from the field after the first night of resumed patrol were alarming. The hunters described a situation that was everyone's worst fear. The vampire population had rebounded fast. Whereas they used to spot one or two a month, the teams who went out that first night reported visuals on more than they could chase down.

They were going to have to put on hip boots, wade in, and get the numbers trimmed down quickly or it was going to get exponentially worse.

The next day after the Sovereigns all over the globe began sharing initial data, Baka walked into Jefferson Unit, took the elevator down to Sublevel 2 and knocked on Rev's door. When Rev looked up and saw who was standing in the outer office, he was sure that his knee jerk reaction gave him away. Whereas Farthing had never met Baka, Sol had known him better than most.

Rev forced his features to appear neutral as he rose to greet the visitor.

Baka extended his hand. "Istvan Baka."

"Baka? I've heard of you."

Baka replied with a small smile. "No doubt."

Rev gestured to a chair facing his desk. "Tell me something truthfully."

"Ask," Baka said as he moved toward the chair.

"Before I sit down and get comfortable, do I need to keep a stake in my hand? I'll hide it under the table for political correctness of course."

Baka raised an eyebrow. "Funny. I wasn't expecting you to be entertaining. The guy who sat in that chair before you was the antithesis of that."

Rev instantly stiffened, feeling defensive about the reputation of his former self. "What do you mean? I'd been led to believe he was a stand-up guy."

"Oh he was," Baka rushed to say, "in every sense of the phrase. He was also serious as a DOA pronouncement."

Rev frowned at that, but supposed the vampire was telling the truth.

"Yes, well, a little levity never hurts."

"I'm a believer."

"So what can I do for you?"

"I've seen the early reports, most of them. New York seems to be hardest hit by the resurgence of the virus."

Rev pursed his lips and steepled his fingers. "Initial assessments point toward that conclusion."

"I'd like to be stationed where I can do the most good. That seems to be here." Baka waited for a reaction before continuing, but Rev said nothing. "If you agree, my wife would be coming with me. She's been working in the field as part of my team. I don't know if you're aware of her, ah, our history, but she has some unique gifts."

"I am aware that your wife would be an asset to any operation lucky enough to get her. We'll take her. You stay in Paris where you can do the most good."

Rev said it with a perfectly deadpan inflection and had to admit he thoroughly enjoyed the look on Baka's face when the vampire apparently thought he was serious.

"I... I..."

The Sovereign decided to let him off the hot seat and released him with a chuckle. "The look on your face was priceless, vampire."

Baka caught on at the first hint of humor and started nodding as if to say, "You got me."

"Joking aside, is that the only reason why you're asking for a transfer to J.U.?"

Baka stared at him for a few beats. "Probably not. My friends are here. And if it's all the same to you, please don't call me vampire."

"When did you get to be a sensitive fella?"

"What makes you think I wasn't always a sensitive fella?"

Rev locked eyes with Baka for a second. "Exactly right. Why would I think otherwise? Just out of curiosity, are you dispersing the rest of your team?"

"You mean...?"

"Animal House."

Baka winced a little at the tag. He knew the kids could be unruly, but for months he'd worked with them on a nightly basis and was acutely aware that they were volunteering their services for free with no motivation other than a little guidance on honor and responsibility from Jean Etienne. He thought they'd outlived the Animal House thing. Or should have.

On the other hand he questioned why he was being resentful and defensive on their behalf. They didn't care what they were called. All they truly cared about was blood and "femmes", particularly when those two things came as a package.

If they had truly understood the multilayered implication of the nickname, they would probably laugh and demand to be called Animal House.

"Well, they agreed to help when the circumstances were considerably different. Factors have changed, as you're aware. To say that the mutation is a game changer is an understatement."

"Go on."

"They've agreed to continue to help, but want more flexibility."

"What does that mean?"

"They, um, want to set their own hours."

"I see. That may present some problems for whichever Sovereign ends up trying to keep them reined in."

"Well..." Baka looked unsure how to proceed.

"Well what?"

"I was hoping you might want to be the Sovereign with the problem of keeping them reined in."

Again, Rev found himself staring at Baka while he thought through all the potential ramifications. "Traveling with a circus, are you?"

"That's one way to put it. It may seem like a motley crew of mixed species and abilities, but the bottom line is that we're vampire hunters."

He took a good long look at Baka as he sifted through Sol's memories. It was definitely not the same Baka that Sol had dealt with. For one thing, he didn't have that creepy amused look about him, like he knew a secret that he wasn't sharing. Trying to talk to a vampire who looks like he knows something you don't makes for high blood pressure and uncomfortable squirmage in one's chair.

Rev sucked in a big breath and let out a long sigh. "That's the hook all right. Hard to turn down. Even if I wanted to." He shook his head. "So we would need married housing for you and…"

"Heaven."

"Yes, Heaven. Nice name. And the crazy kids?"

"They don't really require living arrangements."

"Well, that's a definite plus in their column."

Baka smiled and looked hopeful. "Is that a yes?"

Rev seemed distracted, like he was juggling too many things at once. "How did you get here, by the way?"

"Hitched a ride on a company plane. I'm afraid there may not be enough residual trace of immortality to keep me alive in the passes, according to Jean Etienne's speculation. And my wife isn't willing to chance it. So I fly the old-fashioned way. In a jet."

"Yeah. Monq is still working on the idea for separating a person's particles, transporting them elsewhere, and reassembling them on arrival. If you think traveling the passes comes with risk, just imagine that!" Rev shook his head. "Are you spending the night then?"

"Yes." Rev turned away and seemed to become immediately engrossed in something on his monitor. "Sovereign Farthing?"

"Hmmm?"

"When do you think I might expect an answer regarding my request for transfer?'

Baka could read every emotion that passed over the Sovereign's face – something that never could have been said about Solomon Nememiah. In rapid succession he watched surprise become confusion. That quickly changed to understanding and resolved in a slight embarrassment.

Rev stood up and extended his hand. "Welcome to Jefferson Unit, vam… uh, Baka. We're glad to have you and your crew."

CHAPTER 12

Farnsworth was so unaccustomed to getting calls on her personal phone that it took her a minute to identify the odd buzzing as her phone vibrating on her desk. Looking at the face, she saw that it was a text from Farthing.

I understand it could have gone either way at this time of year, but it seems the weatherman says cold. So bring your coat. And hat. And mittens.

She laughed at the last thing and repeated, "Mittens," under her breath.

"Hmmm? You said something?" Actually it sounded more like sumzing when Genevieve said it.

Farnsworth looked up and blushed like she'd been caught doing something untoward. "Um, well, Sovereign Farthing texted to say I should bring a hat and mittens because it will be cold tonight. For our date."

Genevieve blinked. "And this makes you blush? What is it about hats and coats and the mittens that makes you blush?" She smiled. "Oh. You are planning to make love wearing just hats and mittens?" She said it as offhandedly as if she was asking if they were having Italian or seafood for dinner.

"You say these things to embarrass me, don't you?" Farnsworth's face had gone bright red.

Genevieve blinked. "Embarrass? No." She shook her head like the idea of deliberately setting out to cause her boss embarrassment was unthinkable.

Farnsworth took a deep breath. "I just have to remember you're French and look at things differently. I just thought it was sort of, I don't know, endearing. Nurturing. That he thought about me being cold."

"But of course. He likes you very much."

When Farnsworth arrived at the Whister pad, she was wearing a red dress, a long but stylish wool coat, and she was carrying a large outrageously expensive bag that contained slip on sneakers, a hat that wouldn't ruin her hair for days, and a pair of extravagant red leather gloves with faux Canadian fox fur trim. When she stepped off the elevator she found a date waiting with a smile that lit her up like a shot of bourbon.

The Whister dropped them at The Order's 63rd Street location, which was just four blocks from the newly reopened Café Des Artistes, close enough to walk. When they arrived, Rev leaned over and said something inaudible to the maître d, who responded with a smile and a nod. They were seated in a back corner booth. It was the sort of place where wait staff knew not to interrupt a sentence in progress, to be present when needed without hovering when unwanted. Quiet and elegant for fine dining with anyone. Romantic and seductive when with the right person.

Dinner was one of those two and a half hour experiences that would be remembered when all the ordinary nights of ordinary meals were long forgotten.

Farnsworth had spent the past twenty-four hours vacillating between cancelling and not. On the one hand she thought there couldn't be much harm in going, unless you considered that a date gone wrong with your Unit Sovereign could be big trouble. On the other hand, she felt guilty about being attracted to the young knight recently turned administrator. She thought it was much too soon after Sol's death to be even mildly interested in someone, particularly not someone so junior.

Mixed into that muddle was a constant second guessing of her attractiveness. A little voice of ugly judgment kept prodding, asking, "Why would such a catch be interested in an old, well, at least older woman?"

The fact was that Rev was easy to be with. His company required no effort. It simply felt right. After dessert and coffee, he said, "I'm stuffed. How about you?"

"Overstuffed."

"What do you think about walking around for a little while? Did you bring some other shoes? Not that those aren't nice. Because they are. "

She chuckled. "All is well. My shoes take no offense. And, yes, I did bring other footwear. Per instructions. Meet you at coat check."

"Deal."

Stepping out onto the sidewalk, the crisp air felt good. As they started away she was still buttoning up and pulling on her gloves. While so engaged, Rev waved a cab over and opened the door for her.

When they were inside, he said, "Bergdorf Goodman," to the taxi driver.

Farnsworth smiled and looked intrigued. "We're going shopping?"

He was instantly aware that they'd never been so close together. Not since he'd been reborn. The close quarters of the taxi's back seat seemed awash with a potent intimacy that was theirs and theirs alone. Even if there was a Somalian cab driver singing along to Frank Sinatra music. Off key.

Rev's face was so close to hers when he turned to answer the question that he forgot the question. In fact he forgot everything except how beautiful she was in red and that included the red lipstick that he couldn't seem to look away from.

"Hello?"

He jerked his gaze up to her eyes. "What?"

She laughed. "I said, 'Are we going shopping?'"

"No. It's the starting point on our route."

"We have a route?"

"Yes, ma'am, we do. And we are there." The cab stopped at the curb.

While Rev paid the driver, Farnsworth strolled a few feet toward the display windows to see what high end buyers thought about clothes for summer. Not that she valued their opinion. For the most part she thought they were certifiably insane. But there weren't many places that decked out windows anymore. So why not experience the show?

Rev came up behind her. "You like that?"

"Good gods no. Wouldn't be caught dead in it."

One of the pedestrians on the sidewalk overheard her and sniggered. Seemed she wasn't the only one who questioned the good sense of people who would spend actual money on those clothes.

She leaned over to Rev and said in a low conspiratorial tone, "And especially not at fifteen hundred dollars for a little short sleeved knit sweater. For that it had better have actual gold thread in the weave."

They started strolling. "So what do you spend your money on?"

"My millions?"

He laughed. "Given what I already know about you I wouldn't be that surprised if you hadn't been mastering stock market manipulation in your spare time between one and two in the morning."

She gave him an odd look.

"What?"

She shook her head a little. "Nothing. It's just... That was a really nice compliment."

He stopped and turned toward her with a smile. "Finally. A compliment you're happy to accept. So do I get a thank you or a kiss? Or a kiss *and* a thank you?"

"Thank you, Sovereign Farthing."

Before she knew what was coming next, he'd taken her face between his hands and placed a slow, sincere and deliciously promising kiss on her mouth.

"Thank you, Operations Manager Farnsworth. Can I call you Susan yet?"

She was so stunned by the suddenness of the move and the burn of the kiss that all she could do was concentrate on not reaching up to touch her lips. When she didn't respond, he took her arm and wrapped it under and over the crook of his so that she'd have to walk close.

"Come on. Let's go see what there is to see."

It was out of his mouth before he knew it. He looked at her to see if that would raise an alarm. After all she was the one who had taught him that expression. He reminded himself to be more careful. He couldn't behave as if he was promenading with the love of his life, who had promised to be his wife. He had to behave as if it was a first date.

After a few feet she seemed to come back to life and began pointing out this thing or that about sights or people. Abruptly she glanced his way with a grin and said, "This is fun. Do you bring all your dates on a walk down Fifth Avenue?"

"As you well know, I'm new in town, but even if I wasn't, the answer would be no because I don't go on dates." At first she laughed, but his expression said he wasn't kidding. "I asked somebody who has a reputation for being good with girls what sort of thing would be fun and maybe impress you? He gave me this idea." Something about the fact that he'd wanted to impress her made her stomach do a little jig. "Is it working?"

"Yes. Like I told you. It's fun!"

"And are you impressed?"

She stopped walking which caused a crowd of pedestrians to part and walk around. "Why do you want to impress me? No. Strike that. Just make it simple. Why me?"

He put his arm around her waist and pulled her to the side next to a building. "Why would you question how special you are? You think there are a lot of women like you?"

"Well. Yes."

"Well, you'd be very, very wrong then." He pulled her close and kissed her again, then straightened and looked around. "Come on."

He pulled her around the corner and started heading for a building that was displaying the telltale awning and flags of an uptown hotel. She kept waiting for the voice of the proper mature woman to make it out of her throat, but she was silent. Silent. Excited and thinking, *Oh my gods. What in the abyss am I doing?*

A question sat on the tip of her tongue, "Did you plan this?", but she didn't ask it. She knew he hadn't. She could tell by the way he'd scanned the surroundings. It was a purely spontaneous response to a breathless kiss, the sampling of which, apparently, made him want more.

He wasn't alone in that. Her body was crazy for the guy and responding to him like a rare Stradivarius violin responds to the touch of a virtuoso.

He had an iron grip on her as they maneuvered the revolving door, like he thought she might bolt if he loosened his grip, but it wasn't fear that made him hold on tight. It was anticipation. And arousal. He rushed them toward the desk.

"We'd like a room. "

The desk clerk smiled and glanced at Farnsworth. He couldn't read anything from the bloom in her cheeks because of the chilly breeze that was whipping around Manhattan that night, but the shine in her eyes was a giveaway that he needed to check them in quickly and efficiently. He didn't ask about luggage, which desk clerks do sometimes just for the fun of it. He didn't ask if they wanted two beds. He made a point of saying that service of a limited menu and beverages, including wine, was still available, to which Rev replied, "Please send up a nice merlot."

"Very good, sir."

Rev took the key and began guiding Farnsworth away from the desk. They rounded the end of the long marble counter and turned left, as directed by the desk clerk. He was trying to appear completely controlled and not scare her by walking too fast, but his body was saying he'd better run. On the ride up to the room Rev was hyperaware that she was gripping the lapels of her coat tightly and holding the edges together as if she was afraid she might be asked to remove outer wear at some point.

His mind understood that she thought they were strangers, but his heart and his body believed they were lovers who'd been separated far too long. The charade was cruel to both of them, but necessary if, according to the Powers That Be - with whom he had a passing acquaintance, he wanted to stay incarnate. And he did want to stay incarnate for so many reasons including the high probability of impending carnality with Susan Farnsworth.

As they walked down the hall toward the room she was looking more and more like she was approaching a firing squad. Rev wasn't sure about the best course of action, but he knew he was on shaky ground and that he'd better proceed cautiously. He was halfway surprised that she walked in when he opened the door. Based on her body language, he'd anticipated that she might try a sprint for the fire escape.

Once inside, he turned on the lamps and took off his coat while Farnsworth stared at the bed. He walked over to her, gently gripped her forearms that were holding her coat lapels like her life depended on it, and began slowly walking backwards so that she moved with him, almost like a dance. He maneuvered her across the room until the two of them were standing over the sofa, where he urged her to sit.

She looked down at the sofa and complied, but made no move to loosen her hold on the coat. He sat down close to her and waited for her to look at him. She didn't. She looked everywhere in the room but at him.

"If this was a mistake, I apologize. The last thing, the very last thing, I want is to make you uncomfortable. If you'd like to think of this as simply a quiet place, away from work and all the people who know us, where we can have some wine and get to know each other better? Then that's exactly what this will be."

She looked over at him. "Just wine?"

He smiled. "I don't want to leave you with the impression that it's my first choice, but showing you a good time is what I want most tonight." It would have been impossible to not smile at words so thoughtful. So she smiled. "Can I take your coat or would you rather keep it?"

She looked down at where she was holding the coat together like she'd forgotten she was wearing one. When her eyes lifted to him, she laughed in a self-deprecatory way. "I'm being silly. Right?"

"I don't know. What got you spooked?"

"Spooked? That's an unfortunate choice of words."

A small frown formed and he shook his head in confusion. "I don't...

"You opened the wrong door with an unfortunate word and I made it worse with a bad joke. Terrible joke as a matter of fact."

He opened his mouth to respond, but there was a knock at the door. "Must be wine."

While he went to open the door, she removed her coat.

"Good evening, sir. Where would you like the wine?"

Rev gestured toward the table in the corner.

The tray was carried by a young man wearing a handsome mulberry short coat. He nodded at Farnsworth. "Madame." While opening the wine, he said, "The management instructed room service to include some cheese and a few chocolates."

"That was very nice of them," said Rev as he took the vinyl wallet holding the bill and signed for it.

"Thank you, sir. Will there be anything more?"

"We'll call if we need something else."

The traveling sommelier nodded at Farnsworth again. "Have a good evening."

Rev closed the door behind him and locked it. When he turned back to the sofa, Farnsworth wasn't there. She had gathered up two wine glasses in one hand and the bottle in the other and was headed back toward the sofa.

She poured both glasses and handed one to him as he sat back down. She took a sip and closed her eyes as the taste lingered on her tongue and the slight tinge of burn descended into her system.

"You were saying?" he asked.

"Hmmm?"

"Before. You were saying something about a bad joke."

"Oh." She'd been hoping he'd forgotten so they could start fresh on a new topic. She looked away and started studying various objects in the room again.

"Susan. You can tell me. Whatever it is. I want to know."

She smiled. "I don't think you do."

"I do."

"Not really." She shook her head.

"If you weren't so beautiful, I might be tempted to call you exasperating."

Her smiled died. "I'm not beautiful."

He cocked his head. "Who said?"

She dropped her eyes and took a sip of wine. "I know that people talk about other people at Jefferson Unit. It's like a small town. Everything is everybody's business." He nodded to encourage her to continue. "So maybe you already know that I was engaged?"

"To the former Sovereign. Yes. I did know that. Is that what this...? Are you feeling like...?" Try as he might he couldn't find a way to phrase the question without making things awkward between them. "You talk. I'll listen."

"Well, it wasn't that long ago and I really wasn't ready to think about, um, dating. I may have ventured into this too soon."

"You're having second thoughts about having dinner with me?"

She flashed a big smile that showed white even teeth, a big contrast to her lipstick. "Too late for that. No. Dinner was wonderful. I just wasn't prepared for... ah, this." She used the wine glass she was holding to gesture toward the bed. "It's too soon. He hasn't been gone that long."

There it was. The grandfather of all double binds. There was a part of him, a big part, that was glad she mourned Sol. There was another part that wanted her to just suck it up, get over it, and take off her clothes. At some point he realized she was waiting for him to respond.

"Tell me about him."

That was the last thing she'd expected to hear. It was evident he'd surprised her because her dark eyes flared a little. "Why would you want me to talk about that?"

"Just do." She looked dubious. "We agreed we're here to get to know each other. I've got you all to myself. No phones. No computers. No workmen. No Genevieve. No trainees needing fresh diapers." That made her laugh and damnation if laughter wasn't a great look for her. "It's our chance to say whatever we want without fear of being overheard."

For a minute she just studied him, like she was trying to discern whether or not he was being truthful. "He was extraordinary. Well," she shrugged, "I guess all Sovereigns are extraordinary, by the very definition, but there was so much more. I could talk about all his wonderful qualities, but in the end, what it came down to? Is that we fit. Just as simple as that. He made me feel like I was precious because he'd picked me. He made me glad to be me."

She felt a hot tear slide down her cheek and reached to swipe it away, but Rev caught her hand. He leaned over and kissed her cheek where the tear had left a trail. When he pulled back it wasn't far enough that she couldn't feel his breath on her face. "I can't tell you when is the right time to move on, but I can tell you that's how you make me feel."

"What?" she sniffed.

"You make me feel like there's nothing more important in the world than being with you."

"That doesn't make any sense. You practically just met me. This is our first date."

"I know and I don't care. You're the one."

"The one?"

"The one."

"I want to go."

"All right." He cursed himself silently for pushing. Too much. Too soon. He'd scared her away and it might take forever to get her alone again. He reached for her coat and helped her into it. She gathered up her purse and started for the door without looking back. He followed helplessly wishing he could just go back five minutes and retract everything he'd said that made her ill at ease. "Just tell me one thing," he said to her back. "Do you feel comfortable with me? Like we... fit?"

He'd followed so close that, when she turned around, she practically ran into him. They weren't face to face because he was a good eight inches taller. She dropped her purse on the floor, reached up with both hands, and pulled his face down so that she could press her mouth to his. When his tongue began a thorough exploration, hers tangled with his and she delighted in the groan she elicited.

They cleaved to each other in a way that was far too desperate for a first date. They pulled, pressed and almost clawed with a passion that was staggering. And so unexpected. At least on her part.

Within minutes Farnsworth's wool coat and red dress had joined the purse on the floor. That was when the wave of panic washed over her. "Stop. Stop." She tried to push him away.

He was dumbfounded. "Why?"

"Turn off the lights."

"Turn off the lights? Why?"

"Because I'm forty-four. Not twenty-four."

He stared into her eyes for a few beats before saying, "No."

She gaped. "What do you mean, 'No.'?"

"I want to look at you."

"No you do not."

"Yes. I do." At that point he was grabbing for clothing while she was retreating. It quickly turned into a game of mock chasing around a hotel room with Farnsworth in pretty black and red lingerie. It was so ridiculous she couldn't help laughing.

When he caught her, he pulled her to him, trapping her arms. "I'm not shy about my body. Would it make you feel better if I go first?"

She laughed, but it was hollow and smirking. "Of course you're not shy about your body! First you're a man. And, second, you're only thirty-one!"

"Put on some music. I'll do a strip-tease for you."

She looked at him like he was crazy. "You're past ridiculous," she laughed although there was a part of her that was intrigued.

"If I dance for you naked, you have to agree to let me remove these last pretty things from your beautiful body." He knew he had her when she hesitated. He backed her up until the sofa seat hit the back of her legs, then gave her a little push. She sat and ended up at eye level with his swollen crotch. When he saw that her eyes hadn't left his groin, he reached down and ran a palm over the erection that was clearly outlined by silk and wool blend slacks. Honestly, he wasn't an exhibitionist and didn't know where that came from, but the motion made her tongue peek out and absent-mindedly lick her bottom lip.

He strode to the radio beside the bed, which was a Bose and had beautiful clear sound. After a little tuning he settled on a smooth jazz station and turned around with a devilish smile. Farnsworth responded with a flush, pulled a throw pillow over her midsection and held onto it like a life raft. Everything about what was going on screamed naughty, but she was helpless to end it.

Rev was already coatless. She'd pushed it off his shoulders when they were still by the door. As he watched her closely, observing every reaction, he toed off his shoes, took off socks and threw them behind him. He paid careful attention to where her eyes were tracking and to changes in the rhythmic rise and fall of her chest.

Dancing was certainly not a skill he would claim, but he was flexible and he figured the aspect of clothing removal was more important than actual dancing. So he began moving rhythmically, unbuttoning his shirt as slowly as he advanced on his audience. It seemed that Rev Farthing's body had recorded muscle memory of dance moves. Maybe Sol wasn't a dancer, but Farthing was.

Farnsworth was feeling all sorts of tingling sensations awaking parts that had been dormant for a while. She found herself feeling impatient about the time he was taking to remove his shirt. She was ready to see his exposed upper body.

When he did pull the shirt back, he was standing right in front of her. Her eyes went straight down the hills and valleys of his abs to the dark happy trail that disappeared into his pants. She wanted to lean forward and lick straight up that trail until she reached his nipples while running her hands over that flawless expanse of skin.

He motioned for her to take hold of his right cuff. When she did he pulled away and turned until the shirt landed in her lap, leaving her feeling like she'd just stripped him. Without thinking or taking her eyes away from the floor show, she brought it up to her nose. The scent was shockingly familiar. Starch, Old Spice soap and a hint of cigar, like the little black cigars Sol used to smoke. Underlying all that was something indescribably masculine that got her nether parts even more engaged in the experience at hand.

Still moving to the music, Rev's hips and body were making slow circles, not so exaggerated as to be comical, not so insignificant as to go unnoticed. Her eyes followed his fingers as they undid his belt buckle. He began to draw it out of the waistband loops, painstakingly, agonizingly slowly.

Glancing up at his face she could see that he was clearly enjoying her obvious appreciation of his body and its performance, but he was also smoldering as much as she was. It was by far the most erotic thing she'd ever experienced.

When the belt was halfway out, he extended the buckle to her and nodded. Tentatively she reached out and took it, then pulled until it came free in her hands. He smiled like she'd done something quite exceptional.

He unbuttoned, unzipped, turned around and took a step toward the bed before letting the pants drop to his bare ankles. She already knew he had an eye-catching rear view because she'd been watching him turn around and leave her office several times a day. But the panorama of his bare muscular shoulders and back tapering to his slim waist was a whole new level of lust-driven need to salivate.

When he turned back around to face her, he was wearing nothing but black knit boxers and a smile. He walked forward until his legs were touching hers. One small piece of fabric was the only thing that stood between Rev and nakedness.

"Go on," he said. She shook her head in an exaggerated way just like a little girl. He laughed. "I insist."

His hips began moving again as if to entice her to submit. She was mesmerized. And he knew it. Finally, her desire to see what was under the boxers overrode every bit of warring emotion whether it was caution, anxiety, guilt, or fear. She reached out with both hands and let her fingertips slide under the waistband. The second her hands came in contact with his skin he closed his eyes and subtly thrust his hips forward as if his body was reflexively begging her for more touch.

With her heart beating as fast as if she was riding a roller coaster, she pulled the stretchy material toward her and down so that his cock could spring free. She didn't have so much as three seconds to appreciate the glorious sight of perfect, ample young male in the fullness of arousal before he bent down, tossed the pillow aside and scooped her up.

During the brief time her mind was frozen on a loop of *oh, my, my, my, my, my,* he managed to carry her to bed and place her securely underneath him so that she was trapped by part of his upper body and one of his heavy legs. All thought of protest died as he began an assault of hot and sincere kisses over her neck and face. She had absolutely no desire to be anywhere else doing anything else.

Her body had already been primed by the sensual demonstration of striptease so that she overheated like a pressure cooker with actual contact. When her lips parted to release a moan, he muffled the sound by covering her mouth with his. Thus distracted, he reached under her, released the bra snaps and pulled the fabric away. As he continued to overwhelm her with touches light and firm, kisses passionate and feathery, she had no defense to offer when he lifted far enough away to pull her panties down her legs.

There was a question in her eyes once she was bared to him.

"Beautiful. Perfect for me."

She could tell that he was telling the truth. He really wanted her. In that way. All forty-four years of her.

As he continued making love to her she marveled at how he seemed to know exactly what she wanted and needed. He knew every one of her erogenous zones and explored them like he'd had a Farnsworth instruction manual. It was heady and heavenly. And comfortingly familiar. When she climaxed, she shocked herself by calling out Sol's name.

The instant it left her lips, she realized what she'd said and gasped. Rev had stilled. He lifted his head to see her face and found her eyes wide open and starting to tear up.

"I'm sorry," she began. "So very, very sorry. I know it's you and, oh gods, I don't know how I could have said that."

"Shhhh. It's okay," he murmured in a soothing tone. "Don't be sorry. You just gave me a goal to work toward. Someday you're going to feel that way about me."

What he wanted more than anything was to tell her that she wasn't wrong, that she responded to him like he was her man because he *was* her man. He hadn't really realized just how hard it was going to be to keep that particular secret.

During the night, as Farnsworth lay in his arms in the dark, she told him everything about what had happened at the beach house up to and including the paramedic callously saying to his companion that she could have prevented Sol's death with the correct application of a tourniquet.

He listened silently, her tears falling on the bare skin of his chest, as she poured out the grief and sorrow and guilt. All the while he was thinking that he'd been a selfish bastard, first caught up in getting back to life and then caught up in getting Jefferson Unit up to speed. He hadn't really considered the extent of what she'd been through while he'd been otherwise occupied.

There as they lay together, for the first time, he put himself in her place and tried to imagine what it would have been like if she'd been the one who bled out on the beach on a cold March day while he watched helplessly. He pulled her tighter as his chest constricted and he loved her even more.

Lost in those thoughts he had to go back and piece together what she'd just said.

"What?"

"I said it's time for me to sell the beach house. I don't want to ever be there again. I guess I'll go down this weekend, get the stuff out I want to keep, and talk to a realtor."

"I want to go with you."

After a long pause, she said, "Why?"

"It was a place you loved and it was a place where something life-changing happened to you. I'll take Saturday off and go with you." *After all,* he thought, *what's the point of getting a second chance at life if not to do some things differently? Like take a day off to go on an important errand with your girl.*

"You'll take Saturday off?" She seemed to be considering. "I don't know."

"Why not? Is this a one night stand?"

She sighed and made a sound like a stifled laugh. "No. Nothing like that. It just... I don't know. Seems like it would feel wrong to take somebody else there."

"Tell you what. Let me go with you. If my being there makes you uncomfortable, I'll take a hike. Okay?"

"I can't imagine why you'd want to go. Really. But truthfully, I'd just as soon not face it alone."

"You haven't been back since?"

"No."

"Then I absolutely insist on going."

Things between Rev and Farnsworth were moving at dizzying speeds. She hadn't had a lot of relationships with men, but she knew enough to know that her relationship with Rev was highly unusual.

On Saturday morning at dark early they left Jefferson Unit in her Land Rover. The vehicle was old, but it ran and she loved that it had so much glass. It was the next best thing to being in a convertible.

Rev noticed that she was becoming more and more apprehensive as they drew closer to Cape May.

"I'm with you, Susan. You're not doing this alone."

He saw her face soften as she glanced over at him. "I know. And I'm glad. It would have been harder to come all by myself."

The house smelled a little musty when they opened the door and stepped in. As Farnsworth went through the rites of opening the house, Rev followed her around trying to keep her mind occupied with questions. Like, "How long have you had this place?" "Did you always want a beach house?" "What is it about the beach that you like so much?"

When she took her jewelry box out of the dresser drawer in her bedroom and dropped her pearl necklace inside, he saw the ring he'd given her sitting alone inside one of the pink velvet compartments. That ring wasn't designed to sit inside a beach house jewelry box like a high school memento that had outlived its day and its usefulness. That ring was made for wearing on her finger. He'd known it the moment he first saw it.

Farnsworth glanced at her watch. They still had half an hour before the realtor was to meet them there so she made a pot of coffee and they sat down at the kitchen table to wait. Ten minutes after appointment time, the realtor called to say something urgent had come up and could they possibly reschedule for the next day?

"Just a minute." She put the phone face against her chest to mute the sound and turned to Rev. "She can't come today and wants to know if I can meet her tomorrow instead?"

"If you're asking if I can stay with you until then, the answer is yes."

She nodded, told the realtor they could meet Sunday afternoon instead, and ended the call. When she faced Rev, it was evident that she wasn't sure what to do next.

"So! We're spending the night?" he asked, trying to sound enthusiastic. She looked around nervously and bit her bottom lip. It was heartbreaking to see his supremely confident lady so devastatingly insecure. "Or we could go get a room at that bed and breakfast we passed. Come back tomorrow." When she didn't answer, he added another option. "Or I could go get a room at the B&B if you'd rather."

He watched her chest heave as she took in a deep breath and steadied her resolve. It gave literal meaning to the term "suck it up".

"No. We can stay here. It would be silly to go somewhere else."

Rev wanted to do something to ease the pain he was reading on her face and body language, but didn't know that anything but time, and maybe love, could fix that.

"Let's go back up the highway to that grocery store and get some supplies. I'll make dinner. What would you like?"

That seemed to distract her, at least temporarily. She smiled. "You know how to cook?"

"Not everything, but I have a couple of specialties. Bam!" He made a stage magic gesture with both hands.

She giggled. "Would never have taken you for an Emeril fan."

"Well, while we're driving to the store, I'll tell you about the time I was stuck in a Nicaraguan dump waiting for a guy who was supposed to deliver a Chupacabra report. There was a TV, but the only channel that came in was the cooking channel. For days I had nothing to do but watch that guy and listen to it rain."

"Okay. Going to grab a sweater and then we'll go."

When she came back down, she was wearing a brightly colored hand knit sweater that truly was wearable art and Rev would have thought it was gorgeous on her except for one thing.

"What's that?" He pointed at her chest and looked unhappy.

She looked down. "It's a sweater."

"No. That!"

She looked closer, following the trajectory line to the exact place where he was pointing. The sweater was a highly prized designer item that had been an expensive gift. It was covered with rows of pretty white fleeced, white-faced sheep following each other in rows, except for a single black-faced sheep that was facing outward. "Are you talking about the little black-faced sheep? It's the designer signature."

His eyes rose to meet hers and he realized he probably looked and sounded a little crazy. He shoved a hand over his head. "I guess this sounds crazy and I apologize for that, but could you possibly wear another sweater?"

Farnsworth let her mouth fall open. "Are you afraid of the black-faced sheep on my sweater?"

He looked like he was trying to decide what to say, but never got a chance. She burst into laughter that racked her body. It was a feeling she'd grown unaccustomed to. She held her sides and laughed so hard she actually thought it might make her sore. The fact that Rev looked so humiliated only made it funnier.

Farnsworth wasn't usually the sort of person to find humor in ridicule, but there was something so ludicrous about the battle-hardened vampire hunter being afraid of a little inanimate sheep, part of a woven pattern on a piece of cloth.

"I'm not afraid," he said, failing to sound convincing. "I just don't like it."

She shook her head and started back upstairs to change, chuckling all the way.

She had given him the keys to drive, but said nothing else after coming back down wearing a sweater that was mono color. White. He thought she was making a statement with her choice of substitute.

En route to the store, he said, "I guess it was ridiculous."

"What?" she asked innocently while batting her eyelashes and screwing up her mouth to stifle a giggle.

"Okay. Have it your way. Just keep it up, but you're looking at karma's errand boy."

That phrase completely messed up her determination not to tease him anymore. The laughter started all over again.

"You want to tell me what it's about?"

"What?"

"Being phobic of black-faced sheep?"

He looked away, out the driver's side window, then back at the road, but did not look at her. "No," was all he said, but it was obvious he was pouting. She'd hurt his ego.

Staring at his handsome profile for a few beats, she was thinking that everyone is entitled to a few quirks, a few eccentricities, and a few secrets. "Okay. I know it wasn't that you were bitten by one because they're herbivores. But that's all I'm going to say. Subject closed." True to her word she didn't say anything else about it. Right after one last muffled chuckle.

They argued over whether to use red peppers or green peppers and finally compromised on both. Oddly, even the arguing felt like a glove worn into the exact shape of the hand.

It started to rain just as they made it back to the house, ran up the stairs, and closed the sliding glass door.

Rev grinned. "Good timing."

The temperature dropped a little, but mostly it just felt colder because of the additional damp in the air. He built a fire using wood that Sol had brought in and, again for the thousandth time, wished that he could turn to Farnsworth and remark about the oddity and bitter sweetness of that.

They sat down on the couch in front of the fire together. With dinner a couple of hours away, there wasn't really anything to do but be in the moment. Together.

She decided the best way to handle a silence before it became awkward was to fill it with sound. "So I guess Rev is short for Revenge?"

He angled his body toward her and reached over to finger a stray tendril of dark locks next to her face. "No," he said with a light of amusement dancing in his eyes. "Short for Reverence." And that's what she would call the emotion being projected back at her, but she didn't trust it. Couldn't trust it. People just didn't fall in love so fast.

He leaned over, lowered his voice, and said, "Let's go upstairs."

Her body betrayed her in a series of quivers. She asked herself if she wanted that and the surprising answer was yes. She thought making love to a man who wasn't Sol, in that place of all places, should feel like a betrayal, but it didn't.

Before they arrived she would have said the same thing about teasing and laughter, that it would feel horrible, that it would be an affront to her relationship with the man she loved – the man she would always love. But she didn't feel guilty about laughing with Rev. It didn't make her feel bad at all. It was more like the easing of a giant burden.

Without another word she rose and walked to the stairs.

They made sweet love that afternoon with rain falling on a roof that had been built before modern codes required sound-muting insulation. It was lovely.

It was also eerie that he seemed to know *exactly* what she liked in bed. All the little familiarities that lovers usually learn through time and experiment. Like the fact that she liked her nipples tweaked but not pinched, that she liked oral sex right after a recent shower, that she liked breath *on* her ear, but not tongue *in* her ear, that she liked nipping but not biting.

When they returned to the kitchen to make dinner, it felt as though an exorcism had been done on the house, clearing away ghostly vibrations of unhappy memories. Farnsworth insisted that they do the cooking together. They were making pasta primavera. He was responsible for the primavera and Alfredo sauce, which he finished before her part of the meal, the pasta, was ready.

She turned from the boiling pot on the stove, waving a long wooden spoon, and asked Rev to open a bottle of wine.

"Sure," he smiled. He picked out a bottle of Red Guitar, then walked straight to the trick drawer, kicked the baseboard underneath the bottom cabinet and pulled at the same time.

Her mind raced through every conceivable explanation while her knees threatened to give out from under her. Somehow she managed to stay upright. It couldn't be. But it *had* to be. She couldn't dismiss the possibility out of hand. After all, she worked for an organization where impossible things were as routine as requisitioning printer paper.

While he was facing the counter opening the wine, she came up behind him.

"So," she said in the lightest tone she could manage, "the realtor doesn't come until tomorrow afternoon." He glanced back over his shoulder, but didn't turn around. "So I was thinking we might rent a dune buggy tomorrow morning."

He wheeled on her with wild eyes, his face instantly drained of color and wearing panic like a mask. He grabbed her shoulders and tried to say the word "no" forcefully, but his throat had closed up and he could barely get out a sound that was somewhere between a whisper and a growl.

When he realized how much he'd appeared to overreact, he relaxed his grip on her shoulders. Seeing the expression on her face he knew instantly that it had been a trick. A good one. He released her, dropping his hands and stood up straight.

He clutched his arms around his body as if that would prevent the Powers That Be taking it from him. When a minute had gone by and he was still standing in the beach house kitchen, he started to breathe easier. He had promised that he wouldn't tell anyone, but he hadn't guaranteed that no one would guess.

Beginning to relax, he asked, "How?"

"How did I know?" He nodded slowly. "There's a trick to opening the drawer with the bottle opener." His eyes slid to that drawer and he glared at it like it was a traitor. "But if somebody in this room is going to ask a question that begins with 'how', by all rights it ought to be me."

"I can't tell you anything besides the fact that I'm glad you figured it out. If I could have told you more, I would have. Don't you know I wanted to?" He ran his hand over the top of his head and looked around nervously like he was still expecting lightning to strike. "You have to be the smartest woman alive."

At the same time Rev was beginning to hope that he might have a real second chance at life, it hit Farnsworth that her suspicions were confirmed.

It was real.

He was real.

Sol in a younger, different body.

When the reality hit her, it was all at once. She convulsed, sucking in a gasp as she grabbed for him, exhaling a deluge of tears intermingled with sobs.

"I... missed you. So much." He cradled her head to his chest with one big hand and let her cry while he scattered kisses over the top of her hair. "Do you know how hard it is to lose the person you...?"

"Love?" He pulled back. "The person you love? You do still love me, right?"

She nodded, wondering why she didn't feel traumatized by shock. Her best explanation was that some part of her had recognized him and had been processing it on a subconscious level all along.

"The answer is yeah. I know how I felt when I thought I might not see you again. So, yes. I know. I can't tell you much, but I will tell you that I had to fight my way back here. Part of it was because my job wasn't finished, but a big part of it was because of you." He ran his thumbs across her tearstained cheeks.

The pasta chose that moment to bubble over making a mess of starchy water all over the stove and floor. The cleanup took an hour and the food was inedible, but neither one cared. They were just happy to be with each other.

She was finishing up when Rev returned to the kitchen. He held out two fists. "Which one?"

She smiled indulgently and tapped his left hand.

He shook his head and opened an empty fist. "Nope. Try again."

She tapped his right hand. He held out the engagement ring he'd bought her. "You want to go out for food? Or get married? Or get supper *and* get married?"

She laughed and nodded. "Yes. Both."

"You know you're never going to be able to tell anybody. That it's me."

"Okay. I can keep a secret, but you know I'm not the only one who knows you pretty well. I'd be surprised if at least one other person isn't suspicious."

After a short pause, his jaw clenched and he simply said, "Storm." Then he looked away and sighed. "I guess I haven't taken steps to disguise Sol very well." He ran a hand over his head. "Maybe deep down I really wanted to be found out."

He gave her a devilishly intimate smile and stepped into her, pressing her body into his and brazenly cupping her breast with his palm. "I know I like having *you* know. A lot."

They drove to the beachside roadhouse that was twenty minutes up the highway. Farnsworth said she'd never been, but thought they stayed open late.

The parking lot was crowded for ten o'clock at night. It was the kind of joint that promised a good time, but not necessarily good food. The crowd was mostly twenties and thirties. Lots of people with tans on their faces from windsurfing even in winter. The bar area occupied the middle of the space with pool tables on one side and eating tables on the other.

The minute they walked in Farnsworth noticed that every female of every age stopped what they were doing and turned to look at Rev Farthing. She knew the new body was good-looking, but hadn't thoroughly digested the idea of drop dead beautiful until that moment. She was also self-consciously aware of the age difference. Acutely so.

A blond wearing a half apron, a black fanny pack, and a Harley tank top that revealed way too much bounteous bosom sauntered up to them, smiling at Rev. Without ever once making eye contact with Farnsworth, she said, "Seat yourself, gorgeous." She noticed that even the wording ignored her. 'Seat yourself' instead of seat yourselves.

Rev smiled at her and nodded as he put his hand on the small of Farnsworth's back to guide her toward the "dining room".

It had taken him less time than he would have imagined, prior to finding himself occupying a new body, to get used to having women throw themselves at him. He saw it as harmless, ego-boosting fun. No more. No less.

After a few minutes Ms. Overboobed arrived with two menus and two glasses of water. Again, she managed to leave the menus and the water without making eye contact with Farnsworth. When she left, Rev said, "What looks good to you?"

"I'm so hungry I almost don't care how much grease is in it or how many times the same grease has been used to fry other people's food."

He laughed. "Well I could go the health route and try to take care of this body, but I'm thinking I'll go with the other option which is to do whatever the hel I want. You should take care of *your*self though."

She was just about to ask what he meant by that when the slut slinked back over to their table. Her approach to order taking was the height of informality. She bent over and rested her elbows on the table, which revealed what very little had been left to imagination.

From that pose she tried her very best I'm-interested smile on Rev. "So what are you having, sugar?"

"Half pound burger medium with bacon, shitake mushrooms, hickory sauce, yellow mustard. Three onion rings *on* the burger and heat the bun. Put some fries on the side of that with a ketchup bottle that hasn't been opened. And I'll take a long neck Lone Star."

She grinned. "I like a man who knows what he wants. And what about your...?"

She pointed at Farnsworth with her pencil and glanced her way for the first time.

"My fiancée," he beamed at Farnsworth, finishing Boobs' sentence for her.

Farnsworth smiled and wiggled her ring finger in the air.

Boobs' face fell and she flushed, flummoxed. "Oh, I wouldn't have... What's your order, ma'am?"

"Anything without arsenic." Boobs looked confused. "Bring me the small version of his burger, medium *well*, without the bacon and onion rings, with lettuce and tomato. I'll have a coconut rum with 7 Up now."

When they were alone again Rev said, "That's new. I didn't know you like coconut rum."

"It helped me sleep through a few hard nights after..."

He decided to change the subject. "What was that about arsenic?"

"At least half the female population of this establishment wouldn't shed a tear if I ended dinner with my feet straight up in the air like an exterminated cockroach."

Rev looked sincerely lost. "No clue."

"You can't be oblivious to the way Boobie is coming on to you."

His gaze jerked toward the bar and then slid back to Farnsworth slowly as a snide smile formed on his perfect mouth. "You're jealous of the waitress? Seriously?"

"You need to get with the twenty-first century, old man. They're called wait staff now. Not waitresses."

"Wait staff. Bimbo. Whatever. I can't control other people's minds or their clothing choices or the fact that they choose to run up credit card bills getting grotesque implants, but you've got to know you're the *only* one for me. Now and forever."

She gave him her best heartwarming smile. "Now that I know who I'm with, I *do* know that. That's why I didn't trip her when she walked away."

They laughed and talked, made fun of the juke box music, stuffed themselves with America's favorite toxins, and loved every second of it. When it was time to leave, Farnsworth insisted on paying the check. Rev protested, but she was adamant. So he gave in.

With the pen provided she wrote a note on the back. It read, *I'm famous for giving great tips, but not tonight. – The Gorgeous Sugar's Woman*

She didn't trip the waitperson, but by all that was holy, she didn't tip her either.

CHAPTER 13

Glen was standing in front of his dresser not wearing a stitch, vigorously rubbing excess moisture out of his hair with a towel, when his phone buzzed. He looked over at the face, read the first part of the text, and cursed under his breath.

Z Team was called to the Sovereign's office. Since he was officially a part of Z Team, he assumed that included him. It also presented the potential of a timing catastrophe. He was supposed to be in Sov. Farthing's office in forty-five minutes. The problem was that he was also supposed to be picked up in an hour by the half witch, half demon who he hoped would someday be his mother-in-law.

Which of them would he least like to disappoint? Now there was a riddle for the sphinx. Glen was thinking that, when Monq said everything in life could be distilled to an equation, he hadn't been faced with that particular dilemma. Any way you added the factors, the sum equaled undesirable result.

He stood holding his phone for a few seconds, then replied to the text.

Would it be possible for me to arrive five minutes early for a private word, sir?

Glen watched while the send bar filled and waited until he received confirmation that transmission was complete. When no response dinged in right away, he decided to use the wait time productively and get dressed.

He glanced away from the phone long enough to retrieve faded jeans and a black tee shirt. The clothes were pulled on without Glen diverting attention away from his phone except for the literal blink of an eye when the shirt slid past his face.

Sitting on the side of the bed, he jerked on crew socks, then pushed his feet into short black combat style boots and left the lacings undone. Looking up at his reflection in the mirror that hung over the dresser, he grabbed the comb, pulled it haphazardly through his hair a couple of times and then shook his head so that it didn't look like he'd gone to a lot of trouble. He cared about grooming, but drew a line short of metropussy.

The phone vibrated against the wood of the dresser top and Glen snatched it up faster than a snake strike.

Five minutes face time approved.

His feet knew the way to the Sovereign's office so well that his body would take him there with his mind on auto. Thinking it wouldn't be a good idea to ask to meet five minutes early and be late, he went with the philosophy of better safe than sorry. He exited the elevator at second sublevel, glanced at his watch, and took up a post outside the Sovereign's office ten minutes early. He wasn't taking *any* chances on being late.

The trainee on duty as outer office assistant had a vantage point that gave a partial view of the hall. He looked at Glen quizzically.

"Got a meeting with the big giant head in," he looked at his watch, "seven minutes."

The kid nodded and smiled.

In five minutes Rev opened his door part way and said, "When Sir Catch arrives, show him in."

The kid looked toward Glen. "He's already here, sir."

"Oh." Rev opened the door the rest of the way and saw Glen waiting. He motioned for him to enter and retook his seat behind his desk while he waited for Glen to close the door behind him. "Well?"

"It's about the Z Team meeting, sir."

"Yes? What about it?"

"I'm scheduled to have dinner with the Storms tonight. She, uh, Mrs. Storm, is supposed to pick me up in half an hour or so. I was wondering if I should cancel that engagement?"

"I see." Rev stared at Glen a moment longer. "That won't be necessary. What I have to say to Z Team won't take longer than five minutes." He sighed. "Probably."

"Thank you, sir. Should I wait outside in the hall?"

"No. Just open the door and relax until they get here."

"Yes, sir."

When the other three members of Z Team came strolling in looking like they owned the place and like they wondered what he was doing arriving early, Glen was thinking he wished he'd been told to wait outside. First in was Torrent Finngarick, also known as Torn, followed by Rafael Nightsong, aka Raif, and Gunnar Gustafsven, a.k.a. Gun.

"Come in and close the door behind you." Rev didn't try to disguise his distaste for Z Team. "Got a special assignment for you. You'll be leaving Tuesday at 1500. Sensitive situation in Bulgaria. You'll be escorting a special investigator and insuring her safety."

"*Her* safety?"

Rev gave Torn a look that would have instantaneously shriveled an ordinary guy's testicles to the size of peas. The three seasoned members of Z Team looked at each other. Torn said, "You're no' sendin' us on a squint mission. No' *now*."

The Sovereign looked Torn over. "Orders from the top. We all have somebody we have to answer to. On this mission you'll be taking your orders from the expert who's being sent to the scene to act on behalf of The Order."

Torn's lips pressed together. "'Tis ox leavin's, *Sovereign*." He used the term 'sovereign' sarcastically and with a belligerence that could get him brigged and fined. 'Tis about what happened in Caracas, right? Time to let that go. 'Twas a long time back and a joke to boot."

Rev was hit with splashes of wild color and a memory of being so sick he almost doubled over just from recalling it. He'd been getting steadily better at handling the random remnants of experience his brain had retained. That particular incident must have been a doozy to elicit such a big visceral reaction. He wondered what those animals had done to Rev Farthing in Caracas in another lifetime unknown to him.

"No," he said evenly as the unpleasant feelings began to fade. He rose from his chair slowly and deliberately in a display of authority before placing his palms on his desk. "It's not about Caracas. It's about orders."

Glen stood and stepped in front of Torn. "Sir Finngarick forgot himself and got carried away in the disappointment of being denied an immediate return to hunter duty, sir. It won't happen again."

Rev looked from Glen to Torn and back again. He decided the best option was to allow Glen to defuse. "You'll probably be gone three days, but it could take longer. Pack accordingly. You know the drill." Rev turned toward his computer screen. When no one moved, he looked at them each individually before saying, "Dismissed."

When they were a few feet down the hall, Torn turned on Glen. "What was that kiss ass routine, rookie? And whatever gave you the idea that you fuckin' speak for me?"

What happened next was the last thing in the world that Torn was expecting. Glen placed his palm on Torn's collar bone and shoved him back against the wall. Hard. That apparently effortless move, was accompanied by the low level werewolf snarl that never failed to raise the hair follicles of everyone within earshot.

The next words that came out of Glen's mouth were half spoken, half growled.

"Don't talk to me like that, Elf. I'm not a trainee anymore. And don't even think about being disrespectful to a superior again. I don't care if you have a history. You better get your shit together before you make me sorry I threw in with you."

When Glen released Torn and stepped back, Gun laughed into his hand and said, "Yeah. What he said," which only served to infuriate Glen further.

Glen wheeled on him. "Shut it, Gun. You were the one tasked with defusing this redheaded powder keg." He jerked his head toward Torn. "Where were you in there? The situation had one leg hanging off a cliff. I gave you plenty of time to step in and handle it, but what? You pussied out? Had a petit mal seizure? You scared of this elf?"

Gun was starting to grasp that his new role wasn't a figurehead, that it had teeth and he was supposed to be using them. The realization that the kid had just done the job he was assigned, after he failed to do it, was a creeping humiliation that was manifesting in the reddening of his face. "Now look..."

"Nuh-uh. You're the one looking right now. You want me to play the role of newbie. Sure. I'm your guy. But only if you're walking the walk." He looked over his three team mates. "You want me to respect you? Defer to you? Maybe even admire you? Then start acting like *admirable* Black Swan knights."

It was that scene that Litha came upon. Glen faced off against the rest of his new team just royally dressed down by him. She appeared in the hallway where she was to meet Glen and pick him up, and was now looking at the four of them with apprehension.

"Glen? You ready?"

Hearing the soft voice behind him, he watched three pairs of eyes shift their focus away from him. He didn't turn around immediately, but relaxed his shoulders while continuing the stare down with Z Team. Without looking away from them he let his face morph into a genuine smile right before he said, in fully human tones, "Yes, ma'am. I am. You're right on time."

If the three weren't already speechless, they would have been after seeing Glen turn and saunter over to the beautiful green-eyed witch. He submitted his left wrist while leaving his right thumb hooked in his back pocket. While they watched, Litha snapped the other half of the purple fleece lined handcuffs on Glen just before they disappeared.

Raif whistled softly while Gunnar turned to Torn. "I think you'd better not call him rookie again."

Torn gave him a look that could kill. "Shut it, Gun."

"Come on, Irish," Raif said. "You know he's right. Time for us to grow up maybe. Yeah? Fuck of a thing that it takes a kid going all righteous on us to point it out. "

Torn stared at Raif. "Maybe." He gave Gun a little crooked grin. "But if I'm steppin' over a line, you'll be catchin' fire from Wolfboy right along with me."

"Yeah." Gun nodded like he was seriously contemplating one scenario after another. "You could look at it like that. Or you could just come to the understanding that it's embarrassing for you to have not one, but two babysitters."

Torn's grin fell. Raif laughed softly and pushed with his shoulder as he nudged by.

"Fuckers." Torn looked and sounded like a teenager who'd just been grounded.

The Black Swan Vineyard, Napa Valley

Glen didn't have time to assess Litha's mood in the passes, but as soon as they reached the vineyard and unhooked, he could see something was wrong. She'd brought them straight to the kitchen where an aproned Storm was stirring something that smelled like marinara.

"Something wrong, Litha?"

If Storm had looked over before Glen had voiced the question, he wouldn't have needed to ask. The look on his face said it all, but it was punctuated by a shake of his head.

"Nothing at all," she said with a coolness that didn't quite pass for nonchalance. "Why do you ask?"

Storm shook his head again and turned back to the stove. You wouldn't have to be trained to read signals like a Black Swan knight to know that Litha was lying.

"Why do I ask? Well, it could be the look on your face or the tone of your voice. Or it might be the fact that every single muscle in your body is tight as can be."

"Hey!" Storm turned and pointed the spoon at him. "You don't need to be looking so closely that you're making judgments about the state of my wife's muscles."

"Sorry, Litha. No offense intended."

She glared at Storm and clenched her teeth. "None taken."

Behind her back, Glen held up his hands as if to say, "What gives?"

"Got the word today that retired knights have been recalled to duty." He looked at Litha. "Temporarily."

Glen could have kicked himself for not anticipating that Storm being in danger could be a sensitive subject with Litha after all she'd been through. Glen nodded at Storm almost imperceptibly and walked up behind Litha.

He almost whispered to her back. "Would it be better if I come another night?"

Litha turned around and looked at the spot where Glen's eyes were supposed to be. Then her gaze traveled upward. "When did you get so tall? And, don't be silly. I'm not taking you back until I've stuffed you with pasta and grilled you about my baby."

Glen looked at Storm for an indication of what to do next. Storm just shrugged and gestured for him to sit down at the table.

"You know," she began, "you weren't the only cute one in the hallway."

Glen looked from Litha to Storm, who had tuned into the conversation with an extra dose of interest. "What is she talking about?" he asked Glen like it was an accusation.

Litha knew it was mean to try to rile Storm's jealous tendencies, but she was feeling extra ornery. Before Glen could answer she jumped in. "Who's the edgy one with the dreamy pale blue eyes and the tribal tattoos?"

Storm gaped. "Dreamy blue eyes?" He looked at Glen like he thought Glen had set Litha up on a blind date. Then his brain cleared enough to register the rest of it. "Did you say tattoos? Since when do you like tattoos?"

She didn't look at Storm, but raised a shoulder prettily and left her answer at that. The cell phone she'd left on the kitchen bar rang. Storm looked over at it and announced, "It's Elora."

Normally she would think it was rude to leave a dinner guest to take a phone call, but made an exception for Elora. "I'll take it in the other room."

"Hi." She answered while walking toward the back of the house.

"Just calling to check on you. You seemed pretty upset."

"You're not?"

"Well, yes. Of course it's not ideal, but it's temporary."

Litha clenched her teeth involuntarily. "If I hear that word one more time today..."

"Which word? Temporary?"

"Ugh!"

"Okay. So what's your biggest fear?"

Litha stopped dead still. "You want me to say that out loud?"

"Well, since I'm not Song, that's the only way I'm going to know the answer."

"I don't think I should. It might be inviting, I don't know, inviting... you know."

"No I don't. Are you trying to tell me that you're superstitious?"

"I think superstitious is a weird word for somebody who works for Black Swan to use. Don't you? Really?"

"Okay. Let me start over. Do you have reason to believe that saying something out loud will make it happen?"

"Yes. Sort of. I'm not sure."

"Way to be decisive."

"Fuck off."

"Litha!" Elora started laughing because Litha didn't normally use language like that and it sounded really out of place coming from her.

"Okay. Here it is."

Elora waited for a full minute. "Where it is?"

"I'm working on it. Don't rush me." Elora started humming the Jeopardy clock ditty. "I'm afraid a vampire will..."

When it became clear Litha wasn't going to finish the sentence, Elora said, "Bite him. You're afraid he'll be bitten by a vampire, turn into one, and have to be put down." Litha's silence was confirmation enough. "That's what I thought. See? Here's the thing. You're thinking like a human."

"What do you mean?"

"You're going to know when Storm is on patrol because you're going to move in here with him until this is over. Right?"

"I hadn't thought about it. I guess so."

"So you know when he's out on patrol. You could follow him. You could stay in the pass so that he's visible to you, but you're not visible to him. Or you could weave a protection spell or something like that, right?"

"Elora. If you were here I would have to give you a big kiss."

"No, you would not. Rammel has my lips so swollen they look bee stung. I don't need any more kisses today."

"Too much information. But I love you. And I thank you. You may have saved my marriage."

"Well, as someone once said to me, I live to serve."

"If not my marriage, at least dinner. Glen is here. We're going to try to get to the bottom of why Rosie is AWOL. Call you tomorrow."

When Litha came back to the kitchen, she was a different person. She breezed in with a radiant smile, gave Storm a big "mwah" kiss on the cheek and asked what she could do to help get dinner on the table.

Storm was stunned and relieved at the same time. He didn't know what Elora said to his wife, but she had wrought a bona fide miracle. He didn't dare ask Litha about the change of heart for fear that she might be reminded that she'd been leagues past pissed just minutes before.

With a nonchalance that took acting skills, Storm loaded a giant bowl of fettuccini with thick meat sauce and handed it to Glen, who practically put his face in the food. Litha giggled at the way their guest was inhaling the spicy aroma and making nummy sounds, while shaving fresh parmesan slices onto the Caesar salad she'd just finished tossing.

"It's nice to have you here, Glen," she said turning back to the salad.

He set his bowl down at the chair where he had always parked it for Thursday night dinners and straightened up to look over at Litha. "Yeah," he nodded. "I've missed this."

Storm shut down his cooking station, took off his apron and grabbed the remaining two bowls for himself and Litha. "Sit," he ordered, gesturing toward Glen with one of the bowls he carried. When all three were seated Storm poured Pino Noir into their glasses.

Glen took a sip. "Hmmm. Not bad. I wonder if this is a local wine," he teased.

"Not bad, you say? I challenge you to find better anywhere at any price. We could charge ten times as much for this wine, but we like the idea of knowing a lot of people can afford to open it for a typical Thursday night in the kitchen."

"A man of the people." Glen held up his glass in a toast.

"Hear, hear." Litha joined in raising her glass.

Storm held up his own stem of ruby red liquid and corrected, "A wine for the people."

They clinked, drank and dug into Storm's Neapolitan masterpiece.

Litha turned to Glen. "Tell me something fun. What's your latest news?"

"Got my first assignment right before you picked me up. We, Z Team I mean, are going to Bucharest on Tuesday. Escorting a squint specialist on some unnamed mission. Something The Order wants checked out, I guess.

"Anyhow. This is it. Tuesday night at this time I'll be Sir Catch for real. Knight Errant. Off to see the world on a bona fide version of who let the dogs out."

Storm's eyes twinkled with amusement and something that looked a little like pride. At least that was what Litha thought. She couldn't imagine why Storm would be so much more emotionally engaged with the idea of Glen as hunter than he had been with the idea of Glen as administrator. But there it was.

"Dogs, huh? That's about right. I wish you weren't making your bones with those..."

"Don't say it," Glen interrupted. "They may be exactly what you're thinking, but they're also my team mates now."

Storm was silent as he looked at Glen thoughtfully. He tipped his wine glass, shoved a ridiculous amount of romaine lettuce in his mouth then smiled at Glen while he chewed. Glen read his own interpretation into that response and smiled back while Litha looked from one to the other wondering what was passing between them.

"Is that who you were arguing with when I picked you up?" Litha asked semi-innocently.

Remembering her comments from earlier, Storm's gaze shot to Litha. "That's who you were talking about?!? Gods cursed Z team?!? Dreamy eyes and tattoos?"

Litha stared at Storm wishing to the Seven Legions that she hadn't gone out of her way to get his jealousy juices flowing.

"Yes. It was Z Team," Glen said quietly. Storm and Litha were staring at each other. Neither acknowledged Glen's comment in any way. "I'd offer to leave, but I wouldn't get back until after I have to report tomorrow morning. I'd probably have to walk to the interstate then hitchhike to the airport and gods only know when I'd get a flight to Newark. And with the time difference..."

Glen was desperately hoping to distract them with chatter. The air in the room was heavy. Glen hadn't ever experienced the TV sitcom ideal of nuclear family life, but he imagined that was what it felt like to have parents argue.

Finally, Litha reached over and rested her hand lightly on Storm's knee. "You know I didn't mean any of that. I was mad and worried about you. I guess I wanted to knock you off balance. It was childish. I'm sorry."

Storm looked at Glen. "Would you excuse us for a moment? Don't wait for us. Go ahead and eat."

Glen looked at his food. "Okay, but yours is getting cold."

Storm pulled Litha up as he stood and guided her out the back door onto the porch. He closed the kitchen door, urged her a few feet away, and shoved her against the Italianate stucco wall. His delight at hearing her little gasp when he pressed his body into hers massaged away his jealousy. And he smiled at the sound of her little moans when he rocked against her.

"Tell me I'm the only one for you." She opened her mouth to do exactly that, but didn't get past the first syllable before he covered her mouth with a kiss so heated one would have thought she'd tried to leave him. He broke from the kiss, "Tell me," he demanded.

Litha's heart rate had accelerated so quickly that she was panting. "You're the only one. There could never be anyone, but you."

The part of Litha's brain that was still functioning normally was amazed that someone as strong and confident and beautiful as Storm could need that reassurance. And she was sorry she'd been dumb enough to make him feel emotionally threatened and question her single-minded devotion. That was where her thoughts had gone, when she felt her dress being raised.

"Climb on, baby."

"Storm! What? No! What if Glen...?"

"Glen'll stay put."

He said it like Glen had no mind of his own, but was held in place by Storm's will alone. That last word was punctuated with the pop of practically new raspberry lace panties being rent asunder and cast aside. She felt him open his pants and started to protest further, but didn't get far before he lifted her up. Her legs wrapped around his waist of their own accord just before Litha felt her husband drive into her in one powerful thrust. She wanted to cry out, partly from surprise and partly from pleasure, but she didn't want Glen to hear. Dinner and a sex show. No.

Everything about the incident was out of the ordinary. Storm wasn't the sort of lover who tore panties and impaled her standing up in the great outdoors. He was acting out a claiming, a primitive rite of territorialism. And she was enjoying it. No. Reveling in it.

It didn't last long and didn't need to. It was short, fast, violent and loving. Ten minutes before she would have said that a phrase like violently loving was an oxymoron, but her sexy beast of a husband had just made nonsense of that notion.

He sat her back on her feet with a sweetly lingering kiss that ended with a smug smile of pure satisfaction. Just to be sure she got the message, he ducked down to catch her gaze in his. "And don't forget it."

If she wasn't already married to the man, she would have swooned.

He bent down and retrieved the ruined scrap of lace. After turning it over in his fingers a couple of times, he shoved it down into his pants pocket, but made sure there was just the tiniest hint of raspberry still showing. When Litha realized that he intended to walk back into the house like that, the swoon was replaced with outrage.

"Storm. You are *not* walking around like that's a trophy!"

She reached for it, but he started walking backwards, smiling. "I'm not?"

Litha lunged, but he, of course, was quicker.

Glen looked up to see a smiling Storm rush through the door with Litha right on his tail. Her face was flushed and her lips were swollen. Glen hated himself for noticing that Rosie's mother may have been a fantasy walking. She was Rosie's mother for gods' sake and noticing her attractiveness made him feel tawdry.

"Have fun?" Glen wasn't worried about a smack down. If they could politely excuse themselves to leave him sitting in their kitchen while they were fucking on the patio, he could afford a moment of teasing impertinence.

Storm's answer was a smile broadening into a grin. Litha blushed madly, smacked Storm on the abs with the palm of her hand, and retook her seat at the table.

"Sorry, Glen," she started. "We needed to clear up a misunderstanding. These things happen with married people sometimes."

Glen could think of about a hundred things to say, but wisely, said nothing.

Storm turned to Litha and said, "What's for dessert?" in such a way that made her wonder if the caveman behavior didn't need to be curtailed.

"As a matter of fact, I got a turtle cheesecake from Weingartens."

"Sounds great, doesn't it, Glen?" Storm slapped Glen on the shoulder.

Glen smiled at Litha. "Definitely! Butter pie with chocolate and nuts. What could be better?" Litha stared at Glen for a couple of beats. "What's wrong?"

"Nothing. You've just made me seriously rethink eating that."

"Aw, come on," Glen said good-naturedly, "with your figure you can afford…" At that point in the sentence, Glen's brain reengaged as he realized that Storm was touchy about people noticing Litha's looks. He didn't have to look at Storm to know that he was glaring.

"Yes?" Litha asked. "With my figure I can afford to…?"

"I, ah, lost my train of thought."

Litha looked at the way Storm was glowering at Glen. "I'll bet. Okay. Coffee with your butter pies?"

Both guys said yes.

Glen helped Litha clear, but she shooed him back to the table when she started making coffee.

Storm was lying in wait. "Piecing bits together. Sounds like Litha dropped in on an argument. Standoff, did she say?"

"I don't think she said standoff."

"Hmmm. But there was some disagreement."

"Yes."

"You want to tell me what that was about?"

Glen's eyes slid to Storm's and Storm saw challenge there for the first time in their relationship. "Even if I wanted to tell you, I wouldn't."

"I see." Storm's tone was noncommittal, but inside he was doing a victory dance thinking that Z Team couldn't be luckier if they'd won the lottery. They'd managed to walk off with a new team member who was loyal, tough, and smart all in one package. He hoped they understood that they'd been given a priceless gift.

"So," she said. They both looked at Litha as she set down her coffee cup. "You know it's not an ambush because I told you I was going to ask. What do you know about why Rosie felt like she needed to disappear?"

Glen put his fork down and sat back. "She said that? That she needed to disappear?"

"Yes. Pretty much."

Glen squirmed a little. There was little doubt that the conversation was awkward. The fact that Glen had put his fork down was testament to that!

He wasn't sure how much he should divulge. He couldn't say it was none of their business. Of course Rosie was their business. To some extent Glen was their business. He just wasn't sure how much about Rosie *and* Glen, the couple, was their business.

As he sat deliberating his options he happened to glance at Storm who took a man-sized bite of cheesecake and raised an eyebrow. Since he couldn't decide on a "best" course of action, he decided to lay it out.

"Rosie went with me on an errand I was running for Elora. While we were gone I told her that I'd signed on with Z Team. She didn't like the idea of me being inducted into Hunter Division. At all. So she gave me an ultimatum."

Glen noticed that Storm frowned at that.

"She basically said I needed to choose between her and knighthood. I said I'd spent half my life training for it. I told her I love her, but I'm too young to take a desk job."

Glen saw that Storm and Litha exchanged glances at various points in the story.

"That's pretty much it. I laid it out for her. Then she laid it out for me by saying that I needed to change my mind and call by dinner on the following Thursday night. I didn't."

"You didn't call?" Litha asked.

"I didn't think it would be the best thing for our future to let her dictate what, when, who, and where. So I didn't change my mind and I waited until midnight to call. But she didn't answer. I've called a lot since then. Texted, too. Nothing."

Storm turned to Litha. "Did you know about any of this?"

Litha shook her head. "She wouldn't say anything more than that she had to get away for a while."

"She probably didn't tell us anything because she was ashamed of behaving like such a brat! As she should be!"

Litha gaped. Storm had never criticized Rosie. Not ever. "Storm."

"You can't think that was behavior worthy of a child of two parents who work for Black Swan."

"Well, no, I..."

He interrupted that thought. "Of course she didn't tell us why she was going. She knew that I, for one, would think less of her. I mean, how do you turn to your dad, who happens to be a Black Swan knight, and say, 'My boyfriend threatened to accept an offer of knighthood so I'm running away?' Criminently!"

Glen wasn't sure what he'd been expecting, but Storm's reaction wasn't one of the possibilities on his list of scenarios. "So you're not mad at me?"

Storm looked at Glen like he'd temporarily forgotten he was there. "Why would I be mad at you? It's our daughter who's behaving badly."

"Storm," Litha tried again, "she's really young and inexperienced."

"I agree," Glen said. "And I have a theory."

He had their attention, but waited for them to say they wanted to hear it.

"Well?" Storm was already irritated. No sense poking the bear.

"I know she has your memories." He looked between them. "But I don't think she views them viscerally. To her, your memories are like historical facts."

"You're going to have to give me more. I'm not getting the point, Glen," Litha urged him to continue.

"Okay. Let's say you saw a movie about the Battle of Doe Ford. You may know the facts surrounding the experience, but since you didn't experience it personally, you didn't integrate feelings associated with it and you didn't learn any lessons either. When Rosie views your memories, she does it without real understanding. Like watching a movie about somebody else's life. The events won't resonate unless they're seen in the context of shared experience."

"You're talking about maturity," Litha said.

"In a nutshell, yes. I love her, but she's not as mature as she looks. She's not fourteen months old, but she's not twenty-one either. If she had been a..."

"What were you going to say?" Storm demanded. "Were you going to say if she had been a normal kid?'"

"Well, yeah, I was going to say that. Normal fourteen-year-olds get grounded or have privileges taken away. Their families try to provide a safe place for them to finish percolating – maturity wise – so that, when they go out in the world they can handle themselves. At least that's how it's supposed to work. I think. No personal experience with any of that so I can't be sure.

"But Rosie isn't just physically deceiving. She's powerful and tricky and, you know as well as I do, she can't be controlled."

Storm reached over and took Litha's hand in his. They were silent for a while, considering all that had been said. Finally Storm said, "Litha. Do you know where she is?"

Litha shook her head. "I don't know where she is, but I trust Kellareal to make sure she's safe. He promised her that he wouldn't reveal her location, but she was at least mature enough to ask to be notified if there was an emergency. And it's not true that she can't be controlled. It's just true that *we* can't do it. Kellareal can manage her though."

When Glen looked across the table at Storm, he could swear that Storm looked years older than he had before cheesecake.

"Well," Glen said. "If you do hear from her, will you tell her that I've been trying to reach her and that I'm sorry things were left that way? I think she already knows the rest."

"Of course, Glen," Litha said. "I guess you need to get back. Get ready for your trip?"

"Thanks for being honest with us, Glen. I was really in the dark about what was going on. I'm not pleased, but knowing is better than not knowing."

"Yes, sir."

"Knights don't call each other sir, Catch."

"You're not just a knight to me, sir. You're Rosie's dad."

Storm beamed at Glen.

Litha stood and walked to the bar to grab the handcuffs. "By the time you get back from your assignment, I guess we'll be moved into Jefferson Unit."

Storm's mouth dropped open. "You're moving to J.U. with me?"

With a look of warning, she said, "*Temporarily*."

When Litha returned to the kitchen where she shared a life with her husband, she found him sitting at the table, looking morose.

"What's wrong?"

He lifted eyes that were unmistakably sad. "I miss her. I was just getting to know her and then she was gone. She didn't even say goodbye. Or tell us how long she'd be gone. Or where she is. Or what she's doing."

Litha sighed as she sat down. "Her body and her intellect grew so fast, but she didn't have the chance to learn the little things that the rest of us take for granted, like how to handle disappointment. Or how to compromise."

"Don't you want to check on her? Just to make sure she's okay?"

"I do. Of course I do. And I will if it's something you have to have. But I'd rather give her this. She's asked us to let her have some time alone. Maybe on some level she recognizes that she's missing some key components to being really grown up."

"How long are you willing to give it?"

"I don't have a deadline in mind. Do you?" Storm pursed his lips and looked thoughtful. "Three months? If we haven't gotten a visit or a message or anything by then?"

"Sure. That's fair." She smiled. "What can I do to take your mind off of it?"

CHAPTER 14

1500 Black Swan Hangar, Jefferson Unit, Fort Dixon, New Jersey

Z Team was already boarded and waiting for their walking assignment to arrive. They heard voices coming up the steps. Monq and a woman.

Monq's face appeared first when he entered the cabin. He gave perfunctory nods to Z Team, but bestowed a genuine smile for Glen, who grinned and waved back like a little kid on a field trip. Seeing that exchange, Raif shook his head at the newbie's eagerness and looked out the window with all the bored callousness that comes with eight years of active hunter duty spent in every one of the world's biggest shit holes.

Listening with one ear, it sounded like Monq was apparently introducing the squint to her protectors. Or was it escorts? Sighing, he decided he should probably turn his head and try to look mildly interested. That was the last thought that fired his synapses before he felt his heart slam into his rib cage. *Her.*

"Gods on fire."

Raif said it quietly, but not so quiet that his partner, who was sitting in the chair next to him, didn't hear. That reaction definitely got Torn's curiosity going. "You know her?"

Raif's nostrils flared in reflex to seeing her again. "Yeah. Passing acquaintances. Unfortunately." Raif felt his organs squirm around when he said the word 'unfortunately'. His body had always had adverse responses to lying. It was like his insides protested the fact that his feelings didn't match the words coming out of his mouth. Gods teeth, he didn't need his own intestines calling him on his fabrications. "And you're responsible."

Torn looked at him with incredulity all over his face. "Me? Now why would you be thinkin' I'm responsible for you knowin' the lass?"

Raif sneered at him with a disdain so potent and palpable a lesser man would have recoiled. "Remember speed dating?"

Torn looked from the scowl on Raif's face to Dr. Renaux. When she spotted Raif, her eyes sparked with recognition. She looked away quickly as the reddest full blooming blush he'd ever seen formed on her face and neck.

He barked a laugh in Raif's direction. "Fucked that one up royally, did ye?" He leaned toward Raif and muttered, "All the better for me. I'm startin' to see this assignment could have an upside," he leaned in close enough so that only Raif could hear him whisper, "with rust-colored hair. Skin pigmented like an Impressionist paintin' and dyin' for a master's touch."

Looking irritated, Raif got up and moved across to the other side of the plane where he slammed himself into a recliner, leaned it back, faced toward the window, and closed his eyes.

Torn had been team mates with Raif a long, long time. Long enough to see when every muscle was tense, eyes closed or not. He laughed again with all the impish glee that Irish elves were known for, enjoying the situation. This trip was shaping up to be potentially fun on so many levels.

The plane hadn't been in the air for ten minutes before Torn had moved to sit beside Mercy on one of the long, plush sofas. She looked up from what she was reading when she realized that someone was making himself at home. In close proximity.

"Torn Finngarick." He extended his right hand and gave her the full treatment charming smile.

For just a second Dr. Renaux forgot that she was a grown woman, a professional who was well-respected in her field. She forgot that because, at that limited distance, the elf was so captivating all she could do was stare. She'd heard about the sexual magnetism of Irish elves, but hadn't ever experienced it up close and personal. That combined with the creature's beauty was a powerful and, no doubt, potent package.

She was trying to remember if she'd ever seen a person who appeared to have skin so perfect that it was without pores. That was her wayward wondering when he brought her back to the moment by clearing his throat.

"And you would be Dr. Renaux?" he prompted with patience and a twinkle in his sky-blue eyes.

Apparently the redheaded heartthrob was accustomed to having women go frozen fan girl. Crap. She was so flummoxed he'd had to remind her of her own name. Being struck speechless like an illiterate shepherdess coming face to face with a god was a brand new experience for Mercy. A cautionary tale of male beauty from the ancient myths.

Confronting how preposterous it was for her to be struck dumb by a gorgeous guy dripping sex, she laughed out loud. "Great guess. Yes. Dr. Renaux. Call me Mercy."

He grabbed his chest right over his heart and declared, "Mercy."

Well, beauty wasn't everything. Like she'd never heard that one before.

On hearing the sound of her laughter, Raif opened one eye a slit. Just as he'd expected, it had only taken Torn fifteen minutes to get acquainted and extract playfulness from her. He'd known it was inevitable, but that was fast even for Torn. The bastard was probably giving her the deluxe treatment because he'd seen Raif's reaction and thought there might be a sore to rub salt in.

Torn's reputation with the ladies, especially human women, was notorious, which meant he was admired by men who aspired to a fuck 'em and chuck 'em lifestyle and reviled by the women who'd been fucked. And chucked. It was weird the way women flocked to bad boy elves like gluttons for punishment.

If Torn hadn't been on the plane, Raif would have eventually worked up the courage to approach her and apologize for the way he'd acted the day they'd met. He'd remembered her first name, but not her last. So he couldn't track her down. During their relatively brief exchange he'd been so busy telling her who she was and what was wrong with her that he hadn't found out anything about who she was and why he'd had such a strong visceral reaction to her.

Every chance he got he had used his time off to more or less sneak away to the city. He didn't tell his nosey team mates where he was going or what he was doing. He just let them assume it was something brothel related. Far from it.

Like a sap, he'd walked around the area where the speed date had taken place. He had no logical reason to believe she lived or worked in that area. She could just as easily be an hour away. Probably was. He knew the chances of running into her were a pair of slim and none and accepted that it was an idiotic way to spend rec time.

If the rest of Z Team knew how he was spending his time, he would *never* hear the end of it. They'd be following his sorry soul through lifetimes for the pleasure of tormenting and harassing him about it. That's because they were reprobate bastards. And he had the very fine distinction of fitting right in with them.

He knew it was juvenile to care about being teased over a woman, but he had to live with those shitheads and ridicule gets real old real fast.

Yeah. Every member of Z Team knew that, when it came to the female sex, Torn got first round pick. They knew they might as well sit back and wait for him to make his selection before scoping out who they might want to get to know better.

If Torn had taken a bead on Mercedes Renaux, Raif knew he might as well close his eyes, take a nap, and try to forget that he'd been some perverse combination of asshole and idiot to the only woman of quality he'd talked to in a decade. If you could call that talking. It was more like a verbal assault, which was illegal. She could have actually filed charges.

After the initial shock of realizing they were on the same plane, bound for the same destination, and destined to spend at least a couple of days in the general vicinity of each other, Mercy had *studiously* avoided looking his way.

Which was fine with him.

Really.

"What's that you're readin'?" Torn asked Mercy.

She turned the yellow manual over so he could see the cover.

He grinned. "The Manual! I have no' seen one of those for, well, for a long time. How long have you been workin' for The Order?"

"New hire." She held up the book. "Trying to get up to speed. I just learned about the existence of vampire a week ago. I've been reviewing the data on the events of the past year, the viral 'cure' and all." She put air quotes around 'cure' and smiled. Then she smoothly segued into a different subject like a social pro. "And you're the grand poobah for this outing?"

He laughed. “Grand to be certain, but knights do no’ poobah. We’re equal in the eyes of The Order.” He looked around the plane at his team mates with pride. When his gaze fell on Glen, he halfheartedly threw a gesture in his direction. “Except for the kid. Equal is a ways down the road for him.”

Reaching over to look at the Field Training Manual cover again, Torn asked, “Are ye findin’ it interestin’ then?”

“Oh sure. If I’d found this on the street a week ago I would have thought it’d been dropped by somebody coming from a comic con.”

“And now?”

“Now I’m working on getting my mind to accept that I’m reading non-fiction.”

“How’s it goin’?”

“It’s a struggle.”

“Hmmm. Maybe I can help you with that.”

Torn stood up and raised his heather gray tee shirt, exposing peaches and cream skin stretched over washboard abs that would have been as flawless as his face except for a white scar that ran crisscross.

Unused to having beautiful elves stand in front of her and expose mouth watering abdomens suddenly and without invitation, she stared up at him with wide eyes and a certainty that she was even further out of her element than a mere education on vampire would suggest.

“See this?” He traced the length of the scar with a fingertip.

She nodded. Oh yes. Indeed she did see that.

“Guess how it came to be there,” he demanded.

She thought about refusing to guess, but decided that would be boring and she had vowed when she took the job offer from Black Swan that she had left boring Mercy behind. Forever.

"You were riding a skate-board through a copying office without a shirt on and fell onto the paper cutter when the blade was left open."

His face split into a gorgeous grin that lit the entire jet cabin. "Good guess! But no. I was actually wearin' a shirt when this happened. 'Twas the result of a vamp who'd let his nails grow long and groady like Howard Hughes. Took a swipe at me with his ugly-ass jagged claws and preserved the incident, now frozen forever on my body. As you see."

"Well, three things. First, what a shame your perfection is thus marred. Second, if I'm reading this manual correctly, it's a good thing it wasn't his teeth. Third, you know they make over-the-counter scar reduction cream that could have helped with that."

He grinned, let his shirt fall and dropped back onto the couch next to her. "True, but usin' the scar cream? 'Tis no' very manly now, is it? And I would no' have a conversation starter."

She stared at him. "In other words, you wouldn't have a legitimate excuse to bare your assets to strangers who happen to be female."

His grin morphed into a smile that was both seductive and conspiratorial. He leaned over and lowered his voice so that only she could hear. "You got me."

She looked away, laughed and went back to her reading.

Torn slid down in a sexy devil-may-care slouch, stretched his arms over the back of the sofa behind Mercy's head in a possessive pose and looked over at Raif to see if he was watching. Raif's eyes were closed, but Torn could tell by the tension in his jaw that he'd seen every delicious moment, which made Torn chuckle to himself.

Mercy looked over. "Something funny?"

Torn turned back to her, his eyes going deliberately to her mouth and lingering there in an aggressively intimate display. "I was just thinkin' about my partner over there nappin' in the nappy chair. He told me he had the pleasure of meetin' you. Briefly."

She stiffened visibly and put the book down in her lap, but not before casting a glance toward Raif's form that was reclined if not relaxed. What Torn saw there in the instant of that flicker was a mixture of embarrassment and outrage. But there was also something more than just wounded pride. Just as he'd suspected.

You could say a lot of things about Torrent Finngarick, but he did know women.

Glen broke up the quiet by raising his voice so that everybody could hear him. He was waving a tour guide in the air. "Hey! Let's try to finish this up fast so we can do a little sightseeing before we have to head back."

Torn gave him a blank stare as did Gun, who'd been standing in the galley chatting up the flight attendant. Raif opened one eye before crossing his arms over his midsection and renewing his determination to sleep.

Glen didn't seem fazed that no one responded. He simply resumed his research on tour destinations.

Torn looked at Mercy, who looked at Glen and said, "Sounds good to me."

The elf smiled at her in such an indulgent and amused way that, for just a second, she was tempted to give him a chance at a one nighter. That thought took her gaze in Raif's direction like he was a magnet. Believing that she could look him over without being observed, she let her eyes move slowly over the length of him, from the messy jet black hair to the stubble on his jaw past the partially visible tattoo on his bicep down to the frayed hems of his jeans, all the way to the square toed boots underneath.

She almost jumped when Glen announced that, "They say that there's history underneath every rock in Sozopol. Turn one over and you'll find something left by Greeks, Romans, Thracians, Slavs, Ottomans or Proto-Bulgarians. That's a quote!"

Raif's eyes opened a slit and caught her staring, but not for long. She quickly looked away with a telltale flush of embarrassment creeping up her neck toward her cheeks.

Mercy had done her fair share of traveling. It went with her occupation of choice, but she'd never come close to the way The Order transported their personnel from place to place. That rich-and-famous level of luxury was a new experience.

When Pietra, the flight attendant, wheeled out an entire standing prime rib on a rolling butcher block, Mercy gaped.

"What's the matter?" Torn asked.

"I didn't even know it was possible to cook prime rib on a plane."

Torn laughed. "Well, you ought to get out more." He winked.

Pietra cut the prime rib and served it at the booth-style seating in the front of the plane that could be used for dining or cards. She served a Caesar salad that was the best Mercy had ever tasted along with baskets of popover rolls just out of the oven and smelling divine.

Mercy sat next to Torn with Gun and Glen across from them. Raif sat in the other booth, across the aisle, by himself. Having had the experience of once being the new kid at school, the seating arrangement made her uncomfortable. She wouldn't want her worst enemy to feel ostracized, which probably meant she didn't have any real enemies. When she couldn't stand it any longer, she decided to say something.

"Perhaps someone should go sit with Mr. Nightsong."

The three men looked across the aisle. Gun and Torn just laughed like it was a ridiculous notion, but Glen said, "Would it make you feel better if I go sit with him?"

"Well," she hedged, "I think it would be nice."

Without another word Glen picked up food and paraphernalia and moved across the aisle. When he started to set his plate down across the table, Raif didn't look up, but said, "Fuck off."

Glen promptly picked up his dinner setting and moved back to his original spot. He smiled at Mercy. "Miss me? The gentleman declines and says he prefers to keep his own company this evening."

She returned his good-natured smile, nodded her head and, as thanks, passed him her portion of chocolate mousse that had just been delivered. While she was scowling at Raif, Torn leaned close and said, "Sir Nightsong."

She looked back at him. "What?"

"You called him Mr. Nightsong. When you're in the company of The Order, 'tis *Sir* Nightsong."

"Oh. Of course." She glanced back across the aisle.

"May seem silly to someone who is new to our conventions. The formal observance of service is a small thin', but believe me, he's earned it."

She looked at Torn. "Respect you mean? He's earned respect?"

"Oh, aye." Torn caught Pietra's eye. "Pee, my darlin', will ye be kind enough to pour an Irish whiskey as a chaser for this lovely puddin'?"

She smiled. "You know perfectly well that it's a mousse, Sir Luscious. And, yes, I will bring your nectar of gods."

Mercy looked across the table and crossed her eyes while mouthing, "Sir Luscious."

Gun and Glen rewarded her with a big laugh. Smiling at the shared joke she looked across the aisle and came face to face in a stare with Sir Nightsong. The pale color of his blue irises was so arresting and the intensity of his gaze was so electrifying, she couldn't make herself look away. She had a brief impression of a mouse being held spellbound by a snake.

When she opened her mouth to say something, his eyes dropped to her lips before coming back to her eyes. "I guess we're going to be stuck together for a couple of days. So let's be grown up and have a truce. I'll go first. I apologize for calling you a liar, Sir Nightsong. I guess it turns out that you really *are* a vampire hunter."

He desperately wanted to say something. He knew he *should* say something. All those days that he'd aimlessly loitered around a four square block area of New York he had rehearsed what he was going to say a thousand times. Then he had his chance. There it was. She was staring at him with those big liquid eyes waiting. Waiting. Waiting. While he was dumbstruck.

Pietra stepped in between them to clear Raif's dishes and, in doing so, broke the visual connection.

Mercy realized that her olive branch had been rejected with Raif's abject silence. In some ways it was worse than telling Glen to, "Fuck off."

She was grateful that Pietra's body hid from view the fact that her face and neck had gone chameleon, perfectly reflecting the red color of her humiliation. It only took an instant to make a vow that the great fiery pit would freeze over before she gave him another chance to be decent.

When Pietra left with Raif's dishes, Mercy had turned away and was again involved in conversation with her dinner companions. He'd lost the chance to fake a semblance of civilized behavior. He hadn't left the impression of looking dumbstruck. He'd left the impression of being an asshole. He thought about slapping himself, but it was too late for that, too. It would just raise further questions about his sanity.

Glen was reading from the guide book. "There's a reserve habitat for rare animal species. The reserve is inhabited by fifty types of mammals: noble deer and lopatar – deer, roes, muflons, foxes, jackals, otters and colonies of bats live in the rock caves. The extinct species of mammals are the bear, the lynx and the monk seal."

"I'd go with you if it can be worked out, Glen. I've never taken much time for sightseeing when traveling. It's always about the destination and not the journey. I think it would be fun and I haven't been to a zoo in twenty years."

"It's not a zoo! It's a reserve habitat. Apples and oranges. Think there's a rare Bulgarian animal tee shirt?"

She laughed. "Let's find out."

Eavesdropping on the conversation across the aisle, Raif rolled his eyes and took a sip of the black coffee Pietra had just poured. He was starting to believe that every dick on the plane was a rival. Even the kid. He was thinking that it got dark fast when you were flying away from the sun. And she seemed easy to talk to. He'd never liked flying over oceans at night. How he wished he had found out how easy she was to talk to by talking to her instead of sitting on the other side of the jet sneaking an eavesdrop. He was wishing he'd asked for Benadryl instead of coffee when he heard the rustle next to him. Mercy had stood to return to the lounge seating and left a hint of perfume behind when she passed.

After dinner Mercy had decided to take advantage of one of the luxurious sleeping compartments in the rear. The few hours she could grab in what was left of the nine hour flight would come in handy because the next day would be a full day. Maybe the most important day of her archeological career, even if the work was never published or professionally recognized in any way.

She woke when Pietra announced they were landing. Between the steady vibration of movement and the engine noise, she'd conked out and slept hard. She sat up thanking the gods for the partition that shielded her from being seen sleeping with her mouth open or drooling.

Sitting up and angling her body toward the exterior wall, she looked out the window. Because of the seven hour time difference, the sunrise was just beginning, enough that she could make out the landing strips with farmland on one side and a Black Sea village on the other.

Mercy insisted on supervising the transfer of her equipment from the plane. The Order had provided two identical Audi sedans. The older members of Z Team quickly decided that Glen would drive the car with all the luggage and equipment while the other three and their assignment rode together. Glen seemed to understand that the new guy gets the shit jobs and was okay with it. He took the keys to the equipment car good-naturedly.

Torn grabbed the keys to the people car. "I'll drive."

"Shotgun," Gun said. "I'll navigate."

"Welcome to this century, Gunnar. We do no' need a navigator. The car has navigation."

"Don't like the navigator angle? Okay. How about this? I get shotgun because I have long legs."

"I don't mind sitting in the back," Mercy said.

Torn turned to Raif with an especially bright twinkle in his eye. “I guess you’re stuck sittin’ next to her, brother.”

Raif shrugged as if to say he didn’t care, that he’d done worse.

CHAPTER 15

It's an orangeade sky. Always it's some other guy.

Sozopol, Bulgaria

Not once during the entire drive did Raif look over at Mercy. He stared out his window as if he'd never witnessed anything as fascinating as farming.

Sozopol turned out to be a picturesque fishing town on the coast of the Black Sea, located on a peninsula that boasted one of the most beautiful coves and beaches anywhere in the world. And, just as they say, build a gorgeous beach and resorts are sure to follow. The marina claimed three hundred thirty berths to house yachts and sail craft for the well-heeled.

The ancient Bronze Age town had been rededicated to Apollo by 7th century BCE Greeks. They erected a temple and a statue forty-five feet tall when they renamed it Apollonia. For centuries after that it thrived as a stop on the trade route of sailing vessels, part of the flow of commerce between Rhodes, Corinth, Athens, and Thracian territories. It was vibrant with culture and art, which meant it was also rich and populous.

The Order didn't own a property in Sozopol, but there was a five star hotel, a very pretty five story pink building with white columns overlooking the sea. The exterior was 1940s. The interior was Euromodern.

The little band of paranormal investigator and her escorts was delighted to learn that there was an old-world elegant restaurant and a Russian chef who specialized in Mediterranean fare and sushi – of all things. Some of the contingent were more impressed to find out that there were five bars. So far as Torn was concerned that meant the hotel had its priorities straight.

At the height of the season the place was probably hopping, but at that time of year it was practically deserted. When Mercy asked if they would need dinner reservations, the desk clerk laughed.

After checking in, Mercy just had enough time to shake her clothes out and hang the ones that mattered before the hotel phone rang beside the bed.

"Dr. Renaux?"

"Yes."

"You have guests asking for permission to speak with you on the desk phone. Will you accept the call?"

"Certainly. Put them on."

"Dr. Renaux?" asked a new male voice.

"Yes," she said again.

"This is Professor Yanev from Sofia University and the Minister Igvanotof. We'd like to welcome you personally and perhaps discuss your visit. In private if possible. Would it be inappropriate to ask to come to your room?"

"Are your intentions honorable?" She took the pause in dialogue to mean that either the caller didn't get the joke or his intentions were not honorable. Either way, she was going to find out. "Never mind. It was a poor attempt at humor."

"Oh," he chuckled. "You Americans. Always joking."

"Yes. We're all comedians. I'm in Room 316."

"We shall be at Room 316 momentarily."

Mercy hung up the phone and turned to almost run into Glen who was sharing a connecting room with Gunnar.

"Who was that?" he asked.

"A government representative and an academic. They want to greet me and talk about going to the site. They're on the way up."

Gun came closer and leaned on the door jamb separating the two rooms.

"On the way up?" Glen gaped at her.

"Yes. They want to talk in private. Given what I've learned about The Order that doesn't seem either unusual or unreasonable."

"No, but you gave them your room number?"

"Well, yes. How else would you expect them to find me?"

"How would we expect them to find you?"

"Do you have a repeating problem, Glen?"

"Do you have an absentminded professor problem, Dr. Renaux?"

"What's that supposed to mean?"

"It's supposed to mean this. How are you thinking we're going to protect you if you give out your room number to any stranger who calls up and asks for it?"

She looked thoughtful. "I see what you mean."

"Normally I wouldn't mention this, but I get the feeling you care about other people, so I'm going to share. You didn't just endanger yourself, but us. We could have been caught unaware." She just blinked in response, but he definitely had her attention. He turned to Gun. "Get Raif and Torn. Let's make sure this is up and up." Gun nodded and moved off. Glen looked at Mercy and softened his tone a notch. "It's our job to keep you safe, but you have to be willing to help us out with that. Just a little. Right?"

She nodded. "You are right. Of course. I've never been in a situation where I needed protection. I just didn't think about..."

"You're a smart lady and I'm sure you catch on quick. Don't take any phone calls unless one of us is with you. Don't give out your location to anybody unless we give the okay. Always leave the door between us cracked open so we can be aware of what's going on in here."

"Okay."

When the welcome committee arrived on the third floor, Raif and Torn were waiting in the hallway outside Mercy's room while Glen and Gun waited inside. As the two Bulgarians approached they could see that two rather intimidating individuals were sizing them up. They stopped at 316 and looked over to verify the number on the door.

Just as one of them reached up to knock, Raif and Torn took one each and shoved them against the wall. They were frisked thoroughly, efficiently, and perhaps with more roughness than was necessary.

When they were released, the one with the stupid hat said something in Bulgarian that was most likely about his assailant and most probably uncomplimentary. Both men made readjustments to the business suits they were wearing and looked at Raif and Torn with as much huffiness as they dared.

Without taking his eyes away from them, Torn reached over and tapped on the door with his knuckles. Glen stood in front of Mercy while Gunnar opened the door. Torn's nod was a signal to let the visitors enter.

As Mercy was trying to look around Glen to see what was going on, Glen stepped aside. The two visitors were visibly flustered.

"Hello," she said. "I'm Dr. Renaux. Not much to offer in the way of seating, but please." She gestured toward the chairs.

They sat in the only two chairs, while Mercy sat on the end of the bed.

"Dr. Renaux. Delighted to meet you." His glance at the four knights made the pleasantry sound sarcastic. "I'm Yanev, professor of archeology at Sofia University. And this is the Minister Igvanotof."

The Minister gave a curt nod dripping with displeasure.

Glen and Gunnar made no move to leave, but Raif and Torn were satisfied that the other two could handle the suits so they backed out and closed the door.

She'd received a briefing about her mission. Everyone on the trip was there for a reason and had a part to play. She'd been given instructions to look over the site carefully, listen to the claims, and make a determination as to their validity. The knights had been given much simpler and more concise orders. Escort Dr. Renaux and protect her if necessary.

After assessing the situation and deciding they wouldn't be needed further for Dr. Renaux's meeting, Raif and Torn left to explore the hotel. To a Black Swan knight that meant searching out every conceivable security vulnerability, every possible escape route, and every bar. When the first two tasks were complete, it didn't take them long to find out that one of the five bars was open for business.

In Mercy's suite, Professor Yanev was attempting to persuade her that they were prepared to be attentive to her every need or request. Yanev was fortyish, with weathered skin, bright intelligent dark eyes and extraordinarily white teeth, which were revealed often once he began to relax.

"Tomorrow morning, if that is suitable to you, we will travel to the site and I will give you guidance," he said smiling.

"Professor Yanev..."

"Please, just Yanev."

"All right. Yanev. If there's not time to go today, then tomorrow morning works for me. What time do you have in mind?"

Yanev looked at the Minister Igvanotof and said something. The other man shook his head as he answered. When Yanev looked at her again, he said, "I will be at your disposal."

It seemed they hadn't done any research on Dr. Renaux and just assumed that she didn't speak Bulgarian. What the Minister had actually said was that the earlier they got started the sooner they'd be rid of her and her bulky boys.

"That's very accommodating. How about eight thirty?"

Yanev smiled his very whitest smile. "Yes. Eight thirty outside the front entrance. While we are here, let me ask. Do you have any questions?"

"As a matter of fact I do." Yanev gestured with his head so she continued. "Is the site closed to the public?"

"It is and has been since the discovery."

"Very well. Will there be others there in an official government capacity? Or perhaps others with academic license?"

He looked at Minister Igvanotof, said something, and waited for the answer. The Minister's eyes found Mercy's and he stared at her like he was wondering why she asked the question.

"The Minister says that all access was mysteriously and suddenly closed to all but those who work for your organization. The area is closely guarded, but once inside, there will be no one else present. Other than myself, if you should wish me to remain."

Mercy rewarded her visitors with a gracious smile. "Excellent. I'm so pleased to hear it."

She was also pleased with her acting ability, thinking she hadn't given away, on any level, the fact that the Minister had said that no one of import would be there either before she arrived or during her visit. Mercy was thinking his title should be Minister of Snark. She was tempted to say goodbye in Bulgarian, but the fun of that wouldn't eclipse the intel to be gained by pretending ignorance of the language.

When they left, Glen asked, "Did that go the way you wanted?"

"Yes. More or less. They don't know I understand the language, so the Minister was surely much freer with his low opinion of me than he might have been otherwise."

"Ouch," Glen grinned. "They didn't look you up."

She shook her head slowly. "Hmmm hmm. Not even the easy stuff. The info about how many languages I speak usually comes up pretty close to the top on any search of Dr. Renaux."

Glen grinned bigger. "You Giggled yourself."

Mercy laughed. "I did."

"Was that fun?"

"Of course. Ever done it?"

"No. Black Swan knights don't exist. Didn't you know that?"

"Do now."

"So we've got some time to burn before dinner. You busy? We could play Mad Fowl."

"Thanks," she chuckled. "I'll take a rain check. I want to be ready for tomorrow. I'm as excited and anxious as a kid before a dance recital. So I'm going to take a toes-up until time for dinner."

"Okay. Like I told you, I'm going to leave the adjoining door open a crack. We'll be quiet so you can nap, but... Do not leave your suite. Do not open your door - the one to the hallway. If you need something, come get one of us. If you hear something, yell. Got it?"

"Got it. Yell if I hear something. Knock if I need something."

"Drinks downstairs at six o'clock. I hear the sunset hour is still pretty even looking east, out to sea."

"Spoken like a dedicated tourist. Okay. Meet you downstairs at six."

Glen turned, searching her face for a clue as to whether she was joking or not. She held her straight face in place long enough to convince him that she was serious. When he summoned some patience and opened his mouth to explain why she couldn't do that without violating one of the rules, she gave him a gotcha smile.

"You gonna be trouble?" he asked.

Mercy shook her head as she laughed softly. "No, sir. Trouble is the very last thing I've ever been. In my life."

"Finding that hard to believe, Doc."

"Doc?" She found the idea of being called 'doc' by someone the age of one of her students incredulous. At the same time she fell in love with both the idea behind it and the informality of it.

"You don't really expect me to call you Dr. Renaux?"

She shook her head again and smiled. "No. Doc is fine."

Mercy laid down on top of the covers of the double bed and quickly fell into the deepest sleep she could remember. She woke after a couple of hours and was a little disoriented at first. When she realized how long and how soundly she'd slept, she wondered if it was because, subconsciously, she knew she was protected and completely safe.

She heard the hum of low voices coming from the next room and peeked through the crack in the door. Glen appeared to be trying to teach Gun some card tricks. Mercy smiled to herself thinking the kid was quite a character. She slipped into the bathroom and took a bath that was quick, but hot and relaxing then pulled on jeans and an apricot sweater of the shade that did marvelous things for auburn coloring.

When she was ready, she tapped on the adjoining door.

"Open!" She swung the door wide enough to see the two of them. "You ready?" Glen's upbeat personality was hard to resist.

"It is I. Professor Ready."

"Let's do it then. One spectacular sundown coming up."

The five of them were sitting inside the terrace room looking at the sunset toward the east over the water.

"Nice sundown." As Torn stretched his long legs out in front of him, he winked at Mercy knowing her eyes couldn't help but be drawn to the movement of his body.

She flushed with a slight embarrassment at having been caught looking at his crotch. Raif saw the exchange and cursed under his breath, wishing he could tase his partner's naked balls while he stood with his feet in a tub of water. Thinking about that made his face break into a grin.

Torn looked curious. "What's so funny?"

Raif shook his head. "Private thoughts."

As Torn's comment seeped into her consciousness, Mercy looked over the horizon and had to agree. Though the actual sunset was behind them, the last of the light painted the eastern sky with fiery streaks of orange and yellow fading into charcoal gray where the water met the sky.

"You're right about the view. It's an orangeade sky."

"What's an orangeade?"

Raif was glad Gunnar asked the question. He wanted to hear the answer, but didn't want to openly express that much interest in what the babe thought.

"Hmmm." She finished her swallow of wine cooler. "I did my undergrad at Duke. My roommate, Squoozie, was from Texas. Down there they have a soda called Orangeade. When she drove her car to school every Fall, she'd fill it up with cases of Orangeade and have her clothes shipped." Mercy chuckled as she seemed to be recalling good times.

Glen had perked up when she said her roommate's name. "Her last name wouldn't be Caelian, would it?"

Mercy's eyes widened. "Yes! How did you know that?"

"Well, to be fair, how many Squoozies from Texas could there really be? I know her brother. He works for Black Swan."

"Kay?" Torn asked.

"The same," said Glen.

"Small world." Torn grasped the hurricane glass they had brought his margarita in and took a drink. In a simultaneous flash of impressive coordination, Torn retracted his legs, sat up, and spewed alcoholic beverage on the inner terrace floor. Then half-yelled a disgusted, "Aaah."

"Serves you right for ordering a margarita in a French owned Bulgarian hotel, dumb ass." Gunnar laughed and Raif joined him, enjoying the boorish spectacle more than he should. "At least you managed to aim *away* from us for a change. The last time... Chinese restaurant in Toronto, wasn't it? ...I walked away with a mixture of tequila and elf spit all over my front." Gunnar turned to Glen chuckling and slapped him on the back. "Come to think of it, you should have seen what happened the first time the young werewolf had black beer! That time it was Torn who was getting the old bar towel wipe down."

Mercy's gaze snapped to Glen. "Werewolf?"

"Blah." Torn stuck out his tongue like he thought airing it out would take the offending taste away. "What would you be doin' if you had somethin' unbelievably disgustin' in your mouth?"

Torn knew exactly what Raif and Gunnar were thinking by the way they looked down at their shoes and smiled without saying a word. He was glad they both decided on the polite choice - keeping that thought to themselves.

"You're not ready for civilized company, brother." Gunnar glanced at Mercy and gave him a reproving look.

Torn looked at Mercy. "Aye. 'Tis true enough. Beg your forgiveness, my lady."

Mercy laughed partly because of the 'lady' reference and partly because the beautiful elf was bursting with sexual ardor and magnetism powerful enough to charm the clothes off a girl in public before she even knew she was undressing. The werewolf thing was probably an inside joke.

Glen had been looking at his guide book. "Listen to this. The Beglik Tash. The unique Thracian sanctuary Beglik Tash was discovered in 2003, only thirty km south of Sozopol. It's the earliest Thracian megalith sanctuary along the Black Sea coast. Research has proven that there's been constant human occupation since the end of the Bronze age. It's basically a cult temple to fertility."

He put the guide book down. "Oh come on. We have to go! Haven't you always wanted to stand in the middle of an ancient fertility temple?"

Gun and Torn looked at each other and burst into laughter. Mercy noticed that Raif just looked away.

When Torn quieted, he said, "No, Glen, I can no' say that I have *always* wanted that. Nor can I begin to understand why you would want that. Most of the handsome virile lads I know are wantin' to avoid fertility at any cost." He punctuated that with a wink thrown Mercy's way. She turned her head and worked at hiding a smile because she didn't want Glen to think she was laughing at him.

"Yeah?" Glen said. "Well, most of the handsome virile lads you know don't have two brain cells to rub together."

Torn chuckled. "True enough, younger brother. You've go' me there."

CHAPTER 16

BLACK SWAN FIELD TRAINING MANUAL Chapter 28, #17

Hunter Division personnel are expected to be flexible of body and mind. At times resourcefulness may be a knight's greatest asset. The ability to improvise when necessary is a trait highly prized by The Order.

When it came down to the first night that Storm was joining patrol rotation, Litha had come to the conclusion that she just couldn't do it. She couldn't construct a rationalization big enough or intricate enough or delusional enough to justify spying on her husband. But by the time the dreaded day of first patrol after retirement rolled around, she'd calmed down enough to be at peace with the fact that she'd fallen in love with a famous vampire hunter, who might just have a couple more hunts left in him. After all, he wasn't yet thirty years old. On the one hand, she thought, if he was a surgeon, he'd still be years away from beginning his career. On the other hand, if he was a pro athlete, he'd be long washed up and put out to dry.

Kay gave Storm an amused look. "In some ways this feels more familiar than watching TV with my wife."

They were separating from Ram and Rev, going opposite ways in an alley. Storm looked back over his shoulder at Ram and Rev walking away. On a whim he called out, "Sol!"

Without hesitation, Rev turned and said, "Yeah?" The four of them stood frozen, Storm and Rev staring at each other, Kay and Ram looking back and forth between the two.

Let it never be said that Ram didn't know how to handle a situation delicately. "What the fuck, Stormy?"

"You know, that's a good question, Ram. And well put." Storm didn't take his eyes off Rev. "Something you want to tell us?"

Rev pursed his lips before growling. "No."

"You sure?"

"You gone hard of hearing?"

Storm's gaze was a concentrated challenge, pinning Rev in place, but he moved in close enough for quiet conversation.

"How about clueing us in, brother?" Kay was as calm as the eye of a hurricane as he nudged Storm. "What's going on here?"

"Has it seemed to you that there are things about the new Sovereign that seem familiar? Eerily so?"

"Like what?" Ram asked as he eyed Rev from top to bottom.

"Oh, like the fact that he smokes the same brand of Turkish cigars that Sol used to smoke. And lights them with an old school fluid lighter. Then he puts the lighter down in front of him and turns it around and around the same way Sol used to." Kay turned his attention toward Rev and began regarding him with increased interest. "How about the way he screws up his mouth when he's aggravated or the way he steeples his fingers when he's making a decision?"

Rev lifted his chin in defiance and narrowed his eyes at Storm. "And let's not forget the fact that he took a bead on Farnsworth about thirty seconds after arriving at Jefferson Unit. Doesn't it strike you as a little strange that he handles Sol's job like he knows what he's doing? No. Not like he knows what he's doing. Like he's done it before!"

Ram eased around in front of Rev so that the three veteran members of B Team appeared united as the inquisitors they had just become. They stood in a dimly lit alley with accusation hanging in the air, waiting for Rev to answer.

"Your imagination's just got the better of you, Sir Storm."

"There! Right there. I never met another knight who called me *Sir* Storm. But Sol did." Storm glanced at Kay. "All the time. Called me Mr. Storm when I was a kid. Switched to Sir Storm when I was inducted." He stepped closer to Rev. "When I called Sol's name, you turned around like you'd been answering to that name your whole life."

Ram and Kay were giving Rev looks that said the questions weren't going to go away just by staring Storm down. Finally Rev replied with the cool of an iceberg. "So what are you saying? Exactly? That I'm a body snatcher?"

"What I'm doing right now is asking questions."

"I don't have answers for you."

"Is that because you don't have an answer or because you can't answer?" Rev gave nothing away. Storm blinked twice rapidly. "Well, then there's no harm in sharing this with Simon and the Council."

"NO!" Rev's answer was a little too forceful and a little too quick.

"Start talking."

Rev blew out a breath and looked around at the alley. "Let's go sit down somewhere private." He ran a hand through his hair. "I'll buy a round of drinks and tell you a story. Not about me, mind you. A story about a guy I heard of."

Rev hated the suspicious glances he caught in his peripheral vision as they walked in silence to the basement bar around the corner. Harry's was dark and quiet. Cozy in a masculine sort of way with oak beams and big comfortable red leather booths. And they knew it well because it was also the sort of place where vampire liked to hang out when they'd hunted successfully and were high on some girl's warm, rich Type O.

All four quickly scanned the room, as only veteran hunters would do. Within fifteen seconds any one of the four could have taken a pop quiz on how many people occupied the room, where they were, what they were doing, and something about what they looked like. Complimentary or not.

Ram veered off from the team and headed straight to the bar. He told them to pour four Irish whiskeys. The other three left room for him at one end of a big curved corner booth. He noticed they weren't talking. Just waiting.

"Spirits on the way," he said, sliding in.

Storm looked at Rev. "So? You were going to tell us a story? About a guy?"

Rev looked around the room knowing that stalling was futile. He'd used every step of the walk between the alley and the bar trying to decide the best way to get the knights to move on to another subject without losing claim to the fine young body he currently occupied. Of course, he knew they'd be pit bulls going for a bone until they were satisfied.

The bartender's young helper arrived with a tray and began setting glasses in front of them. When he was gone, Storm turned to Rev. "Well?"

Rev looked up, "What was the question?"

Storm narrowed his eyes. "Kay. Weren't you in my interrogation class?"

"I think so," Kay said. "We were fifteen maybe? What about it?"

"Do you remember them teaching us that if a subject asked to have the question repeated it meant that they were stalling so they had time to work on the lie that they were about to tell?"

Kay looked at Rev with speculation. "You know, since you mention it, I do remember that."

Rev took in a big breath and let it out forcefully. "All right, but don't get bent out of shape about the back story. I have to set the stage."

"Set the stage," Storm said drily. Rev nodded. "Rammel. Are you keeping an eye on the patrons sharing this fine establishment?"

"On guard." Ram's seat on the end of the booth had the best view of the door and the room in general.

Looking back at Rev, Storm said, "By all means then, set the stage."

"Do you believe in the afterlife?"

Storm and Kay exchanged glances. Ram said, "Great Paddy."

Rev looked at Ram with lines formed between his brows. "Is that an answer?"

"Aye. O'course."

"Okay. I'll play along," Storm said. "I wouldn't say I 'believe', but I would say I'm keeping an open mind."

Rev looked at Kay who said, "No. I think Elora's fairy stories are likelier."

"Elftales," Ram corrected Kay with a small scowl forming between his brows. There might be a new politically correct way to think of his brother-in-law's people, but old bias dies hard.

"Whatever," Kay said. "We're just a walking mass of electrical impulses. When the plug is pulled, we're done."

"Kind of a bleak outlook." Rev was looking at Kay like he was surprised to hear that view coming from the big berserker.

"Works for me. So we're really going to debate mythology?"

"One person's mythology is somebody else's religion."

Kay opened his mouth to respond, but Storm cut him off. "Enough. Let's get to the story. About a guy? Remember?"

"Yes. It's related. So here goes.

"There was a guy who died and went to the, uh, afterlife. And it was nice enough, but he couldn't enjoy it because he'd left unfinished business. Serious unfinished business." Rev paused for a minute for that to soak in. "So he started kicking up a fuss. At first the people in charge ignored him, told him to take another hit of feel good and try to relax into the new digs. They said he'd adjust soon enough and everything would be hunky dory."

Rev looked around the table. The knights were focused on what he was saying and waiting for him to get to the part where he started to either make sense or relate to any situation they could imagine.

"Here's the thing though. Time went by and he didn't adjust or relax. Just the opposite, in fact. The people who were trying to enjoy their 'reward', " he put the word 'reward' in air quotes, "started complaining that he was disturbing them."

Rev rolled his eyes like he was experiencing a memory. "Well, how many times can you do the hokey pokey? Really!"

He looked around the other three knights and noticed they were looking wary.

"Okay. Let's just say that this guy didn't fit in. At all. And he was getting a reputation as a troublemaker, which was fine with him because that was his plan. He hoped that, if he raised enough stink, they'd send him back where he belonged." Rev looked around the table. "And that's what happened. End of story."

Storm, Ram, and Kay looked back and forth between themselves for a minute.

"End of story?" Storm asked.

"Yes."

"But you said he died."

"Yes." Rev looked straight into Storm's eyes like he was trying to will him to understand.

Ram shook his head, said, "Fuck," then followed a big swallow of whiskey with an exaggerated hiss.

"Look. I'm trying to work with you here, but you're not giving us much. How is this guy going to be sent back if his body is…" Storm stopped midsentence. His eyes widened momentarily and then he started shaking his head.

"What?" Ram asked. Storm continued to stare at Rev like he'd seen a ghost. Ram turned to Kay. "What?"

Kay downed his whiskey in one drink and said, "If I'm following, I think the implication is that an old Sovereign might occupy a new Sovereign's body if he went to heaven and raised hel."

Ram's head jerked to Rev and his eyes flicked over the part of his body that could be seen above the table.

Storm put his elbows on the table and leaned in. "That's some story." Rev nodded. "I guess the guy was told the deal came with conditions?"

"Yes." A single blink was the only movement in Rev's face.

"And I'm going to hazard a guess that one of those conditions was that the guy wasn't to tell anybody."

Rev shrugged. "That's what I heard."

Kay looked at Storm with open-mouthed astonishment. "You're not buying this. It's preposterous!"

Storm studied Kay for a minute, then lowered his voice. "That word isn't in Black Swan vocabulary." Kay pulled back and frowned. "And you know it."

"So," Ram started, "would that guy be wearin' flesh belongin' to some other poor bastard?"

Rev looked up and met Ram's gaze. "The other poor bastard was done with the mortal coil, but it was fresh enough to be reparable by the powers that be."

"Great Fuckin' Paddy," Ram said under his breath while looking a little horrified. "You mean they can just hand your body off like a used car?"

Storm's shoulders were raised by the big breath he inhaled and let out. "There's no rule against answering questions is there?"

"Not if they're not specific," Rev answered.

"I was picked up at my parents' house and driven to the San Francisco unit. You know what kind of car I arrived in?"

As Rev listened to the question, his face softened. He smiled at Storm with a fondness that made him seem so familiar. "I'll make a guess and say it was a sedan."

The tension that Ram and Kay had been holding dissolved into laughter and comfortable slumping into the leather seat.

Ram looked at Kay and repeated, "A sedan!" through chuckles.

As Storm watched Rev slowly rotate the whiskey tumbler on the table in front of him, he felt a twinge of disappointment grip his heart. He realized that, on some unconscious level, he'd been hoping that the answer would be the opposite of Occam's Razor. That, instead of the simplest explanation being the right one, the most farfetched and wholly unbelievable explanation would be the truth of it.

Rev didn't react to Ram's and Kay's ridicule. He just continued to stare at the glass he was turning. Almost too quietly to be heard, he said, "Yeah. I'm guessing sedan. A navy blue DeSoto." He raised his eyes to Storm, who didn't have enough warning to stop the emotions that rushed forward. Before he could shut it down, his eyes had started to water.

Kay and Ram, whose ridicule had stopped abruptly with the very specific naming of the vehicle, both looked away from Storm to save him the embarrassment of being caught misting. Storm swiped at his eyes and sucked it up. "Wow."

Some of the rigidity left Rev's expression when he smiled and nodded. "The best education money can buy and that's the best you have to offer?"

Kay looked at Storm. "You believe him?" It sounded more like an accusation than a question.

Storm ignored Kay. "Does Farnsworth know?"

Rev grinned so big it made Storm have second thoughts about his conclusion. "Let me put it this way. We're engaged."

"Great Fuckin' Paddy." Remembering that he was the designated watcher, Ram looked toward the door and made direct eye contact with one of two vampire, who had been scanning the room while deciding whether or not to stay. He forced himself to look away and pretend to be casual, but the vampire had detected the subtle way Ram's body came to attention. That and the fact that the men occupying the corner booth fit the profile to a tee.

If he'd been a new vampire, the eye lock wouldn't have been accidental. All the reports that had come in made it clear that the mutated virus had created much more aggressive behavior. In the past, when given a choice of fight or flight, vampire almost always chose flight. Not anymore.

The vamp who had caught Ram's eye was seventy-five years old and had a strong preference for flight. Knowing how to recognize knights of the Black Swan was undoubtedly one of the reasons why he'd lived so long. Every vamp who made it to a one year anniversary had heard the stories, the legends, and been admonished with a list of things to look for, but some were able to control blood lust well enough to pay attention to surroundings. And some weren't.

Black Swan Knights travel in packs of four. Sometimes they separate into pairs, but one pair will never be very far away from the other – usually within earshot. They tend to stand out from the larger population, partly because they are at the peak of physical perfection and fitness, but also because they cannot help but exude an air of danger or warning.

As Ram turned back to the group, he picked up his whiskey glass and tapped it lightly on the table three times to get the attention of the others. He lowered his voice.

"Do no' look at the door. Two biters on the premises and I'm thinkin' one has made us. Get ready for a run down. If they go they're goin' to have a jump on us."

Storm casually leaned over to remove his wallet from his pocket. He withdrew a large bill, but barely had time to throw it on the table when the vamps bolted. Ram and Kay were on the outer edges of the booth. They both moved fast, but Ram, being smaller and lighter, was faster.

As it happened, four blocks away at 42nd and 7th, three trainees were enjoying a rec night away from Jefferson Unit. Kristoph Falcon, Rolfe Wakenmann, and new transferee, Sinclair Harvest, were sitting at a deli window table, eating sandwiches piled outrageously high with meat, enough for a small, normal family to make a meal of.

Falcon was getting more satisfaction than he should out of telling Sin all about Wakey having to read romantic poems to half the trainees as part of a punishment for disrespecting someone's sexual preference. Out loud.

During a break in the conversation, Falcon happened to be looking out the window and thinking that punishment isn't always bad. He and Wakey had impressed the shit out of Sin when the Whister pilots had taken a back seat and let the two of them fly the trip to Manhattan.

Anybody who doesn't believe in fate either isn't very old or hasn't been paying attention. Because it was at that moment, when Falcon had looked away from the other boys, that he saw two figures run past on the sidewalk just on the other side of the glass. That alone may not have been extraordinary or remarkable for midtown Manhattan. What credited the incident with the hand of fate was the fact that one of the vampire looked straight into Kris Falcon's eyes during the split second they ran past. It took less time than that for Falcon to register what he'd seen. Some classes were more worthy of his attention than others.

He stood up so fast he knocked his chair over. Sin and Wakey looked at him like he was possessed until he said the word vampire without moving his lips, like a ventriloquist.

Who knows what would have happened had it not been for the history of knights that came before? Perhaps things would have gone differently, but the fact was that every trainee had heard the story of how Elora Laiken had slain a vampire with a toothpick. Perhaps that story sat on the edge of every trainee's consciousness. No one can ever know for sure.

All we do know is that, on the way to the exit that night, Falcon reached out and grabbed the table's wooden plaque holder that told the wait staff what number had been assigned to a diner's order. It had a round base and a dowel extending straight up from the center like a flag pole.

Being a potential knight meant that Wakey was pretty fast on the uptake. He must have thought it was a pretty good idea because he grabbed another from the table by the door. The deli manager came out onto the sidewalk to yell after them about not paying the bill, but the boys' focus had turned very single-minded.

Being young, conditioned like Olympic athletes, and without the muscular bulk of knights a decade older, they were lightning fast. Faster than the vampire who had hoped they were out of danger after they'd managed to lose two braces of Black Swan knights.

The vampire knew there were three kids running behind them, but never suspected they might be the goal because they knew the score. Hunters come in groups of two or four grown men, not three kids. So they ducked into an alley, as vampire so often do.

"How could we just lose them into thin air? Are we losin' our touch then?" Ram was a little exasperated because he wasn't used to letting prey get away. "Great Paddy. We've turned into heavy-hooved has-beens."

"Don't be melodramatic, Rammel. Everybody loses vamps now and then."

"Noooooo. They do no'. 'Tis ne'er happened to *us* before."

Storm and Kay both gaped at Ram like he was nuts. "It happened the very night your wife did that stupid ass move with the toothpick. Remember? We left her alone to do a rundown and then... We. Lost. Them."

Ram chewed on his lip. "Paddy! Unbunch the knickers, man. So maybe it happened one time."

Kay just shook his head. "Nothing changes."

"Let's split up and take a look around. Three blocks on either side. What do you think?" Storm was so accustomed to making suggestions as to how B Team should proceed in the field that he didn't even think about the fact that he was in the presence of an acting Sovereign and seriously outranked.

Before anyone responded, Rev's phone vibrated against his hip. He looked at it and said, "It's Mr. Barrock."

Ram looked at Kay and mouthed, "Who?"

Opening the phone he said, "Farthing here."

There were several pauses between which Rev alternated between staccato grunts and cursing under his breath. Finally he said, "We're close by and on our way. Send clean up and we'll take care of the rest."

He ended the call, shoved the phone in his pocket and said, "Seems we've got a situation."

Seven minutes later, Rev and three members of B Team arrived at the location where they'd been directed. Storm nodded at Kris and Wakey. He remembered them from the Battle for Jefferson Unit. Given the fact that they'd won medals protecting Elora and flying injured personnel away in a Whister, it would have been impossible to forget them. They nodded back.

"Well, gentlemen," he said, feeling like he was channeling Sol. "What do we have here?"

They stepped away so that he could see the two corpses their bodies had been concealing. Both former vampire had strange sticks coming out of their chests with round wooden blocks on the end. Storm studied the phenomenon as best he could in the dim light.

Ram leaned over and asked with an incredulity thick as syrup. "Are those…?"

Wakey spoke up. "The little flag flyers for your deli order. Sir."

"Great Paddy."

Ram looked at Kay who deadpanned, "It seems we've stood and talked like this before."

"That song is no' from your era, Danny Disco."

"It's Disco Danny. Can you ever get it right, Rammel?"

"Who in Paddy's name cares whether 'tis fuckin' Danny Disco or fuckin' Disco Danny, berserker?"

"Knock it off," Storm said before turning back to the boys. "You want to tell us what happened?"

"Aye," Ram chimed in. "You kiddos got some 'splainin' to do."

"Rammel! I said knock it off!" Storm was getting more insistent.

"Fine. Do no' be goin' berserk on us." Ram smiled at Kay who eased into a wide stance and rolled his eyes.

"Well..." Wakey began.

"Before you start..." Storm glanced at Rev and then waved toward the trainees. "This is Mr. Falcon and Mr. Wakenmann. They won medals for heroism during the assassination attempt that destroyed Jefferson Unit. Or a large part of it.

"Why don't you introduce your friend?"

Kris and Wakey both looked at Sin like they hadn't seen him before. Kris finally spoke up. "Sinclair Harvest, sir."

Kris looked back at Storm. "I think he already knows who all of you are." Sin's head nodded up and down. He looked like he was star struck.

Storm looked at Wakey. "Okay. Go on."

"Well, we were getting a bite at the Koch Deli over on 7th. I got a pastrami on toasted rye with spicy brown mustard that was this tall." He left a space between his hands. "Falcon had just been sharing with the new guy how Sovereign Nememiah made me read love poems to all the guys and then apologize to Crisp." When his gaze scanned the older men and stopped on Rev's glower, Wakey decided to edit the less pertinent details.

"All of a sudden Falcon jumps up and says, 'Vampire', like this." He said it with his lips pulled tight and his tongue held motionless so that the formation of vowels was almost impossible. "We got up to follow him. I noticed he grabbed one of the wooden number holders. I figured out why he did it so I grabbed one, too. You know they're always talking about resourcefulness in tactics class.

"So Falcon went tearing out the door after the vamps who were running and we went tearing out the door after him, but we had to work hard at it because, man, the fucker is fast!" When Wakey realized he'd said the word 'fucker', he stiffened and went wide-eyed. "Um, sorry about the language, sir." He directed the apology to Storm, but glanced over at the others.

Storm said, "That's okay this time, but remember you're training to be a knight and The Order expects you to exercise befitting decorum."

Storm gave Ram a pointed look as he said it. Ram replied by locking his gaze and mouthing, "Fucker." As much as he hated to do it, Storm couldn't help a little smile. There was something charming about the way Ram remained the same. Neither marriage nor aging nor being proclaimed father of a king could make Rammel stodgy, and that indomitable spark of life and fun was oddly comforting to Storm.

"So you were saying that Falcon here is fast on his feet." Storm made a little circular gesture with his hand, signaling that Wakenmann should pick up the story where he stopped.

"Like wind, sir. Even in those boots he wears because chicks like the look."

Rev made a huffing sound that caused Wakey to look his way. Seeing that the guy was glaring even more, and, who would have thought that possible? Wakey redoubled his intention to continue with the relevant stuff.

"So Sin and I had to pump like devils to keep him in sight. I guess the vamps turned into this alley because when we got here Falcon was engaged with both, trying to find an in without getting bitten. And I've just got to say that's a lot harder than it sounds."

He turned toward Falcon and Harvest who acknowledged by nodding solemnly. At the same time

Ram and Kay exchanged similar nods double punctuating their younger counterpart's declaration.

Storm looked at Falcon. "Is this true, Mr. Falcon? You deliberately ran down and engaged two vampire in the field without authorization and without backup?"

When it was put that way, it sounded downright shameful. There was a time when Falcon would have stared Storm down and dared him to a challenge, but that was before a deep and abiding respect for these hunters had begun to grow in his heart. He didn't want to disappoint Sir Storm so he found himself looking down at his feet when he said, "Yes, sir."

Storm continued quietly, with measured words. "And did you think that was a good idea?"

Falcon didn't answer right away. When he did, he spoke as quietly as Storm. "I guess I wasn't really thinking about anything except vampire running. I guess I didn't think just sitting there eating our sandwiches was an option. In the back of my mind I was thinking that those vampire could be the end of somebody's sister or daughter or girlfriend. And that I could stop them." His eyes flickered and he added, "Maybe."

"That's all very true. The thing is this. What about you? You're somebody's brother. You're somebody's son. You're somebody's friend." That last word was punctuated with a nod toward the other two trainees. "You can't start thinking of yourself as dispensable. Not only are you important to some other people, but The Order has invested a lot of time and money in you. And you could have easily squandered that investment tonight by being a loose cannon."

Falcon didn't say anything. The other boys looked away.

"What's worse is that you led your friends into a situation. Once you rushed in, they had no choice but to follow you. They *had* to get your back. So it wasn't just yourself that you risked. It was them, too." Storm watched Falcon's face carefully and was satisfied with the impact his words were evidently having on the kid. "Here's something they don't usually tell hunters until it's time for field duty. Before you embark on a patrol you have to be one hundred percent certain that you've sorted out your feelings about your duty to your team members and Black Swan.

"You know how hard it was to try and fight while avoiding coming in contact with a fang? Especially when the opponent is all about *trying* to bite you? What you haven't been told in class is that, if one of you *does* get bitten, you have to be prepared to dispatch your friend, who sometimes feels like a brother to you. With the new virus it has to be done within minutes. No time for regrets, recriminations, or even goodbyes.

"Thank the gods I've never had to do it, but I've heard stories about what happens to guys who've had to execute their own partner. It breaks them. For life."

While Storm gave the boys a literal street education, Rev felt tremors going through his body like the old wives' tales about somebody walking on your grave. And he wondered for the thousandth time since returning to life as Farthing just how much residual memory his body had retained.

"You see these two guys?" Storm pointed to Ram and Kay. "I've been with them since I was younger than you are and I love them more than you can begin to imagine. I'd have no trouble trading my life for either one of them. Hel. It would almost be easy. But having to *kill* one of them? Hold him in my arms and watch the light go out of his eyes? I don't see myself coming back from that."

It was silent when Storm stopped speaking, like an eerie impossible quiet had settled around them like a shroud. Not just in the alleyway, but in the city. There was no traffic noise, no music, nothing but the sounds of their own breathing and heartbeats.

"In short, there's a lot more to being a Black Swan knight than you know and you're *not* ready for it. Are you hearing me?"

Falcon looked more than reprimanded. He looked devastated, like he'd just walked himself through the image of having to dispatch one of his friends. He nodded his head at Storm solemnly. "Yes, sir."

Storm sighed. "Okay, enough lecture for now. I want to know how you identified them as vamps to begin with."

Falcon made a visible effort to recover himself and get his thoughts back together. "We were sitting at a table by the window. I just happened to look up when they ran by and one of them looked right at me. There's really no mistaking those eyes."

Ram unconsciously nodded an affirmation.

"Like I said, I wasn't thinking about anything except making sure they didn't get away. After three blocks or so they slowed down and looked behind them. I guess they saw that I was running toward them, but didn't think I was coming for *them*. Or didn't think I was much of a threat. So they stopped and turned in here.

"I didn't stop running. I did an airborne roundhouse thinking I'd knock one off his feet and maybe have a chance to stake the other while the one down was figuring things out."

At that Ram raised his hands and let them flop against his thighs to convey his own two cents' worth of disgust.

Storm said, "Continue."

"I grabbed the one still standing by the back of his collar and smashed his face into the wall. Hard. I'd hoped to stun him so I could take a good aim with my little stick.

I was afraid I only had one shot because it would likely splinter and break with repeated stabs.

"It's just that the one on the ground didn't stay down long enough. He grabbed me from behind and I guess he was about to chow down. Then I heard Sin. I guess he was running and making this sound like a growl. He got a fistful of the vamp's hair and pulled him back off me.

"That left me free to concentrate on the fu..., uh, biter in front of me. I didn't look back, just had to trust that Sin and Wakey had the other one handled.

"I danced around with him for a bit, him trying to bite me, me trying to get ahold of him *and* avoid the fangs. Which are damn ugly, by the way. I wasn't getting anywhere fast until these two..." He stopped, motioning to his friends, a tone of unmistakable pride creeping into his retelling at that point. "They got him from behind and held him still for me. So all I had to do was jam the twig into the right spot.

"That's the story."

For a time the three members of B Team who were present stood motionless, just looking at the rookies. Undoubtedly they were seeing themselves and replaying a hundred such encounters in their minds. They'd survived long careers as vampire hunters. Each one of them was secretly wondering how much of that had been luck.

The veterans could see that the boys were trying to be cool and casual about the informal debriefing, but they could also see that the kids were jazzed, almost vibrating visibly. They knew firsthand what sort of adrenaline rush accompanies a victorious skirmish with vampire. And they hoped these kids would never find out what the other kinds of skirmish, the non-victorious sort, felt like.

Finally Storm turned to Rev. "Got anything you want to add, Sovereign?"

Rev didn't take his eyes away from the boys.

"Yes. First, who paid the bill at the deli?" The kids looked at each other, shook their heads and gave Rev a guilty look. "Next lesson. Somebody is always designated bill payer. That means he's got his hand on enough to throw down and cover the debt. Now, go pay your bill. Tell the manager there was an emergency, that you never intended to run out on the check, and that you're sorry if it caused an inconvenience. If there's any trouble, call me." He held his hand out until Falcon handed over his phone. Rev programmed his contact number in and returned it. "Do not tell a soul about this incident and be in my office tomorrow morning at 11:30." Wakey started to say something then stopped. "Question, Mr. Wakenmann?"

"I was just wondering if that means we're excused from class?"

Rev sighed. "Yes. It does. Go straight to the midtown Whister pad. Your night out is over."

All three boys mumbled, "Yes, sir," and began walking away.

"Hey," Ram's voice stopped them. "E'en with all the fuckups and the maybes and the chances, you still did good tonight. Maybe saved somebody from bein' eaten. Maybe saved somebody else from turnin' vamp. Does no' mean 'twas wise, mind you."

The kids smiled as they turned around and kept walking.

"Rammel," Storm said. "nobody was *ever* soft on us."

"Tellin' kids their instincts are good. 'Tis no' the same thin' as bein' soft."

"I had just been thinking that fatherhood hadn't changed you. I was wrong." Storm looked at Rev. "So what now, Sovereign?"

"Let's call it in to clean up." He looked over to see the boys turning out of the end of the alley. "Seems like

Elora's been relieved of the responsibility of picking three trainees. Looks like they picked themselves."

When Kay had finished the call for clean up, Rev said, "Let's wait for the truck. Then maybe I'll buy you three another drink. To celebrate my engagement."

Storm narrowed his eyes. "Did you tell her?"

"Couldn't do that. Against the rules. She put it together herself and warned me that, if she could do it, other people – like you – might do the same."

Storm whistled low. "You're a lucky son-of-a-bitch, boss."

"Watch that language."

"I could use a whiskey," said Ram.

"See? Nothing changes," said Kay.

Elora turned over and looked at the clock. The red digital display was either wrong or time was moving very, very slowly. It wasn't long after she'd fallen into Jefferson Unit before she realized that she'd gotten herself mixed up with a rough crowd. She'd known since before she'd admitted to being Rammel Hawking's mate that the one thing she could not do was wait at home and hope B Team survived the night.

For cripes' sake, that was how she ended up maneuvering her way onto B Team to begin with – so she could watch out for guys who looked a lot bigger, stronger, faster, but were in fact, far more vulnerable physically.

Ram was supposed to be on patrol from eight to two. She'd had time to get right with the thing and get a grip on being a big girl about it and thought she had. So she kissed her husband goodbye, gave Helm a bath, put him to bed, and spent a couple of hours catching up on the baby book. Future generations were going to want to know that the king could blow bubbles with mashed carrots.

A good night's sleep wasn't an option. She had a baby who'd be demanding attention, a change of clothes, and breakfast – in that order – in just a few hours. If that wasn't enough of a motivation, there was a sharp group of trainees housed in the dormitory downstairs who'd be showing up for fight school, as they liked to call it, bright eyed, rested and ready. Fitful, sleepless nights were just out of the question, but the more she stared at the ceiling talking to herself about why she needed to go to sleep, the more wide awake she became.

By midnight she was up and pacing back and forth trying not to see images of roaring vampire with long sharp fangs or the long jagged, freshly stitched path of the knife wound that cut Ram from stem to stern. If he was a normal husband with a normal job, she could just call to make sure he was okay, but Black Swan had phone silence rules for good reason. A knight couldn't be distracted by a phone call in the middle of a vampire encounter. The results could be disastrous. For that reason, only the Sovereign could be reached by phone in the field and then, only for emergency reasons.

By the time she heard movement at the front door she had worked herself into a frenzy bordering on hysterics. Ram hadn't even closed the door before she had grabbed him into an embrace that was punishing to a native of Loti Dimension.

"Hey, now. Ease up just a bit. I'll no' be able to fuck you senseless if most of my bones are pulverized."

"Oh, sorry, sorry, sorry." She relaxed her hold and covered his face and neck in kisses.

Ram chuckled. "Do no' take this the wrong way, but what is this about?"

She pulled back so that she could search his face for evidence of injury. When she was satisfied there was none, she ripped his Ramones shirt right down the middle.

"Hold on! Great Paddy, woman! That shirt was a classic! Have you gone barkin' mad?"

She stared into his eyes until he stopped speaking, then her gaze jerked down to the buttons of his jeans. Her inspection of his chest and torso had revealed nothing but beautifully whole skin. No new wounds. But she had to be sure his entire body was unmolested.

When Ram saw where her train of thought was going, he said, "Stop! I ne'er thought the day would come when I'd be sayin' do no' e'en think about takin' my pants off, but do no' e'en think about takin' my pants off." She reached for his waistband. He backed up a step. "Do no' make me do somethin' you will regret."

She stopped. "Like what?"

"Like rubbin' your eyebrows the wrong way."

"You wouldn't. I hate that."

"Aye, I know and I would despise takin' advantage of intimate knowledge, but I will use the tools at my disposal if you persist in this most unbecomin' behavior."

Her shoulders sagged. "Are you okay?"

"Indeed. Good as Irish gold."

"If you're lying, I will find out."

"Aye, but findin' out is best when 'tis consensual."

"Okay. You have a point." She bit into her lower lip and tears sprang to her eyes. "I was going crazy."

"Aye. I can see that."

"I can't do it, Ram. I couldn't do it before we were us and I *really* can't do it now."

"Why do we no' step away from the door? Perhaps we might share an inch of wine and discuss the matter."

He sat her down on the living room sofa, poured two glasses of wine a little deeper than the inch that was mentioned and returned to sit next to her.

"Are you beginnin' to feel more like yourself?"

"Yes. Do you want to tell me about your night?"

"Aye. But first I'd like to know what has your feathers flyin' all over the house."

Elora had been set to tell Ram exactly how worried she'd been, but seeing that he was cavalier, she quickly got her wits about her and hatched a plan. Two nights hence she would be the one going out without him. She strongly suspected that when she returned after her patrol, he would be in a much better frame of mind to understand what her problem was and why she was distraught.

"Nothing. It was silly. Probably PMS. Now that you're here, it's all good. So tell me everything."

And that is what he did.

Up to a point.

He told her all about losing the pair of vamps only to learn that they'd been found by three of her trainees. At one point in the story he had to give her a minute to slow her heart rate and catch her breath. There clearly was a good reason why the kids called her "mother".

When he reached the part of the story where Rev had proclaimed that the three trainees were bound to skip two years and go into rotation, Elora started shaking her head violently.

"No," she said. "He can't have them."

Ram said nothing. He took a long drink of wine, licked his lips, set the glass down and slid closer to Elora. Softly trailing his knuckles along her jaw line he said, "You know I'm sensin' a pattern here. Seem you do no' like the idea of your peeps or your chickadees in situations that could prove hazardous to health."

"I don't," she said in a matter-of-fact tone as she looked at her wine glass and took another drink.

"Well, 'tis no' a thin' either strange or unusual about that. 'Tis only natural."

"Exactly."

"Except that your peeps and chickadees are no' automobile salesmen. There's a good reason why the job comes with a big life insurance policy. 'Tis dangerous. You know that. Our business is savin' the world. Lots of perks, but there's a downside, too."

"Are you patronizing me, Rammel?"

"No' at all."

"I need to go to bed."

"Music to my elfin ears."

CHAPTER 17

Sozopol, Bulgaria

Mercy descended the grand staircase, reminiscent of another day in hotel pageantry. When she and her two shadows reached the elevators, she had kept walking. Glen and Gun looked at each other and followed without asking questions. After all, they were there to escort and protect. Not direct. She kept walking until she reached the staircase, which was open and not at the end of the hall behind a closed door.

"Hey. I like your kippers," Glen called from behind.

Mercy stopped and turned around. "My what?"

"Your," he was motioning in the direction of her lower body, "kippers".

"Glen, I don't have any kippers on me and you couldn't possibly be hungry enough to hallucinate me dripping in herring."

"Herring?"

Her eyes narrowed. "Are we talking about the same thing?"

"I'm talking about the pants you're wearing with all the pockets. Aren't they called kippers?"

She shook her head, turned around and started back down the stairs. "They're called pants, Glen. But thank you. I'm pleased you like them."

Glen looked at Gunnar who couldn't hold his laughter in another second. "Kippers?"

"Like you're an expert on women's clothing?"

"Well..." Gun started.

"Shut it, old man," Glen trotted down the stairs behind Dr. Renaux.

The three joined Torn and Raif who had already commandeered a round table with two features to its credit. It was in a corner near an exit, always a favorite of Black Swan knights. And, if you were on the side of the table with your back to the room, it had a marvelous view of the morning sun rising over the Black Sea.

Mercy sat looking and sounding cheerful. "Hmmm. Nice view. So what looks good?"

"Good Bulgarian food?" mumbled Raif.

Torn smirked at him and turned his attention to Mercy. "They've got that thin' where they smash bread, milk, and cheese up with sugar and butter. Looks disgustin', but we were told before you came down that kids love it."

"Popara," she said.

"Forgot you've been 'round this part of the world. We should be askin' you what to get."

"Well they've got these things that are sort of like grilled breakfast sandwiches. Brioche meets minced meat and eggs and cheese. In any combination you like."

"Sold," Glen said. "I'll take three."

"I'll just have some more of that negarche cake," Gun added. "With coffee."

"Breakfast of champions." Mercy smiled at him in mock approval.

"Exactly," replied Gun. He offered Mercy a high five either not realizing that she was being sarcastic or not caring. Without missing a beat she gave him a high five and rattled her coffee cup, hoping to get the attention of a waiter.

"Hey," she said, then followed that with something in Bulgarian.

"You have to tell us what you said. We can't be responsible for you if we don't know what you're saying to people."

"Why not?" She tipped her chin and asked the question playfully.

"Because," Torn began, "if, for instance, you were to say, 'in exactly ten minutes my friends will be openin' fire on passersby on the coastline walkway below', then we would need to prepare for bein overrun with hotel security, local police, and perhaps the Bulgarian military as well. If you said, 'Show me the way to the Ladies', then we could relax. Except for Glen, who will be accompanyin' you as far as is seemly."

"I see your point. But how would you know if I was telling the truth about what I said? What if I made up something outrageous, but told you that I requested cheese bread?"

"Because Black Swan knights are highly trained in matters of communication. We're practically livin' lie detectors."

"I see. Very well then. I said, 'We're not tourists, you know. And you're burning daylight!'"

Torn thumped the table and grinned. "And that, gentlemen, is the truth."

Raif looked down his nose at her. "You said 'burning daylight'?"

Mercy looked around. "Did anybody hear that? It sounded like a voice coming from nearby."

Torn chuckled softly and clapped Raif on the shoulder.

When everyone had been served some sort of morning caffeinated beverage, Mercy took a few sips of coffee, listened to the easy banter between team mates, and when it grew quiet for a minute, put voice to the question that had been on her mind.

"If you, as knights I mean, are so great at reading people, I'd like you to give me your impression of Professor Yanov and Minister Igvanotof."

Gunnar spoke up. "Yanov is cheesy and Igahblahblah needs to get laid. Badly."

Mercy chuckled. "Anybody else? Anything useful?"

"What's your concern? Your reason for askin'?"

Mercy looked at Torn. "Just wanted to hear another perspective. Igvanotof...", she looked at Gun pointedly when she said it, "might have just been having a bad day. Or a bad life. Or there might be some other reason why he was behaving cold at best and hostile at worst."

"Look around," Glen said. "The dining room is deserted. We might not be tourists, but that doesn't mean they wouldn't *love* it if we were."

Mercy looked at Glen for a minute and slowly started to smile. "So. You're a boy wonder, Glendennon Catch."

"I wouldn't say that exactly. No." He looked over at Gun. "But I do have more than two brain cells to rub together."

Gun gaped. "I'll slap you down, boy."

"Punchline perfect. Gun. Can I have a ba-DA-bump?"

Mercy cut in to steer the kiddos back on topic. "You're saying that if The Order exercises its power to shut this down, closes the site, gag order on everybody who knows, millions of tourist dollars remain forever floating just out of reach in the Minister's imagination. So he has good reason to be displeased with us."

"Yes. That's what I'm saying."

She sat looking solemn while she considered that. "No wonder they thought I needed an 'escort'." She put the word 'escort' in air quotes. "Are you armed? Just curious."

Torn smiled his killer Irish smile. "Beautiful lady. Black Swan knights are always armed. Even when we're no' carryin' weapons."

She wasn't exactly sure what he meant by that, but any related question fled her mind because their food arrived just then. When the waiter had delivered everything satisfactorily and retreated to the place where waiters go and cannot be accessed by patrons, Torn said, "There's no' a need to worry for your safety. Nothin' will be happenin' to you. Or even us for that matter. Think about it. If they wiped us all out mysteriously, there'd be fifty investigators here within hours. If they wiped us out straightforward-like, there'd be an army here within days.

"Either way it would no' be a smart choice and, although BlahBlah seems an unhappy man, he does no' strike me as a stupid man."

"Okay, well, thank you for the analysis. That helps me know how to deal with him."

Half an hour later they met Professor Yanov and Minister Igvanotof at the entrance to the hotel. Yanov left his car and walked over to greet them with a smile while Igvanotof sat in the vehicle and stared straight ahead. Yanov suggested the two Order vehicles follow them to the site.

Mercy waited with a sullen Raif and a silent Gun while Torn and Glen brought the cars around from the garage.

Raif eyed her surreptitiously the entire time, thinking that archeologists are supposed to be old men who resemble the bones that fascinate them. Not fresh and freckle-faced beauties with hair that blazes under direct sunlight. They're not supposed to wear bright yellow sweaters over their khaki pants and hiking boots. And they're really not supposed to carry backpacks made of shiny evening gown material.

Every time he thought he'd looked enough and tried to drag his eyes away, something new drew his interest. Lost in thought staring at the swelling curves under the sunny sweater, he was caught off guard when she suddenly turned toward him in what seemed to him like a blaze of glory. The way her hair had swept off her shoulder caused his eyes to go there and get stuck.

"What?!?" She challenged him with a piercing look.

He brought his eyes level with her and blinked, then shook his head and looked away.

"Here they are," said Gunnar.

Mercy threw Raif one last reprimanding look before letting Gunnar guide her to the car.

Sitting in the back seat, it was impossible for Raif to fold his long legs so that he didn't encroach on Mercy's half of the space. Whenever a bump would bring his knee in contact with hers, she made a show of jerking away, sometimes harrumphing as well just to punctuate her revulsion at the idea of touching. The fact was that a car full of four people didn't reduce the awkward feeling of intimacy that was created by being trapped in a small space with a man who smelled a little like heavenly cologne, a little like a summer night breeze, and a lot like his own uniquely masculine scent. Her body was hyperaware of the proximity and seemed to have its own agenda regarding Rafael Nightsong.

They traveled on a cliff side mountainous road that curved in and out offering occasional picturesque views of the sea below. All in all it took only fifteen minutes to get there, even with the extremely slow speeds. They came to a stop in a small graveled car park carved, or blasted rather, from the mountainside in front of a monastery built many centuries before there were cars or a need to park them. The parking lot wasn't deserted, as she'd expected. There was a port-a-potty and six or seven vehicles already parked and deserted before their little caravan pulled in.

When the car came to a stop, Mercy was the first one out. Whether that was because of eagerness to get to her work or her eagerness to get away from the discomfort of Raif's nearness was irrelevant. She wanted out. Right away.

Mercy strode quickly toward the lead vehicle from which Professor Yanov and Minister Igvanotof were emerging. The side nearest her was the driver's, which was preferential since that meant she would encounter Yanov first.

He flashed his ready grin as he stood up straight and closed the car door. "It's a fine morning for mysteries. Is it not?"

She smiled in return. "Indeed it is and I couldn't be more ready."

"This way then." He gestured for her to accompany him.

As if she hadn't done her homework, Yanov proceeded to explain that the site, perched high above the town of Sozopol, was what remained of the fifth century monastery. Relics found under the altar had been moved to the National Museum. So there wasn't much left to see.

"Where are the remains of interest?"

Yanov grinned. "Come this way."

He was walking toward the edge of the cliff where there appeared to be nothing but a guard rail so flimsy it wouldn't stop a determined bicycle, and a few men standing around, ostensibly for the purpose of guarding the site.

When they reached the edge of the cliff, she could see that scaffolding had been built on the mountainside with supports driven deep into the rock. It was a good thing she wasn't afraid of heights.

They'd created a catwalk path to the cave entrance.

Yanov spoke to everyone in their little group. "Safety first." He grabbed a helmet off a bench and strapped it on. "No admittance without helmets. There is nothing to worry you, but the caves are classified as unstable because there is occasional seismic activity."

"How in the world was this found to begin with?" Mercy asked while the knights were choosing helmets that fit and putting them on.

"Oh. It's an interesting story. For some years, probably centuries, scrub trees have grown here and there on the cliff side. A few months ago a small earthquake loosened some of the rock and the trees fell away into the sea, which made the caves visible from the sea.

"Two boys, teenagers, were fishing together in a row boat and noticed. I don't know how or why word of that spread to the Ministry of Antiquities or what exactly led them to fund further investigation." He turned to Minister Igvanotof. "Do you know?"

The Minister shrugged and looked away as if that was an actual answer to the question.

In turn, Yanov shrugged and smiled at Dr. Renaux, then continued. "When the skeletons were discovered, the site was shut down immediately. I suppose someone working in the Department of Antiquities contacted your organization? I don't know. All I know is that authority changed hands within hours and I was sworn to secrecy.

"Very strange. Huh?" Mercy agreed that if she had been in his position she would think the whole thing more than strange. "I know you brought some of your own equipment. These men," he waved toward the men standing by the guard rail, "are here to carry what you need."

"Thank you. Let me see what we have first and then decide."

"Very good. With your permission I will lead the way."

"Right behind you." Mercy turned and looked over her four escorts, ostensibly to indicate that she was forging ahead.

She heard laughter behind her and turned to see Torn looking at Gunnar. It wouldn't take a human lie detector to guess that Gun was afraid of heights. She reached past Torn with a glare, grabbed Gun's wrist and pulled him forward so that he was next to her on the mountain side. Hopefully his psyche would accept the fake security of having a cliff on one side and Mercy on the other.

She leaned into him and whispered, "Okay?"

It was far too cool for the telltale sweat she saw trailing from Gun's temple. He nodded. In a stronger voice she said, "Gunnar. Please take my hand so that the heights don't make me feel unsteady."

She didn't wait for his agreement, but grabbed onto his bear paw of a hand and squeezed. The look he gave her fell somewhere between gratitude and adoration.

Raif quietly watched her extraordinary display of empathy and kindness and castigated himself for being the world's worst judge of character. She couldn't possibly be more different than he'd originally thought when he'd first seen her at the great speed dating fuckup.

Glen leaned over to Raif and said, "I'm not fond of adventures that begin with warnings about unstable mountains."

Raif looked over, smirked, said, "Well, kid. You wanted to be a knight. This is the gig. You get what you get," then walked off.

"Hey," Glen yelled after him. "Thanks for the pep talk." Raif waved his hand without looking back. Glen started forward. When he passed Igvanotof leaning against a rock wall, he said, "Are you coming?"

Igvanotof shrugged and never looked directly at Glen.

Entering the mouth of the cavern, one by one they switched on their head lamps. The chamber with the two skeletons was located about twenty-five feet inside. The stone ceiling was high enough to allow even Gunnar to stand upright, but the chamber where Mercy needed to work was really too small for four knights, one local and an archeologist.

"For starters, I'm going to need more light and less people," she said.

"We had lights powered by generator, but when the inquiry stopped they were removed. "

Mercy nodded. "How long would it take to get them back again?"

Yanov pursed his lips. "A day."

Mercy heaved a big sigh. "See if you can make it happen in four hours. No gas powered generators. We don't want to be breathing those fumes in this enclosed space."

Yanov stepped out on the catwalk where he could get a signal and make a call.

"I'm not going to be able to get very far without more light. There's only so much I can do with these." Mercy pointed to the headlamps on their helmets. "And it's pretty much already been done."

"What do you want to do?" Glen asked.

"Go wait outside in the sunshine, I guess, "

"Good news!" Yanov returned sounding pleased. "We can have more lights here in two hours."

They spent the next three hours sitting on the rocks of ruins part way up a mountain overlooking the

Black Sea. Some might feel that there are worst ways to spend a morning, but Dr. Renaux was antsy about having a closer look around her assignment and at least three of the four knights felt their time was being wasted babysitting a redhead and two skeletons when they should be on rotation for vampire hunting. So, all in all, the time passed slowly.

After a couple of hours, Glen opened the trunk of the equipment car and produced bottled waters for everybody. He made a delivery stop, handing over three bottles to Mercy, Torn, and Gun then turned and headed toward where Raif sat on an outcropping alone.

Raif had situated himself on a flat rock where he could watch Dr. Renaux surreptitiously without having to listen to the flirting going on with Torn. He hadn't missed the fact that the two of them had been putting on a mating dance show ever since she'd boarded the plane in New Jersey. It was a wonder that he'd been able to eat while watching the cutesy display the two of them put on at breakfast.

When he'd tried to join in the conversation, she'd mocked him, turning to Torn with wide eyes and blinking exaggeratedly. *Did you hear something?* Torn had laughed and winked and encouraged her. Traitor.

Raif was sure that, later that night, he'd hear Torn sneaking off down the hallway for a clandestine screwing of Dr. Renaux. That is, if it didn't turn out that her prim rigidity made entry impossible. As much as he wanted to tell himself he didn't care, he knew he was wishing that he was the one who'd get to find out whether that feminine body felt cold as steel or soft, warm and pliable.

He was lost in those thoughts when Glen walked up and held up a plastic bottle. "Water?"

Raif looked up, then reached out to take it. "Thanks."

"You always so antisocial?"

"I'm not antisocial. I'm just not into small talk."

"Oh. Small talk. I can see that," Glen said thoughtfully.

"Something else?" Raif asked like Glen's presence was an irritant.

"No. Just thought I'd try to get to know you better. Since we're going to be team mates and all."

"Not much to know."

"I'm betting there is. You strike me as a complicated sort."

Raif barked out a belligerent laugh, looked at Glen and shook his head. "You know, kid. I've been called a lot of things since I've been wearing a Z Team brand on my hindquarters, but 'complicated' is a new one."

"Yeah? Fits though, doesn't it?"

Raif raised his chin and looked down his nose with a ghost of a smile. "I'm not much of a talker. Why don't you tell me *your* story?"

Glen wasn't the least put off by the hint of a challenge and didn't hesitate.

"Okay. One of my grandfathers is a werewolf. I don't shift, but I have some of the characteristics, like the vocal cords. I'm not a second son, but they made an exception for me because they thought I fit the profile. I do except that I'm not as angry as most." That got a laugh out of Raif.

"I got a big break because of Elora Laiken's dog. It was a right place, right time kind of deal. She used to take him out in the courtpark for a run and play. The dog and I hit it off. So she started tapping me to dogsit when she had to be away.

"When B Team got transferred to Edinburgh on temporary assignment, they took me along as dogwalker. There was a lot more to that job than just walking the dog. But anyway, while I was there, I learned a lot about Order business, made some pretty wonderful fucking contacts, and got to date my share of fae girls.

"About a year ago, when we had to mount a rescue mission for Lady Laiken, I got put in charge. After that people started treating me differently. Did the temporary Sovereign thing when Nememiah died. Hated it.

"I'm head over heels in love with an Order brat. Sir Storm's daughter. But she's disappeared, deliberately, because we had a fight - about me throwing in with Z Team actually. Now I don't have any way of reaching her. It sucks." He pushed his thumb into the valley near his heart where his rib cage came together. "Makes my heart hurt when I think about it. So I'm trying not to.

"That's my story. Your turn."

Raif gave Glen a sideways look and smiled. "You'd be great at speed dating." They heard a truck downshifting like it was struggling up the last part of the steep road. "I'm thinking that must be the professor's enlightenment."

Glen laughed. "Enlightenment. That's a good one. Don't think you're off the hook. I gave you my story. Now you owe me yours."

Raif stood up and raised his hand to rest for a second on the slope of Glen's trapezius. "Some night when I've had enough tequila to loosen the shyness."

"It's a date," Glen said.

They walked together toward the truck. The driver and his helper were heading toward the rear to open up the back doors. When they started unloading the lights and generators, they were joined by a couple of other men who had, apparently, been hanging around for the purpose of assisting with such a task, should the need arise.

When Glen and Raif began to help lift one of the generators, there was a rapid conversation in Bulgarian that resulted in an unmistakable impression that the help of the foreign visitors was not needed or welcome.

Raif lifted his palms and backed away. "Fine. Have it your way."

When they rejoined the others, Glen said, "What about lunch? You think they have taco trucks here?"

Torn's eyes danced with lively elfin amusement. "I do no' believe they will be comin' 'round with tacos, but if such a vehicle did turn up, I must know, would you actually eat from it?"

Glen's hand rubbed over his torso and looked around. "Depends on how much longer until food."

Torn laughed and said to the others, "We forgot we have a team member with the special needs of a boyo still growin'."

After another forty-five minutes, Yanov made his way across the gravel lot toward Dr. Renaux and company. "The lights are working. Are you ready to begin?"

"Yes, thank you." Mercy stood up. With a glance in Glen's direction, she turned to Yanov. "Do you think we might ask someone to go for takeout lunch? The Order will pay of course." She looked to Torn for confirmation of that and he nodded.

Raif despised the fact that she'd come to the conclusion that Torn was the guy to ask. Officially, it was Gun who had been appointed leader by Storm, even though Black Swan teams had a tradition of not naming leaders.

"Yes. The truck drivers will stop and place an order at an establishment that will deliver. We will let your, uh, party know when sustenance has arrived."

"Sustenance!" Glen's exclamation was so full of joy and enthusiasm it made the others chuckle. "Great word, Professor. And just what I had in mind. I'm needing some serious protein and I wouldn't mind a few carbs to go with that."

Yanov didn't really understand Americans, but smiled and pretended comprehension. He spoke to the truck drivers who nodded ascent and started back down the mountain with a rumble and a grind of gears.

The four knights agreed that, since there was only one way into the cave, there was no need to have everyone hovering over Dr. Renaux at once. In fact, they reasoned that they might be more effective if they were in a position to see what was coming. So they agreed that they would rotate duties. Two would take up a position at the edge of the scaffolding, where the site was cordoned off from view. From that vantage point, they could see the parking lot, part of the road that ascended to the monastery ruins, with the catwalk and cave entrance behind them. One would remain at the cave entrance and another would stay with their charge while she carried out her mission.

In determining who would do what first, they used typical Z Team protocol – rock, paper, scissors. The winners of the first round would compete for who chose first until each knight had an initial assignment, as decided by Fate. Every two hours they would change places. The person in the cave would go to the catwalk entrance. The person at the mouth of the cave would guard Dr. Renaux.

The first round was decided. Torn and Gun would take up position at the catwalk with Raif at cave entrance, and Glen with the beautiful archeologist. They had barely gotten her equipment set up where and how she wanted it when, just an hour into the plan, lunch arrived in a car that gave the term "beater" a whole new meaning. In addition to sounding like it was dragging its muffler, the paint job it needed ten years before – and every one since then, had been skipped. At present it was simply past saving.

Torn announced the dinner bell to Raif who relayed the news to Glen and Mercy. She laughed when she saw that Glen was exercising a good deal of restraint to stop himself from running her down.

"Hungry?" she teased. His answer was a groan. "All right. All Right. Go on and eat."

"I can't leave you," he pleaded.

"Oh? So you need me to go with you? What's in it for me?"

Glen narrowed his eyes. "I can't offer my body if that's what you're getting at. Rosie would kill me."

Suppressing the smile that wanted to erupt in response to Glen's refusal of sex that hadn't been requested, a few images of the sort of guy who *was* her type flickered across the screen of her imagination.

"Rosie? Who's Rosie?"

Another groan, louder this time. "Okay. Here's what's in it for you. If you'll accompany me to lunch, like a good professor of archeology, I'll tell you the whole story. And it's a good one."

Without further delay, she put her tools down and wiped her hands on the brown canvas apron she was wearing. "I can't resist a good story. Especially if love is involved. There is love involved, right?"

He showed her a grin that made her think Rosie was a lucky girl. "Oh yeah."

Lunch was served in a pan. Not a disposable takeout container, but an actual pan. It was a dish called moussaka, a casserole of potatoes, ground meat, and tomatoes flavored with sea salt and bay leaves, topped with white sauce. Each one of them was given a pan big enough to feed a family of three.

The Minister, conspicuously absent from lunch, seemed to come and go according to an agenda known only to him.

By the time Mercy had eaten a third and was stuffed, Glen had finished his.

When she passed the rest of hers over, he grinned like it was Yule and said, "No sense in letting perfectly good Bulgarian pan lunch go to waste."

Yanov said that, knowing how Americans love sweets, they had included pieces of Turkish baklava.

When Glen grabbed as many pieces as he could hold in his hand, Torn said, "Do no' eat that. Sugar will make you soft."

Glen sneered at Torn. "When I start getting soft, we'll talk about modifying my eating habits. Until then, you mind your dessert and I'll mind mine."

"Very well. When the time comes that you can no' keep up, do no' say no one warned you about the pitfalls of indiscriminate eatin'."

"Duly noted," Glen said with his mouth full of baklava.

"Okay," Mercy stood. "You guys can stay here, bask in the sun and have an after-lunch nap if you want, but I have work to do."

"Does this mean lunch is officially over?"

"It is for me," she said and started away.

Naturally they all got up and followed. Where she went, they went until she was safely back at Jefferson Unit. When Glen reached the edge of the catwalk he stopped.

"What are you doin', rookie? You're in the cave," Torn said.

Glen held up his watch and turned the face toward Torn. "Nope. It's been two hours. Raif's in the cave. You're at the entrance. Gunnar and I are here."

"May be technically true, but 'tis no' in the spirit of the arrangement. Lunch is no' supposed to figure in."

"I'm okay with truth that's technical. No such stipulations were made."

"And you're a stickler for rules, are you?"

"When it works to my advantage, yeah."

Raif watched Mercy walk away as if she had zero interest in juvenile squabbles between knights. She bent down when she reached the cave entrance to retrieve the helmet she'd left there, put it on, and disappeared inside.

"Let him have his fun," Raif said. "I'll go in the cave and you take the entrance. Or exit as the case may be."

Torn gave Glen a pointed look, but followed Raif.

When they were out of earshot, Gun said, "You may want to rethink baiting your team mates, kid. Those guys have long memories and a well-developed sense of justice. It may seem like fun and games right now, but teams have a way of evening things up and out."

Glen scowled a little. "So now you're telling me I've thrown in with three bitter, vindictive, vengeful old trolls with no sense of humor?"

Gun laughed out loud. "Yep. That about covers it."

Hearing someone's approach, Mercy looked up right into Raif's gaze which was so pale blue, so piercing, and so compelling she forgot to look away. Not wanting to be first to blink, Raif continued to stare until Mercy shook herself internally and averted her eyes wishing she'd remembered to glare at him.

Looking around, he moved to a spot that he apparently found suitable. He leaned his big body against the cave's rock wall and crossed his arms over his chest. The spot he'd settled on just happened to be right in front of where Mercy was working so that she couldn't help but be aware of his presence.

Between Yanov hovering and Raif loitering within peripheral vision, it was hard to concentrate. The knight was a major distraction, but she couldn't give him the satisfaction of telling him that.

After a half hour or so, she looked up, "Dr. Yanov?"

"Madame?"

"I need to take another look at the reports you'd submitted prior to our arrival. Do you have them with you?"

"Of course. They are in the auto." As he left to retrieve the satchel with the documents, they could hear the slight echo of his steps all the way to the entrance followed by a vocal exchange that must have been Yanov telling Torn where he was going and what he was going to do.

All the while Raif stared at Mercy as if he was studying a specimen on a lab slide. She could feel it. Her entire nervous system was reacting with an uncomfortable prickle. When she thought she couldn't stand one more exasperating second, she looked up with wild eyes and said, "What ?!?"

On cue, as if the mountain objected to her tone or the timbre of her question, the ground began shaking. Raif's gaze jerked to Mercy. He was feeling exactly the same thing he was reading on her face - shock. Even a veteran Black Swan knight, trained to react instantly to any foe or peril, is only human. And freezing in place is the way most humans react when the ground starts moving underneath them.

The last thing anyone expects is a betrayal by the earth beneath our feet. We take it for granted believing that, when faith in everything else has failed us, we can still rely on the floor of our shared habitat to remain stable and be our guaranteed constant. It's a covenant with our environment that is unshakeable right up until the moment that it shakes right out from under us.

It probably only took three seconds for Raif's mind to sort through the possibilities and fire back the word "earthquake", but that three seconds represented a lot of waste from the perspective of how much reaction time was available. The rumble was growing so loud that he couldn't hear Mercy's panicked shriek, but he saw the heaving almost knock her off her feet.

A quick glance behind him told him all he needed to know about which way to go. There wasn't much deciding. The tunnel was caving in between them and the entrance. With only one way to go, he grabbed Mercy and pulled her deeper into the cavern as they heard the grind and thud of thousands of pounds of rock and debris falling in behind them.

As they hurried further into the darkness, stumbling over uneven ground and tripping over loose rocks, the dust began to catch up with them so that they were coughing and trying to run at the same time. Then, just as it had begun – with no warning, the cavern grew silent as a tomb.

The instant that Mercy had that thought she regretted the use of the particular phrase 'silent as a tomb'.

When they stopped, their lungs went through three stages of recovery – coughing, then panting, and finally normal breathing.

If not for the headlamps on their helmets, they would have been experiencing a darkness more complete than most people ever see. When Mercy turned her head toward Raif, the lamp on the front of her helmet lit his face. She then did the single thing most unexpected and most inappropriate, given their situation. She laughed.

"What is so fucking funny?" her companion wanted to know.

She was still chuckling. "Your face is completely covered with dust and the way your eyes are peeking out, it just, I don't know, struck me as comical."

"Comical. You should see *you*."

"Then why aren't you laughing?"

"Because I'm sane."

"Oh don't even think about going there because that is *so* up for debate."

"Okay, look, before you go off on one of your little tangents..."

On the other side of the rubble, Gunnar and Glen had their hands full trying to rescue Torn. When the tunnel began to close he was forced onto the catwalk that was being supported by scaffolding. The scaffolding was the first thing to go, It came apart and fell down the mountain like it had been made of Tinker Toys. Fortunately Torn was able to grab onto a couple of feet of protruding rebar that had been sunk into the cliff wall to support the scaffolding.

The only thing keeping him from a long fall to a painful death was his grip and the strength of his biceps, which were burning from holding up his weight while he screamed for his team mates to do something.

"Hold on, we've got it under control," Gun yelled back.

"Are you bat droppin's mad, Gunnar? You do *no'* have it under control. My hands are slippin' and in another minute I'm likely to be meetin' Paddy, whose name I have taken in vain on an hourly basis most of my life."

Gun turned around to look at Glen and say, "What in hel's name should we do?, but Glen wasn't there. He looked at Yanov, who was frozen in indecision with all the color gone from his face.

Glen came jogging up with a spool of cable that had been left to connect the lights to the generators.

"What's that for?" Gun asked.

"I'm making a lasso out of this cable. Feed it to me."

"You know how to do that?"

"Yep."

"Would you two wankers stop fuckin' around and get me down?!? This is no' funny!"

Glen yelled back. "Okay. Get ready. I'm gonna rope your head."

"You're what?!?" Torn was one notch past hysterical.

"Rope your head. Here it comes."

"NO! WAIT!"

The cable had gone sailing through the air and smacked Torn on the side of the face before it slid by and kept going.

"You're gonna have to suck it up and help, Torn. When it comes by next time, let go with one hand so you can grab the cable and put it around your waist."

"LET GO?!? THAT'S YOUR PLAN?!?"

"Stop being such a baby. You're not the only one who needs rescuing, you know. Here it comes. Man up and grab the rope. Maybe you'd have more energy if you'd had some sugar with lunch."

There was no time to reply to that when Torn saw the makeshift cable lasso flying toward his face again. He pressed his lips together, let go with his left hand, reached for it and caught it. He shoved the circle over his shoulder and brought his left arm through before taking hold of the rebar again. He took three deep breaths, then tightened his grip with his left hand, let go with his right hand and pulled the cable so that it slipped past his right shoulder.

Glen had been poised, waiting for that exact moment. When he saw the loop clear Torn's other shoulder he jerked the cable so that it tightened around him.

"Gun. Grab this cable on the ground behind me. If he lets go, the only thing that's going to keep him from hitting bottom is the hold we've got. And prepare yourself. Since we don't have gloves, it's going to cut into our hands and hurt like the devil."

"Don't worry, brother. I'm right behind you," Gun said.

"Torn!" Glen shouted. "We've got you. You're gonna have to let go. It's gonna be scary because you'll drop a little ways at first and then swing, but it's okay. Just like rappelling. We're not gonna let you go. You may smack into the side of this mountain, but you're to survive it. You understand me?"

Torn knew he didn't have a choice. His hands were sweaty from the fear and they'd be slipping even if he still had the strength to hold himself up. Which he didn't.

"Do no' let me go!" And with that his hands slipped off the rebar.

As Glen predicted, he dropped and swung like a pendulum across the face wall. Fortunately he stayed close enough to the wall so that the impact didn't break bones. He was able to use his legs to create a braking effect and stop the swing back, just like rappelling – as Glen had said.. When his body came to a rest, his team mates started to pull him up.

Yanov and the other government employees who had been working as guards had grabbed the cable to help pull Torn up. The cord bit into their hands and stung, but after seven long minutes of pain and strain, they brought Torn up and over the top of the flimsy little guardrail.

He collapsed on the sand and gravel parking lot, as did Glen and Gun.

Yanov said something to Glen in Bulgarian, which he didn't understand, then remembered he needed to speak English. "Give me your keys. He needs water."

Without sitting up, Glen dug into his pants pocket and retrieved the keys to the equipment vehicle. Yanov had seen him take bottled waters out of the trunk so he went straight there hoping to find more. And, yes, there was a carton of twenty-four minus those that Glen had passed out at lunch. He grabbed an armful and hurried back to the knights as fast as he could.

Glen crawled over and raised Torn's upper body enough so he could drink water without choking. He slowly gave Torn water until he'd consumed two entire bottles.

Torn looked around, "Where's...?" Then he remembered. "Oh gods no."

Glen and Gun looked at each other, then at Yanov. "We're going to need your best engineers to figure out how to dig them out before they run out of air."

Yanov's sad eyes didn't change expression and he stood unmoving. "Forgive me for saying so, but it seems very unlikely that..."

"I don't know how you do things here," Gun said, "but *we* don't leave people behind until we're absolutely sure they can't be saved. Right now we're not sure of anything except that our people are trapped and we can't see or hear them."

"I understand and am very sorry to be the one to inform you, but I do not believe the Bulgarian government will incur the expense. Even if they would..."

"Even if they would? What?"

"The scaffolding would have to be rebuilt to support heavy digging equipment. Even with funding and permission to proceed, I don't think it could be accomplished in time, while sufficient air remains."

Glen scowled at Yanov. "I've seen reports of mine collapses on the news. Don't they have a way of boring through rubble to communicate with people who might be trapped? And to run an oxygen hose?"

Yanov cocked his head to the side like he was interested. "Truthfully I cannot answer those questions. That is far outside my area of expertise and I'm not familiar with new developments in the field."

Glen turned to Gun. "You gonna call it in?" Gun stared at Glen. "You're the honcho."

Gun shook his head while continuing to stare at Glen. "That's ludicrous. I'm 'honcho' in name only. When Torn's not in charge," he glanced at Torn, who was still lying on his back staring at the sky like he'd seen a miracle, "that would be you."

"Me?"

"Not to mention the fact that, of the three of us, which one actually knows the Director personally?"

Glen returned Gun's stare that was half determination and half plea then turned aside pulling out his phone as he walked away.

Gun walked over and squatted next to Torn. Without looking over at Gun Torn asked, "The kid makin' the call?"

"Yeah."

"I feel funny no' knowin' if Raif is alive or hurt or... Well, just no' knowin'. I was just thinkin' about the first time I met him. We were about the same age Glen is now. We'd both been in trouble and were bein' sent to the Yucatan on chupacabra duty as a punishment.

"I remember my Sovereign sayin' with a smile that there's only one thin' worse than goin' after vampire and that's chupa huntin'. Nasty creatures to be sure. Wily and way too many teeth for a species that lives on land.

"Raif and I, we got on the same plane in Phoenix and," he stopped and chuckled like he was reliving a good time, "you remember when they used to have the big reclinin' chairs on tracks so that the seatin' could be reconfigured?"

Gun nodded. "Yeah, I do."

"Well, we hit turbulence in flight. The truly frightenin' sort that reminds you that human bein's are no' meant to be sling shottin' around the globe in a hunk of metal. A hunk of metal whose integrity depends on whether or no' some welder had a fight with his wife.

"So I was grippin' the arm rests with white knuckles and tellin' Paddy I'd be a good boy if I lived to tell the tale. All the while, bins and compartments 'round the plane were flyin' open and slammin' shut.

"Then I hear this war cry whoop. I look over and see that Raif has released the brake that kept his chair in place. So every time the plane shifted, his chair would run up and back on the tracks. He'd slide one way and come to a slammin' stop like bumper cars. Then slide back the other. He was laughin' so hard.

"Naturally I did no' want to be left out. So I looked around for the release on my own chair. In seconds the two of us were ridin' the storm out. Literally." Torn chuckled again. "I forgot all about bein' afraid. He made big fun out of scary flyin'.

"You know it was right after that that somebody decided the chairs should no' be on tracks.

"He was so full o' life back then. Three years later, we'd both hit the wall of foolishness past which there is no tolerance. We were both assigned to Z Team in Marrakesh, but I did no' know he'd also be there until I looked up and saw him comin'. I was so pissin' glad to see him. I could no' keep the grin off my face.

"At the time, the other two on Z Team were old fuckups in their mid-thirties who'd been assigned to that cesspool so long they did no' even bother to bathe. After Raif had a day or so to get his bearin's, he realized what kind of consequence we'd got ourselves into. So you know what he said?

"Well, here we are, brother and, no doubt, we deserve it. So let us go find out who imports tequila and get tattoos."

They heard steps crunching on gravel and looked up to see Glen approaching. "The Director says they'll take it from here. He says everything that can be done will be done, for us to sit tight at the hotel after we get Torn cleared by medics. They'll keep us informed. Play by play."

"The Director said 'play by play'?"

"No. That was a paraphrase. Sue me."

"I do no' need to be poked and prodded by medics. I need Margaritas."

"Yeah? Then how come you're still lying down in a parking lot looking like your body just smacked into the side of a mountain?"

"You're a funny kid. He's a funny kid, is he no', Gun?"

"Hysterical, Torn. Let's get you to the car and then decide about the clinic."

"I'm no' goin' anywhere."

"What do you mean?"

"I'm no' leavin' here until Raif comes out of that hole."

Gun and Glen looked at each other. Gun cleared his throat. "I get the sentiment, brother. I love him, too. But setting up camp here in this parking lot? It's not going to bring him back sooner."

"No' the point and you know it."

"What is the point, then?"

Torn didn't answer. After a long pause, Glen said, "Do you feel like it would be kind of a betrayal to leave?"

Torn didn't answer, but Glen could see his jaw clenched.

Glen nodded, mostly to himself. "Here's the deal. Our orders," he motioned between Gun and himself, "are to take you to a hospital and make sure there's no concussion or breakage. After that, we've been told to go to the hotel and wait. That's exactly what we're going to do even if we have to drug you to get you to the car."

Torn shot a death glare at Glen, who had started to look and sound a lot like authority.

Glen continued. "However, after we've gotten a med green light, and, after you've gone back to the hotel for a nap and a meal, I'll bring you back here until it gets dark."

Torn seemed to be thinking about that. "Paddy. He's goin' to be cold in there. That hole feels like a meat locker."

"Well," Gun said. "He's not alone. Maybe they'll call a survival truce and keep each other warm."

CHAPTER 18

"My little *tangents*!" She shouted as if the incredulity of it couldn't be grasped by the human brain.

"You know, this is *exactly* why they don't allow women in mines."

Mercy gaped. "You're saying you think the collapse is my fault? Because I'm a woman?!? You're supposed to be an educated person, regardless of appearance to the contrary. I know that you of all people do not believe that superstitious nonsense."

He turned to her with an expression that was so smug it was smarmy. "I wasn't talking about that. I'm talking about the fact that no one wants to die with fucking yammering and shrieking hurting their ears." His face was inches away from hers by the time he finished his tirade. "Bitches and their runny mouths!"

"You really are an imbecile, you know that?"

"Maybe, but this imbecile is your only hope of getting out of here alive, Your Royal Cuntness."

"You did *not* just say that."

"I did." He got right in her face and grinned as he said it, but she didn't miss the way his eyes lowered to her mouth and lingered there a little too long.

She backed away a couple of feet and regarded him warily. After a lengthy pause, she responded with a quiet calm he hadn't expected. "That really was an ugly thing to say."

He turned his back to her and took a deep breath. When he felt like he had his emotions under control, he turned back.

"I was trying to tell you that we need to take care of a couple of things. First, are you hurt?"

She stopped and took inventory. There was a stinging on her leg. She angled the headlamp toward it. When she put the light on it, she could see that it was a scrape that needed some cleaning and some antibiotic salve, but not stitches.

Raif bent to take a close look. "Is that the worst of it?"

"Yes. You?"

"I'm fine."

"Really fine or macho fine?"

He looked up at her. "I have no idea what 'macho fine' is?"

"It's that thing men do when they don't want to make an effort to communicate or when they feel all depends on preserving a delusion of being super-human."

"Delusion, huh. Got it all figured out, don't you?"

"Is that what you're doing? Are you hurt somewhere?"

He turned a smile her way that she could read as wicked even through the dust. "Are you wanting an excuse to check me over? Inch by inch?"

"Okay. Not hurt. I believe you. What's second on your agenda?"

"Second is preserving what little resources we have. One of us needs to switch off the helmet light. That will make the light we've got last twice as long."

"Good idea. I'll do it."

"Okay."

"What do you mean 'okay'?"

"I mean okay. How many ways are there to take that?"

"You're supposed to say, 'I wouldn't hear of it. I'll switch mine off first.' That would be the gentlemanly thing to do."

"Yeah, well, I have no aspirations to be a gentleman. Unless you mean it in the sense of being a frequent patron of strip clubs."

"What a surprise!" She said with as much sarcasm as she could infuse into three words. "Exactly what I would expect from somebody who couldn't get a *real* date if his life depended on it. Naturally you would have to resort to looking at women who are being *paid* to let you look."

He gaped. "It shouldn't surprise me that your first reaction to this predicament is to act like a raving bitch."

"You, on the other hand, haven't missed a beat. You're still the same dick I know and loathe."

"You're calling me a dick?" He barked out a laugh riddled with ridicule. "What's it like to be the only woman in history so caustic that she could bring down a mountain WITH A SINGLE WORD!!"

By the time he finished that sentence he was yelling. He braced for her next volley of insult and barb, but instead saw that her face had gone slack and her bottom lip trembled.

"Holy shit. I didn't mean..." Raif had no idea how to go about damming up an impending burst of female emotional turmoil. The idea of making a woman feel better was far outside his skill set and even farther outside his comfort zone. "You know that was just trash talk, right? You can't really start an earthquake like that."

She sniffed and looked away. "I know that. You don't get a doctorate in archeology without learning a little geology along the way." She tried for haughty, but was quivering on the inside because she wasn't entirely sure that she didn't cause the quake. Sometimes an unfortunate pairing of timbre with the right note on the scale can create a vibration that destabilizes...

"You know they're going to do everything humanly possible to get us out of here."

"Would you mind looking to your right?"

"Why?"

"So I can see what's there. The only light we have between us moves with your head. I think I might as well sit down because there's no place to go."

He looked to the right. The ground next to the wall was uneven and the floor of the cavern featured a variety of embedded sharp rocks. He looked to the left and found a small spot where the floor looked like smooth sand.

"Right there," he said, pointing to the spot with his headlamp. "We can rest for a little bit."

"Rest for a little bit before what?"

He shrugged. "Nothing concrete, but it's not give up the ghost time until we've surveyed our options. When I was a kid I was fascinated by the Knights Templar. I remember something about some of these old mountain monasteries having escape tunnels underneath. They were always getting raided by thieves..."

"And the Pope, himself."

"Yeah. Maybe not the Pope *himself*, but at least his minions. Anyway if this happened to be one of those..."

"Then we might come to a way out if we go farther in."

Raif shrugged and nodded, bracing in expectation of verbal abuse. He knew she was going to tell him it was a truly stupid idea.

"You're a lot smarter than you look, you know that?"

That was just about the last thing he expected to hear from Dr. Renaux.

"I thought I was an imbecile."

She giggled and he had to admit he liked the sound of it a lot better when it was directed toward him and not Torn.

"Maybe you're an imbecile who has his moments."

They sat down a foot apart on the small patch of smooth ground and put their backs against the cold cavern wall. Unlike an overstuffed sofa, it wasn't going to warm up from body heat after a while.

"I don't want you to get your hopes up or anything. Odds are greatly in favor of us dying in here, hating each other. I don't know which will get us first: lack of air, lack of water, or lack of food."

"Don't sugarcoat it." He shrugged as if to say it was what it was and no apology should be necessary. "Well, just look at it this way. I'm a cheap date."

Raif laughed in an open and unguarded way that seemed antithetical to everything she'd learned about him up to that point. "Hey," he said. "It's our second date and we're escalating. Maybe next time we can cause the entire universe to implode."

She giggled again. "What you said about us hating each other..." She let that sentence trail off and die.

"Yeah?"

"We can't do anything about the air or water or food, but we don't have to die hating each other." Raif didn't respond. "So tell me something. What was it about me that made you hate me instantly? On sight? I mean at the, um, speed date lunch."

He let out a big sigh and didn't answer right away. "I didn't hate you. Far from it. That... behavior. It was more like a preemptive strike."

"Preemptive strike? I don't get it."

"You asking to hear my sob story?"

"Uh. Sure. I'm not otherwise occupied."

"Well, like I said I don't think there's a rat's ass chance of us getting out of here still breathing, but just in case, can we agree that what happens in the cave collapse stays in the cave collapse?"

She turned her head toward him and smiled. She couldn't read his expression because the helmet light was shining in her eyes, but he appreciated that smile, even if it was covered with teeny bits of ground up rock.

"Sure," she said.

"Okay. Here goes. I was in an awkward place when I first started noticing girls. They made fun of me and I learned not to trust them."

When it sounded like he might not say more, she prompted. "What do you mean by awkward place?"

He'd never talked to anybody about his damage. Not even Torn. But sitting there in the abject blackness next to Dr. Renaux, whose faint scent could still be detected under the dust coating, it all just came bubbling up like a geyser.

"My mother left my dad with a promising career as an aerospace engineer and two little boys who looked just like her. I don't know why she left. If Dad knew, he never said.

"You hear about people who go into depression and then bounce back. Well, he just did the first part. No bounce back. He knocked around odd jobs for a few years making just enough to get by. When I was thirteen, he got a job working daytime security at a private school for rich kids, the kind who are already wearing Ivy League sweatshirts because they know where they're going to college *and* that they're going to get in.

"One of the perks of the job was free tuition and books for my brother and me. We got free tuition and books, but not the stuff that would help us fit in. Like wardrobe and good haircuts. We were trashy kids who lived in a rundown trailer park, or community as they preferred to call it. And we looked like what we were.

"My older brother managed it better. He was a lot more easygoing, good natured about the teasing. Eventually his peers decided he was more or less cool, like their mascot James Dean or something. I don't know. Let's just say that my adjustment had sharper edges.

"Long story short, I figured out early that I liked girls and wanted some of what they had to offer. Unfortunately the admiration wasn't mutual."

"That's... hard to believe." Mercy ventured in a soft voice after he was silent for a bit.

Raif really didn't know what to say to that. So he went on.

"The girls... They looked so clean and shiny and smelled so good, not like perfume, more like the smell of wholesome. I don't know. It's hard to explain. They looked like they'd been taken care of. Of course they were. Taken care of that is. And I wanted to be close to that.

"When I tried to get close enough to talk to them, they looked at me like I'd gotten lost on my way to the back door. Sometimes they laughed. One girl, I remember, just sniffed. *Sniffed*. And turned away like I wasn't there."

Mercy could hear the emotion in his voice and could almost imagine the way he must have felt as a little lost boy.

"The other news is that, about the same time, everybody was starting to figure out that I was good in school. Despite rumors of me being a imbecile," his helmet light turned toward Mercy pointedly, "I was good enough to compete with the brainiacs. Right before I turned fourteen, Black Swan found me and I was out of there. Had *no* reason to want to stay.

"Fast forward to speed dating because of a bet I lost to Torn. First, I'd had a bad night. A really bad night. When I first saw you sitting there at that speed dating table, what I saw was what I imagined one of those girls might look like all grown up. Prim and proper and entitled and sure that nobody who wasn't fourth generation Yale was good enough to talk to her. So I lashed out."

"Preemptive strike."

He turned toward her thinking there was no reason to hold back. He didn't have any reason not to tell the whole story.

"Yeah. Seeing you sitting there almost knocked me over. I wanted you to like me so much and I was so sure that you were going to make me feel like a walking piece of shit...

"The thing is that, right after I blew the place up, I realized that maybe I hadn't been fair. I hadn't even given you a chance to say hello before I shut down all the possibilities. I deliberately put you on the defensive, but it wasn't you I was mad at. I figured that out."

"You did?"

"Yeah. For all the good it did. You were already long gone when I got my shit together and I didn't know anything about you. I remembered your first name, but not your last name. I was being so intent on not looking and feeling like a fool, again, that I left myself without any way to find you. Like an idiot."

"You wanted to find me?" She sounded like it was the strangest thing she'd ever heard, but she also sounded enthralled, which encouraged him to continue.

"Yeah. For all the good it did. So - and believe me I know how lame this is going to sound - I started going back there on days off. I'd just walk around the area hoping that maybe you lived or worked close to where that restaurant was." He laughed. "I got to know the neighborhood really well. I could mark on a map every single place to sit down or urinate. I could write a guidebook and call it *Looking for Mercy in Midtown*."

She'd been studying him quietly, soaking it all in, almost afraid to move. "Catchy title. And not a bad strategy either. Just so happens I work *and* live within a few blocks of there. It's probably surprising that you never saw me."

"Wow."

"Yes. So I've got to ask something. What were you planning to do if you saw me?"

He stared for a few seconds with the light shining in her eyes then put his head back against the wall and laughed. "You give me more credit than I deserve if you think there was a plan. Sometimes I rehearsed apologies, but when you tried to talk to me on the plane I had a brain freeze. Maybe I would have chickened out and just become a stalker."

"Wait. You had a brain freeze on the plane when I tried to talk to you? I thought you were just being an asshole."

"I can't blame you for thinking that. It wasn't my best impression."

"Yeah. But you looked for me? Tried to find me? To apologize?"

"Well... partly."

"What's the other part?"

After several moments of silence passed, he said, "It's your turn. Tell me about you."

"What about me?"

"You can start with, 'I was born...', and take it from there."

"I'm a long-winded teacher-type. You might be sorry you opened that door."

"I'll take my chances."

"Alright. My adoptive parents were killed when I was a baby. I was raised by a grandmother who hadn't been particularly impressed with the idea of adopting and had been very vocal with my parents about that. I know because at least once a day she reiterated that she'd warned them against adopting and pointed out that she'd been right because look how badly things had all turned out for her. She was saddled with some faceless stranger's kid.

"She went through the motions of care, but not the motions of love. So I knew I was missing something and I wanted that something I was missing.

"By second grade I had figured out that I was smart and that I could get positive recognition by doing smart things. I might not have had parents who doted, but I could stand on the fringes of approval if I pleased my teachers. So I studied. Hard. And eventually put myself through graduate school on scholarship and stipend."

"We have something in common then. We both pretty much raised ourselves. Mine were absent. Yours were dead. From a kid's point of view, it's about the same."

Mercy was thinking that the following day was her birthday and that she was the only person alive who knew that and cared. When she didn't respond right away, he pressed on.

"How did you end up at Columbia?"

"Luck. Mostly. In the early sixties, spy satellites found about ten thousand archeological sites in the Middle East. Lost cities with roads and canals. All 'undiscovered'." She put the word 'undiscovered' in air quotes although he didn't see that since his helmet light wasn't on her at the time. "Some of them were as big as a hundred and fifty acres. So archeologists all over the world began petitioning the governments of Turkey, Iraq and Syria for permits to excavate and investigate. It took nearly forty years to get in, but I was lucky enough to get taken on as assistant slash intern at one of the sites that was permitted to dig.

"I was there for a little over three years. One day my boss handed me a letter. It said there was an opening at Columbia. I remember looking up at him with a question on my face. That's when he offered to recommend me if I wanted it." The smile on her face revealed that she was reliving that day as she told the story. "Well, I'd never lived anywhere like New York, but the opportunity seemed like a gift from the gods. I think I might have squealed," she laughed, "which both embarrassed and pleased the man I worked for. He was a famous guy, at least in circles frequented by archeology academics, attached to de Gaulle in Paris. Very prestigious. I knew a recommendation from him would go a long way.

"He told me to keep the champagne corked until there was an actual offer, which was good advice, of course."

"But you got it."

She smiled. "But I got it."

He reached over and pulled away a tiny piece of rubble hanging from her eyebrow. "And now you're here."

"Now I'm here."

"Yeah. Tell me how that happened."

"Stays in the collapsed cavern, right?"

"Right."

"Okay. If we get out of here alive, you have to forget everything I've said. I was pretty disillusioned after the speed dating incident. I didn't come away from that feeling excited about the prospect of connecting with the opposite sex. So I gave up on the idea of maybe meeting somebody. Ever. And decided I needed to make some big changes in my life. Do something different..."

"Wait. Hold it right there. You're saying you were so upset about that scene with me that you gave up on the idea of dating?"

"I think you underestimate your heartthrob worthiness, Sir Nightsong."

"Dr. Renaux. You thought about me." He said it like he couldn't really believe what he was hearing.

"Call me Mercy. Yes. I thought about you."

"In a good way. Right?"

"I wouldn't go that far." He chuckled. "The experience was so horrible that I rededicated myself to work, but that didn't seem to be filling the…"

"Hole?"

She could tell that he was smiling an infuriating smile. "Was your development arrested at age thirteen?"

He laughed. "Probably."

"Anyway, I got a message from a man named Monq. It was so intriguing I had to check it out. I guess that's what archeologists do. We get intrigued by mysteries and have to go where they lead.

"He told me about vampire and, naturally, I thought he was a loon. Right up to the moment when a kid materialized out right next to my chair and showed me fangs.

"I'm still not sure why I didn't die of a heart attack on the spot. Seems like I should have, but I didn't even faint. Or scream. Isn't that what women are supposed to do? That's what women *always* do in movies."

The sound of his soft laugh came closer to making her heart skip than the vampire had. "Sooooo. Either you're special or they got it wrong."

"Which one? Right now I'm feeling like a disappointment to my gender. No fainting. No screaming."

"You want me to pick?"

"Yeah. You set up the parameters. Now choose."

"You're special." Although she couldn't see it, his smile became a grin. "*And* they got it wrong." She laughed. "So Monq figured a trick vampire show is worth a thousand words." She nodded. "And it worked."

"And it worked."

"And now you're here on this grand adventure that will probably end in our deaths."

"Hmmm. Nothing funny about that."

He took her by the hand and pulled her to her feet. "It has its drawbacks. But it's not all bad either. Finally found a way to get you alone. "

Sir Nightsong couldn't have surprised her more if he'd started singing "Dixie". He started moving forward being careful to keep the light where she could see in front of her.

"Anybody ever mentioned that it's hard to get a read on you, Nightsong? You're kind of a moving target."

"Nobody's ever said that in so many words. I have had a couple of people tell me I'm not worth trying to decipher. I think the exact words were along the lines of 'fuck off'."

"Can't imagine why anyone would ever have *that* reaction."

He chuckled. "You don't have to forget the… uh, incident. But I do think you should let me out of the penalty box. Since mine will probably be the last face you ever see and all."

"I can't see your face. When it's not dark, there's a light shining in my eyes."

After twenty minutes of moving further into the cavern they noticed three things. The cavernous space was getting larger instead of smaller. The air was getting thicker instead of thinner. And they could hear some noise ahead that sounded like an engine.

"Listen."

"What is it?"

He shook his head back and forth. "Let's go find out."

"Famous last words."

After several minutes of forging ahead they noticed that, with every few steps, they were able to discern a fourth factor in their ever changing equation. The cavern was getting lighter instead of darker. The engine noise was also getting louder. A faint glimmer of hope was starting to take root in their minds.

What they found at the end of their short journey seemed both miraculous and magical. The cavern opened up into a circular space about forty feet in diameter. The far side featured light coming from above and a small waterfall that fell into a pool.

They looked at each other.

"Good news or bad news?" Raif asked.

"Bad news first," she replied.

"It's a dead end with no way out."

"I don't like the bad news."

"Exactly why it's called bad news."

"What's the good news?"

"We're not going to die of thirst. Assuming that water is good to drink. We can shut the helmet light off thereby doubling our ability to light the darkness. Again. And, last but not least…"

"Yes?"

"We can wash the mountain off so I can see your beautiful face before I die."'

She cocked her head. "You think I'm beautiful?"

"Well… Not *now*." She hit him on the arm while he laughed. "I meant that in theory your beauty will be restored when you're cleaned off."

"Oh. In theory." She sat down on the ground.

He sat down in front of her. "Hey. You know what though? Seriously?"

"What?"

"I think we should try to use what time we have left well."

She looked around. "Doing what?"

"Fucking." She picked up a pebble near her hand and tossed it so that it landed against his abs. "Hey. What was that for?"

"Fucking? Really?"

"Yeah. Look, I know I'm not a ladies' elf like Finngarick. Maybe I'm not your death by sex fantasy, but *you're* mine."

Mercy gaped, not knowing whether he was serious about the sex or the fantasy or any of it. And she seriously wasn't about to let him know that the face she saw in her most erotic nocturnal moments was his.

"I don't know you well enough to be able to tell when you're joking and when you're not."

He nodded like he was mulling that over. "I get that. So we'll make it easy. I'm half joking about the fleshy friction. I'm perfectly serious about the fantasy part."

She stared at him for a while trying to figure out if he was telling the truth about telling the truth. "If you're being honest, about the fantasy part, then thank you. It's nice to go out on a high note."

Reaching for her bronze taffeta back pack that would never be stylish, or clean, again, she began digging around inside. After a few seconds she said, "Yes! I thought so!"

"What?"

She withdrew a packaged rectangular item and held it aloft. "A protein bar! Don't worry. I'm giving you half."

"Protein bar." He made a face. "Those things leave an aftertaste like road kill."

"First, it's food. Second, you're actually going to complain about the taste now? When it could be your last meal? Third, how do you know what road kill tastes like? Fourth, strike that last question. I don't want to know. But if that's really how you feel, I'll just eat the whole thing myself."

He launched himself at her feet and sat on his knees, holding his curled hands up like begging paws.

She had to hand it to him. The guy wasn't just drop dead gorgeous in an exotic and bad boy way. He could also be cute with cross currents of little boy that called to her nurturing instincts. He was a mystery, an unlikely combination of traits that was near irresistible to a professional mystery chaser.

Rolling her eyes, she unwrapped the bar. What she revealed looked a little like jerky pressed with straw. She broke off half and started to hand it to him, but he leaned forward and opened his mouth. She extended the half bar toward his mouth, expecting him to take a bite, but he took the entire piece and began chewing while grinning. Mercy wasn't sure whether to be appalled, amused or amazed that his mouth was that big. But she wasn't going to insist on manners when they were spending their last hours in a cave together.

Raif walked over to the pool to try the water. He leaned down to smell first. When it passed that test, he dipped his hand in for a taste. "Well, I'll be a..."

"What? What is it?" She came up behind.

"It's warm." He looked up at her. "Mercy, you're a good luck charm. There must be a fissure underneath leading to some volcanic activity down deep."

She stared at his upturned face for a beat before she started laughing. "Got to give it up for your attitude, Raif. Not everyone would call this situation lucky."

His face split into a grin that she knew would be heart stopping if his face was clean. "Let's go in."

"In?" She looked at the water dubiously while Raif stood up and started stripping off clothes.

"Come on. We're both freezing. The water will warm us up. It's like a natural hot tub."

"I don't know."

"What don't you know, Mercy? If there was ever a time to throw caution aside, this has got to be it."

He was making good points both about the chill and the caution. She grabbed the hem of her sweater and pulled upward.

CHAPTER 19

Farnsworth looked at her phone. It was a text from Rev. *Dinner at my place tonight. 8. Don't get caught up and be late.*

She smiled at the phone thinking she was the most blessed woman who ever lived. How many could say they lost their love, but got him back again? One. So far as she knew. *Okay. What shall I wear?*

Rev: *Little as possible.*

It was a private joke that didn't seem to get old.

She set the alarm on her phone so that, if she did get caught up in work, she'd have a warning and know when to quit. It was a good thing she'd had the foresight because she was in the middle of looking at the reconciliation of the clinic budget when she heard the chime.

At precisely eight she knocked on Rev's door. The Sovereign's quarters were a little bigger and more luxurious than any other residence at the Unit, but they still wouldn't be called palatial. She noticed the stainless steel room-service style cart sitting next to the dining table, which could seat four, but was set for two.

"You didn't cook?" she teased.

"I'm afraid that if I impress you any more you're going to spontaneously combust."

"I'd laugh at that, but can't argue. You are extremely impressive."

"Nice to have a woman who appreciates the extent of my wonderfulness. Have I ever told you that you look good in red?"

She smiled. "Uh-huh. What are we having? Smells good."

"It's a surprise. One of several."

She raised an eyebrow. "Oh?"

"Mashed potatoes smothered in flank steak smothered in onions. I guess it's a theme dish."

"Uh-huh. What's the safe word?"

"Hmmm?"

"Nothing. So we're eating light. Going dainty?" she quipped.

"There's asparagus spears," he said defensively. "But I'm a working knight right now, which means I have to have *real* food that will help me stay in shape."

"And not get flabby like you used to be?"

She snickered. But he didn't look like he appreciated her attempt at humor. In fact, he'd gone still and was looking far too serious. "We can't joke like that or talk like that. Not even when we're alone together. If we do, we'll get comfortable with it and, sooner or later, there'll be a slip. That slip could lead to questions and that, for all I know, could lead to the end of... this."

A chill settled around her as she confronted the possibility of losing him all over again. She folded her arms protectively around her middle to still the trembling and hoped he didn't see it. After all, if she couldn't talk about what had happened, that meant she also couldn't tell him about how much she feared losing him again.

"I understand." She nodded slowly. "You're right. I've got some work to do editing my words. I don't know how to guard my thoughts though. Sounds hard."

"Believe me. It is."

"Don't worry. Hard is what we do for a living, right?"

"Right." His face had softened as she expertly diffused the issue. "Let's eat."

Over dinner Rev told her some of what happened with the trainees on his night patrolling. Farnsworth shared that Kristoph Falcon was hopelessly enraptured by her assistant and that he found a reason to come to the office every day.

"That's going nowhere. There's got to be a six year age difference," he shook his head chuckling. When he looked up and saw that all the color had drained from his fiancée's face, he realized too late what he had said. "Wait. I didn't mean... You know I didn't. Cripes. Just shoot me now."

"Well, it's out there. How you really feel," she said quietly. "I'd rather know than not know."

He stood up so fast she didn't have time to track the movement as she was pulled up and into his hard body. She would have liked to be the sort of woman who could simply give herself over to melting against him and shedding a few tears, but she wouldn't. She might have felt comforted, but right or wrong, her self-esteem would have suffered.

"Look at me." She stared at his chest. "Look at me." After a few beats she managed to raise her eyes. "The reason why I didn't think about the difference in our ages when I said that is because I don't think about the difference in our ages. As far as I'm concerned it doesn't exist. When I look at you what I see is my beautiful, sexy woman who's soon to be my beautiful, sexy bride. I see everything I ever wanted in my future all rolled into a soft package with just the right curves in just the right places.

"The way I feel about you can't be reduced to numbers. Please tell me you understand that."

She nodded and pressed her cheek into his chest so he couldn't see how much work it took to keep her tear ducts dry. He stood and held her, swaying back and forth, sensing that she needed reassurance.

After some time, when she was satisfied that order had been restored in her world, she said, "What's for dessert?"

He smiled and kissed the top of her head. "Peach cobbler. It's being kept warm with that candle thing." He nodded toward the cart. "Got coffee, too."

"And another surprise?"

He looked down at her. "Yep. Have a seat."

He refused to tell her what the surprise was until she'd eaten her cobbler and made the requisite yummy sounds. He took the dessert plates away and set them on the cart.

"More coffee?"

"Enough! I can't stand it one minute longer!"

"I never realized how impatient you are."

"Impatient? I have the patience of Jonswil."

"Uh-huh." Reaching toward a nearby chest with a long arm, he opened the top drawer and withdrew a file.

She looked both intrigued and ill at ease. "What is it?"

"Something that Storm had apparently put in motion when he was still acting as temporary administrator. This came in last night when I was out with B Team, but I wanted to make sure you had some privacy when you received it."

"What on earth?"

He nodded toward the file. "Open it."

She looked down at the manila folder where her finger was resting heavily. It was hard to read what Rev's brown eyes were trying to convey. Intensity? Hope? Worry? She took a surreptitious deep breath and opened the folder.

On the left hand side, a candid photo was attached. It was a determined-looking young woman in an urban landscape, walking purposefully across what appeared to be a square. She wore a form fitted white shirt with exaggerated cuffs, a black knee length skirt, and had a heavy-looking brief style bag strapped cross body. It was a sunny day that picked up streaks of red in her auburn hair and, even though the photographer wasn't close when the picture was taken, there was an impression of freckles across her nose and cheekbones.

Farnsworth's first reaction was to wonder why her fiancé was showing her a photo of another woman. Another woman who was beautiful and much younger. She glanced up at him for a reaction, but he just lowered his eyes to the folder to indicate that she should continue.

When she'd finished studying the photo, her eyes moved to the right hand side of the folder and the first page of documents therein. There was a name at the top and next to that a birth date that made her breath catch. She looked back at the photo again and then reflexively clutched the folder to her bosom as if some part of her spirit hoped she could make up for twenty-eight years of separation and empty arms by doing so.

At first she'd thought she felt tears spring to her eyes, but none fell. When the first wave of shock subsided, she continued reading.

Mercedes Renaux.

Her adoptive parents were killed when she was a baby before she ever met them. She'd then been raised by a widowed grandmother who had admonished her son and daughter-in-law, in writing, not to adopt, but rather to graciously accept their childless state as fate and look toward hobbies to fill their time. A copy of that letter appeared in the file. Gods knew how The Order had obtained it.

It seemed the girl had an indomitable spirit. She wasn't particularly social, but she did well in school and eventually put herself through a Ph.D. program with scholarship and living frugally on a tiny stipend. That led to a field assistant/internship, which led to the teaching appointment at Columbia.

When Farnsworth had a chance to digest the information, she looked up.

Rev said, "I'm guessing the father had red hair and freckles?" She nodded. "Looks good on her. And so do your features and your legs." He pointed to the photo. "That's the same way you carry your shoulders when you're going somewhere with a mission to accomplish. I see you stamped all over her."

Farnsworth smiled through a haze and a cyclone of confusing emotions. "I want to see her." Rev's smile faded and he sat back in his chair, his mouth gone into a thin line. "What aren't you telling me?"

"Well," he began slowly, "the news is mixed. The good news is that she works for us."

"Black Swan?" Farnsworth was nothing less than astonished.

"Just came on recently. As in last week. She's on assignment in Bulgaria."

Little lines appeared between her brows. "What kind of assignment?"

"It's right up her alley. An archeology thing requiring her particular specialty. Something that needed to be looked into before the information gets out to the general public. I sent Z Team with her."

"Z Team!?!" Rev almost laughed. It seemed Farnsworth held roughly the same opinion of The Order's notorious bad boys as he did. "To escort and protect. You know, they have their flaws, but they can be trusted to do a job like that." She snorted her disagreement. "Well, there's more."

She didn't know if he was pausing for dramatic effect or if it was really so bad he couldn't bring himself to just come out with it. "Well?"

"Well... There was an accident at the site. A partial collapse of a tunnel and..." Rev didn't like the way Farnsworth's chest was suddenly rising and falling rapidly.

"And?"

"And she and one of the knights are missing."

"I need to go there." She stood and began looking around for her things. When Rev didn't move from his chair, her eyes flashed. "Now!"

"Susan, I can't get you there at this time of night. If you're serious about wanting to go..."

"No! Not *wanting* to go! *Needing* to go!"

"Okay, then. If you're serious about needing to go, then we can figure out a transport tomorrow morning."

"No. Tonight."

"Tonight?"

"You heard me."

"That's impossible."

"Impossible? Don't you dare say that to me! Nothing is impossible when The Order wants to make it happen. Nothing!" She picked up her sweater jacket and purse. "I've given my life to this organization and never asked for one damn thing in return. Until now. Get me transport tonight."

Rev stood up slowly and pulled his phone from his pocket. He touched the face a couple of times before looking at her face. He looked away quickly.

"Sorry to get you up in the middle of the night but I need a plane here, fueled up with fresh pilots, ready to fly to Bulgaria. And it couldn't wait until morning." Pause. "I'll wait. Thanks." Pause. "I'll owe you. Okay. Goodnight."

He ended the call and looked up. "Tvelgar says there's a plane that was going to overnight in Chicago. They can scramble around, get a fresh alternate crew, and be here in three hours."

"Thank you." She hugged him tight. "For everything. For the, uh, file and for getting me there. I've got to go pack."

"Okay. I'll meet you down at the front entrance," he looked at his watch, "at ten thirty."

"You don't have to see me off, Rev. I'm a big girl."

"I don't plan to see you off, Susan. I'm going with you."

"You can't go *with* me. There's too much to do here."

"Maybe this Sovereign learned some valuable lessons about how to live life from mistakes the last one made. I'm going with you."

She couldn't protest too much when she needed and wanted him to go so badly. Grabbing him around the waist, she planted kisses at eye level, on his shirt above his heart. "Thank you. That... means the world to me." That was the tearful tipping point. A person could only contain so much emotion without spill over. She looked embarrassed about the stray tear that she swiped away.

"Check the weather before you pack."

"I know."

Rev watched her close the door. His next call was to the Laiken-Hawking residence. Ram answered.

"It's Farthing."

"Oh?"

"I need to speak to both of you."

"You mean now? Where?"

"I could come to you if that's easiest."

"Suppose so. We'll freshen the coffee."

"Be there in five."

"One thin'. No matter what, no yellin' is allowed. There's a baby that will no' hesitate to interrupt a meetin' no matter how important we say 'tis."

"If there's to be any yelling, it will not be originated or instigated by me."

"Who is it?" Elora had muted the TV.

"'Tis the new Sovereign. He wants to see us both now and he's comin' here."

Five minutes later, Rev was lowering himself into a chair at the kitchen nook table with a mug of coffee.

"Something's come up and I need to respectfully request a slight amendment to our agreement. Just for the next few days. I wouldn't ask if it wasn't important. Well, hel, I may as well tell you. It's not going to be a secret.

"Farnsworth had a baby when she was a teenager. Her parents made her give it up. We located the girl, er, woman and it turns out she's a recent recruit. Works for us."

"Paddy," Ram supplied.

"Indeed. Based right here out of Jefferson Unit."

"'Tis a small world."

"Yeah. Thing is, Headquarters sent her on assignment to Bulgaria. I sent Z Team to escort her. There was a tunnel collapse and now Farnsworth's daughter, who she just learned about half an hour ago, is missing, along with Sir Nightsong."

"Great Paddy. The Fates seem to have taken a bead on the poor woman."

"Would seem so. Long story short, she's going tonight and I'm going with her."

Elora looked confused. "No disrespect, sir, and maybe it's not my business, but why would you be going with Farnsworth? There are other people who know her better."

"I doubt it. We're engaged." Rev looked at Ram and gave a tiny shake of the head.

"Wow," she said. "That was fast."

"Succinctly put, Lady Laiken, but you know how it is. The heart wants what the heart wants."

"Wow," she repeated. Elora seemed lost in thought for a few seconds, but then reengaged with the moment at hand. "So how can we help?"

"Well, I'm scheduled to patrol with B Team tonight. I was hoping you could get a babysitter and..."

"Yes. We'll do it."

Ram looked at her like he didn't know her. "Do you no' think we should talk it over, just the two of us?"

"Normally yes, but I've given this a lot of thought. I was going to bring it up after my patrol tonight when you'd had a chance to find out firsthand just how hard it is to sit home and not know what's going on. This latest crisis has just moved my schedule ahead by a day."

"Your schedule," Ram repeated drily. "I was actually goin' to have a talk with *you* today and let you know that I'm goin' out tonight instead of you. I am no' likin' the idea of my child's mother in the field. Particularly no' in light of the way these new biters are behavin'. Allegedly."

Elora gaped at him and Ram knew the flush in her cheeks was never a sign that an argument was going his way.

"You mean you were planning to make me fight my way onto B Team a *second* time?" She outrage-whispered so as not to wake Helm. "As for 'badly behaving biters', that's exactly the point I was going to make and my practical demonstration couldn't be more apropos to your phrasing."

"What demonstration?"

"You know how Helm is going through a biting phase?" Elora turned to Rev to catch him up with a summary. "When the baby doesn't get what he wants when he wants it, sometimes he turns red in the face, screams, and bites like a little pit bull. Three days ago he bit Ram on the shoulder." She turned to Ram, who was wearing a gray metal band tee. "Come on. Show our guest how it looks after three days."

Ram hesitated for a couple of seconds, eyeing her in challenge, but finally acquiesced and pulled the short sleeve up above his shoulder to reveal the bite mark . It was ugly. Helm had made a mold of his teeth out of his daddy's flesh. It was bruised all around and had the red telltale signs of beginning infection.

"Your baby did that?" Rev asked incredulously.

Ram nodded.

"It looks worse, Ram. When we're done here, you're going to go down to the clinic and have them take a look." Elora continued. "But back to my demonstration. Tonight, right here in this very high chair," she pointed to the chair for dramatic effect, "the child threw a similar tantrum - which had Hawking stamped all over it, by the way - and he bit the bejuices out of *my* forearm."

She then pulled up her sleeve and turned her arm over so they could both see that, from any and every angle, there was no sign she'd been touched.

Ram grabbed her arm and gave it a close inspection and then insisted on doing the same with the other arm. When he was satisfied with the inspection, he shrugged. "So you're a fast healer."

"No. The point goes much deeper than that. It's not that Helm bit me and I recovered quickly. It's that he didn't do any damage to begin with. Unless you count the fact that I think less of him and question his love."

Ignoring that last part, Ram said, "So you're tryin' to say you can no' be hurt?" He made a rude noise. "Talkin' to the wrong person, love. You're forgettin' that I happened to be there when we almost lost you to vampire bites. Made a righteous mess of that beautiful body if I'm recallin' correctly."

"I'm not forgetting that. But *you're* forgetting that, number one, I wasn't out with a team. I was alone. And number two, I wasn't taken down by vampire. It was a fellow knight, which is why I didn't see it coming." Ram responded by slumping down in his chair and starting to thump a nervous rhythm on the table with his hand. "Don't you see, Ram, if I'm on patrol, I can protect you. When the four of us are together, I may be able to protect Kay and Storm as well. That's why I wanted to be a knight to begin with."

Ram sighed deeply. He was going to give in for all the same reasons he had given in the first time. "That's why you wanted to be a knight?"

"Rammel, if something happened to you, I would never forgive you for going out without me because I would always know that I might have prevented it if I'd been there. I owe that to you, to me, to Helm, and to B Team."

"Are you plannin' to play every card in your deck?"

Elora raised her chin and smiled. "I'm not playing, Ram. I'm standing by my man."

"You know there's a reason why Great Paddy ne'er married."

Elora cocked her head and looked at Ram thoughtfully. "You *do* know there's no Great Paddy, don't you, Ram?"

"What do you mean?"

Rev interjected. "If this is settled, I need to go throw a couple of things in a bag." He started toward the door and turned back. "Oh and take one of the kids we're moving up with you. Have them take turns. They might as well learn from the best. They've already been informed and will be waiting for your instructions." He closed the door and was gone.

Ram and Elora looked at each other.

"I think he paid us a compliment. He implied we're the best. I did no' know that Sovereign types know how to be nice."

"He's not being nice, Ram. He's planning to put my kids on the streets years before they're ready."

Ram's face softened. He took her hands, pulled her up out of her chair and repositioned her on his lap. "Well, see, here's the thin'. In your eyes they'll ne'er be ready whether they're eighteen or forty. Same thin's goin' to happen with Helm someday. When it comes to life, lettin' 'em go 'tis definitely in the hard column. But sometime you have to do it.

"Now I happen to know that they could no' possibly have had a better teacher. You've given them every possible advantage to help them do the work and stay alive. This crop of trainees comin' out of Jefferson Unit? In the whole history of Black Swan there's ne'er been a bunch so well-prepared."

She turned her face into his and smiled just a little. "Yeah?"

"'Tis Paddy's own truth. Now which one will we take with us tonight? And we need to get a babysitter. 'Tis on The Order's tab."

CHAPTER 20

"Wait. Condom."

He gaped at her. "I don't have a condom, Mercedes. Who do you think I was planning on fucking? One of my team members? Or maybe the buttoned-up bitch who was looking at me like I was something pulled out of a stopped-up drain?"

"You did not just say that."

"I... didn't. Well, I guess I did. But I was talking about how I saw things *before*. Not how I see things *now*."

"How do you see things now, Raif?" Her voice was soft and he loved the way her mouth formed his name. He'd never thought it was a particularly good name before, but he was starting to really appreciate the sound of it.

He looked at her with a question in his eyes. "I see the most beautiful girl who's soft and naked, ready for me, and looking at me like I'm candy." He moved his hands up and down the sides of her bare body under the water like he was double checking to make sure she wasn't an illusion. "Do you like my name?"

There was confusion on her face. "Do you have ADD?"

"Maybe. I don't know. But do you like my name? And would it be a problem if I do have ADD? Never mind. Forget that. It's the other thing I want to know. About my name."

"All right. Your name."

She looked away and seemed to be gathering her thoughts. She thought it was an odd conversation to have in a naked embrace with a man who was essentially a stranger.

"No," he said. She brought her gaze back to his face not understanding what he was saying 'no' to. "No diplomacy or tact or Miss Manners. Just tell me how you feel about my name. The real deal right now."

When she looked back at him, her eyes looked as liquid as the reflection of the navy blue water in the pool that surrounded them. "I don't know why you want to know what I think about your name, but I'll tell you what I think. No one has ever had a name more beautiful than yours. If you say it altogether, it sounds like what it is – a song. If you break it down to just your nickname, it sounds like a lover's contented sigh. Now why do you want to know?"

He wasn't sure he could articulate why his heart had forced the question out of his mouth, but he *was* sure that he was dumbstruck by her answer. She was perched partly on a flat rock that formed a natural step, with her legs around his hips. The water was warm and clean and heavenly, but nothing was as heavenly as the beauty he held in his hands. He looked down with hooded eyes. "Kiss me."

"If there's no condom, I don't think kissing is a great idea. It could lead to things condoms are designed for."

All of a sudden he started laughing under her. "You think we'll die from an STD before we starve to death?"

"Well... no, but that's not the only reason people use them. What about pregnancy?"

"You're not on birth control? You weren't kidding about giving up on love, were you? Okay." He ran his hand down his face, his pale eyes sparkling in the ray of late afternoon sun that came through the cavern ceiling above. "Let's have the mature, planned parenthood conversation. Take the one in ten thousand chance that we live through this and combine that with the one in a hundred chance that you'd get pregnant… What we have is essentially zero probability."

"Keyword is 'essentially'."

"Then I hope he has your brains."

After the pause of a few heartbeats the worry lines cleared from her brow and she smiled. "I hope *she* has your smile. And your eyes. And your…"

Stopping that thought in progress, he covered the fountain of words with a kiss that was undoubtedly to die for.

With the help of buoyancy, he held her with one hand and brought the other up to caress and tease a nipple that jutted proudly stiff from being out of the warm water. He pulled her up and into position where he poised at her opening. Listening to her greedy whimper made his head fall backward. When he opened his eyes a sliver to get a look at the expression on her face, he was spellbound by the hunger there, but that wasn't all he saw. His eye was also drawn to a ledge that hadn't been apparent from other vantage points because of the way it blended into the shadows.

Tired of waiting, Mercy pushed her pelvis forward with an eagerness that took what was left of his breath away and caused her to hiss in a mixture of pain and pleasure.

"Mercy," he groaned. "You're tight as a virgin."

"That's because my girl parts are out of practice," she panted.

When her body began to adjust to his size, he gradually increased the pace of his thrusts until they were churning the water into waves and sloshing over the sides. All the while he reveled in her response to him. Her uninhibited vocalizations echoed and reverberated again and again, creating a virtual sound chamber of eroticism. It sounded like he was making love to a dozen Mercys at once, which made his senses feel bombarded with sexual pleasure. The result was that he was harder and fuller than he had ever guessed was possible. Sooner than he would have liked, he jerked in release and buried his face in the crook of wet skin at her neck.

After the sound died and the water calmed, they were both starting to feel the drain. The adrenaline spike may have helped get them out of the way of the collapse, but there was a price to pay for it.

"Hmmm," Mercy said in a way that was too drowsy.

Raif knew how easy it would be for both of them to just go to sleep in the warm water, but there was stuff to do. "Come on." He pulled back and lifted her away at the same time. "Got to get out and get dressed."

"Nooooo. It's cold out there. It's warm in here. I'm staying. You should stay, too. Don't go."

At that moment in time he would have given her just about anything she could ask for. Anything, but that.

"No can do. Get your lovely bounteous ass moving."

"Raif! First, my ass is *not* bounteous if you mean that the way it sounds. Second, we don't have towels. That means we'll have to put our clothes on while we're still wet and then the clothes will be wet. And stay that way! In the *cold* air! Just let me stay here. I might as well die comfortable."

He grabbed her face between his hands. "You're not going to die, Mercy. Got a new plan, but it requires cooperation from you."

Tiny lines formed when her brows drew together. "What kind of plan?"

He groaned. "I'm supposed to be protecting you. Remember? I can't do my job if you're always questioning me. I don't interfere with your work, do I? So can't you just trust me and do what I say?"

"No. What kind of plan?"

"There might be a way out. We need to explore the possibility."

She looked around confused. "What way out? We're in a rock walled tube."

"Well," he pulled her toward him, turned her around, and angled her head just so. "If you look right there, I think there's a ledge that might lead to another cavern, and that one might go to the surface. It could be the monastery tunnel we were hoping for and can only be seen from this position. If you're just looking around, it's hidden in the shadows."

She turned to face him and narrowed her eyes. "When did you know there was a way out?"

"Right before you sat down on my cock."

Her lips parted and her eyes flashed. "And you didn't tell me?"

He barked out a laugh. "Sweetheart. I'm a man. You really expected me to say, 'Stop the fucking! I've just found a way out?' And give up my fantasy?" He was shaking his head. "Noooooo. Not likely. Clearly you have no idea how good you feel when you're wrapped around me."

"You! Gambler!" She was spitting mad and it sounded like an accusation, but not a very bad one. At least not to his way of thinking.

"Gambler?"

"You gambled with our bodies and our future."

He looked confused. "How?"

"STDs? Remember?"

"Mercy, I have never barebacked before. In. My. Life." His face spread into a sardonic smile that was hypnotizing. "And It. Was. Good."

When her brain was able to function again, she said, "Well, that's not the only problem, is it? What if we get out of here only to find out that I'M PREGNANT! How would you feel about your 'fantasy' then?"

"Is this a trick question?"

She scowled. "How could it be a trick question?"

"Doesn't matter. Told you the truth the first time. If we made a baby, I would hope he had your brains and I would hope you don't really love New York because I wouldn't want us to raise our kid there."

That took the wind out of her sails. She stood there blinking.

As he gathered up his clothes, he said, "Hey. What are you gonna have to eat when we get back to the hotel? I'm thinking steaks. Maybe three."

She had to give him points for optimism. "You *do* have ADD, don't you?"

"I don't know. Maybe. Is it important? Do you want to talk about it right now?"

"No. I do not want to talk about it right now. I want to get out of here right now and then get far away from you. I don't know what made me forget that you're certifiable."

"Probably my smile. Or maybe my eyes."

"GAH!"

She scrambled out of the pool, shrieked at the cold, grabbed her dingy-looking backpack off the ground and gave it a brush like that would actually have some effect.

She pulled on her clothes as fast as she could, letting the burst of anger warm her and fuel her resolve. What aggravated her as much as anything was the delicious soreness between her legs and the fact that her nipples were still sensitive and reacting to the touch of cloth. If it had been a fond farewell to life on Earth, it wouldn't have been a terrible way to go. But she would die in earnest before she ever let him know she felt that way.

When Farnsworth and Farthing arrived at the hotel in Sozopol, it was such a circus they couldn't get close to the front entrance. They told their driver to let them out and walked the rest of the way with their luggage.

What spoke to Farnsworth's state of mind more than anything was the fact that she had not contacted the hotel ahead of their arrival. For her, it was an inconceivable error of omission, the sort of mistake she would *never* make if she'd been handling travel arrangements for someone else.

They stepped up to the desk and asked for a room. The desk clerk had the nerve to look amused. "Reservation?"

Rev looked at Farnsworth who looked stricken and shook her head.

"We don't have a reservation. Any room will do," he said.

"I'm sorry, sir. The hotel is full to capacity. There's a hostel a few miles away that may still have beds."

"No. We're going to stay here. We'll work something out with some of your present guests."

The clerk raised an eyebrow. "You know some of our guests?"

"Probably most of them." He looked at his watch. "And I also know where I'll find them at this time of night. Do you have a place where we can leave our luggage for an hour?"

"Of course." He rang the bell on the counter and a bellman appeared within seconds to stow their bags behind his counter.

They wound their way through the crowded bar filled with people who either worked for The Order or had been contracted on short notice, at great expense. They found Torn, Gunnar, and Glen in a corner looking glum and nursing liquids in small glasses. The expressions on their faces quickly ran the span from recognition to surprise to confusion. As they looked back and forth between Rev and Farnsworth, noting the Sovereign's protective hand on the small of the Operations Manager's back, it was clear they had a question about the relationship.

"I can see you're relieved to see us," Rev deadpanned. "Finngarick. Glad to see you survived your run in with Mount Balzak."

Torn, who had imbibed on top of the pain meds he'd been given at the hospital, was days away from sober. He collapsed onto the table and started beating it with his palm while he laughed. "Ball sack. There's a mountain named ball sack. And I ran into it?"

"Gods Almighty," Rev said.

Glen snatched Torn's drink away.

Torn became serious very quickly, "Hey!"

"They didn't tell us he shouldn't drink, sir," Glen began by way of explanation. "But clearly that is the case. We, uh, weren't expecting you. What a surprise."

"Well, it so happens that it's more personal than business. We need to stay here and they don't have any more rooms."

Glen just realized they hadn't invited the new arrivals to sit. He rose. "Sorry, sir. Please sit down. You, too, Ms. Farnsworth. These two were just going to head upstairs, right, Gun? Can you handle him by yourself?"

"Wouldn't be the first time."

"Just a minute," Rev put in. "Before you go, we need to shuffle accommodations."

"Oh sure," Glen looked at Gun. "The adjoining room next to ours isn't being used at the moment. It's where, um, where Dr. Renaux was staying."

Glen saw Rev's hand tighten on Farnsworth's arm as she sniffed and looked away.

Glen had to help Gun get Torn to his feet and drape his arm over Gunnar's shoulders.

As soon as they were gone, Rev said, "We're anxious for word about the survivors of the collapse."

Glen thought that making an assumption of survival was overly optimistic, but wasn't going to correct the Sovereign.

"Nothing. Some guy from Salzburg got here tonight. He's going to be in charge. I guess they've lined people up to start rebuilding the scaffolding at first light. Then they're going to try to run a drill past the rubble and check for signs of life. That's all we know." Glen raked a hand down the front of his face and Rev noted that he'd never seen Glen look really tired.

"Long day."

Glen looked over at Rev. "Yes, sir. Long day."

CHAPTER 21

It was getting dark fast as they began their ascent. Raif climbed ahead of her and stopped to give her a hand up to the first ledge. She was thankful for the hiking boots with tire tread soles because the rock was slick from damp-loving mold.

Mercy made a promise to herself and the gods. If she did survive the ordeal, she would never complain about being tired ever again. Not after finding out what tired actually means as in depleted, can't go on, nothing left, and thinking that death would be preferable to making another step.

Seeing that she was tapped out, Raif was continually encouraging. "You're doing great. Slow and steady." Pause. "Know you're tired, but you can do this." Pause. "Yeah. That's the trick."

He even managed to get a momentary rise out of her when he said, "That's my girl."

She was still mad. Beauty and great sex didn't make up for the fact that he was an oaf who was bossy. A bossy oaf. But she did think it was endearing that he was so concerned for her safety and that he kept uttering little words and phrases of praise to urge her on.

By the time they had partially scaled the wall and pulled themselves onto the ledge, it was dark.

Raif switched on his helmet lamp then said, "You switch yours on, too. I want you to see every step before you put your foot down."

There wasn't as much room overhead as in the lower tunnel. They didn't need to crouch, but it definitely felt more claustrophobic. They were also on an incline and it was steep enough that they were both getting winded.

"Does it strike you as being rather perfect for a natural formation?" Mercy asked.

"Was thinking the same thing. We may have just lucked into finding one of the tunnels the Templar chroniclers wrote about. Wish it was light. If the sun was up, we'd be able to tell if light was coming in from somewhere.

With every step the sound of the waterfall became more faint until the utter silence overtook them. The fact that they could hear nothing but their steps and their own breathing was depressing and debilitating, causing them to doubt the effort altogether. Not being able to see anything unless their headlamps were pointed directly at it made things seem even worse.

Raif stopped so suddenly Mercy ran into his back.

"What is it?"

"Thought I heard something. You hear anything?"

"I'm not sure," she said. "What am I listening for?"

He didn't answer the question. He just said, "Come on," but the excitement in his voice was contagious and gave her just enough of a surge of energy to make another few steps. "There. You hear that."

She listened hard. "Is that a dog barking?"

He grinned. "That's exactly what that is."

"You did it." She sounded amazed.

"Not yet," he said. "But it looks really promising."

They took another couple of steps, but it was like turning the volume down on the barking. So they went back to where it was loudest.

Raif looked straight overhead and thought there was a break in the ceiling which was a few feet overhead. "How strong are you?"

"Um, I don't know. Average?"

"Okay. I've got to get up there and the only way that's going to happen is if you can give me a boost."

"A boost! You've got to weigh two hundred and fifty pounds."

"Well, I'm not Lou Alcinder."

"You mean Kareem Abdul Jabbar?"

"Whatever. So you're a basketball fan?"

"What does that…? Can we get back on topic? You need another plan. I'm not going to be able to hoist your big body."

"You don't have to *hoist* me. Just *boost* me." He pushed a damp strand of hair back from her face. She was too tired to retreat from his touch, or so she told herself, so she let his fingers linger on her cheek.

"Why don't you give me a boost instead?

"First because you have too much weight in your lower body and not enough strength in your upper body to pull yourself up."

"Thanks."

"And even if you could do that, which you can't, you wouldn't be able to pull me up. So unless you were planning to leave me behind?"

"Let me think on it."

"Look," he held his arm straight up. "It's not that far from my hands. Four feet maybe. I can get aloft by a couple of feet and you can get me another two feet with a well-timed boost. With just a little effort I should be able to get a hold. If it turns out that it's an opening and, if I can get through it, I'll pull you up."

"How are you going to do that, genius? By my math I figure that leaves me at least two feet short of being able to reach your hand." He grabbed her shoulders and turned her around. "Raif! What are you doing?"

"Taking your backpack. End to end it's two feet long. If I get up, I'll lower it. You grab on and this whole thing will be history."

"I don't like it."

"It's all we got, babe."

She tried to ignore the shudder that went through her body when he called her 'babe', telling herself it was just the cold seeping all the way to the marrow.

Strapping the backpack cross body over his neck, he put one arm through the strap then showed her how to cup her hands for his foot. "So here's what's going to happen. I'm going to crouch down like this with one foot in your hands. I'm going to concentrate all my effort into one big spring. With an assist from you it'll be enough."

"Okay. So when do I?"

"Get ready. I'll count to three. On three you'll feel the pressure from my foot. Don't let me push your hands down. You push my leg up instead. Like you're throwing me skyward."

"Raif, I..."

"Mercy. Don't be scared. It sounds more Cirque du Soleil than it is. And the worst thing that can happen is that it doesn't work."

"I know, but that *is* the worst thing that can happen."

He laughed softly. "Tell you what. Why don't *you* count to three?" She nodded. "You ready?" She nodded. "One." She started breathing heavy like she was trying to move a boulder. "Two." He could feel her muscles quivering even though she wasn't holding up any weight to speak of. At the last second, he said something about the gods that didn't involve cursing. "Three."

He exploded toward the ceiling and Mercy did her part. Live weight in motion is a lot easier to keep in motion than she thought. Her head lamp jerked up and found him hanging onto something by one hand while punching at something with the other. She heard him grunt and saw him lift himself up so that his shoulders disappeared from view. Within a couple of seconds his torso and legs followed and for one panic-stricken moment she realized she was alone in the cave.

Then she heard his laughter coming from above and a sob erupted from her core. She hadn't *really* believed they'd get out and thought Raif was just trying to keep their minds off of the inevitable.

His light appeared at the opening above her. "Hey. There's no crying in collapsed cave rescues. Grab onto this horrible girly imitation of a backpack and come on up." She laughed and grabbed on. "Don't let go."

She wasn't used to holding up her own weight, but Raif caught hold of her arm when she was a couple of feet off the ground. Having boobs pulled over rock wasn't especially pleasant, but it was *so* much better than the alternative that she didn't care. He pulled her up and on top of him, her back to his front, cushioning her body from the hard, cold ground. His arms came around her as they both lay catching their breath, looking up at the October stars, and thanking the gods for giving them another chance at life.

He turned his head and nuzzled her ear. "You didn't really think we were getting out, did you?"

"No," she said quietly. After a minute she asked, "Did you ever really think we wouldn't?"

"No."

"Why?"

He didn't answer right away. She wasn't sure if he didn't know or if he was choosing his words carefully. For a change. "You made me feel too alive to die."

She let that soak in, slowly, deeply.

He rolled her away gently and heaved himself to his feet. "I think it's colder out here than it was in *there*." After scanning their surroundings as best he could in the dark, he said, "Looks like we got two choices. We can try to find the road, but it will be slow going on this terrain and in the dark. Or we can huddle up together and try to stay warm until the sun comes up tomorrow morning."

"I'm not sure I can move."

"Not an answer, babe."

"Add meanness to your bad qualities."

"Okay. What'll it be? Ladies' choice."

"It's too cold to just sit here."

"Then we have a winner. Choice number two it is." He reached down to help her up. Instead of taking his hand, she gave up a groan that lasted a full minute. "The hard part's over. You survived. When we get back to the hotel, you can take a bath and get in bed. Or eat and bathe and get in bed."

She groaned again for good measure as she was pulled to her feet.

"But somebody's going to need to watch you if you get in a bath to make sure you don't slide under the water and drown. I volunteer."

"Ha."

It was just before midnight when they made it to the road that led to Sozopol. There weren't a lot of vehicles on the road, but they did manage to get a flatbed truck to stop. Mercy told the driver they were going to the hotel. He said he could drop them close to there. So they climbed on the back.

Raif sat with his back to the cab, legs out in front of him. Mercy sat next to him, but slumped over on his lap and was asleep within a couple of minutes in spite of the cold.

CHAPTER 22

When Elora and Ram strode onto the Whister pad with Kris Falcon in tow, Storm and Kay looked surprised, but pleased.

"Guess who's comin' to patrol?"

"Don't take this the wrong way," Storm said as he leaned over to give Elora a kiss on the cheek, "but where's the Sovereign?"

Elora opened her mouth to answer, but Ram beat her to it. "Gone doin' important Sovereign shit."

Elora shrugged and gestured toward Falcon, smiling like a proud mom. "We have orders to show this knight-to-be how it's done."

"In fact," Ram added, "the man said he was to learn from the best. Meanin' us." Kay chuckled. "Sincerely.'Tis Paddy's own truth is it no', Elora?"

"Aye, Ram. 'Tis Paddy's own truth," she answered. Ram beamed like he'd won a cake walk. "Sir Storm. Sir Caelian. I believe you've both met Kristoph Falcon?" Storm nodded and acknowledged Falcon with a chin lift.

"Sir," Falcon said as he offered his hand to Storm and then Kay.

Storm leveled Falcon with a look that said he had x-ray vision. "You carrying weapons tonight?"

"Yes, sir. Just what the Lady Laiken told me to bring."

"And that would be."

He pulled up his jeans legs to reveal a stake in each boot and lifted the back of his jacket to reveal a laser snub nose. One of the new wood bullet models that Monq had just cleared for testing.

Storm turned to Elora. "Who's he sticking to?"

She looked at Falcon, then at Storm. "Well, I'd like for him to go with you because he's already learned most of what I have to teach him. On the other hand, I want to deliver him back here safe at the end of the night."

The pilot stepped out onto the Whister pad and grinned at Falcon. "You flying tonight, kid?"

Falcon grinned. "Sure, Mac. You're my wingman?"

"Nah. Just your co-pilot." Mac smiled and nodded to B Team before boarding the Whister and starting the check.

"Wait," Kay said. "That kid is going to pilot a Whister? The same one we're riding on?"

The other three exchanged a laugh.

"Come on," Storm said. "I'll tell you the story on the way."

By and large the night was uneventful except for encountering the four teenage immortals on patrol in the same district. They stopped to say hello. After a couple of minutes B Team realized that Falcon and Animal House had drifted a few yards away and were involved in a conversation that could have passed for a bunch of human kids.

Members of B Team smiled at each other. There was something uniquely Black Swan about one of their future vampire hunters engaged in sidewalk banter with vampire who passed for teens even if they were hundreds of years old.

They knew that any night out could be their last. Maybe that was what made them feel so alive.

CHAPTER 23

As promised, the truck driver dropped Rev and Mercy two blocks from the hotel. Raif had to carry her because she couldn't stay awake long enough to stand up. He was thanking Black Swan for a grueling physical training regime every step of the way. It was just before one o'clock when they walked into the lobby of the hotel. It was surprisingly busy considering the hour and that it had been more or less empty when they'd left that morning. No one seemed to notice them. So Raif headed for the elevator with a dogged determination, all thought of steaks gone from his mind.

He set her on her feet in front of her door like she was precious cargo and fished the card key out of the battered back pack. He opened the door for her. "You need help getting to bed?"

She hesitated. "No. Thank you. For everything."

"See you tomorrow." He kissed the top of her head knowing it would be the last time she ever let him get that close and backed away.

Mercy turned on the light switch and found two surprised and sleepy-looking people sitting up in bed. "Sorry." She assumed she had the wrong room and turned to leave, but caught sight of her own toiletries bag hanging in the bath. She turned around, so tired she could barely form thoughts, much less words. "Who are you? And what are you doing in my room?"

Farnsworth stood, wearing a loose silk cami with pajama bottoms to match. She approached, looking at Mercy like she was a ghost. Farnsworth knew that it wasn't the ideal time to come clean with her daughter, whom she could see was dead on her feet, but there was also a nagging sense that beginning their relationship with deflection or lies would be a bigger mistake. "There were no more rooms in the hotel. And we're here because I'm your mother. This is your boss, Sovereign Rev Farthing."

Mercy's eyes flicked to Rev and back to the woman talking gibberish.

Farnsworth's impulse was to want to selfishly gush out everything that had led to that moment, but it was plain that her daughter was barely hanging onto consciousness. So she decided to let Mercy be the one to decide how much she wanted to know and when. Her expression never wavered from a look of shell shock. She simply turned around and left the hotel room without saying a word.

Raif had just stripped out of his clothes. He was too tired to get in the shower. So he did what was, in his mind, the next best thing. He was pulling on a clean pair of boxers when he heard a soft knock on the door.

He opened it to find Mercy standing there.

"What's wrong?"

She walked straight into his body and he put his arms around her reflexively. "There's a strange woman in my room who says she's my mother. Can I sleep in here?"

"Yeah. Of course, baby."

He shut the door behind her and helped her strip down to underwear. Then he pulled back the covers, got in and turned off the light, noting that Torn was snoring through the whole thing.

As she climbed in and nestled into his side like she was made to be there, he said, "Are you sure you wouldn't rather sleep in Torn's bed?"

She snorted. "Why would you ask me that?"

"Because girls like you always end up with some other guy."

"Shut up and go to sleep."

He grinned in the darkness and pulled her closer.

The next day the hotel cleared out pretty quickly once it became known that the missing couple was safe. Rev and Farnsworth moved to another room. Raif woke to the sounds of low voices.

Torn was saying, "Woke up with a mother of all hangovers and, Great Glorious Paddy, there they were. Sleepin' like angels. Much as I want to know what transpired durin' the night, I do no' have the heart to disturb a slumber so sound."

"When they wake up, tell Dr. Renaux that her room has been vacated and is ready for her with clean sheets and towels. Here's her card key. I think she left it."

Glen closed the door and Torn sat down on the side of his bed facing his partner and the surprise bedmate.

Raif was on his back with Mercy asleep on his chest. His arms were wrapped around her in what looked like a protective embrace. He opened one eye a sliver and looked at Torn.

Torn smiled like a Cheshire cat. "Got lucky, did ye?"

Raif's gaze swept over the state of Torn's swollen and bruised face and took in the bandages. "When are you going to learn that no means no?"

Between the hangover and whole body soreness, the last thing in the world Torn needed was to laugh, which of course meant that everything was funnier than usual. So he laughed, but the sounds he made were more, Ow Ow Ow than Ha Ha Ha.

That in turn made Raif laugh. Without opening her eyes, Mercy reached behind her and shoved a pillow in his face. "Quiet. Both of you. Go somewhere else."

"This is *our* room," Torn said.

That made Mercy raise her head and look around. "Oh. Yeah."

Raif patted the blanket covering her ass. "Glen came by. He said your room is all yours. No more strange people. Nice clean linens. And he left your key card."

She let out a noncommittal huff that gave no indication of her plans.

"Sooooo," Raif began. "What would you like to do?"

"Be left alone to sleep."

"Well, we could do that. Or I could help you get to your own room where you could have a nice bath and put on some clean clothes. And while you were doing that I could order some room service. Coffee. Juice. Sugary pastries."

She pulled back just far enough so that she could see his face. "What happened to steaks? I thought you wanted steaks."

He grinned. "We'll see what they have in the way of aged filet."

"Okay," she said. "If I agree to get out of this bed, you agree to get me room service."

"That's the deal."

She started to pull back the covers, but stopped. "Make him turn around. And I have to go to the bathroom. I'll never make it all the way to my room."

"Our facilities are your facilities." Raif made a motion to Torn to turn around and his partner complied without hesitation or complaint.

When he heard the bath door close, Torn turned to Raif with a scathing smile.

"What?"

"Two words," answered Torn. "Pussy. Whipped."

"Call it what you want, brother. I'm taking whatever she's giving and calling myself the luckiest son-of-a-bitch alive."

Torn shook his head. "Out of all of us. Ne'er figured you to be the first man down."

CHAPTER 24

When Mercy emerged from the bath in clean clothes, wet hair, and no makeup, she didn't feel the least glamorous, but she did feel a little less like dead person walking. The room smelled like a banquet. Raif had pretty much ordered one of everything the kitchen had to offer and looked ready to eat anything she didn't. They'd run out of surfaces and put a lot of the plates on top of the bed.

She smiled shyly. "Thank you. This looks wonderful."

He pushed out a chair. "Have a seat. What will you have first?"

"Um. Is that cranberry juice?"

He looked where she pointed. "Could be. It's red." She tried it and smiled. "Guess what?"

"What?"

"It's our first real meal together."

"You don't count half a protein bar."

"Okay. It's our first meal together with furniture involved." She smiled as she chewed a piece of cheesy bread. "You take good care of me."

"Glad you noticed."

"Who's taking care of you?"

He stopped dead still. "What do you mean?"

"Who's making sure you got enough sleep, got a shower, got breakfast? I'm not used to being a taker. Doesn't feel right."

Raif's eyes traveled down her body suggestively. "Well, if you're saying you'd like to return some favors..." She giggled and he looked mesmerized. "Is that a yes?"

She took a forkful of something that looked like hash. "It's a maybe," she smiled with a teasing flirtatiousness she didn't even know she had in her.

Seeing that look directed at him, Raif felt like all the blood in his body rushed to his groin. If he didn't know how badly she needed to replenish her body's reserves, he would have lunged at her. That, plus there was business to take care of first.

"If that look means what I think it means, then I'm your guy."

She stopped with her fork in the air. "You're my guy?" He nodded. "But you're putting conditions on that? You're my guy, but only if I'm looking at you with a promise of carnal delight?"

Raif lips parted in reaction to paralysis of tongue while he tried to sort out what he was supposed to say.

"You should see your face," she laughed. "I'm just kidding. Don't look so scared. I'm not making a claim on you or anything like that."

Raif stood and started stacking all the food, some on the little desk-table, some on the dresser. She watched dumbfounded as he carefully built towers of food. First a plate, then a stainless steel cover, then a plate, and so on until he'd cleared the entire bed. Then he took the plate Mercy was working on and set it on the nightstand before sitting beside her. Close beside her.

"Mercy, do you want to make a claim on me?" Her lips parted and her eyes moved to his lips before coming back to his beautifully pale eyes. "Say yes. Because that's what I want. Hel yes I'm your guy. Whether you're looking at me like you want to eat me or looking at me like you want to kill me." He smiled. "Which, in its own way, is almost as cute."

He reached over, took her hands in his, and intertwined their fingers. "Sir Nightsong." Gods he liked the way that sounded. "Let's talk about the speed dating thing."

He groaned and closed his eyes. "Not again. I told you I..."

"Just listen. I heard your story. It's only fair you hear mine." With clear reluctance, he nodded. "I'm not an overly emotional person. The way you made me feel that day, well I hated you for it. I practically ran out of there. I was out on the streets, crying and not able to stop. It was so humiliating to put on a spectacle like that. In front of all those strangers. The way people looked at me. Curiosity. Sympathy. Disdain. I hated you for that, too.

"So, like I told you, I went back to work and decided that dating isn't all it's cracked up to be. I told myself that I had what most people want, fulfilling self-actualizing work. I threw myself into mentoring grad students and volunteered to serve on a couple of boards. I'd been busy before, but I was determined to fill every minute of every day."

She stopped and looked away. He didn't say anything, but squeezed her hand in a gesture of encouragement.

"The thing is," she looked up at him, "it still didn't get you out of my mind." Raif's face went slack at that revelation. That was, apparently, the last thing he'd expected to hear. "I despised you for rejecting me the way you did, but I was also, I don't know how I should describe it, obsessed I guess."

Raif's face was as full of wonder as if he was witnessing a miracle. "You were obsessed with *me*?"

"Yes." She nodded.

"That's... awesome. Also sick and perverted. But go on."

She laughed. "Anyway, as the time went by I couldn't recall your face in detail. All that remained was an impression of black hair, pale eyes, naughty boy beauty."

He stifled a laugh. "Naughty boy beauty? Please, I'm begging, never say that in front of other people or I'll have to commit honor suicide."

Mercy rolled her eyes. "Do you want me to finish or not?"

"I do," he said and closed the inch between them so that they were sitting as close as two people can sit.

"That's pretty much it. The supreme irony is I took this job thinking it would be the very thing I needed to finally get you out of my head and stop obsessing about you. You know the rest. I got on that plane and there you were."

"Can I ask a couple of questions?"

She suddenly looked guarded. "Like what?"

"All the flirting with my partner?"

"Oh." He could see the blush start to rise in her cheeks. *Fascinating.* He reached up and trailed a fingertip down her face to see if it made her skin hot to the touch. "That was my insurance policy to be certain I didn't give away that I was attracted to you and making an even bigger fool of myself."

That answer seemed to please him immensely. "Women are evil."

"Nah. Just me."

"Next question. Are you claiming me?"

In a move that took the breath from her body, Raif pulled her up and rearranged her on the bed, on her back, and tucked underneath him. He buried his face in her neck and inhaled her scent, then started nibbling, which made her gasp, her body arching toward him in a ritual of reflex as old as the race.

"Not letting you up until you say it."

She started laughing at the way her body responded to him so completely and immediately, as if her genetic particles were reaching out in hopes of combining with his.

"Yes."

He lifted his head up so he could look into her face. "Yes?" She nodded, looking at his lips with a hunger that was both invitation and demand. "You and me? Exclusive. Right?"

"Right."

He gave her the kiss she was asking for. She didn't know that kisses could be so thorough or last so long. Or that they could communicate so much feeling. She felt the swell in his jeans grind against her. Her body rocked upward in response.

With a frustrated growl and without warning, he tore away from the kiss and practically leapt from the bed. That left Mercy staring in confusion and wondering what the devil just happened. She was learning that Raif liked to do things fast and abrupt. No grass growing under his feet.

"Duty calling, babe. We got business to take care of first."

"What business?" He looked at his watch. "We're expected downstairs in twenty minutes for debriefing."

"What does that mean?"

"Means we have to go tell our story to our boss and my team mates. You have just enough time to finish eating and get some clothes on. I'm going to take a shower while you do that, then I'll go down with you."

She sat up and scowled. "That woman. Who was in here last night. She said the man with her is my boss."

Raif looked interested in that. "What was his name?"

"Um, I don't know. I was tired and it's kind of hazy."

"About my size? Buzzed hair? Brown eyes?"

Mercy nodded. "That seems right."

Raif whistled long and low. "Guess we'll find out soon enough." He took hold of the door knob. "Back in fifteen minutes."

When Mercy walked down the hallway with Raif, she was more than happy to stop at the elevator and make good use of it. There was a lot to be said for a few hours' sleep, a good breakfast, and being clean, but she still felt like she'd been run over by a semi.

When they got off the elevator Glen was waiting to walk them to the room that had been reserved for their use. There were four others waiting: Torn, Gun, Rev, and Farnsworth. Rev was at the far end of the oblong table. At the end nearest the door, two chairs were situated side by side. Assuming that they were meant to sit in those two, Raif pulled out one of the chairs for Mercy.

She looked up at him for reassurance, silently communicating that this was her first debriefing. He nodded almost imperceptibly and, when they were seated, he reached for her hand under the table. Her eyes kept going to the handsome woman sitting at the end. She knew that woman was lying about being her mother because, for one thing, she wasn't nearly old enough. That woman looked no more than ten years older than she, if that.

Glen pointed at the coffee service. Looking between Raif and Mercy, he asked if he could get them anything.

"Black. No sugar," said Raif.

Glen looked at Mercy. "Water. Please."

While Glen was busy with his volunteer mission of filling beverage requests, Rev decided to get the party started.

"This is not a formal procedure, just co-workers eager to hear what happened. It goes without saying that we're very happy and relieved to have you back, but frankly, your sudden appearance in the middle of the night is, if not a miracle, at least a mystery." Glen took his seat again after delivering drinks. "I'm going to ask you to simply tell us how you came to be here. If we have questions, we'll try to save them until the end, but make no promises. Sir Nightsong. Dr Renaux. You have the floor."

Raif cleared his throat. "I was the one taking a turn inside the burial chamber with Dr. Renaux when the quake occurred. Professor Yanov had left to retrieve documents at Dr. Renaux's request. So we were the only two." He glanced at Mercy, almost like he was asking for confirmation. "When I realized what was happening, I saw that the cavern was collapsing between the exit and our location. The only possibility of survival was to go deeper into the mountain. So I grabbed Dr. Renaux and we ran for it.

"We lost our footing a few times when the ground heaved under us. One of those resulted in a scrape on Dr. Renaux's leg, but it wasn't deep. That was the only injury we sustained, other than the minor bruises and soreness that you might expect from repeated falls.

"When it was over, we stopped to let our minds catch up to what had happened and outline our options."

Raif told the rest of the story with surprisingly vivid detail, leaving out any mention of interaction between the two of them. Mercy could tell that he must have performed the activity of debriefing many times because he did it with such obvious ease.

At one point she was horrified to realize she was nodding off. The combination of still being tired, knowing that she was safe and secure, and the comfort of listening to Raif's voice was lulling her to sleep like a lullaby. She jerked up when her head started to droop toward her chest.

"Are we putting you to sleep, Dr. Renaux?" Rev sounded amused.

"I'm sorry. I..."

Raif cut her off. "When we're sitting here in this nice clean climate controlled room with a nice breakfast under our belts, perhaps my telling doesn't adequately convey what she's been through. Of course she's tired. She should be upstairs sleeping right now."

Rev was studying Raif with interest. "No offense was intended." He turned his gaze on Mercy. "Would you like to be excused, Dr. Renaux? Sir Catch will escort you to your room if this is too much too soon."

"No," she said simply and quietly. Raif leaned over and whispered something in her ear. "No... sir." She looked at Glen. "Is the coffee option still open? All the way? Cream and three sugars."

Raif smiled at that and committed it to memory. Glen quickly and expertly prepared a cup of coffee to her specifications and set it down in front of her.

"Dr. Renaux," Rev addressed her again. "Do you have anything you'd like to add?"

She looked at Raif and suddenly found tears filling her eyes. It surprised her more than anyone. Worse, it seemed her throat had closed up and she was finding it hard to talk. He looked at her with worry and was squeezing her hand harder. She remembered Raif telling her that something similar happened to him on the plane when she'd made an overture.

She held up her index finger to indicate that she needed a minute to pull herself together. All the men except for Raif looked away, thinking they would spare her embarrassment. After a few minutes the stream of tears slowed and she was able to speak in broken sentences. Glen, who was considerate to a fault, gathered up the paper napkins on the coffee service tray and laid them in front of Mercy. She immediately grabbed one and used it like a tissue.

"I just want to say that..." She pressed her lips together tightly to try to contain the turbulent emotion, but to her dismay her body was out of her control. She was overcome with waves of feeling that had to be released and could only find release in tears. "I was sure we were going to die."

She looked over and smiled at Raif through her tears. Everybody in the room knew that they were witnessing two miracles. The first was being in the presence of a couple who had escaped certain entombment, against all odds. The second was being in the presence of a couple who had fallen in love, against all odds.

"But Raif... Raif joked about dying, a lot. But the whole time he acted like we were lucky to be alive."

A look passed between Torn and Gun that said, "Who is she talking about?"

"And we are. Lucky to be alive. All because of him. There's no one else like him."

Farnsworth was silently crying at that point. Glen might have been resisting the urge.

"No doubt that's true," Rev said, recalling every word he, in both incarnations, had ever thought or said about the members of Z Team. The fact that it turned out that one of the miscreants saved his soon-to-be-stepdaughter's life only underscored the fact that life is strange. "Anybody else have questions?"

"Aye. Ask 'em where they spent the night last night."

Raif practically lunged at Torn thinking he would rip the shit eating skin from the fucker's face. Torn would normally open his arms in a smarmy challenge, but he really wasn't in good enough physical shape, after his own ordeal, to be goading his partner into an MMA match. So when he saw Raif coming for him, he didn't cower, but his eyes did flare as he braced for a world of pain.

Fortunately for Torn, Gunnar was sitting between them and tackled Raif to the ground. "Rafael! Stop! He's hurt. On the D.L." That made Raif still. "He's hurt," Gun repeated. "You'll have to take it out of his hide after he's had a chance to mend."

Farnsworth looked at Rev. "Does this sort of thing happen often?"

Rev shook his head. "Only with this bunch. Thorn. In. My. Side."

"Okay. Get off me," Raif said. He stood up and got in Torn's face. "Apologize to her."

"Why?" Torn said.

"You tried to embarrass her."

Torn looked at Mercy sheepishly. "Sorry. You know I like you." He winked at Mercy and Raif lunged for him.

"Fucker!"

It took both Gun and Glen to get him to the ground that time. The only thing that restored order was Mercy leaning over Raif, as he was on his back, pinned down by two of his team mates. She said, "You know I don't care who knows that I was sleeping in your bed last night. You're my guy and I want everybody to know it."

At that all the straining and tension left Raif. He went still on the floor, completely relaxed. Glen and Gun eased up.

"You good?" Gun asked.

Raif nodded and smiled. "I'm good. I'm her guy." He looked toward Torn. "But you better control that loud-mouthed moron because the next thing he says is going to put him in traction."

Gun turned to Torn. "You got that, loud-mouthed moron?"

"Aye. 'Tis no much fun here anyway. I'm ready for a pre-lunch whiskey."

As they were filing out of the room, Glen was saying, "You're not having any whiskey until you turn over those pain pills."

The four who were left in the room stared at each other for a minute. Finally, Raif leaned toward Mercy. "Would you like to hear what she has to say?"

Mercy took a long time to answer, staring at Farnsworth the whole time. At length, she nodded.

"Would you like us to leave the two of you alone?"

She shook her head immediately. Raif looked at Farnsworth as if to say, "Well. Here's your chance. It's now or never."

Slowly Farnsworth got up, walked the length of the room, and sat down on Mercy's other side. With a quiet calm she said, "I'd like to tell you the story if that's alright."

Mercy studied the woman's face for a few seconds and nodded.

Farnsworth began by saying, "My name is Susan Farnsworth. I also work for The Order, which is how I was able to find you."

She went on to relay the entire story. How young she'd been when her parents made the decision for her. How they and the adoption staff had persuaded her with the argument that she had no way to raise a child and that a couple of means who wanted a baby would be the best thing, they would dote and spoil and overeducate.

"In a perfect world." Mercy found her voice. "That's what's supposed to happen in a perfect world. My adoptive parents were killed in a car accident when I was still a baby. I was raised by a widowed grandmother who didn't want me and could barely stand the sight of me. The relationship was neglectful at best and abusive at worst."

Farnsworth let out an almost inaudible whimper.

Mercy pressed on. "Why now? Why did you decide to look for me now?"

"They said the records would be closed to protect the adoptive parents and you. They insisted that it would be the best thing for you to be left alone and said that, if you wanted to find me when you were an adult, you would. The former Sovereign convinced me that I would never be at peace until I looked for you."

Mercy's eyes went to Rev. "And you're in a relationship?"

Rev blinked once slowly. He wasn't accustomed to being addressed in that tone by people who worked for him. He took a deep breath and remembered that it was a peculiarly unique circumstance. "She's my fiancée."

Raif's gaze jerked between Rev and Farnsworth, but he kept quiet, wisely enough.

Farnsworth spoke to Mercy again. "I wish things had been different for you. Gods know I wanted things to be different for you. I'd change the past if I could. Believe me.

"I know it's a lot to take in. I'm not asking for more or less than you have to give, than you *want* to give. Whether or not you want to be my daughter, I am your mother. You can do whatever you want with that information. But I have love I want to give you. I hope that, after you've had a chance to think about it, you might want to explore that. Lunch maybe?"

Mercy responded with a derisive laugh. "Lunch?" She almost sneered before getting up and walking out of the room.

Raif looked at Farnsworth with sympathy. "Sorry," he said, before following after Mercy.

When the two of them were alone, Rev said, "Well. That went better than I expected."

Farnsworth looked at him like he was crazy.

Mercy went back to bed. She was too agitated to go to sleep immediately. When Raif crawled in and spooned behind her, she relaxed into his warmth and the security of his embrace. She slept, but had fitful dreams and woke just before the sun was setting. The bed was empty.

She caught her reflection in the mirror as she walked into the bathroom. Crying and then going to sleep right after didn't result in her best look. She murmured something about Quasimodo and turned on the shower. As the hot water ran over her body, slowly relaxing more of the tension of the past day, she replayed what Farnsworth had said over and over. She tried to picture herself in the same situation, which was hard to do since she'd never had a teenage love affair or parents who wielded almost absolute power over her.

The suggestion of lunch seemed ridiculous at the time, but after giving it some thought, she was beginning to wonder what it would hurt.

She'd blamed Farnsworth for not trying to find her, but Mercy hadn't taken any steps to try to look for her parents either. She didn't have a way of doing that as a child under her grandmother's care, but she certainly could have initiated a search as an adult. Why hadn't she? Because she was too busy? Because she was afraid of what she'd find?

She had to admit it took a certain amount of courage for the woman to look for her. There was something to be said for that. As she was drying off, she heard the suite door close and smiled.

Raif knocked softly on the door. She opened it a crack.

"Can I come in?" he grinned.

"What's in it for me?"

"Open up and I'll show you."

She laughed and flung the door open. He had her gathered into his arms and was deepening a hello kiss when she felt him tug at the towel wrapped around her. Every intimate encounter with Raif, no matter how brief, brought a new range of sensual response. She learned that being completely naked with a man who was completely dressed was titillating.

He tightened his hands around her waist and lifted. Her legs automatically wound around him as he began walking them toward the bed. He laid her on the bed as carefully as if she was made of glass and sat up on his knees, still between her legs, while he pulled his shirt over his head and undid his jeans. He was commando, which was the dichotomy she was coming to expect with Raif. On the one hand, she wasn't sure she wanted to commit to a guy who didn't wear underwear. On the other hand, she thought there was something wild and feral about it that was exciting.

"What?" he asked. She shook her head. "Nothing doing. Tell me." She shook her head. "Tell me now!" He started tickling.

"Okay. I was just thinking about your lack of, um, underwear."

He looked down at the impressive hard on protruding from the opening in his jeans. "Yeah. What about it? I'm not wearing any."

She laughed. "I can see that."

"You don't like the bare look?"

"No I don't," she said seriously, then smiled brightly as she jack knifed up and pulled him back down with her. "I love it!"

Raif responded with a promising smile. He started at her forehead and began working his way down her body slowly with kisses and licks and nibbles and nuzzles. Some made her gasp. Some made her laugh softly. Some made her whole body jerk in response. She lost patience and tried to hurry him along, but he refused.

"This is the first time I'm making love to you in a bed and I'm going to savor every agonizingly slow second of it."

"Is there anything I can say to get you where I want you right now?"

"No," he said as he blew a breath across her pubic area.

"How about please?" He stopped for a second and she took that as an indication that she could be on to something. "Please." He looked up at her. So she started a mantra of begging until he gave up, grinning, and looking at her with something in his eyes that wasn't just lust.

She wouldn't have thought it was possible to penetrate so slowly. When she wiggled and thrust, he held her hips still with his hands, which from her point of view was frustrating and wicked sexy at the same time. He slid out and in with a measured precision, with the tiniest increases, until she was ready to scream. But she didn't scream. She bit him on his pec.

"Ow," he laughed. "You little minx! What is it you're trying to say? Use your words."

"Harder."

"Oh. Harder!" He complied and thrust so hard it lifted her completely off the mattress.

"Faster."

"Faster, too? Demanding." He let go of her hips and brought it. It was hard. It was fast. And she was in ecstasy.

When he was close to coming, he reached down and stimulated her nub just enough to send her over the edge. He thrust twice more after she felt the hot release pumping into her. He collapsed to the side and smiled over at her, looking proud and pleased with eyes shining brightly. "That what you had in mind, Professor?"

"You get an A+."

He chuckled. "What was the best thing that's ever happened to you? In your life?"

She paused. "I don't know."

"Okay then. Ask me."

"Raif. What was the best thing that has ever happened to you in your life?"

"It was this morning, when you told everybody that I'm yours. It... I don't know, it made something crack inside." He turned his face toward her. "Almost like I heard it. Here's this perfectly shiny, beautiful smart accomplished woman," he leaned in and sniffed, "who smells so good, and she just told everybody flat out that I'm her guy. It was the most amazing moment in my life." He looked away, smiled, and turned back to her. "Let's do it again!"

She laughed. "Anytime you want. Call the TV stations." Mercy couldn't remember ever having enjoyed anything as much as that look of happiness on Raif's face. "So do you recommend speed dating?"

His smile melted away as his features grew perfectly serious. His eyes tracked his fingers slowly trailing up her rib cage. "I think maybe when people are supposed to be together, Fate finds a way. If they had a chance speed dating and blew it, but they're really supposed to be together, then Fate will arrange for them to work for the same secret society and be trapped inside a mountain together." He looked up and met her eyes.

Mercy was thinking that was perhaps the most romantic thing that any man had ever said to any woman. At least it worked for her.

All of a sudden he twisted around to look at the bedside clock.

"Oh shit! We're supposed to be somewhere."

She was confused. Again. Why was he always bounding out of bed and insisting they had someplace to be?

"Come on. Come on. Come on," he said hurriedly. "Did you bring a dress?"

"A dress? To a dig? No. I didn't bring a dress."

"Okay. Just put on something."

"I don't want to go out. I'm going to have dinner in here tonight."

Raif was shaking his head back and forth. "No. No. No. You're not. I have plans."

"You do?"

"Plans that involve your cooperation."

"You might as well find out now. I'm not big on surprises."

"Fair enough. Just this once then. After this, no more surprises."

"Somehow I don't think I can trust you to keep your word on this issue."

"All's fair in love and surprises."

"You're not going to let me stay in tonight, are you?"

"Not a chance."

She heaved a big sigh. "I guess I'll get dressed."

"Have I told you that you look good in yellow?"

"Have I told you I'm serious about the ADD thing?"

"Does it matter?"

"Not in the least. The only thing I own that's yellow is the sweater I had on in the cave and it's going to be the gasoline rag for the next bonfire."

"Whatever you wear will be almost as perfect as when you're not wearing anything."

She disappeared into the bathroom, put on enough makeup to resemble the living, and finally settled on clean skinny jeans and a pink gauze top. She threw her hair up into a messy top knot and left some tendrils hanging down.

"Best I can do on short notice," she said when she opened the door and stepped out of the bath.

He pulled her into a slow dance pose and spun her around. "Just like I said. Beautiful." He let go and pulled his phone from his pocket. "Hang on a sec." He texted something, then said. "Good. Let's go."

Mercy paused at the elevator debating about taking the stairs then pushed the button. For the second time that day, Glen was waiting when they got off the elevator. He backed up a few feet and held up his hand. Raif, who had hold of her arm, pulled her to a stop.

"When one of our escorts says to wait you have to do what he says."

"Only if his name is Simon," she quipped.

"What's going on?" Raif just smiled enigmatically. "Whatever's going on, is there food involved? Please just tell me there's food involved."

Glen was emphatic. "Food. Is. Involved."

He held up a finger, pulled his phone from his pocket and said. "Right this way my lady. Dinner awaits in the terrace room."

"Sounds good," Raif said, refusing to look at her.

They walked through the lobby, past reception, through the main restaurant to the entrance of the terrace room at the back. When she reached the doors, they swung open and six people yelled, "Surprise!"

There was a large round table in the center of the room set with seven places. All around the periphery were long tables covered in white linens and birthday cakes with candles blazing. Twenty-eight of them in all. The first had one candle. The second had two candles.

When her mind caught up, her gaze sought out Farnsworth. Raif leaned over and whispered in her ear. "It was her idea. One for every year she missed being with you. She wants you to know she thought about you every birthday and wanted to be with you."

Mercy leaned down and blew out the candle on the first cake. Looking around she realized she was going to have to hurry if she was going to blow out all the candles before the last ones went out on their own. So she started hurrying. First Raif joined her in blowing them out quickly. Then Glen.

The three of them moved as fast as they could from cake to cake, blowing and bumping into each other, with Mercy doing as much giggling as blowing. They barely made it to the last cake and no one knew for sure if it was breath or time that put them out.

She looked over at Farnsworth who was smiling so brightly she looked like she had an aura around her. Mercy turned and put her face in Raif's chest and mumbled something. His arms came around her automatically. "What? I couldn't hear you. Say it again."

All her life Mercy had wanted somebody to know it was her birthday and care. That night was the first time it had ever been acknowledged by someone other than herself. It was a makeup celebration. As close to a do-over as was possible.

She raised her face from Raif's chest and said, "I have a mom."

He laughed. "Yeah. You're a lucky girl." He hugged her and said. "I'd like to hear you say that again. Make an announcement, like you did for me. Tell everybody, including her." He ducked down to look at her eye to eye. "What have you got to lose?"

She smiled, turned and said brightly in full voice. "Hey everybody! I have a mom!"

Farnsworth's sob of relief and happiness, was drowned out by clapping and cheering and a horrible rendition of "Happy Birthday to You". At the end of that Mercy decided she might tolerate a quick hug from her mother.

She reached out to give Farnsworth a friendly, but reserved pat. Farnsworth wanted to respect the boundary Mercy was establishing, but her body must have felt overdue to have that baby in an embrace. Without warning Mercy was pulled into a hug that took her breath away, not because it was physically crushing, but because her own body recognized the kinship and the authenticity of the emotion. After a few heartbeats, she relaxed into it and even returned it.

EPILOGUE

Two weeks later.

Mercy had the key to her mother's beach house in her hand. She and Raif were loaded up, ready to leave for two fabulous days and nights away. They were in the parking garage saying goodbye to her mom and stepdad-to-be.

Rev stopped Raif. "There's a trick to the kitchen drawer where she keeps the wine opener. You have to kick the baseboard and pull at the same time."

Raif grinned. "Is this a joke?"

"Gods' truth. You'll see."

"Okay, then. Thanks for the tip."

Farnsworth was still standing there ten minutes later giving them instructions on how to open up, how to close up, where to go for food, etc.

When they were finally in the SUV and ready to pull away, Rev said, "No dune buggies. Promise me."

Raif shrugged. "Promise."

Their first night at the beach house. After they'd made the drive and meticulously followed instructions for opening up, they'd had dinner and, in the process, discovered that there was a nice selection of wine. They also verified that there was indeed a trick to the wine opener drawer.

Later, they sat on the floor in front of a small fire with their backs supported by the sofa feeling full of good food, warmed by great wine, and perfectly contented as if life didn't get better.

"Want to hear some irony?"

"I have a feeling I'm not supposed to say no."

She ignored that. "I've been thinking about the speed date."

"Oh, here we go again."

"No, really. I've been thinking how ironic it is that we caused a big enough scene to shut the place down and make everybody there question whether or not they wanted to pursue a possible relationship with the opposite sex. Yet…"

"Yet. Here we are. Together."

She laughed. "And the bigger irony is that, out of all the people who were speed dating that day? We're probably the only ones who *are* together."

"Life is strange."

"Indeed."

"I've been wondering about one thing."

"What?" Mercy asked.

"The whole Sozopol vampire discovery is a moot point now, but did you get far enough into it to have an idea what you were going to report?"

"Yes. Since the vampire virus is carried in the bloodstream and depends on the bloodstream, we're centuries too late to know if they were vampire or not. But the truth is that, even if I said there was indisputable proof, I don't think it would change a thing."

Raif wrinkled his brow and looked confused. "Why not?"

"I've actually given this some thought. As someone who recently needed to be convinced that vampire exists, I had a personal demonstration. Even after a vampire materialized out of thin air, right next to me, and basically showed me his fangs while going, "Awrrrrr," I *still* resisted believing it.

"I've got a name for it. The Phenomenon of Familiarity. People don't want to give up their beliefs. Once a belief has taken hold in our minds, most of us will cling to it like a life raft even in the face of incontrovertible evidence. As if we think that, if we change our minds we might somehow cease to be."

Raif was quiet for a while so she assumed he was absorbing her thoughts because they were so deep. When he spoke, he said, "He didn't really say 'awrrrrr', did he?"

PLEASE LEAVE YOUR REVIEW.

Indie authors such as myself depend on reviews for retailer visibility. You can support my effort to bring you fresh stories by writing as few as twenty words and I thank you in advance.

Visit me at http://VictoriaDanann.me

COMING AUGUST 31, 2014

Book One of the new series, *Exiled*.

NEED MORE GREAT PARANORMAL ROMANCE?

Try my friend, Kym Grosso's, Immortals of New Orleans Series.

Walk on the wild side

with hot wolves,

hot vampires,

and

out-of-control witches

when they come together in the heat of the bayou city

for adventure and erotic romance.

www.kymgrosso.com

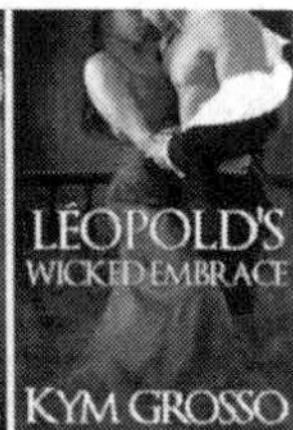

Need more Paranormal Romance?
Follow the VC Warriors in
"The Protectors Series" by
International Best Selling Author
Teresa Gabelman
THE PROTECTORS
DAMON
TERESA GABELMAN
THE PROTECTORS
JARED
TERESA GABELMAN
THE PROTECTORS
DUNCAN
TERESA GABELMAN
INTERNATIONAL BESTSELLING AUTHOR
THE PROTECTORS
SID
TERESA GABELMAN
INTERNATIONAL BESTSELLING AUTHOR
www.TeresaGabelman.com

Made in the USA
Lexington, KY
16 January 2019